An Infamous Army

known and best-loved of all historical novelists, making the Regency period her own. Her first novel, *The Black Moth*, published in 1921, was written at the age of fifteen to amuse her convalescent brother; her last was *My Lord John*. Although most famous for her historical novels, she also wrote twelve detective stories. Georgette Heyer died in 1974 at the age of seventy-one.

An Infamous Army

Georgette Heyer

Arrow Books

The Random House Group Limited
20 Vauxhall Bridge Road, London, SW1V 2SA

www.randomhouse.co.uk

a company within The Random House Group Limited can be
www.randomhouse.co.uk/offices.htm

The Random House Group Limited Reg. No. 954009

A CIP catalogue record for that book
is available from the British Library

arrow books

Published by Arrow Books in 2004

9 10 8

Copyright © Georgette Heyer, 1937

First published in the United Kingdom in 1937 by William Heinemann

Addresses for com   e found at:

T

ISBN 9780099465768

The Random House Group Limited supports The Forest Stewardship Council
(FSC®), the leading international forest certification organisation.
Our books carrying the FSC label are printed on FSC® certified paper. FSC is the
only forest certification scheme endorsed by the leading environmental
organisations, including Greenpeace. Our paper procurement policy can
be found at www.randomhouse.co.uk/environment

Printed in Great Britain by CPI Bookmarque, Croydon, CR0 4TD
Typeset by SX Composing DTP, Rayleigh, Essex

'I have got an infamous army;
Very weak and ill-equipped,
And a very inexperienced staff.'
Wellington to Lt Gen Lord Stewart, G.C.B.
8th May 1815

Author's Note

In writing this story I have realised an ambition which, though I fear it may have been presumptuous, I could not resist attempting. Apart from the epic nature of the subject, the spectre of Thackeray must loom over anyone wishing to tackle the battle of Waterloo. It would not allow me to set pen to paper until I banished it, at last, with the reflection that no one, after all, would judge a minor poet by Shakespeare's standard of excellence. I should add, perhaps, that it is many years since I read *Vanity Fair*; and although I have encroached on Thackeray's preserves, at least I have stolen nothing from him.

With regard to the Bibliography published at the end of this book, to obviate the necessity of appending a somewhat tedious list of authorities, I have limited it to those works which, in writing a novel, and not a history, I have found most useful. Works dealing with the purely tactical aspect of the campaign have been omitted; so too have many minor accounts; and a host of biographies, memoirs, and periodicals which, though not primarily concerned with any of the personages figuring in this story, contained, here and there, stray items of information about them. It will further be seen that, with the exception of Houssaye, no French authorities have been given: the French point of view was not relevant to my purpose. On the other hand, certain works have been included which, though they do not deal with the Waterloo campaign, were invaluable for the light they throw on Wellington's character, and the customs obtaining in his army.

Wherever possible, I have allowed the Duke to speak for himself, borrowing freely from the twelve volumes of his Despatches. If it should be objected that I should not have made him say in 1815 what he wrote in 1808, or said many years after Waterloo, I can only hope that, since his own words, whether spoken or written, were so infinitely superior to any which I could have put into his mouth, I may be pardoned for the occasional chronological inexactitudes thus entailed.

GEORGETTE HEYER

One

The youthful gentleman in the scarlet coat with blue facings and gold lace, who was seated in the window of Lady Worth's drawing-room, idly looking down into the street, ceased for a moment to pay any attention to the conversation that was in progress. Among the passers-by, a Bruxelloise in a black mantilla had caught his eye. She was lovely enough to be watched the whole way down the street. Besides, the conversation in the salon was very dull: just the same stuff that was being said all over Brussels.

'I own, one can be more comfortable now that Lord Hill is here, but I wish the Duke would come!'

The Bruxelloise had cast a roguish dark eye up at the window as she passed; the gentleman in scarlet did not even hear this remark, delivered by Lady Worth in an anxious tone which made her morning visitors look grave for a minute.

The Earl of Worth said dryly: 'To be sure, my love: so do we all.'

Georgiana Lennox, who was seated on the sofa with her hands clasped on top of her muff, subscribed to her hostess's sentiments with a sigh, but smiled at the Earl's words, and reminded him that there was one person at least in Brussels who did not wish for the Duke's arrival. 'My dear sir, the Prince is in the most dreadful huff! No other word for it! Only fancy! He scolded me for wanting the Duke to make haste – as though I could not trust *him* to account for Bonaparte, if you please!'

'How awkward for you!' said Lady Worth. 'What did you say?'

'Oh, I said nothing that was not true, I assure you! I like the Prince very well, but it is a little too much to suppose that a mere boy is capable of taking the field against Bonaparte. Why, what experience has he had? I might as well consider my brother March a fit commander. Indeed, he was on the Duke's Staff for longer than the Prince.'

'Is it true that the Prince and his father don't agree?' asked Sir Peregrine Taverner, a fair young man in a blue coat with very large silver buttons. 'I heard –'

A plump gentleman of cheerful and inquisitive mien broke into the conversation with all the air of an incorrigible gossip-monger. 'Quite true! The Prince is all for the English, of course, and that don't suit Frog's notions at all. Frog, you know, is what I call the King. I believe it to be a fact that the Prince is much easier in English or French than he is in Dutch! I heard that there was a capital quarrel the other day, which ended with the Prince telling Frog in good round terms that if he hadn't wished him to make his friends among the English he shouldn't have had him reared in England, or have sent him out to learn his soldiering in the Peninsula. Off he went, leaving Papa and Brother Fred without a word to say, and of course poured out the whole story to Colborne. I daresay Colborne don't care how soon he goes back to his regiment. I would not be Orange's military secretary for something!'

The Bruxelloise had passed from Lord Hay's range of vision; there was nothing left to look at but the pointed gables and nankeen-yellow front of a house on the opposite side of the street. Lord Hay, overhearing the last remark, turned his head, and asked innocently: 'Oh, did Sir John tell you so, Mr Creevey?'

An involuntary smile flickered on Judith Worth's lips; the curled ostrich plumes in Lady Georgiana's hat quivered; she raised her muff to her face. The company was allowed a moment to reflect upon the imaginary spectacle of more than six feet of taciturnity in the handsome shape of Sir John Colborne, Colonel of the Fighting 52nd, unburdening his soul to Mr Creevey.

Mr Creevey was not in the least abashed. He shook a finger at the young Guardsman, and replied with a knowing look: 'Oh, you must not think I am going to divulge *all* the sources of my information, Lord Hay!'

'I like the Prince of Orange,' declared Hay. 'He's a rattling good fellow.'

'Oh, as to that – !'

Lady Worth, aware that Mr Creevey's opinion of the Prince would hardly please Lord Hay, intervened with the observation that his brother, Prince Frederick, seemed to be a fine young man.

'Stiff as a poker,' said Hay. 'Prussian style. They call him the Stabs-Captain.'

'He's nice enough to look at,' conceded Lady Georgiana, adjusting the folds of her olive-brown pelisse. 'But he's only eighteen, and can't signify.'

'Georgy!' protected Hay.

She laughed. 'Well, but you don't signify either, Hay: you know you don't! You are just a boy.'

'Wait until we go into action!'

'Certainly, yes! You will perform prodigies, and be mentioned in despatches, I have no doubt at all. I daresay the Duke will write of you in the most glowing terms. "General Maitland's ADC, Ensign Lord Hay –"'

There was a general laugh.

' "I have every reason to be satisfied with the conduct of Ensign Lord Hay," ' said Hay in a prim voice. 'Old Hookey writing in glowing terms! That's good!'

'Hush, now! I won't hear a word against the Duke. He is quite the greatest man in the world.'

It was not to be expected that Mr Creevey, a confirmed Whig, could allow this generous estimate to pass unchallenged. Under cover of the noise of cheerful argument, Sir Peregrine Taverner moved to where his brother-in-law stood in front of the fire, and said in a low voice: 'I suppose you don't know when the Duke is expected in Brussels, Worth?'

'No, how should I?' replied Worth in his cool way.

'I thought you might have heard from your brother.'

'Your sister had a letter from him a week ago, but he did not know when he wrote when the Duke would be free to leave Vienna.'

'He ought to be here. However, I'm told that since Lord Hill came out the Prince has not been talking any more of invading France. I suppose it's true he was sent to keep the Prince quiet?'

'I expect your information is quite as good as mine, my dear Peregrine.'

Sir Peregrine Taverner had attained the mature age of twenty-three, had been three years married, and two years out of the Earl of Worth's guardianship, and was, besides, the father of a pair of hopeful children, but he still stood a little in awe of his brother-in-law. He accepted the snub with a sigh, and merely said: 'One can't help feeling anxious, you know. After all, Worth, I'm a family man now.'

The Earl smiled. 'Very true.'

'I don't think, if I had known Boney would get away from Elba, I should have taken a house in Brussels at all. You must admit it is not a comfortable situation for a civilian to be in.' He ended on a slightly disconsolate note, his gaze wandering to the scarlet splendour of Lord Hay.

'In fact,' said the Earl, 'you would like very much to buy yourself a pair of colours.'

Sir Peregrine grinned sheepishly. 'Well, yes, I would. One feels confoundedly out of it. At least, I daresay you don't, because you are a military man yourself.'

'My dear Perry, I sold out years ago!' The Earl turned away from his young relative as he spoke, for Lady Georgiana had got up to take her leave.

Beside Judith Worth's golden magnificence, Lady Georgiana seemed very tiny. She submitted to having her pelisse buttoned close to her throat by her tall friend, for even on this 4th day of April the weather still remained chilly; stood on tiptoe to kiss Judith's cheek; promised herself the pleasure of meeting her at Lady Charlotte Greville's that evening; and went off under Hay's escort to join her mother, the Duchess of Richmond, at the Marquis d'Assche's house at the corner of the Park.

Since Mr Creevey showed no immediate disposition to go away, Lady Worth sat down again, and made kind enquiries after his wife and stepdaughters. One of the Misses Ord, he confided, had become engaged to be married. Lady Worth exclaimed suitably, and Mr Creevey, beaming all over his kindly face, disclosed the name of the fortunate man. It was Hamilton; yes, Major Andrew Hamilton, of the Adjutant-General's Staff: an excellent fellow! Between themselves, Hamilton kept him pretty well informed of what was going on. He got all the news from France, but under pledge of strict secrecy. Lady Worth would understand that his lips were sealed. 'And you too,' he added, fixing his penetrating gaze upon her, 'I daresay *you* have information for your private ear, eh?'

'I?' said Lady Worth. 'My dear Mr Creevey, none in the world! What can you be thinking of?'

He looked arch. 'Come, come, isn't Colonel Audley with the Great Man?'

'My brother-in-law! Yes, certainly he is in Vienna, but I assure you he doesn't tell me any secrets. We don't even know when we may expect to see him here.'

He was disappointed, for news, titbits of scandal, interesting confidences whispered behind sheltering hands, were the breath of life to him. However, since there was nothing to be learned from his hostess, he had to content himself with settling down to what he called a comfortable prose with her. He had already told her, upon his first coming into her salon, of a singular occurrence, but he could not resist adverting to it again: it was so very remarkable. Sir Peregrine had not been present when he had first related the circumstance, so he nodded to him and said: 'You will have heard of the new arrivals, I daresay. I was telling your good sister about them.'

'The King?' said Peregrine. 'The French King, I mean? Is he really coming to Brussels? I did hear a rumour, but someone said it was no such thing.'

5

'Oh, the King!' Mr Creevey waved his Sacred Majesty aside with one plump hand. 'I was not referring to him – though I have reason to believe he will remain in Ghent for the present. Paltry fellow, ain't he? No, no something a little more singular – or so it seemed to me. Three of Boney's old Marshals, no less! I had the good fortune to see them all arrive, not ten days ago. There was Marmont, who went to the Hôtel d'Angleterre; Berthier, to the Duc d'Aremberg's; and Victor – now where do you suppose? Why, to the Hôtel Wellington, of all places in the world!'

'How ironic!' remarked Worth, who had come back into the room from seeing his other guests off. 'Is it true, or just one of your stories, Creevey?'

'No, no, I promise you it's quite true! I knew you would enjoy the joke.'

Lady Worth, who had accorded the tale at this second hearing no more than a polite smile, said in a reflective tone: 'It is certainly very odd to think of Marmont in particular being in the English camp.'

'The Allied camp, my love,' corrected the Earl, with a sardonic smile.

'Well, yes,' she admitted, 'but you know I can't bring myself to believe that the Dutch–Belgian troops count for much, while as for the Prussians, the only one I have laid eyes on is General Röder, and – well – !' She made an expressive gesture. 'He is always so stiff, and takes such stupid offence at trifles, that it puts me out of all patience with him.'

'Yes, *he* will never do for the Duke,' agreed Mr Creevey. 'Hamilton was telling me there is no dealing with him at all. He thinks himself insulted if any of our officers remain seated in his presence. Such stuff! A man who sets so much store by all that ceremonious nonsense won't do for the Duke's Headquarters. They couldn't have made a worse choice of Commissioner. There's another man, too, who they say will never do for the Duke.' He nodded, and pronounced: 'Our respected Quartermaster-General!'

'Oh, poor Sir Hudson Lowe! He is very stiff also,' said Lady

Worth. 'People say he is an efficient officer, however.'

'I daresay he may be, but you know how it is with these fellows who have served with the Prussians: there's no doing anything with them. Well, no doubt we shall see some changes when the Beau arrives from Vienna.'

'If only he would arrive! It is very uncomfortable with him so far away. One cannot help feeling uneasy. Now that all communication with Paris has been stopped, war seems so very close. Then Lord Fitzroy Somerset and all the Embassy people being refused passports to come across the frontier, and having to embark from Dieppe! When our Chargé d'Affaires is treated like that it is very bad, you must allow.'

'Yes,' interjected Peregrine, 'and the best of our troops being in America! That is what is so shocking! I don't see how any of them can be brought back in time to be of the least use. When I saw the Prince he was in expectation of war breaking out at any moment.'

'No chance of that, I assure you. Young Frog don't know what he's talking about. Meanwhile, we have some very fine regiments quartered here, you know.'

'We have some very young and inexperienced troops,' said Worth. 'Happily, the cavalry did not go to America.'

'Of course, you were a hussar yourself, but you must know very well there's no sense in cavalry without infantry,' replied Peregrine knowledgeably. 'Only to think of all the Peninsular veterans shipped off to that curst American war! Nothing was ever so badly contrived.'

'It is easy to be wise after the event, my dear Perry.'

Lady Worth, who had listened to many such discussions, interposed to give the conversation a turn towards less controversial subjects. She was assisted very readily by Mr Creevey, who had some entertaining scandal to relate, and for the remainder of his visit nothing was talked of but social topics.

Of these there were many, since Brussels overflowed with English visitors. The English had been confined to their own island for so long that upon the Emperor Napoleon's abdication and retirement to Elba they had flocked abroad. The presence of an Army of Occupation in the Low Countries made Brussels a desirable goal. Several provident Mamas conveyed marriageable daughters across the Channel in the wake of the Guards, while pleasure-seeking ladies such as Caroline Lamb and Lady Vidal packed up their most daring gauzes and established their courts in houses hired for an indefinite term in the best part of Brussels.

The presence of the Guards was not, of course, the only attraction offered by Brussels. Mr Creevey, for instance, had brought his good lady to a snug little apartment in the Rue du Musée for her health's sake. Others had come to take part in the festivities attendant upon the long-exiled William of Orange's instatement as King of the Netherlands.

This gentleman, whom Mr Creevey and his friends called the Frog, had been well known in London; and his elder son, the Hereditary Prince of Orange, was a hopeful young man of engaging manners, and a reputation for dashing gallantry in the field, who had lately enjoyed a brief engagement to the Princess Charlotte of Wales. The breaking off of the engagement by that strong-minded damsel, though it had made his Highness appear a trifle ridiculous in English eyes, and had afforded huge gratification to Mr Creevey and his friends, did not seem to have cast any sort of cloud over the Prince's spirits. It was felt that gaiety would attend his footsteps; nor were the seekers after pleasure destined to be disappointed. Within its old ramparts, Brussels became the centre of all that was fashionable and light hearted. King William, a somewhat uninspiring figure, was proclaimed with due pomp at Brussels, and if his new subjects, who had been quite content under the Bonapartist régime, regarded with misgiving their fusion with their Dutch neighbours, this was not allowed to appear upon the surface. The Hereditary Prince, who spoke English and French better than his native tongue, and who announced himself quite incapable of supporting the rigours of life at The Hague, achieved a certain amount of popularity which might have been more lasting had he not let it plainly be seen that although he liked his father's Belgian subjects better than his Dutch ones, he preferred the English to them all. The truth was, he was never seen but in the society of his English friends, a circumstance which had caused so much annoyance to be felt that the one man who was known to have influence over him was petitioned to write exhorting him to more diplomatic behaviour. It was a chill December day when M. Fagel brought his Highness a letter from the English Ambassador in Paris, and there was nothing in the austere contents of the missive to make the day seem warmer. A letter of reproof from his Grace the Duke of Wellington, however politely worded it might be, was never likely to produce in the recipient any other sensation than that of having been plunged into unpleasantly cold water. The Prince, with some bitter animad-versions upon tale-bearers in general, and his father in particular, sat down to write a promise to his mentor of exemplary conduct, and proceeded thereafter to fulfil it by entering heart and soul into the social life of Brussels.

But except for a strong Bonapartist faction the Bruxellois also liked the English. Gold flowed from careless English fingers into Belgian pockets; English visitors were making Brussels the gayest town in Europe, and the Bruxellois welcomed them with open arms. They would welcome the Duke of Wellington too when at last he should arrive. He had been received with enormous enthusiasm a year before, when he had visited Belgium on his way to Paris. He was Europe's great man, and the Bruxellois had accorded him an almost hysterical reception, even cheering two very youthful and self-conscious aides-de-camp of his who had occupied his box at the opera one evening. There had been a mistake, of course, but it showed the goodwill of the Bruxellois. The Bonapartists naturally could not be expected to share in these transports, but it was decidedly not the moment for a Bonapartist to proclaim himself, and these gentry had to be content with holding aloof from the many fêtes, and pinning their secret faith to the Emperor's star.

The news of Napoleon's landing in the south of France had

had a momentarily sobering effect upon the merrymakers, but in spite of rumours and alarms the theatre parties, the concerts, and the balls had still gone on, and only a few prudent souls had left Brussels.

There was however, a general feeling of uneasiness. Vienna, where the Duke of Wellington was attending the Congress, was a long way from Brussels, and whatever the Prince of Orange's personal daring might be it was not felt that two years spent in the Peninsula as one of the Duke's aides-de-camp were enough to qualify a young gentleman not yet twenty-four for the command of an army to be pitted against Napoleon Bonaparte. Indeed, the Prince's first impetuous actions, and the somewhat indiscreet language he held, alarmed serious people not a little. The Prince entertained no doubt of being able to account for Bonaparte; he talked of invading France at the head of the Allied troops; wrote imperative demands to England for more men and more munitions; invited General Kleist to march his Prussians along the Meuse to effect a junction with him; and showed himself in general to be so magnificently oblivious of the fact that England was not at war with France, that the embarrassed Government in some haste despatched Lieutenant-General Lord Hill to explain the peculiar delicacy of the situation to him.

The choice of mentor was a happy one. A trifle elated, the Prince of Orange was in a brittle mood, ready to resent the least interference in his authority. General Clinton, whom he disliked, and Sir Hudson Lowe, whom he thought a Prussianised martinet, found themselves unable to influence his judgment, and succeeded only in offending. But no one had ever been known to take offence at Daddy Hill. He arrived in Brussels looking more like a country squire than a distinguished general, and took the jealous young commander gently in hand. The anxious breathed again; the Prince of Orange might be in a little huff at the prospect of being soon relieved of his command, but he was no longer refractory, and was soon able to write to Lord Bathurst, in London, announcing the gratifying intelligence that although it would have been mortifying to him to give up his command to anyone else, to the Duke he could do it with pleasure; and could even engage to serve him with as great a zeal as when he had been his aide-de-camp.

'*I shall never forget that period of my life,*' wrote the Prince, forgetting his injuries in a burst of enthusiasm. '*I owe everything to it; and if I now may hope to be of use to my country it is to the experience I acquired under him that I have to attribute it.*'

Such a frame of mind augured well for the future; but the task of controlling the Prince's martial activities continued to be a difficult one. The British Ambassador to The Hague transferred his establishment to Brussels with the principal motive of assisting Lord Hill in his duty, and found it so arduous that he more than once wrote to the Duke to tell him how necessary was his presence in Brussels. '*You will see that I have spared no efforts to keep the Prince quiet,*' wrote Sir Charles Stuart in his plain style . . . '*Under these circumstances I leave you to judge of the extreme importance we all attach to your early arrival.*'

Meanwhile, though the Congress at Vienna might declare Napoleon to be *hors la loi*, every day saw French Royalists hurrying a little ignominiously over the frontier. Louis XVIII, yet another of Europe's uninspiring monarchs, removed his Court from Paris to Ghent, and placidly explained that he had been all the while impelled, in France, to employ untrustworthy persons because none whom he could trust were fit to be employed. Certainly it did not seem as though anyone except his nephew, the Duc d'Angoulême, had made the least push to be of use in the late crisis. That gentleman had raised a mixed force at Nîmes, and was skirmishing in the south of France, egged on by a masterful wife. His brother, the Duc de Berri, who had accompanied his uncle into Belgium, found less dangerous employment in holding slightly farcical reviews of the handful of Royalist troops under his command at Alost.

These proceedings were not comforting to the anxious, but the proximity of the Prussian Army was more reassuring. But as General Kleist's notions of feeding this Army consisted very simply of causing it to subsist upon the country in which it was quartered, the King of the Netherlands, who held quite different views on the subject, and was besides on bad terms with his wife's Prussian relatives, refused to permit of its crossing the Meuse. This not unnaturally led to a good deal of bad feeling.

'Your Lordship's presence is extremely necessary to combine the measures of the heterogeneous force which is destined to defend this country,' wrote Sir Charles Stuart to the Duke, with diplomatic restraint.

Everyone agreed that the Duke's presence was necessary; everyone was sure that once he was in command all the disputes and the difficulties would be immediately settled, even Mr Creevey, who had not been used to set much store by any of 'those damned Wellesleys'.

It was wonderful what a change was gradually coming over Mr Creevey's opinions; extraordinary to hear him adverting to the Duke's past victories in Spain, just as though he had never declared them to have been grossly exaggerated. He was still a little patronising about the Duke, but he was going to feel very much safer, tied as he was to Brussels by an ailing wife, when the Duke was at the head of the Army.

But he though it very strange that Worth should have had no news from his brother in Vienna. Probe as he might, nothing could be elicited. Colonel Audley had not mentioned the subject of his Chief's coming.

Mr Creevey was forced to go away unsatisfied. Sir Peregrine lingered. 'I must say, I agree with him, that it's odd of Charles not to have told you when he expects to be here,' he complained.

'My dear Perry, I daresay he might not know,' said Lady Worth.

'Well, when one considers that he has been on the Duke's personal staff since he went back to the Peninsula after your marriage in August of 1812 it seems quite extraordinary he should be so little in Wellington's confidence,' said Sir Peregrine.

His sister drew her worktable towards her, and began to occupy herself with a piece of embroidery. 'Perhaps the Duke himself is uncertain. Depend upon it, he will be here soon enough. It is very worrying, but he must know what he is about.'

He took a turn about the room. 'I wish I knew what I should do!' he exclaimed presently. 'It's all very well for you to laugh, Judith, but it's curst awkward! Of course, if I were a single man I should join as a volunteer. However, that won't do.'

'No, indeed!' said Judith, rather startled.

'Worth, what do you mean to do? Do you stay?'

'Oh, I think so!' replied the Earl.

Sir Peregrine's brow lightened. 'Oh! Well, if you judge it to be safe – I don't suppose you would keep Judith and the child here if you did not?'

'I don't suppose I should,' agreed the Earl.

'What does Harriet wish to do?' enquired Lady Worth.

'Oh, if it can be considered safe for the children, she don't wish to go!' Sir Peregrine caught sight of his reflection in the mirror over the fireplace, and gave the starched folds of his cravat a dissatisfied twitch. Before his marriage he had aspired to dizzy heights of dandyism, and although he now lived for the greater part of the year on his estates in Yorkshire, he was still inclined to spend much thought and time on his dress. 'This new man of mine is no good at all!' he said, with some annoyance. 'Just look at my cravat!'

'Is that really necessary!' said the Earl. 'For the past hour I have been at considerable pains not to look at it.'

A grin dispersed Sir Peregrin's worried frown. 'Oh, be damned to you, Worth! I'll tell you what it is, you did a great deal for me when I was your ward, but if you had taught me the way you have of tying your cravats I should have been more grateful than ever I was for any of the rest of the curst interfering things you did.'

'Very handsomely put, Perry. But the art is inborn, and can't be taught.'

Sir Peregrine made a derisive sound, and, abandoning the attempt to improve the set of his cravat, turned from the mirror. He glanced down at his sister, tranquilly sewing, and said in a burst of confidence: 'You know, I can't help being worried. *I* don't want to run home, but the thing is that Harriet is in a delicate situation again.'

'Good God, already?' exclaimed Judith.

'Yes, and you see what an anxious position it puts me in. I would not have her upset for the world. However, it seems certain Boney can't move against us yet. I shall wait until the Duke comes before I decide. That will be best.'

The Earl agreed to it with a solemnity only belied by the quivering of a muscle at the corner of his mouth. Sir Peregrine adjured him to let him have any reliable news he might chance to hear and took himself off, his mind apparently relieved of its care.

His sister was left to enjoy a laugh at his expense. 'Julian, I think you must have taken leave of your senses when you permitted Perry to marry Harriet! Two children, and another expected! It is quite absurd! He is only a child himself.'

'Very true, but you should consider that if he were not married we should have him enlisting as a volunteer.'

The thought sobered her. She put down her embroidery. 'I suppose we should.' She hesitated, her fine blue eyes raised to Worth's face. 'Well, Julian, our morning visitors have all talked a great deal, but you have said nothing.'

'I was under the impression that I said everything that was civil.'

'Just so, and nothing to the point. I wish you will tell me what you think. Do we stay?'

'Not if you wish to go home, my dear.'

She shook her head. 'You are to be the judge. I don't care for myself, but there is little Julian to be recollected, you know.'

'I don't forget him. Antwerp is, after all, comfortably close. But if you choose I will convey you both to England.'

She cast him a shrewd look. 'You are extremely obliging, sir! Thank you, I know you a little too well to accept that offer. You would no sooner have set me down in England than you would return here, odious wretch!'

He laughed. 'To tell you the truth, Judith, I think it will be interesting to be in Brussels this spring.'

'Yes,' she agreed. 'But what will happen?'

'I know no more than the next man.'

'I suppose war is certain? Will the Duke be a match for Bonaparte, do you think?'

'That is what we are going to see, my dear.'

'Everyone speaks as though his arrival will make all quite safe – indeed, I do myself – but though he was so successful in Spain he has never fought against Bonaparte himself, has he?'

'A circumstance which makes the situation of even more interest,' said Worth.

'Well!' She resumed her stitching. 'You are very cool. We shall stay then. Indeed, I should be very sorry to go just when Charles is to join us.'

The Earl put up his quizzing-glass. 'Ah! May I inquire, my love, whether you are making plans for Charles's future welfare?'

Down went the embroidery; her ladyship raised an indignant rueful pair of eyes to his face. 'You are the most odious man that I have ever met!' she declared. 'Of course I don't make plans for Charles! It sounds like some horrid, match-making Mama. How in the world did you guess?'

'Some explanation of your extreme kindness towards Miss Devenish seemed to be called for. That was the likeliest that presented itself to me.'

'Well, but don't you think her a charming girl, Julian?'

'I daresay. You know my taste runs to Amazons.'

Her ladyship ignored this with obvious dignity. 'She is extremely pretty, with such obliging manners, and a general sweetness of disposition which makes me feel her to be so very eligible.'

'I will allow all that to be true.'

'You are thinking of Mr Fisher. I know the evils of her situation, but recollect that Mr Fisher is her uncle only by marriage! He is a little vulgar perhaps – well, very vulgar, if you like! – but I am sure a kind, worthy man who has treated her quite as though she were his own daughter, and will leave the whole of his fortune to her.'

'That certainly is a consideration,' said Worth.

'Her own birth, though not noble, is perfectly respectable, you know. Her family is an old one – but it does not signify talking, after all! Charles will make his own choice.'

'Just what I was about to remark, my dear.'

'Don't alarm yourself! I have no notion of throwing poor Lucy at his head, I assure you. But I shall own myself surprised if he does not take a liking to her.'

'I perceive,' said the Earl, faintly amused, 'that life in Brussels is going to be even more interesting than I had expected.'

Two

When Judith, on setting out for Lady Charlotte Greville's evening party, desired Worth to direct the coachman to call at Mr Fisher's for the purpose of picking up Miss Devenish, she could not help looking a little conscious. She avoided his ironic gaze, but when he settled himself beside her, and the carriage moved forward over the pavé, said defensively: 'Really, it is not remarkable that I should take Lucy with me.'

'Certainly not,' agreed Worth. 'I made no remark.'

'Mrs Fisher does not like to go into company, you know, and the poor child would be very dull if no one offered to escort her.'

'Very true.'

Judith cast a smouldering glance at his profile. 'I do not think,' she said, 'that I have ever met so provoking a person as you.'

He smiled, but said nothing, and upon the carriage's drawing up presently in front of a respectable-looking house in one of the quiet streets off the Place Royale, got down to hand his wife's protégée into the carriage.

She did not keep him waiting for many seconds, but came out of the house, escorted by her uncle, a little stout man of cheerful vulgarity who bowed very low to the Earl, and uttered profuse thanks and protestations. He was answered with the cool civility of a stranger, but Lady Worth, leaning forward, said everything that was kind, enquired after Mrs Fisher, who had lately been confined to the house by a feverish cold, and engaged herself to take good care of Miss Devenish.

'Your ladyship is never backward in any attention – most flattering distinction! I am all obligation!' he said, bowing to her. 'It is just as it should be, for I'm sure Lucy is fit to move in the first circles – ay, and to make a good match into the bargain, eh, Lucy? Ah, she don't like me to quiz her about it: she is blushing, I daresay, only it is too dark to see.'

Judith could not but feel a little vexation that he should expose himself so to Worth, but she passed it off with tact. Miss Devenish was handed into the carriage, the Earl followed her, and in a moment they were off, leaving Mr Fisher bowing farewell upon the pavement.

'Dear Lady Worth, this is very kind of you!' said Miss Devenish, in a pretty, low voice. 'My aunt desired her compliments. I did not keep you waiting, I hope?'

'No, indeed. I only hope it won't prove an insipid evening. I believe there may be dancing, and I suppose all the world and his wife will be there.'

It certainly seemed so. When they arrived, Lady Charlotte's salons were already crowded. The English predominated, but there were any number of distinguished foreigners present. Here and there were to be seen the blue of a Dutch uniform, and the smart rifle-green of a Belgian dragoon; and everywhere you should chance to look you might be sure of encountering the sight of scarlet: vivid splashes of scarlet, throwing into insignificance all the ladies' pale muslins, and every civilian gentleman's more sober coat. Civilian gentlemen were plainly at a discount, and the young lady who could not show at least one scarlet uniform enslaved was unhappy indeed. Wits and savants went by the board; the crowd was thickest about Lord Hill, who had dropped in for half an hour. His round face wore its usual placid smile; he was replying with inexhaustible patience and good humour to the anxious inquiries of the females clustering round him. Dear Lord Hill! So kind, so dependable! He was not like the Duke, of course, but one need not pack one's trunks and order the horses to be put to for an instant flight to Antwerp while he was there to pledge one his word the Corsican Monster was still in Paris.

He had just reassured the Annesley sisters, two ethereal blondes, whose very ringlets were appealing. When Worth's party came into the room, they had moved away from Lord Hill, and were standing near the door, a lovely fragile pair, so like, so dotingly fond!

They were both married, the younger, Catharine, being one of the season's brides, with a most unexceptionable young husband to her credit, Lord John Somerset, temporarily attached to the Prince of the Orange's personal staff. It was strange that Catharine, decidedly her sister's inferior in beauty and brain, should have done so much better for herself in the marriage market. Poor Frances, with her infinite capacity for hero-worship, had made but a sad business of it after all, for a less inspiring figure than her tow-headed, chattering, awkward Mr Webster would have been hard to find. You could hardly blame her for having fallen so deeply in love with Lord Byron. Quite an *affaire* that had been, while it lasted. Happily that had not been for very long – though long enough, if Catharine's indiscreet tongue were to be trusted, to enable her to secure one of the poet's precious locks of hair. That was more than Caro Lamb could boast of, poor soul.

She too was in Brussels, quite scandalising the old-fashioned with her gossamer gauzes, always damped to make them cling close to her limbs, generally dropping off one thin shoulder, and allowing the interested an intimate view of her shape. Old Lady Mount Norris was ready to stake her reputation on Caroline's wearing under her gauze dresses not a stitch of clothing beyond an Invisible Petticoat. Well, her own daughter might possess a lock of Byron's hair, but one was able to thank God she did not flaunt herself abroad next door to naked.

Lord Byron was not in Brussels. Perhaps he was too taken up with that queer, serious bride of his; perhaps he knew that even a poet as beautiful and as sinister as himself would not make much of a mark in Brussels on the eve of war.

His marriage had been a great shock to Caro Lamb, said the gossipers. Poor thing, one was truly sorry for her, however ridiculous she might have made herself. It was quite her own fault that she now looked so haggard. She was unbecomingly thin too; every lady was agreed on that. Sprite? Ariel? Well, one had always thought such nicknames absurd; one really never had admired her. Only gentlemen were sometimes so silly!

There were quite a number of gentlemen round Lady Caroline, all being regrettably silly. A murmur from Miss Devenish reached Lady Worth's ears: 'Oh! she's so lovely! I like just to look at her!'

Judith hoped that she was not uncharitable, but had no wish to exchange more than a smile and a bow with Lady Caroline. One was not a prude, but really that lilac gauze was perfectly transparent! And if it came to loveliness, Judith considered her protégée quite as well worth looking at as any lady in the room. If her eyelashes were not as long and curling as Lady Frances Webster's the eyes themselves were decidedly more brilliant, and of such a dove-like softness! Her shape, though she might conceal it with discretion, was quite as good as Caro Lamb's; and her glossy brown curls were certainly thicker than Caroline's short feathery ringlets. Above all, her expression was charming, her smile so spontaneous, the look of grave reflection in her eye so particularly becoming! She dressed, moreover, with great propriety of taste, expensively but never extravagantly. Any man might congratulate himself on acquiring such a bride.

These reflections were interrupted by the necessity of exchanging civilities with the Marquise d'Assche. Judith turned from her presently to find Miss Devenish waiting to engage her attention.

'Dear Lady Worth,' said Miss Devenish, 'you know everyone, I believe. Only tell me who is that beautiful creature come into the room with Lady Vidal. Is it very wrong? – I could not but gasp and think to myself: "Oh, if I had but that hair!" Everyone is cast into the shade!'

'Good gracious, whom in the world can you have seen?' said Judith, smiling with a little amusement. However, when her eyes followed the direction of Miss Devenish's worshipful gaze, the smile quickly faded. 'Good God!' she said. 'I had no idea that she was back in Brussels! Well, Lucy, if you are looking at the lady with the head of hair like my best copper coalscuttle, let me tell you that she is none other than Barbara Childe.'

'Lady Barbara!' breathed Miss Devenish. 'I wondered – You must know that I never till now set eyes on her. Yes, one can see the likeness: she is a little like her brother, Lord Vidal, is she not?'

'More like Lord George, I should say. You do not know him: a wild young man, I am afraid; very like his sister.'

Miss Devenish made no reply to this observation, her attention remaining fixed upon the two ladies who had come into the salon.

The elder, Lady Vidal, was a handsome brunette, whose air, dress, and deportment all proclaimed the lady of fashion. She was accompanied by her husband, the Marquis of Vidal, a fleshy man, with a shock of reddish hair, a permanent crease between thick, sandy brows, and a rather pouting mouth.

Beside Lady Vidal, and with her hand lightly resting on the arm of an officer in Dutch–Belgian uniform, stood the object of Miss Devenish's eager scrutiny.

Lady Barbara Childe was no longer in the first flush of her youth. She was twenty-five years old, and had been three years a widow. Having married to oblige her family at the age of seventeen, she had had the good fortune to lose a husband three times as old as herself within five years of having married him. Her mourning had been of the most perfunctory: indeed, she was thought to have grieved more over the death of her father, an expensive nobleman of selfish habits, and an unsavoury reputation. But the truth was she did not grieve much over anyone. She was heartless.

It was the decision of all who knew her, and of many who did not. No one could deny her beauty, or her charm, but both were acknowledged to be deadly. Her conquests were innumerable; men fell so desperately in love with her that they became wan with desire, and very often did extremely foolish things when they discovered that she did not care the snap of her fingers for them. Young Mr Vane had actually drunk himself to death; and poor Sir Henry Drew had bought himself a pair of colours and gone off to the Peninsula with the declared intention of being killed, which he very soon was; while, more shocking than all the rest, Bab had allowed her destructive green eyes to drift towards Philip Darcy, with the result that poor dear Marianne, who had been his faithful wife for ten years, now sat weeping at home, quite neglected.

It was a mystery to the ladies what the gentlemen found so alluring in those green eyes, with their deceptive look of candour. For green they were, let who would call them blue. Bab had only to put on a green dress for there to be no doubt at all about it. They were set under most delicately arched brows, and were fringed by lashes which had obviously been darkened. That outrageously burnished head of hair might be natural, but those black lashes undoubtedly were not. Nor, agreed the waspish, was that lovely complexion. In fact, the Lady Barbara Childe, beyond all other iniquities, painted her face.

It became apparent to those who were gazing at her that the Lady Barbara had not, on this night of April, stopped at that. One foot was thrust a little forward from under the frills of a yellow-spangled gown, and it was seen that the Lady Barbara, wearing Grecian sandals, had painted her toenails gold.

Miss Devenish was heard to give a gasp. Lady Sarah Lennox, on the arm of General Maitland, said: 'Gracious, only look at Bab's feet! She learned that trick in Paris, of course.'

'Dashing, by Jove!' said the General appreciatively.

'Very, very fast!' said Lady Sarah. 'Shocking!'

It was not the least part of Barbara's charm that having arrayed herself in a startling costume she contrived thereafter to seem wholly unconscious of the appearance she presented. She was never seen to pat her curls into place, or to cast an anxious glance towards the mirror. No less a personage than Mr Brummell had taught her this magnificent unconcern. 'Once having assured yourself that your dress is perfect in every detail,' had pronounced that oracle, 'you must not give it another thought. No one, I fancy, has ever seen me finger my cravat, twitch at the lapels of my coat, or smooth creases from my sleeve.'

So the Lady Barbara, in a shimmering golden gown of spangles which clung to her tall shape as though it had been moulded to it, with her gold toenails, and her cluster of red curls threaded with a golden fillet, was apparently quite oblivious of being the most daringly dressed lady in the room. Fifty pairs of eyes were fixed upon her, some in patent disapproval, some in equally patent admiration, and she did not betray by as much as a flicker of an eyelid that she was aware of being a cynosure. That dreadfully disarming smile of hers swept across her face, and she moved towards Lady Worth, and held out her hand, saying in her oddly boyish voice: 'How do you do? Is your little boy well?'

In spite of the fact that Judith had been by no means pleased, three months before, to see her infant son entranced by the Lady Barbara's charms, this speech could not but gratify her. 'Very well, thank you,' she replied. 'Have you been back in Brussels long?'

'No, two days only.'

'I did not know you have the intention of returning.'

'Oh – ! London was confoundedly flat,' said Bab carelessly.

Miss Devenish, who had never before heard such a mannish expression on a lady's lips, stared. Lady Barbara glanced down at her from her graceful height, and then looked at Judith, her brows asking a question. A little unwillingly – but, after all, it was not likely that Bab would waste more than two minutes of her time on little Lucy Devenish – Judith made the necessary introduction. The smile and the hand were bestowed; Barbara made a movement with her fan, including in the group the officer on whose arm she had entered the salon. 'Lady Worth, do you known M. le Capitaine Comte de Lavisse?'

'I believe we have met,' acknowledged Judith, devoutly hoping that Brussels' most notorious rake would not take one of his dangerous fancies to the damsel in her charge.

However, the Captain Count's dark eyes betrayed no more than a fleeting interest in Miss Devenish, and before any introduction could be made a young gentleman with embryonic whiskers, and a sandy head at lamentable difference with his scarlet dress coat, joined them.

'Hallo, Bab!' said Lord Harry Alastair. 'Servant, Lady Worth! Miss Devenish, do you know they are dancing in the other room? May I have the honour?'

Judith, smiling a gracious permission, could not but feel that the path of a chaperon was a hard one. The reputation of the Alastairs, from Dominic, Duke of Avon, down to his granddaughter, Barbara, was not such as to lead a conscientious duenna to observe with pleasure her charge being borne off by any one of them. She comforted herself with the reflection that Lord Harry, an eighteen-year-old Ensign could hardly be considered dangerous. Had it been Lord George, now! But Lord George, happily, was not in Belgium.

By the time Lord Harry had escorted Miss Devenish to the ballroom, the inevitable crowd had gathered round his sister. Lady Worth escaped from it, but not before she had been asked (inevitably, she thought) for news from Vienna.

Rumours and counter-rumours were as usual being circulated; the English in Brussels seemed to be poised for flight; and the only thing that would infallibly reassure the timorous was the certain news of the Duke's arrival.

It was easy to see what Brussels would make of him when he did come. 'The pedestal is ready for the hero,' said Judith, with rather a provocative smile. 'And *we* are all ready to kneel and worship at the base. I hope he may be worthy of our admiration.'

General Maitland, to whom she had addressed this remark, said: 'Do you know him, Lady Worth?'

'I have not that pleasure. Pray do not mention it, but I have never so much as laid eyes on him. Is it not shocking?'

'Oh!' said the General.

She raised her brows. 'What am I to understand by that, if you please? Shall I be disappointed? I warn you, I expect a demi-god!'

'Demi-god,' repeated the General, stroking one beautiful whisker. 'Well, I don't know. Shouldn't have called him so myself.'

'Ah, I am to be disappointed! I feared as much.'

'No – no,' said the General. 'Not disappointed. He is a very able commander.'

'That sounds a little flat, I confess. Is it only the ladies who worship him? Do not his soldiers?'

'Oh no, nothing like that!' said the General, relieved to be able to answer a plain question. 'I believe they rather like him than not: they like to see his hook nose among them at any rate; but they don't worship him. Don't think he'd care for it if they did.'

She was interested. 'You present me with a new picture, General. My brother-in-law is quite devoted to him, I believe.'

'Audley? Well, he's one of his family, you see.' He observed a bewildered look on her face, and added: 'On his staff, I should say. That's another matter altogether. His staff know him better than the rest of us.'

'This is more promising. He is unapproachable. A demi-god should certainly be so.'

He laughed suddenly. 'No, no, *you* won't find him un-approachable, Lady Worth, I pledge you my word!'

Their conversation was interrupted by Sarah and Georgiana Lennox, who came up to them with their arms entwined. The General greeted the elder sister with such a warm smile that Lady Worth was satisfied that rumour had not lied about his purpose of re-marriage. Lady Sarah went off on his arm; Georgiana remained beside Judith, watching the shifting crowd for a few moments. She presently said in rather a thoughtful voice: 'Do you see that Bab Childe is back?'

'Yes, I have been speaking to her.'

'I must say, I wish she had stayed away,' confided Georgiana. 'It is the oddest thing, because, for myself, I don't dislike her, but wherever she is there is always some horrid trouble, or unhappiness. Even Mama, who is never silly, is a little afraid she may cast her eyes in March's direction. Of course, we don't breathe a word of such a thing at home, but it's perfectly true.'

'What, that your brother –'

'Oh no, no, but that Mama fears he *might*! One can't blame her. There does seem to be something about Bab which drives quite sensible men distracted. Dreadful, isn't it?'

'I think it is.'

'Yes, so do I,' said Georgiana regretfully. 'I wish I had it.'

Judith could not help laughing, but she assured her vivacious young friend that she was very well as she was. 'All the nicest men pay their court to Georgy,' she said. 'It is men like the Comte de Lavisse who run after Lady Barbara.'

'Yes,' sighed Georgiana, looking pensively in the direction of the Count. 'Very true. Of course one would not wish to be admired by such a person.'

This sentiment was echoed by the Lady Barbara's brother, much later in the evening. As his carriage conveyed him and his ladies home to the Rue Ducale he said in a peevish tone that he wondered Bab could bear to have that foreign fellow for ever at her elbow.

She only laughed, but his wife, who had been yawning in her corner of the carriage, said sharply: 'If you mean Lavisse, I am sure I don't know why you should. I only wish Bab may not play fast and loose with him. I believe he is extremely rich.'

This argument was one that could not but appeal to the Marquis. He was silent for a few moments, but presently said: 'I don't know about that, but I can tell you his reputation doesn't bear looking into.'

'If it comes to that, Bab's own reputation is not above reproach!'

Another gurgle of laughter came from the opposite corner of the carriage. The Marquis said severely: 'It's all very well to laugh. No doubt it amuses you to make your name a byword. For my part, I have had enough of your scandals.'

'Oh, pray spare us a homily!' said his wife, yawning again.

'Don't be anxious, Vidal! They're laying odds against

Lavisse's staying the course for more than a month.'

The carriage passed over an uneven stretch of pavé. Unpleasantly jolted, the Marquis said angrily: 'Upon my word! Do you like to have your name bandied about? Your affairs made the subject of bets?'

'I don't care,' replied Barbara indifferently. 'No, I think I like it.'

'You're shameless! Who told you this?'

'Harry.'

'I might have known it! Pretty news to recount to his sister!'

'Oh lord, why shouldn't he?' said Lady Vidal. 'You'll be a bigger fool than I take you for, Bab, if you let Lavisse slip through your fingers.'

'I don't let them slip,' retorted Barbara. 'I drop them. I daresay I shall drop him too.'

'Be careful he doesn't drop you!' said her ladyship.

The carriage had drawn up before one of the large houses in the Rue Ducale, facing the Park. As the footman opened the door, Barbara murmured: 'Oh no, do you think he will? That would be interesting.'

Her sister-in-law forbore to answer this, but, alighting from the carriage, passed into the house. Barbara followed her, but paused only to say goodnight before picking up her candle and going upstairs to her bedroom.

She had not, however, seen the last of Lady Vidal, who came tapping on her door half an hour later, and entered with the air of one who proposed to remain some while. Barbara was seated before the mirror, her flaming head rising out of the foam of sea-green gauze which constituted her dressing-gown. 'Oh, what the deuce, Gussie?' she said.

'Send your girl away: I want to talk to you,' commanded Augusta, settling herself in the most comfortable chair in the room.

Barbara gave an impatient sigh, but obeyed. As the door closed behind the maid, she said: 'Well, what is it? Are you going to urge me to marry Etienne? I wish you may not put yourself to so much trouble.'

'You might do worse,' said Augusta.

'To be sure I might. We are agreed, then.'

'You known, you should be thinking seriously of marriage. You're twenty-five, my dear.'

'Ah, marriage is a bore!'

'If you mean husbands are bores, I'm sure I heartily agree with you,' responded Augusta. 'They have to be endured for the sake of the blessings attached to them. Single, one has neither standing nor consequence.'

'I'll tell you what, Gussie: the best is to be a widow – a dashing widow!'

'So you may think while you still possess pretensions to beauty. No longer, I assure you. As for "dashing", that brings me to another thing I had to say. I believe I'm no prude, but those gilded toenails of yours are the outside of enough, Bab.'

Barbara lifted a fold of the gauze to observe her bare feet. 'Pretty, aren't they?'

'Vidal informs me he has seen none but French women (and those of a certain class) with painted nails.'

'Oh, famous!'

Barbara seemed to be so genuinely delighted by this piece of news that Lady Vidal thought it wiser to leave the subject. 'That's as may be. What is more important is what you mean to do with your future. If you take my advice, you'll marry Lavisse.'

'No, he would be the devil of a husband.'

'And you the devil of a wife, my dear.'

'True. I will live and die a widow.'

'Pray don't talk such stuff to me!' said Augusta tartly. 'If you let slip all opportunities of getting a husband I shall think you are a great fool.'

Barbara laughed, and getting up from the stool before her dressing table, strolled across the room to a small cupboard and opened it. 'Very well! Let us look about us! Shall I set my cap at dear Gordon? I could fancy him, I believe.'

'Sir Alexander? Don't be absurd! A boy!'

Barbara had taken a medicine bottle from the cupboard and

was measuring some of its contents into a glass. She paused, and wrinkled her brow. 'General Maitland? That would be suitable: he is a widower.'

'He is as good as promised to Sarah Lennox.'

'That's no objection – if I want him. No, I don't think I do. I'll tell you what, Gussie, I'll have the Adjutant-General!'

'Good God, that would not last long! They call him the Fire-eater. You would be for ever quarrelling. I wish you would be serious! You need not marry a soldier, after all.'

'Yes, yes, if I marry it must be a soldier. I am quite determined. The Army is all the rage. And when have I ever been behind the mode? Consider, too, the range of possibilities! Only think of the Guards positively massed in the neighbourhood. I have only to drive to Enghien to find an eligible *parti*. The cavalry, too! All the Household Troops are under orders to sail, and I had always a liking for a well set-up Life Guardsman.'

'That means we shall have George here, I suppose,' said Augusta, without any appearance of gratification.

'Yes, but never mind that! What do you say to a gallant hussar? The 10th are coming out and they wear such charming clothes! I have had a riding dress made à la hussar, in the palest green, all frogged and laced with silver. Ravishing!'

'You will set the town by the ears!'

'Who cares?'

'*You* may not, but it is not very agreeable for us. I wish you would consider me a little before you put Vidal out of temper.'

Barbara came back into the middle of the room, holding the glass containing her potion. 'Where's the use? If I don't, George will. Vidal is such a dull dog!'

Augusta gave a laugh. 'I had rather have him than George, at all events. What are you taking there?'

'Only my laudanum drops,' replied Barbara, tossing off the mixture.

'Well, I take them myself, but I have the excuse of nervous headaches. *You* never had such a thing in your life. If you would be less restless –'

'Well, I won't, I can't! This is nothing: it helps me to sleep. Who was the demure lass dancing with Harry? She came with Lady Worth, I think.'

'Oh, that chit! She's of no account; I can't conceive what should possess Lady Worth to take her under her wing. There is an uncle, or some such thing. A very vulgar person, connected with Trade. Of course, if Harry is to lose his head in that direction it will be only what one might have expected, but I must say I think we might be spared that at least. I can tell you this, if you and your brothers create any odious scandals, Vidal will insist on returning to England. He is of two minds now.'

'Why? Is he afraid of me, or only of Boney?'

'Both, I daresay. I have no notion of staying here if Bonaparte does march on Brussels, as they all say he will. And if I go you must also.'

Barbara shed her sea-green wrap and got into bed. The light of the candles beside her had the effect of making her eyes and hair glow vividly. 'Don't think it! I shall stay. A war will be exciting. I like that!'

'You can scarcely remain alone in Brussels!'

Barbara snuggled down among a superfluity of pillows. 'Who lives will see!

'*I* should not care to do so in your situation.'

A gleam shot into the half-closed eyes; they looked sideways at Augusta. 'Dearest Gussie! So respectable!' Barbara murmured.

Three

Lady Worth walked into her breakfast-parlour on the morning of April 5th, to find that she was not, as she had supposed, the first to enter it. A cocked hat had been tossed on to a chair, and a gentleman in the white net pantaloons and blue frock-coat of a staff officer was sitting on the floor, busily engaged in making paper boats for Lord Temperley. Lord Temperley was standing beside him, a stern frown on his countenance betokening the rapt interest of a young gentleman just two years old.

'Well!' cried Judith.

The staff officer looked quick up, and jumped to his feet. He was a man in the mid-thirties, with smiling grey eyes, and a mobile, well-shaped mouth.

Lady Worth seized him by both hands. 'My dear Charles! of all the delightful surprises! But when did you arrive? How pleased I am to see you! Have you breakfasted? Where is your baggage?'

Colonel Audley responded to this welcome by putting an arm round his sister-in-law's waist and kissing her cheek. 'No need to ask you how you do: you look famous! I got in last night, too late to knock you up.'

'How can you be so absurd? Don't tell me you put up at an hôtel!'

'No, at the Duke's.'

'He is here too? Really in Brussels at last?'

'Why certainly! We are all of us here – the Duke, Fremantle, young Lennox, and your humble servant.' A tug at his sash recalled his attention to his nephew. 'Sir! I beg pardon! The boat – of course!'

The boat was soon finished, and put into his lordship's fat little hand. Prompted by his Mama, he uttered a laconic word of thanks, and was borne off by his nurse.

Colonel Audley readjusted his sash. 'I must tell you that I find my nephew improved out of all recognition, Judith. When I last had the pleasure of meeting him, he covered me with confusion by bursting into a howl of dismay. But nothing could have been more gentlemanlike than his reception of me today.'

She smiled. 'I hope it may be true. He is not always so, I confess. To my mind he is excessively like his father in his dislike of strangers. Worth, of course, would have you believe quite otherwise. Sit down, and let me give you some coffee. Have you seen Worth yet?'

'Not a sign of him. Tell me all the news! What has been happening here? How do you go on?'

'But my dear Charles, *I* have no news! It is to you that we look for that. Don't you know that for weeks past we have been positively hanging upon your arrival, eagerly searching your wretchedly brief letters for the least grain of interesting intelligence?'

He looked surprised, and a little amused. 'What in the world would you have me tell you? I had thought the deliberations of the Congress were pretty well known.'

'Charles!' said her ladyship, in a despairing voice, 'you have been at the very hub of the world, surrounded by Emperors and Statesmen, and you ask me what I would have you tell me!'

'Oh, I can tell you a deal about the Emperors,' offered the Colonel. 'Alexander, now, is – let us say – a trifle difficult.'

He was interrupted. 'Tell me immediately what you have been doing!' commanded Judith.

'Dancing,' he replied.

'Dancing!'

'And dining.'

'You are most provoking. Are you pledged to secrecy? If so, of course I won't ask you any awkward questions.'

'Not in the least,' said the Colonel cheerfully. 'Life in Vienna was one long ball. I have been devoting a great part of my time to the quadrille. *L'Eté, la Poule, la grande ronde* – I have all the steps, I assure you.'

'You must be a very odd sort of an aide-de-camp!' she remarked. 'Does not the Duke object?'

'Object?' said the Colonel. 'Of course not! He likes it. William Lennox would tell you that the excellence of his *pas de zéphyr* is the only thing that has more than once saved him from reprimand.'

'But seriously, Charles –?'

'On my honour!'

She was quite dumbfounded by this unexpected light cast upon the proceedings at Vienna, but before she could express her astonishment her husband came into the room, and the subject was forgotten in the greeting between the brothers, and the exchange of questions.

'You have been travelling fast,' the Earl said, as he presently took his seat at the table. 'Stuart spoke of the Duke's still being in Vienna only the other day.'

'Yes, shockingly fast. We even had to stop for lard to grease the wheels. But with such a shriek going up for the Beau from here, what did you expect?' said the Colonel, with a twinkle. 'Anyone would imagine Boney to be only a day's march off from the noise you have been making.'

The Earl smiled, but merely said: 'Are you rejoining the Regiment, or do you remain on the Staff?'

'Oh, all of us old hands remain, except perhaps March, who will probably stay with the Prince of Orange. Lennox goes back to his regiment, of course. He is only a youngster, and the Beau wants his old officers with him. What about my horses, Worth? You had my letter?'

'Yes, and wrote immediately to England. Jackson has procured you three good hunters, and there is a bay mare I bought for you last week.'

'Good!' said the Colonel. 'I shall probably get forage allowance for four horses. Tell me how you have been going on here! Who's this fellow, Hudson Lowe, who knows all there is to be known about handling armies?'

'Oh, you've seen him already, have you? I suppose you know he is your Quartermaster-General? Whether he will deal with the Duke is a question yet to be decided.'

'My dear fellow, it was decided within five minutes of his presenting himself this morning,' said the Colonel, passing his cup and saucer to Lady Worth. 'I left him instructing the Beau, and talking about his experience. Old Hookey as stiff as a poker, and glaring at him, with one of his crashing snubs just ripe to be delivered. I slipped away. Fremantle's on duty, poor devil!'

'Crashing snubs? Is the Duke a bad-tempered man?' enquired Judith. 'That must be a sad blow to us all!'

'Oh no, I wouldn't call him *bad*-tempered!' replied the Colonel. 'He gets peevish, you know – a trifle crusty, when things don't go just as he wishes. I wish they may get Murray back from America in time to take this fellow Lowe's place: we can't have him putting old Hookey out every day of the week: comes too hard on the wretched staff.'

Judith gave him back his cup and saucer. 'But, Charles, this is shocking! You depict a cross, querulous person, and we have been expecting a demi-god.'

'Demi-god! Well, so he is, the instant he goes into action,' said the Colonel. He drank his coffee, and said, 'Who is here, Worth? Any troops arrived yet from England?'

'Very few. We have really only the remains of Graham's detachment still, the same that Orange has had under his command the whole winter. There are the 1st Guards, the Coldstream, and the 3rd Scots; all 2nd battalions. The 52nd is here, a part of the 95th – but you must know the regiments as well as I do! There's no English cavalry at all, only that of the German Legion.'

The Colonel nodded. 'They'll come.'

'Under Combermere?'

'Oh, surely! We can't do without old Stapleton Cotton's long face among us. But tell me! who are all these schoolboys on the staff, and where did they spring from? Scarcely a name one knows on the Quartermaster-General's staff, or the Adjutant-General's either, for that matter!'

'I thought myself there were a number of remarkably inexperienced young gentlemen calling themselves Deputy-Assistants – but when the Duke takes a lad of fifteen into his family one is left to suppose he likes a staff just out of the nursery. By the by, I suppose you know you have arrived in time to assist at festivities at the Hôtel de Ville tonight? There's to be a fête in honour of the King and Queen of the Netherlands. Does the Duke go?'

'Oh yes, we always go to fêtes!' replied the Colonel. 'What is it to be? Dancing, supper – the usual thing? That reminds me: I must have some new boots. Is there anyone in the town who can be trusted to make me a pair of hessians?'

This question led to a discussion of the shops in Brussels, and the more pressing needs of an officer on the Duke of Wellington's staff. These seemed to consist mostly of articles of wearing apparel suitable for galas, and Lady Worth was left presently to reflect on the incomprehensibility of the male sex, which, upon the eve of war, was apparently concerned solely with the price of silver lace, and the cut of a hessian boot.

The Colonel had declared his dress clothes to be worn to rags, but when he presented himself in readiness to set forth to the Hôtel de Ville that evening his sister-in-law had no fault to find with his appearance beyond regretting, with a sigh, that his present occupation made the wearing of his hussar uniform ineligible. Nothing could have been better than the set of his coat across his shoulders, nothing more resplendent than his fringed sash, nothing more effulgent than his hessians with their swinging tassels. The Colonel was blessed with a good leg, and had nothing to fear from sheathing it in a skin-tight net pantaloon. His curling brown locks had been brushed into a state of pleasing disorder, known as the style *au coup de vent*; his

35

whiskers were neatly trimmed; he carried his cocked hat under one arm; and altogether presented to his sister-in-law's critical gaze a very handsome picture.

That he was quite unaware of it naturally did not detract from his charm. Judith, observing him with a little complacency, decided that if Miss Devenish failed to succumb to the twinkle in the Colonel's open grey eyes, or to the attraction of his easy, frank manners, she must be hard indeed to please.

Miss Devenish would be present this evening, Judith having been at considerable pains to procure invitation tickets for her and for Mrs Fisher.

The Earl of Worth's small party arrived at the Hôtel de Ville shortly after eight o'clock, to find a long line of carriages setting down their burdens one after another, and the interior of the building already teeming with guests. The ante-rooms were crowded, and (said Colonel Audley) as hot as any in Vienna; and her ladyship, having had her train of lilac crape twice trodden on, was very glad to pass into the ballroom. Here matters were a little better, the room being of huge proportions. Down one side of it were tall windows, with statues on pedestals set in each, while on the opposite side were corresponding embrasures, each one curtained, and emblazoned with the letter W in a scroll.

A great many of the guests were of Belgian or of Dutch nationality, but Lady Worth soon discovered English acquaintances among them, and was presently busy presenting Colonel Audley to those who had not yet met him, or recalling him to the remembrances of those who had. She did not perceive Miss Devenish in the room, but since she had taken up a position near the main entrance, she had little doubt of observing her arrival. Meanwhile, Colonel Audley remained beside her, and might have continued shaking hands, greeting old friends, and being made known to smiling strangers for any length of time, had not an interruption occurred which immediately attracted the attention of everyone present.

A pronounced stir was taking place in the ante-room; a loud, whooping laugh was heard, and the next moment a well-made

36

gentleman in a plain evening dress embellished with a number of Orders walked into the ballroom, escorted by the Mayor of Brussels, and a suite composed of senior officers in various glittering dress uniforms. The ribbon of the Garter relieved the severity of the gentleman's dress, but except for his carriage there was little to proclaim the military man. Beside the gilded splendour of a German Hussar, and the scarlet brilliance of an English Guardsman, he looked almost out of place. He had rather sparse mouse-coloured hair, a little grizzled at the temples; a mouth pursed slightly in repose, but just now open in laughter; and a pair of chilly blue eyes set under strongly marked brows. The eyes must have immediately attracted attention had this not been inevitably claimed by his incredible nose. That high-bridged bony feature dominated his face and made it at once remarkable. It lent majesty to the countenance and terror to its owner's frown. It was a proud, masterful nose, the nose of one who would brook no interference, and permit few liberties. It was also a famous nose, and anyone beholding it would have had to be very dull-witted not to have realised at once that it belonged to the Duke of Wellington.

Lady Worth grasped its significance, but could scarcely believe that quite the most soberly-dressed gentleman in the room (if you let out of account that casual sprinkling of Orders) could really be the Field-Marshal himself. Even Lord Hill, at his elbow, was more resplendent, while any Cornet of Hussars would have cast him in the shade.

That was Lady Worth's first impression, but a second, following it swiftly, at once corrected it. The Duke had no need of silver lace or a scarlet-and-gold coat to attract the eye. He had a presence which made itself felt the instant he entered the room. He stood surrounded by his general staff, and they became no more than a splendid background for his trim figure. It was very odd, reflected Lady Worth, watching him, for his height was no more than average, and he did not bear himself with any extraordinary dignity. Indeed, there seemed to be very little pomp about him. He was shaking hands briskly with the Belgian

37

notables presented by the Mayor; he was laughing again, and really, his laugh was over-loud, not unlike the neighing of a horse.

He came further into the ballroom, pausing to greet individuals, and, catching sight of Colonel Audley, said in a quick, resonant voice: 'Ah, there you are, Audley! One of my family, Baron – Colonel Audley, who has been with me in Vienna, and will show us all how they perform the *grande ronde* there.'

'Why, Charles, how do you do?' exclaimed the Duchess of Richmond, giving him her hand. 'And Lady Worth! My dear Duke, I think you have not met Charles's sister-in-law. Lady Worth, the Duke of Wellington!'

Judith found herself under the piercing scrutiny of the Duke's deep-set eyes, which surveyed her with an expression of decided approbation. She would have bowed merely, but he took her hand in a firm grasp, and shook it, saying: 'Delighted! You must let me tell you how delighted I am to meet Audley's sister. Do you make a long stay in Brussels? Eh? Yes? That's capital! I shall hope for a better acquaintance.'

Judith said something graceful, and as his Grace seemed inclined to linger, presented her husband. A brief How-de-do? was exchanged; other people pressed forward to claim the Duke's attention; and he passed on, bowing to one person, shaking hands with another, calling out: 'Hallo, how are you? Glad to see you!' to a third. Unlike the figure of her imagination, he seemed very much at home in a ballroom, quite accessible, cheerful to the verge of jocularity, and ready to be pleased. Such remarks of his as reached Lady Worth's ears were none of them profound, and when the anxious besought his opinion of the political situation he replied with a joviality which had almost the effect of making him appear to be a little stupid.

Lady Worth was still looking after the Duke when she caught sight of Miss Devenish, standing not many paces distant, beside her aunt. Judith noticed with satisfaction that she was in her best looks, her hair very prettily dressed, her cheeks faintly flushed, and her large eyes glowing. She had just decided not to seem to be in too great a hurry to introduce Charles, when his voice said in her ear: 'Who is that?'

Nothing, thought Judith, could have been more opportune! Lucy was far too unaffected to have purposely placed herself beside a plain young female in a dress of particularly harsh puce, but the effect could not have been more advantageous to her. How right she had been to advise the child to wear her white satin! It was no wonder that she had caught Charles's eye. She replied in a careless tone: 'Oh, that is a young friend of mine, a Miss Devenish.'

'Will you present me?'

'Why, certainly! She is pretty, is she not?'

'Pretty!' repeated the Colonel. 'She is the loveliest creature I ever beheld in my life!'

Prejudiced as Judith was in Miss Devenish's favour, this encomium seemed to be to her somewhat exaggerated. Charles sounded quite serious too: in fact, oddly serious. She turned her head, and found to her surprise that he was not looking in Miss Devenish's direction, but towards the big double doorway.

'Why, Charles, whom can you be staring at?' she began, but broke off as her gaze followed his. It was quite obvious whom Colonel Audley was staring at. He was staring at a vision in palest green satin draped in a cloud of silver net. The Lady Barbara Childe had arrived, and was standing directly beneath a huge chandelier, just inside the ballroom. The candlelight touched her hair with fire, and made the emerald spray she wore in it gleam vividly. The heavy folds of satin clung to her form, and clearly revealed the long, lovely line of a leg, a little advanced beyond its fellow. Shoulders and breast were bare, if you ignored a scarf of silver net, which (thought Lady Worth) was easily done. Any woman would have agreed that the bodice of the wretched creature's gown was cut indecently low, while as for petticoats, Lady Worth for one would have owned herself surprised to learn that Barbara was wearing as much as a stitch beneath her satin and her net.

A glance at Colonel Audley's face was enough to inform her that this disgraceful circumstance was not likely to weigh with him as it should.

His hand came up to grasp her elbow, not ungently, but with a certain urgency. 'Miss Devenish, did you say?'

'No, I did not!' replied Judith crossly. She recollected herself, and added with an attempt to conceal her annoyance: 'You are looking at the wrong lady. That is Barbara Childe. I daresay you may have heard of her.'

'So that is Barbara Childe!' he said. 'Are you acquainted with her? Will you present me?'

'Well, really, Charles, my acquaintance with her is of the slightest. You know, she is not quite the thing. I will allow her to be excessively handsome, but I believe you would be disappointed if you knew her.'

'Impossible!' he replied.

Judith looked wildly round in search of inspiration, and encountered only the mocking eyes of her lord. She met that quizzical glance with one of entreaty not unmixed with indignation. The Earl took snuff with a wonderful air of abstraction.

Help came from an unexpected quarter. Those standing by the door fell back; the orchestra struck up *William of Nassau*; the King and Queen of the Netherlands had arrived.

There could be no question of performing introductions at such a moment. As the ushers came in, the crowd parted, till an avenue was formed; their Majesties were announced; every lady sank in a deep curtsy; and in walked King William, a stout gentleman, with his stout Queen beside him, and behind him his two sons.

Majesty was in an affable mood, smiling broadly, ready to have any number of presentations made, and to be extremely gracious to everyone; but the Princes attracted more attention. The younger, Frederick, was a fine young man, with not inconsiderable pretensions to good looks. He bore himself stiffly, and favoured his acquaintances with an inclination of the head, accompanied by a small, regal smile.

His brother, the Prince of Orange, though arrayed in all the magnificence of a general's dress uniform, was a much less impressive figure. He was very thin and held himself badly, and his good-humoured countenance bore a slight resemblance to that of a startled faun. His smile, however, was disarming, and a marked tendency to wink at cronies whom he observed in the crowd could not but endear him to his more unceremonious friends. When he caught sight of Colonel Audley, an expression of delight leapt to his rather prominent eyes, and he waved to him; and when the Duke of Wellington, having bowed punctiliously over the King's hand, turned to pay his respects to him, he frustrated any attempt at formality by starting forward, and taking the Duke's hand with all the reverence of a junior officer honoured by a great man.

'I hope I see your Royal Highness in good health?' said the Duke.

'I am so glad to see you, sir,' stammered his Royal Highness. 'I would have reported at your house this morning, but I did not know – I was at Braine-le-Comte – you must forgive me!'

The Duke's face relaxed. 'I shall be happy to see your Highness tomorrow, if that should be convenient to you.'

'Yes, of course, sir!' his Highness assured him.

Majesty, listening indulgently to this interchange, intervened to draw the Duke's attention to his younger son. The Prince of Orange seized the opportunity to efface himself, and would have slipped away in search of more congenial companionship had not the signal for the dancing to begin been given at that moment. He was obliged to lead the opening quadrille with the Duchesse de Beaufort, and to dance a couple of waltzes with Madame d'Ursel and Madame d'Assche. After that, he considered his duty conscientiously performed, and disappeared from the ballroom into one of the adjoining rooms where refreshment and kindred spirits were to be found.

He entered between looped curtains to find a small but convivial party assembled there. Lord March, a fresh-faced young man with grave eyes and a quick smile, was leaning on a chair back, adjuring Colonel Audley, seated on the edge of the table, and Colonel Fremantle, lounging against the wall, to make a clean breast of their doings in Vienna. The fourth member of the group was Sir Alexander Gordon, a young man with a winning personality, who was engaged in filling his glass from a decanter.

'Charles!' cried the Prince, coming forward in his impetuous style. 'My dear fellow, how are you?'

Colonel Audley stood up. 'Sir!' he said.

The Prince wrung his hand. 'Now, don't, I beg you! I am so pleased you are here! Do not let us have any ceremony! This is like Spain: we need only Canning, and Fitzroy to walk in asking, "Where's Slender Billy?" and we are again the old family.'

'That's all very well, but you've become a great man since I saw you last,' objected Colonel Audley. 'I think – yes, I think a Royal Tiger.'

A general laugh greeted this old Headquarters' joke. The Prince said: 'You can't call *me* a Tiger: I am not a visitor to the camp! But have you seen the real Tigers? *Mon Dieu*, do you remember we called the Duc d'Angoulême a Royal Tiger? But, my dear Charles – my dear Fremantle – the Duc de Berri! No, really, you would not believe! You must see him drilling his men to appreciate him. He flies into a passion and almost falls off his horse. But on my honour!'

'*No*, sir!' protested March.

'I swear it!' He accepted a glass of wine from Gordon, and perched himself on the arm of a chair. 'Confusion to Boney!' he said, and drank. 'And General Röder!' he resumed.

'Confusion to him too, sir?' murmured Gordon.

'No – yes! The worst of our Tigers! Have you met General Röder, Charles? He doesn't like the British, he doesn't like the Dutch, he doesn't like the Belgians, he doesn't like the French, he doesn't even like your humble servant. So here is confusion to General Röder!'

While this toast was being drunk, a pleasant-faced officer in Dutch uniform had peeped round the curtain and then come into the room. He was considerably older than any of the young men drinking confusion to the unfortunate Prussian Commissioner, but was hailed by them with cheerful affection.

'Hallo, Baron! Come in!' said Audley. 'How are you?'

'Glass of wine with you, Baron?' Fremantle held up the decanter invitingly.

'Constant! We are drinking confusion to General von Röder. Join us immediately!' commanded his Royal master.

The Baron Constant de Rebecque glanced swiftly over his shoulder. He accepted a glass of wine, but said in very good English: 'I beg of you, sir – ! Consider where you are, and who you are, and – very well, very well, here is confusion to him, then! And now will you recollect, sir, that this is a fête for their Majesties, and it is expected that you will conduct yourself *en prince*! Your absence will be noticed: his Majesty will be displeased.'

The Prince shrugged his shoulders. 'It is absurd. I will not spend all the evening being civil to the Tigers, and I will not conduct myself *en prince* if that means I must not drink a glass of wine with my friends.'

'Sir, you are also the General in Command of the Army, and not any more a junior aide-de-camp.'

The Prince patted his arm. 'Constant, *mon pauvre*, you have not seen – you have not heard! You are dreaming, in fact. Go and look who is here tonight. My poor command is quite at an end.'

'*Mon Prince*, you are still in command, and you must mingle with your guests.'

'That's quite true, sir,' said Fremantle. 'The Duke hasn't taken over the command yet. Duty calls you, General!'

At this moment, and while the Prince still looked recalcitrant, a very tall man with the buff collar and silver lace of the 52nd Regiment appeared between the curtains, and stood silently surveying the group. He was Saxon fair, with ice-blue eyes, a high-bridged nose, and a fighting chin, and was built on splendid lines that were marred only by the droop of his right shoulder, the joint of which had become anchylosed, from a wound incurred in the Peninsula. At sight of him, Lord March straightened himself instinctively, and Colonel Fremantle jumped up from his chair.

The Prince turned his head, and pulled a grimace. 'You need not tell me! You are looking for me. First my quarter-master-general, and now my military secretary. Your health, Sir John!'

'Thank you, sir,' said Colonel Colborne in his slow deep voice. A smile crept into his eyes. 'I thought I should find you with the riffraff of the staff,' he remarked. 'If I were your Highness, I would return to the ballroom.'

'Because my father will be displeased,' said the Prince. 'I have that by heart.'

'No,' replied Sir John. 'Because his Majesty is more than likely to request the Duke to speak to you, sir.'

'Oh, *mon Dieu*!' exclaimed the Prince, preparing for instant flight. 'You are entirely right! Charles, my hôtel is in the Rue de Brabant! I charge you, don't forget! I will go and do my duty, and dance with all the ugly old women. Would you like to be presented to a fat *Frau*? No? Well, then, *au revoir*!'

'Stay a moment!' said Colonel Audley suddenly. 'Do that for me, sir, will you?'

The Prince paused in the doorway, looking back with a laugh in his eyes. 'What, present you to a fat *Frau*?'

'No, to the Lady Barbara Childe.'

The Prince's brow shot up; a low whistle broke from Lord March; Colonel Fremantle said solicitously: 'My poor fellow, you are not yourself. Take my advice and go quietly home to bed.'

Audley reddened, but only said: 'I am perfectly serious. I have been trying for the past hour to get an introduction, but there's no coming near her for the crowd round her. *You* could present me, sir, if you would.'

'Steal into the supper-room and change the tickets on the tables,' suggested March flippantly.

'Don't do it, sir!' recommended Fremantle.

The Prince laughed. 'But Charles, this is the road to ruin! Really, you wish it?'

'Most earnestly, sir.'

'Come, then, but mind, I am not to be blamed for the consequences!'

Colonel Audley had not exaggerated the difficulty of approaching Barbara Childe. When she left the dancing-floor on the arm of her partner she became engulfed in a crowd of impatient supplicants who would scarcely give place to any under the rank of a general. All had, however, to fall back before the Prince of Orange, who led Colonel Audley up to her ladyship, and said with his appealing smile: 'Lady Barbara, I want to present to you a friend of mine who desires beyond anything this introduction. Colonel Audley – Lady Barbara Childe!'

Colonel Audley bowed, and looked up to find the Lady Barbara's brilliant gaze upon him. There was candid speculation in it, a tolerant smile just parted the lady's lips. The Colonel returned the look, smiled, and said in his pleasant voice: 'How do you do?'

'How do you do?' responded Barbara slowly, still looking at him.

Four

The Colonel, finding a gloved hand held out to him, took it in his, and bent his head to kiss it. Barbara looked down at it with a little bewilderment, as though she wondered why she had extended it.

'Do please grant the Colonel one waltz!' said the Prince, amusement quivering in his voice.

He moved away. The Comte de Lavisse said in English: 'But how should that be possible, one asks oneself?'

'May I have the honour?' said the Colonel.

'But no!' objected the Count. 'This leads to an affair of the most sanguinary! I shall immediately send my friends to call upon you!'

'We shall all send our friends to call upon you!' declared an office of the 1st Guards. 'Audley, this is piracy! Those wishing to dance with Lady Bab must present their credentials a full week beforehand!'

Captain Chalmers, of the 52nd, said: 'Send him about his business, Bab! These staff officers are not at all the thing. Stick the Light Division!'

'These Light Division men, Lady Barbara,' said Colonel Audley, 'fancy themselves more important than the rest of the Army put together. I tell you in confidence, but you know it is a fact that they brag shockingly.'

'An insult!' declared Chalmers. 'An insult from a staff officer! Bab, I appeal to your sense of justice!'

Barbara laughed, and, laying her hand on Colonel Audley's

arm, said: 'Oh, the wishes of Royalty are tantamount to commands, gentlemen.' She kissed her hand to her court, and walked back on to the floor with Colonel Audley.

He danced well, and she as though by instinct. Neither spoke for one or two turns, but presently Barbara raised her eyes to his face, and asked abruptly: 'Why did you look at me *so*?'

He smiled down at her. 'I don't know how I looked. I have been wanting to dance with you all evening. Does every man say that to you?'

'Yes,' she replied nonchalantly.

'I was afraid it must be so. I wish I might think of something to say to you which would interest you by its novelty.'

'Oh! . . . Can you not?'

'No. If I said the only thing I can think of to say you would find it abominably commonplace.'

'Should I? What is it?'

'I love you,' replied the Colonel.

Momentary surprise, which caused her wonderful eyes to fly upwards to his again, gave place immediately to frank amusement. Her enchanting gurgle of laughter escaped her; she said: 'You are wrong. The unexpected cannot be commonplace.'

'Was it unexpected? I had not thought that possible.'

'Certainly. At the end of a week I might expect you to say just that, but you have said it within ten minutes of making my acquaintance, and so have taken my breath away. Go on: I like to be surprised.'

'That is all,' said the Colonel.

Again she cast him that considering glance. 'You are very clever, or very simple. Which is it?'

'I haven't a notion,' replied the Colonel.

'Ah! Is this strategy – from a staff officer?'

'No, it is the truth.'

'But, my friend, you are fantastic! You will next be making me an offer!'

He nodded. She saw the twinkle in his eye and responded to it. 'Let us sit down. I don't care to dance any more. Who are you?'

47

He compelled her to continue dancing the length of the room, and then led her off the floor to the entrance doors, and through them into the first antechamber.

'My name is Charles Audley; my army rank lieutenant-colonel; my regimental rank, major. What else shall I tell you?'

She interrupted him. 'Audley . . . Oh, I have it! You are Worth's brother. Why did the Prince present you to me?'

'Because I asked him to. That was my only strategy.'

She sat down upon a couch against the wall, and with a movement of her hand invited him to take his place beside her. He did so, and after a moment she said with her odd, boyish curtness: 'I think I never saw you before tonight, did I?'

'Never. I have been employed in the Peninsula, and later in Paris and Vienna. But I have a little the advantage of you. *You*, I daresay, had never heard of me before, but *I* had heard of you.'

'That's horrid!' she said quickly.

'Why?'

'Oh! People never say nice things about me. What have you been told?'

'That you were beautiful.'

'And?'

'And disastrous.'

'I don't mind that, but should not you take care?'

'You are forgetting that I am a soldier, and therefore inured to risks.'

She laughed. 'You've a confoundedly ready tongue! Come, take me back into the ballroom: my reputation won't stand all this sitting about in antechambers, I can tell you.'

He rose at once, but said: 'I wonder why you chose to tell me that?'

She too was on her feet; she had to look up to meet his eyes, but only a little. 'You don't like it, do you?'

'No. I don't.'

'Nevertheless, it is the truth. I play fair, you see.'

He looked at her for a moment, half smiling, then raised his head, and held up a finger. 'Listen! Do you know that waltz they are playing? It has been the rage in Vienna. Will you dance with me again?'

A shade of admiration came into her eyes; she said appreciatively: 'The deuce take it! I believe – yes, I believe that was a snub! But you must not snub me!'

He turned towards her, and took both hands in a strong clasp. 'Don't speak ill of yourself, and I won't. There!' He raised her hands one after another to his lips, and lightly kissed them. 'My dance, I think, Lady Barbara?'

They went back into the ballroom; the Colonel's arm encircled that supple waist; a gloved hand lay light as a feather on his shoulder; Barbara murmured: 'You waltz charmingly, Colonel.'

'So do you, Lady Barbara.'

She stole a mischievous glance up at his face. 'That was to be expected. It is still thought a trifle *fast* in England, you know.'

From a little distance, Georgiana Lennox, circling round very dashingly with Lord Hay, caught sight of them, and promptly exclaimed: 'Oh, how infamous!'

'Where? Who?' demanded Hay.

'Over there, stupid! Don't you see? Bab Childe has seized on one of the nicest men in Brussels! Of all the wretched pieces of work! I do think she might be content with her odious Lavisse, and not steal Charles Audley as well!'

'Lucky devil!' said Hay.

'Sir!' Georgiana in outraged accents. 'Take me back to Mama this instant, if you please!'

'Oh lord!' gasped Hay ruefully. 'I didn't mean it, Georgy, really I didn't!'

She allowed herself to be mollified, but remarked sagely: 'You may think him lucky, but I expect Lady Worth won't.'

She was quite right. From the harbour of Sir Henry Clinton's gallant arm, Judith too had perceived her brother-in-law and his partner. That the couple could waltz better than any other in the room, and were attracting some attention, afforded her not the slightest gratification. She had observed the look on Colonel

Audley's face, and although she had never before seen him wear that particular expression she had not the least doubt of its significance.

Sir Henry, noticing the direction of her troubled gaze, manoeuvred that he too might see what had caught her eye. He said: 'Your brother-in-law, is it not, Lady Worth?'

'Yes,' she acknowledged.

'Dances very well, I see. All the Duke's family do, of course. But he will be making enemies if he monopolises Bab Childe.'

'Monopolises her?' faltered Judith. 'Is not this the first time he has danced with her?'

'Oh no! He was dancing with her the last waltz. My wife tells me the young fellows form up in column for the honour of obtaining the lady's hand.'

'Charles is fortunate, then,' said Judith.

'If you choose to call it fortunate,' said Sir Henry, giving her a somewhat shrewd look. 'I don't want to see any of my staff entangled in that direction. She has a very unsettling effect, from what I can discover. One of Barnes's boys lost his head badly over her, and is now of about as much use to Barnes as my wife's little spaniel would be.'

'I wonder who introduced Charles to her?'

Sir Henry laughed shortly. 'I can tell you that, dear lady. The Prince of Orange.'

Judith pursued the subject no further. Sir Henry's differences with the Prince made it tactless to introduce that ebullient young gentleman's name into any conversation with his second-in-command.

Colonel Audley relinquished Barbara presently, and discovering a disinclination in himself to dance with anyone else, went away in search of other amusement. This was not hard to find, for he had many friends present, and was able to spend a pleasant hour wandering about the ballroom and the adjoining salons, exchanging greetings and news with his acquaintances.

Two suppers were being served at midnight, the one a select affair given by the King to his more distinguished guests; the other a less select and more informal entertainment held in an adjoining salon. The Earl and Countess of Worth were of the first party; so, too, was Colonel Audley, in his character of aide-de-camp. He was about to join the stream of people passing through the ballroom to the King's supper parlour, and was standing by the entrance to one of the apartments leading out of the main antechamber, when the curtains obscuring the room behind him were thrust back, and Miss Devenish came out, almost running, her cheeks flushed, and one hand clasping to her shoulder a torn frill of lace.

So precipitate was her arrival in the antechamber that she nearly collided with Colonel Audley and recoiled with an exclamation on her lips and appearance of great confusion.

Colonel Audley had turned, with a word of apology for obstructing the way. Miss Devenish, still clutching her torn frill, said in a breathless voice: 'It is of no consequence. It was quite my fault. I beg your pardon – I was going in search of my aunt!'

Colonel Audley glanced from this agitated little lady towards the room from which she had fled in such haste, and took a step towards the entrance. Miss Devenish put out her hand quickly to stop him: 'Oh, please!' she said. 'I don't wish – I am being very stupid. So vexing! I have had the misfortune to tear my lace, and must get it pinned up.'

Colonel Audley took her trembling hand in his, and held it in a comfortingly firm clasp. 'My dear ma'am, what has happened to distress you?' he asked. 'Is there anything I can do?'

'Oh no, indeed! You are very kind, but it was nothing – really nothing at all! If I could find my aunt – it is time to be going in to supper, I believe.'

Colonel Audley glanced towards the ballroom. 'We will do our best to discover her, but I am afraid it will be a difficult task,' he said. 'Does she expect you to join her in the supper-room?'

'Oh yes! That is, nothing was said, but of course she would expect me. I was to have gone in with a – a gentleman, only . . .' She broke off, blushing more furiously that ever.

'Only that perhaps the gentleman had had a trifle too much

to drink, and so forgot himself,' finished the Colonel in a matter-of-fact voice.

Miss Devenish gave a gasp, and looked quickly up into his face. The smile in his eyes seemed to reassure her. She said: 'Yes, that was it. Oh, how singular it must appear to you! But indeed –'

'It doesn't appear in the least singular to me,' he interrupted. 'But your lace! That is a more serious matter. If you had a pin – or even two pins – in your reticule, and could trust to my bungling fingers, I believe I could set it to rights.'

The fright had by this time died out of her eyes. A smile quivered on her lips. She replied: 'I have a pin – two pins – but are you sure you can?'

'No,' said the Colonel. 'But I am sure I can try. Give me your pins.'

She glanced round, but they were alone in the antechamber. 'Thank you: you are very obliging!' she said and opened her reticule.

The pins once discovered, it was a matter of a minute or two only before the frills were in place again. Miss Devenish was quite astonished by the Colonel's deediness. 'I made sure you would prick me at least!' she said merrily. 'But I am quite in your debt! Thank you!'

He offered his arm. 'May I take you to your aunt, if we can find her?'

'Oh – ! I should be very happy: but am I not trespassing on your time?'

'How should you be? Perhaps your aunt may be waiting for you in the ballroom.'

No trace, however, of Mrs Fisher was to be found there, nor was she discovered in the corridor leading to the second supper-room.

'I am afraid there is nothing for it but for you to accept me in place of your other supper partner,' said the Colonel. 'Your aunt must have gone in already, and from what I have seen of the crowd there you will be lucky indeed if you contrive to find her. Shall we go in?'

She looked doubtfully at him. 'But are you sure you are not expected in the other room? I thought – someone told me – that nearly all the staff officers were invited, and you are one, are you not?'

'I am, but no one will care a button whether I sup in the other room or not, I assure you,' replied the Colonel. 'It will be very dull, if I know these staff functions.'

'Will it?'

'Oh, I give you my word! It will last an interminable time, and a great many people will made interminable speeches. I should infinitely prefer to sup with you.'

Miss Devenish smiled. 'I shall be very happy to go with you,' she said. 'Indeed, I think I should feel wretchedly lost by myself. There are so many people!'

They fell in with the slow-moving stream of guests, and presently found themselves in a large, brilliantly-lit room set out with any number of tables, and already bewilderingly full of people. As they paused within the room, looking about them for a couple of vacant places, Miss Devenish exclaimed: 'Oh, there she is!' and started towards a table near the door, at which was seated a stout, good-humoured-looking lady in purple sarsnet and a turban.

'There you are, my love!' said Mrs Fisher. 'I came in early to be sure of obtaining a good place. Well, and are you enjoying yourself? For my part I find the rooms very hot, but I daresay young people don't notice such things. You had better sit down while you may. I assure you I have been quite put to it to keep these seats for you.'

Miss Devenish turned to Colonel Audley. 'Thank you so very much! You need not miss your engagement in the other room after all, you see.'

Mrs Fisher, having favoured the Colonel with a sleepy yet shrewd scrutiny, interposed to invite him most hospitably to join her at the table. 'I would not go into the other room if I were you,' she told him. 'I daresay they will be making speeches for as much as a couple of hours.'

'Just what I have been saying to your niece, ma'am,' he replied, pulling out a chair for Miss Devenish.

As he did so a hand smote him on the shoulder. 'Hallo, Charles! How are you? What are you doing here? I thought you were supping in state! Judith and Worth are.'

The Colonel turned. 'Hallo, Perry!' he said, shaking hands. 'How do you do, Lady Taverner? Yes, I ought to be in the other room, but I missed Worth, and so came here instead. Are you staying long in Brussels? Do you like it?'

'Oh, pretty fair! 'Evening, ma'am – 'evening, Miss Devenish. Look, Harriet, there's Dawson waving to us: he has secured a table. Charles, are you staying with Worth? Oh then, I shall see you!'

He passed on, and the Colonel turned back to Miss Devenish to find her staring at him in the liveliest surprise. He could not help laughing. 'But what have I done? What have I said?' he asked.

'Oh! nothing, of course! But I had no idea you were Colonel Audley until Sir Peregrine spoke to you. Lady Worth is such a particular friend of mine!'

Mrs Fisher interposed to say in rather a bewildered voice: 'My love, what is all this? Surely you have been introduced!'

'No,' admitted Miss Devenish. 'I came upon Colonel Audley quite by accident.'

'But we were as good as introduced, ma'am,' said the Colonel, 'for I distinctly remember my sister telling me that she would present me to Miss Devenish. But just then the King and Queen arrived, and the opportunity was lost.'

Mrs Fisher smiled indulgently, but remarked that she had never known her niece to be so shatterbrained.

A couple of hours later Lady Worth, coming back into the ballroom on her husband's arm, was dumbfounded by the sight of Colonel Audley waltzing with Miss Devenish.

'Oh, so you contrived it, did you?' said Worth, also observing this circumstance.

'I did no such thing!' replied Judith. 'In fact, I had quite made up my mind it would be useless to present him to poor Lucy, straight from Bab Childe's clutches! But was there ever such a provoking man? Not but what I am very glad to see him with Lucy. Even you will admit that *that* would be preferable to an entanglement with Lady Barbara! I wonder who introduced him to her?'

She was soon to learn from the lady herself in what manner the Colonel had become acquainted with Miss Devenish, for Lucy joined her presently and confided the story to her sympathetic ear.

'Very disagreeable for you,' said Judith. 'I am glad Charles was at hand to be of assistance.'

'He was so very kind! But I am afraid you must have been wondering what had become of him. Was it very wrong of me to let him have supper with us?'

Judith started. 'So that was where he was! To be sure, I could not see him at any of the tables, but there was such a crowd I might easily miss him. I make no doubt he had a much more agreeable time of it with you.'

'We had a very cosy party,' replied Miss Devenish, 'if only my aunt had not found the heat so oppressive! Colonel Audley has such pleasant, open manners that he makes one feel one has known him all one's life.'

Lady Worth agreed to it, and had the satisfaction, during their drive home, of hearing Colonel Audley comment favourably on Miss Devenish. 'A very charming, unaffected girl,' he said.

'I am glad you were able to be of service to her.'

'Pinning up her lace? No very great matter,' replied the Colonel.

'I understood she had a disagreeable adventure: some young man (she would not tell me his name) was ungentlemanly enough to force his attentions upon her, surely?'

'Oh, I had nothing to do with that!' said the Colonel. 'He was probably in his cups, and meant no serious harm.'

'She is unfortunately situated in having an aunt too indolent to chaperon her as she should, and an uncle whose birth and

55

manners cannot add to her consequence. The fact of her being an heiress makes her very generally sought after!'

'An enviable position!' said the Colonel.

'Ah, you do not know! But I was an heiress myself, and I can tell you it was sometimes a very unenviable position.'

Worth said, with a note of amusement in his voice: '*My* position was certainly so, but that *you* experienced anything but the most profound enjoyment comes as news to me.'

She was betrayed into a laugh, but said: 'Well, perhaps I did enjoy teasing you at least, but recollect that I was never a shy creature like Lucy.'

'I recollect that perfectly,' said the Earl.

'Is Miss Devenish shy? I did not find her so,' said the Colonel. 'Shy girls are the devil, for they won't talk, and have such a habit of blushing that one is for ever thinking one has said something shocking. I found Miss Devenish perfectly conversable.'

Judith was satisfied. The Colonel, though ready to discuss the fête, had apparently forgotten Barbara Childe's existence. Not one word of admiration for her crossed his lips; her name was not mentioned.

'Julian, what a mercy! I don't believe he can have liked her after all!' confided her ladyship later, in the privacy of her own bedroom. 'Indeed, I might have trusted to his excellent good sense. Did you notice that he did not once speak of her?'

'I did,' replied the Earl somewhat grimly.

'Well?'

He looked at her, smiling, and took her chin in his hand. 'You are an ever-constant source of delight to me, my love. Did you know?' he said, kissing her.

Judith returned this embrace with great readiness, but asked: 'Why? Have I said something silly?'

'Very silly,' Worth assured her tenderly.

'How horrid you are! Tell me at once!'

'My adorable simpleton, Charles induced no less a personage than the Prince of Orange to present him to the most striking woman in the room, seized not one but two waltzes which I have not the least doubt were bespoken days ago by less fortunate suitors, and comes away at the end of the evening with apparently not one word to say of a lady whom even you will admit to be of quite extraordinary beauty.'

'Oh!' she said. 'Is that a bad sign, do you think?'

'The worst!' he answered.

She was shaken, but said stoutly: 'Well, I don't believe it. Charles has great good sense. I am perfectly at ease.'

Had she been privileged to observe Colonel Audley's actions not very many hours later her faith in his good sense might have suffered a shock. The Colonel's staff training had made him expert in obtaining desired information, and he had not wasted his time at the fête. While his sister-in-law still lay sleeping, he was up, and in the Earl's stables. Seven o'clock saw him cantering gently down the Allée Verte, beyond the walls of the town, mounted on a blood mare reserved for his brother's exclusive use.

Nor was this energy wasted. The edge had scarcely gone from the mare's morning freshness before the Colonel was rewarded by the sight of a slim figure, in a habit of cerulean blue, cantering ahead of him, unattended by any groom, and mounted on a raking grey hunter.

The Colonel gave the mare her head, and in two minutes was abreast of the grey. Lady Barbara, hearing the flying hooves, had turned her head, and immediately urged the grey to a gallop. Down the deserted Allée raced the horses, between two rows of thick lime trees, and with the still waters of the canal shining on their left.

'To the bridge!' called Barbara.

The Colonel held the mare in a little. 'Done! What will you wager?'

'Anything you please!' she said recklessly.

'Too rash! I might take an unfair advantage!'

'Pooh!' she returned.

They flew on, side by side, until in the distance the bridge leading over the canal to the Laekon road came into sight. Then the Colonel relaxed his grip and allowed the Doll to lengthen her stride. For a moment or two the grey kept abreast, but the pace was too swift for her to hold. The mare pulled ahead, flashed on up the avenue, was checked just short of the bridge, and reached it, dancing on her hooves and snatching a little at the bit.

Barbara came up like a thunderbolt, and reined in, panting. 'Oh, by God! Three lengths!' she called out. 'What do I lose?'

The Colonel leaned forward in the saddle to pat the Doll's neck. Under the brim of his low-cocked hat his eyes laughed into Barbara's. 'I wish it might be your heart!'

'My dear sir, don't you know I haven't one? Come now! In all seriousness?'

He looked at her thoughtfully. She had had the audacity to cram over her flaming curls a hat like an English officer's forage cap. She wore it at a raffish angle, the leathern peak almost obscuring the vision of one merry eye. Her habit was severely plain, with no more than two rows of silver buttons adorning it, but the cravat round her throat was deeply edged with lace, its ends thrust through a buttonhole.

'One of your gloves,' said the Colonel, and held out his hand.

She pulled it off at once, and tossed it to him. He caught it, and tucked it into the breast of his coat.

She wheeled her mount, and prepared to retrace her steps. The Colonel fell in beside her at a walking pace.

'Do you collect gloves, Colonel?'

'I have not up till now,' he replied. 'But a glove is a satisfactory keepsake, you know. Something of the wearer always remains with it.'

'Let me tell you that a gallant man would have let me win!' she said, with a touch of raillery.

He turned his head. 'Are you in general so spoilt?'

'Of course! I'm Bab Childe!' she replied, opening her eyes at him.

'And challenged me to a race in the expectation of being permitted to win?'

Her mouth lifted a little at the corners; the one eye he could see glinted provocatively. 'What do you think?'

'I think you are too good a sportsman, Lady Barbara.'

'Am I? I wonder?' Her gaze flitted to the Doll; she said appreciatively: 'I like a man to be a judge of horseflesh. What's her breeding?'

'I haven't a notion,' replied the Colonel. 'To tell you the truth, she is out of my brother's stable.'

'I thought I knew her. But this is abominable! How was I to guess you would steal one of Worth's horses? I consider you to have won almost by a trick! She's the devil to go, isn't she? Does he know you have her out?'

'Not yet,' admitted the Colonel. 'My dependence is all on his being still too delighted at having me restored to him to object.'

She laughed. 'You deserve to be thrown out of doors! I believe that to be the mare he habitually rides himself!'

'Oh, it won't come to that!' said the Colonel. 'I shall implore my sister-in-law's intercession. That is a nice fellow you have there.'

She passed her hand over the grey's neck. 'Yes, this is Coup de Grâce. We are in the same case, only that while you stole your lady, I have been lent this gentleman.'

'Whom does he belong to?' asked the Colonel, running an eye over his points. 'He may have a French name, but I'll swear he's of English breeding.'

'Captain de Lavisse bought him in England last year,' she replied with one of her sidelong looks.

'Did he?' said the Colonel. 'Captain de Lavisse – is he the man who was standing beside you last night, when I first met you?'

'I don't recollect, but it is very probable. He is in the 5th National Militia: Count Bylandt's brigade, stationed somewhere near Nivelles – Buzet, I think. He has estates north of Ghent, and a truly delightful house in the Rue d'Aremberg, here in Brussels.'

'A gentleman of consequence evidently.'

'Fabulously rich!' said Barbara with an ecstatic sigh, and touching the grey's flank with her heel, went ahead with a brisk trot.

He rode after; both horses broke into a canter, and their riders covered some distance under the limes without speaking. Barbara presently turned her head and asked bluntly: 'Did you ride this way, and at this hour, to meet me?'

'Yes, of course.'

She looked a little amused. 'How did you know I rode here before breakfast?'

'Something you said last night gave me the clue, and I discovered the rest.'

'The deuce you did! I had thought very few people knew of this habit of mine. Don't betray me, if you please. I don't want an escort.'

'Shall I go?' enquired the Colonel with uplifted brows.

She reined in again to walk. 'No. You have had the luck to encounter me in a charming mood, which is not a thing that happens every day of the week. I warn you, I have the most damnable temper, and it is generally at its worst before breakfast.'

'Oh, that is capital!' declared the Colonel. 'You show me how I can be of real service to you. I will engage to be here to quarrel with you any morning you may wish for a sparring partner.'

'I think,' she said quite seriously, 'that you would not make a good sparring partner. You would spare me too much.'

'Not I!'

She did not answer. A solitary horseman, cantering down the avenue towards them, had caught her attention. As he drew nearer, she turned to the Colonel with one of her wicked looks, and said: 'You are about to meet the Captain Count de Lavisse. Shall you like that? He is quite charming!'

'Then obviously I shall,' he answered. 'But I thought you said he was stationed at Nivelles?'

'Oh, he has leave, I suppose!' she said carelessly.

The Captain Count, very smart in a blue uniform with a scarlet-and-white collar, and a broad-topped shako, set at an angle on his handsome head, drew rein before them, and saluted with a flourish. 'Well met, Bab! Your servant, *mon Colonel*!'

The Colonel just touched his hat in acknowledgment of this magnificent salute, but the lady blew a kiss from the tips of her fingers. 'Let me make you known to each other,' she offered.

The Count flung up a hand. 'Unnecessary! We have met already, and there is between us an unpaid score. I accuse you of *volerie*, Colonel, and demand instant reparation!'

'Your waltzes, were they?' said the Colonel. 'My sympathy is unbounded, believe me, but what can I do? The Duke is devilish down on duelling, or I should be happy to oblige. You will have to accept my profound apologies.'

'This is dissimulation of the most base! I am assured that you would serve me again the same *tour* – if you could!' said the Count gaily. His eyes rested for an instant on Barbara's ungloved right hand. He made no comment, but there was a gleam of understanding in the glance he flashed at the Colonel. He wheeled his horse, and fell in beside Barbara. Across her, he addressed Colonel Audley: 'Your first visit to Brussels?'

'No; I was here last year for a short space. A delightful town, Count.'

The Count bowed. 'A compliment indeed – from one who has known Vienna! Our endeavours must be united to preserve it from the Corsican *maraudeur*.'

'*Your* endeavours may be,' remarked Barbara, 'but I have met some who wish quite otherwise.'

He stiffened. 'Persons of no consequence, I assure you!'

'By no means!'

'Madame, when the time comes you shall see how the suspected Belgians shall comport themselves!' He threw a somewhat darkling look at Colonel Audley, and added: 'Rest assured, we are aware what *malveillants* reports have been spread of us in England, and by whom! Is it not so, *mon Colonel*? Have you not been warned that our sympathies are with Bonaparte, that we are, in effect, *indignes de confiance*?'

The Colonel responded with easy tact, but lost no time in turning the conversation into less dangerous channels. A civil interchange was maintained throughout the remainder of the ride, but the Lady Barbara, suddenly capricious, was silent. Only when they arrived at Vidal's house in the Rue Ducale did she seem to recover from her mood of abstraction. She gave the Colonel her hand then, and the shadow of a tantalising smile. 'Do you really care to quarrel with me, Colonel?'

'Above all things!'

'You have not met my brother and his wife, I think? They are holding a soirée here tomorrow evening. It will be confoundedly boring, but come!'

'Thank you: I shall not fail.'

A few minutes later, Barbara dropped into a chair at her brother's breakfast table, and tossed her forage cap on to another. Vidal said peevishly: 'I suppose you have been making yourself remarkable. If you choose to ride out before breakfast, you may for all I care, but I wish you will not go unescorted!'

'No such thing! I was escorted – I was doubly escorted! Tell me all you know of Charles Audley, Robert.'

'I don't know anything of him. How should I?'

'A younger son, with no prospects,' said Augusta trenchantly.

'But with such charm of manner, Gussie!'

'I daresay.'

'And such delightful smiling eyes!'

'Good God, Bab, what is all this?'

'Oh, I have had the most enchanting morning!' Barbara sighed. 'They rode on either side of me, Etienne and this new suitor of mine, and how they disliked one another! I have invited Charles Audley to your party, by the way.'

'Oh, very well! But what is the matter with you? What is there in all this to put you in such spirits?'

'I have lost my heart – to a younger son!'

'Now you are being absurd. You will be tired of him in a week,' said Augusta with a shrug.

Five

From the Rue Ducale, with its houses facing the Park and backing on to the ramparts of the town, to Worth's residence off the Rue de Bellevue, was not far. Colonel Audley arrived in good time for breakfast, laughing off his sister-in-law's demand to know what could have possessed him to ride out so early after a late night, listened meekly to some pithy comments from his brother on his appropriation of the Doll, swallowed his breakfast, and made off on foot to the Duke of Wellington's Headquarters in the Rue Royale. This broad street lay on the opposite side of the Park to the Rue Ducale, its houses over-looking it. Two of these made up the British Headquarters, but the guard posted outside consisted merely of Belgian gendarmerie, the Duke, whose tact in handling foreigners rarely deserted him, having professed himself perfectly satisfied with such an arrangement.

The Duke, when Colonel Audley arrived, was closeted with the Prince of Orange, who had brought with him a welter of reports, letters for his Grace from Lord Bathurst, the English Secretary for War, and his own instructions from the British Commander-in-Chief, his Royal Highness the Duke of York. Colonel Audley, learning of this circumstance from Lord March, whom he met in the hall, ran upstairs to a large apartment on the first floor overlooking the Park, where he found two of his fellow aides-de-camp, in curiously informal attire, kicking their heels.

A stranger, unaware of the Duke of Wellington's indifference to the manner in which his officers chose to dress themselves, might have found it difficult that either of the two gentlemen in the outer office could be an aide-de-camp on duty. Fremantle, lounging in a chair with his legs thrust out before him, was certainly wearing a frock-coat, but had no sash; while Colonel the Honourable Sir Alexander Gordon, who was seated in the window, engaged in waving to acquaintances passing in the street below, was frankly civilian in appearance, his frock-coat being (he said) quite unfit for further service.

Fremantle was looking harassed, but Gordon's sunny temper seemed to be unimpaired.

'In the immortal words of our colleague, Colin Campbell,' he was saying, as Colonel Audley strolled in, ' *"Je voudrais si je coudrais mais je ne cannais pas!"* '

'Don't be so damned cheerful!' begged Fremantle. His jaundiced eye alighted on Colonel Audley's immaculate staff dress. 'Lord, aren't we military this morning!' he remarked. 'That ought to please the Beau: we have had one snap already about officers presenting themselves for duty in improper dress.'

'Oh!' said Audley. 'Crusty, is he?'

'Yes, and he'll be worse by the time he's done with all Slender Billy's lists and requisitions and morning states,' replied Fremantle, with a jerk of his head towards the door leading to the Duke's office.

Gordon, who was looking down into the street, announced: 'Here comes old Lowe. I wonder whether he's realised yet that the Duke doesn't like being told how he ought to equip his army? Someone ought to drop him a hint.'

'Fidgety old fool!' said Fremantle. 'There'll be an explosion if he cites the Prussians to the Beau again. I'm glad *I'm* not going to Ghent.'

'Ghent? Who is going to Ghent?' asked Audley.

'You are, my boy,' replied Fremantle comfortably.

'When?'

'Tonight or tomorrow. Don't know for certain. The news is that Harrowby and Torrens are arriving from London today for

64

a conference with the Duke. He is going with them to Ghent, to pay his respects to the French king.'

'Damnation!' exclaimed Audley. 'Why the devil must it be me?'

'Ask his lordship. Daresay he noticed your fine new dress uniform last night. He must know mine ain't fit to be taken into Court circles. Why shouldn't you want to go to Ghent, anyway? Very nice place, so I'm told.'

'He's got an assignation with the Fatal Widow!' said Gordon. 'That's why he's so beautifully dressed! New boots too. And just look at our elegant sash!'

Colonel Audley was saved from further ribaldry by the sudden opening of the door into the inner sanctum. The Duke came out, escorting the Prince of Orange. He did not, at first glance, appear to be out of humour, nor did the Prince bear the pallid look of one who had had the ill-luck to find his Grace in a bad temper.

However, when the Duke returned from seeing his youthful visitor off, there was a frosty look in his eye, and no trace of the joviality which had surprised Lady Worth at the Hôtel de Ville. He had, at the fête, given everyone to understand that he was entirely carefree, and perfectly satisfied with all the preparations for war which had been made.

But the Duke at a ball and the Duke in his office were two very different persons. Lord Bathurst, in London, had been quite anxious to see him at the head of the Army as any in Brussels, but Lord Bathurst was shortly going to be made to realise that his Grace's arrival in Belgium was not to be a matter of unmixed joy for officials at home.

For the Duke was not in the least satisfied with the preparations he found, and did not hesitate to inform Lord Bathurst that he considered the Army to be in a bad way. He had received disquieting accounts of the Belgian troops, thought the English not what they ought to be, and expressed a wish to have forty thousand good British infantry sent him, with not less than a hundred and fifty pieces of field artillery, fully horsed. It did not appear to his Grace that a clear view of the situation was being taken in England. '*You have not called out the militia, or announced such an intention in your message to Parliament,*' he complained. '*. . . and how we are to make out 150,000 men, or even the 60,000 of the defensive part of the treaty of Chaumont, appears not to have been considered.*' His boldly-flowing pen travelled on faster. He wanted, besides good British infantry, spring wagons, musketball cartridge carts, entrenching-tool carts, the whole Corps of Sappers and Miners, all the Staff Corps, and forty pontoons, immediately, fully horsed. '*Without these equipments,*' he concluded bluntly, '*military operations are out of the question.*'

Yes, the Duke might not yet have taken over the command of the Army, but he was already making his presence felt. General Count von Gneisenau, the Prussian Chief-of-Staff, whom his Grace had visited at Aix-la-Chapelle on his journey from Vienna, also had a letter, written in firm French, to digest. General Gneisenau had proposed a plan, in the event of an attack by the French, of which the Duke flatly disapproved. Nothing could have been more civil than the letter the Duke wrote from Brussels on April 5th, presenting a counter-plan for the General's consideration, but if his Excellency, reading those polite phrases, imagined that a request to him to '*take these reasons into consideration, and to let me know your determination,*' meant that his lordship was prepared to follow any other military determination than his own, he had a great deal yet to learn of the Duke's character.

A copy of this suave missive was enclosed in the despatch to Bathurst, a formal note sent off to the Duke of Brunswick, and the returns presented by the Prince spread out on the table.

The Duke's aides-de-camp might groan at his crustiness, but no one could deny that there was enough to try the patience of even the sweetest-tempered general.

Of his Peninsular veterans only a small percentage was to be found in Belgium, the rest being still in America. His quartermaster-general was also in America, and in his place he found Sir Hudson Lowe, who was a stranger to him, and, however able an officer, not in the least the sort of man he wanted to have under him. The Prussians were going to be difficult too; General Gneisenau, a person of somewhat rough manners, evidently mistrusted him; and the Commissioner, General von Röder, was doing nothing to promote a good understanding between the two headquarters. That would have to be attended to: probably matters would go more smoothly now that old Blücher was to take over the command from Kleist; but the hostility of the King of the Netherlands towards his Prussian allies meant that his lordship would have the devil of a task to keep the peace between them. He suspected that King William was going to prove himself an impossible fellow to deal with, while as for the Dutch–Belgic troops, a more disaffected set he hoped to see. The only hope of making something of them would be to mix them with his own men, but it was plain that that suggestion had not been liked. Then there was the Prince of Orange, a nice enough boy, and with a good understanding, but quite inexperienced. He would have to be given a command, of course: that was inevitable, but damned unfortunate. It was a maxim of the Duke's that an army of stags commanded by a lion was better than an army of lions commanded by a stag. The Prince would have to be kept as much under his own eye as possible. He must be warned, moreover, to be on his guard with several of his generals. But he had a good man in Constant de Rebecque, and another in General Perponcher, who had seen service with the British in the Peninsula, and had done well with the Portuguese Legion formed at Oporto in 1808.

'*Your Lordship's presence is extremely necessary to combine the measures of the heterogeneous force which is destined to defend this country,*' had written Sir Charles Stuart, and it did not seem that he had exaggerated the difficulties of the situation. When the Anglo-Allied Army was at last brought together it would be found to be heterogeneous enough to daunt any commander with less cool confidence than the Duke. A large proportion of the force would consist of Dutch–Belgic troops, many of them veterans who had fought under the Eagles, and as many more young soldiers never before under fire. In addition, a contingent from Nassau had been promised; and the Duke of Brunswick, the Princess of Wales's brother, was to place himself and his Black Brunswickers at the Duke's orders. There was to be a Hanoverian contingent also, tolerably good troops: but his lordship had found in Spain that the Germans had a shockingly bad habit of deserting, which made them troublesome. That did not apply so much to the King's German Legion, of course: those stout soldiers were as good as any English ones; and they had good commanders too: Count Alten; old Arendtschildt, the model of a hussar leader; Ompteda, with his large dreamy eyes at such odd variance with his soldierly ability; Du Plat, always to be relied on to keep his head. His lordship was not so sure of this new fellow, Major-General Dörnberg, commanding a brigade of Light Dragoons; his lordship was not acquainted with him, and in his present mood his lordship was not inclined to look favourably upon strangers.

Besides all these foreign troops, there were the British, who must be used as a stiffening to the whole. The devil of it was there were not enough of them, and too many of the regiments now in Belgium were composed of young and untried soldiers. If he only had his old Peninsular Army he would have nothing to complain of. He could have gone anywhere, done anything with those fellows. His lordship had not been accustomed in Spain, to such flattering language about his troops, but the truth was his lordship was always more apt to condemn faults than to praise excellence. He had said some pretty harsh things of his Peninsular veterans in his time, but in his grudging way he valued them, and wished he had them in Belgium now. His lordship, in one of his bitter moods, might say that they had all enlisted for drink, but anyone else rash enough to speak disparagingly of them would very soon learn his mistake. Acrid disparagement of his troops was his lordship's sole prerogative.

Well, such Peninsular regiments as were available would have to be sent out. In the force at present under Orange's command were only the second battalions of three of these, and a detachment of the 95th Rifles. There were the Guards, of course, who would certainly maintain their high reputation, but his lordship's mouth turned down at the corners as he ran over the lists of the remaining regiments. Young troops for the most part, inexperienced except for their brief campaign under Graham in Holland. He would have to get good officers into them, and hope for the best, but the fact was he had under his hand the nucleus of what bade fair to be, in his estimation, an infamous army.

There were other, minor vexations to try his patience, notably the absence of his military secretary. When he left Paris for Vienna, Lord Fitzroy Somerset had remained there as chargé d'affaires, and was now in Ghent. He missed his quiet competence damnably; he must have him back: someone must be chosen to assist Stuart with the King of France in his stead; Colonel Hervey's brother Lionel, perhaps. He must have Colin Campbell too, and must prevail upon Colquhoun Grant to come out as Head of the Intelligence Department. With him and Waters he should do very well in that direction, but from the look of it he would be obliged to make a clean sweep of all these youngsters at present filling staff appointments, and, in his opinion, quite unfit for such duties. He must come to a plain understanding, also, with King William, on the question of the troops to be employed on garrison duty. All the chief posts would have to be held by the British: his instructions from London were perfectly precise on that point, and he agreed with them, though it was already evident that King William did not.

Taking one thing with another, his present position was unenviable, and the future dark with difficulties. A superhuman task lay before him, as bad as any he had ever tackled, but although he might complain peevishly of lack of support from England, of wretched troops in Belgium, of the impossibility of dealing with King William, of the damned folly of that fellow Lowe, no real doubts of his ability to deal with the situation assailed him.

'I never in my life gave up anything that I once undertook,' said his lordship, in one of his rare moments of expansiveness.

Fremantle came into the room with some papers for him to look over. He took them, and remembered that he had been devilish short with Fremantle this morning, for some slight fault. He had not meant to be, but it was unthinkable that he should say so; he could not do it: to admit that he had been in the wrong was totally against his principles. The nearest he could ever bring himself to it was to invite the unfortunate to dinner, or, if that were ineligible (as in Fremantle's case it was, since he would dine with him in the ordinary way), to say something pleasant to him, to show that the whole affair was forgotten.

'I'll tell you what, Fremantle!' he remarked in his incisive way. 'We must give a ball. Find out what days are left free. It will have to be towards the end of the month, for it won't do if I clash with anyone else.'

'They say that the Catalani is coming to Brussels, sir,' suggested Fremantle.

'That's capital: we'll have a concert as well, and engage her to sing at it. But, mind, fix the figure before you settle with the woman; I hear she's as mercenary as the devil.' He picked up his pen again, and bent over his table, but added as Fremantle was leaving the room: 'You can have my box, if you mean to go to the theatre tonight: I shan't be using it. Take the curricle.'

So Colonel Fremantle was able to report in the outer office that his lordship's temper was on the mend. But within half an hour, his lordship, glaring at his quartermaster-general, was snapping out one of his hasty snubs. 'Sir Hudson, I have commanded a far larger army in the field than any Prussian general, and I am not to learn from their service how to equip an army!'

One would have thought this would have stopped the damned fellow, but no! in a few moments he was at it again.

'*Sir Hudson Lowe will not do for the Duke,*' wrote Major-General Torrens next day, to London, with diplomatic restraint.

Lord Harrowby, and Major-General Torrens, arriving on April 6th to confer with him, found that there was much that would not do for the Duke, and much that he required from

England with the greatest possible despatch. His lordship – it was strange how that title stuck to him – might be uncomfortably blunt in his manner, but the very fact of his knowing so positively what he wanted, showed how sure was his grasp on the situation. And, after all, General Torrens had dealt with him for long enough to know, before ever he reached Brussels, that he was going to hear some very plain truths from him.

But his criticisms were not merely destructive: what he said to the delegates from London left them in no doubt of his energetic competence. The news he brought from Vienna was quite as good as could have been expected. The treaty between Great Britain, Austria, Russia, and Prussia had been signed; there had been a little trouble over the question of subsidies; but his lordship was able to report that the Russians and Austrians were mobilising in large numbers; and even that the Emperor of Russia had expressed a wish (though not a very strong one) to have him with him. 'But I should prefer to carry a musket!' said his lordship, with a neigh of sardonic laughter.

For their part, Lord Harrowby and Sir Henry Torrens had brought soothing intelligence from home. All the available cavalry were under orders, and some already marching for embarkation to Ostend; of the infantry, in addition to the corps and detachments already despatched, and now in Belgium, about two thousand effectives were to proceed from a rendez-vous in the Downs to Ostend. The Government was willing, and indeed anxious, to meet his lordship's requirements in every possible way.

His lordship stated these with disconcerting alacrity. He wanted equipment, and ammunition; he wanted field artillery, and horses; he wanted the militia called out: 'Nothing can be done with a small and inefficient force,' said his lordship uncompromisingly. 'The war will linger on, and will end to our disadvantage.'

Harrowby began to explain the constitutional difficulties attached to calling out the militia. It was plain that his lordship made very little of these, but he was not one to waste his time in

71

fruitless argument. He had another scheme, already proposed by him in a despatch to Lord Castlereagh. He thought it would be advisable to try to get twelve or fourteen thousand Portuguese troops into the Netherlands. 'We can mix them with ours, and do what we please with them,' he said. 'They become very nearly as good as our own.'

Upon the following day, a third visitor from London appeared in the person of the Duke's brother, the Marquis Wellesley. The Marquis was fifty-five years old, and nine years senior to the Duke. There was not much resemblance between the brothers, but strong ties of affection had survived the strain put on them by the younger man's rise to heights beyond the elder's reach. It had been Richard, not Arthur, who was to have been the great man of the family; it was Richard who had set Arthur's feet on the ladder of his career, and had fostered his early progress from rung to rung. But Arthur, his feet once firmly planted, had climbed the ladder so fast that Richard had been left far behind him. It was only twenty-eight years since Richard had written to remind the Duke of Rutland of a younger brother of his, whom his Grace had been so kind as to take into his consideration for a commission in the Army. '*He is here, at this moment, and perfectly idle,*' Richard had written. '*It is a matter of indifference to me what commission he gets, providing he gets it soon.*' Richard, with his brilliant mind and scholarship, had been a coming man in those days, Arthur a youth of no more than ordinary promise. Seventeen years later, a Major-General, he had been made a Knight Companion of the Bath, and after that the honours had fallen so thick upon him that it had been difficult to keep count of them. He had been created in swift succession Viscount Wellington of Talavera, Earl of Wellington, then Marquis, and lastly duke; he was a Spanish Grandee of the First Class, Duke of Ciudad Rodrigo, Duke of Victoria, a Knight of the Garter, of the Golden Fleece, of the Order of Maria Theresa, of the Russian Order of Saint George, of the Prussian Order of the Black Eagle, of the Swedish Order of the Sword. An Emperor had lately clapped him on the shoulder, saying: '*C'est pour vous encore sauver le monde!*'

and yet he remained, reflected Richard, with a faint, whimsical smile, the same unaffected creature he had ever been. Nor had he outgrown his boyhood's admiration of Richard. 'A wonderful man,' he called him, and honestly believed it.

The Marquis was a wonderfully handsome man, at all events, with large, far-sighted eyes under heavily-marked dark brows, an aquiline nose, with delicate, up-cut nostrils, a fine, rather thin-lipped mouth, and a lacquered skin of alabaster. He had beauti-ful manners too, a natural stateliness tempered by charm, and an instinct for ceremonial. No sudden cracks of loud laughter broke from him; he had never been known to utter hasty, harshly-worded snubs; and his stateliness never became mere stiffness. The Duke, on the other hand, could be absurdly stiff, and pain-fully rude, while his ungraciousness towards those whom he disliked was proverbial. He had no taste for pomp, very little for creature comforts, and although he had been christened Beau Douro in the Peninsula on account of a certain neatness and propriety of dress, he set no store by personal adornment. He was outspoken to a fault; his mind ran between straight and clearly defined lines; and he knew nothing of dissimulation. Ask him a question, and you might be sure of receiving an honest answer – though perhaps not the one you had hoped to hear, for his lordship, unconcerned with considerations of personal popularity, was rigorously concerned with the truth, and with what he saw to be his clear duty. Tact, such as his brother possessed, he did not employ; and when the members of His Majesty's Government acted, in his judgment, foolishly, he told them so with very little more ceremony than he would have used with one of his own officers.

He met his elder brother with frank delight, gave his hand a quick shake, and said briskly: 'Glad to see you, Wellesley! How d'ye do?'

'How do *you* do?' returned the Marquis, holding his hand a moment longer.

'We are in a damned bad case,' replied the Duke bluntly.

The Marquis did not make the mistake of taking this to mean

that his brother envisaged defeat at Bonaparte's hands; he knew that it was merely the prelude to one of Arthur's trenchant and comprehensive complaints of the Government's supine behaviour. Already, and though he had not been in his presence above a minute, he was aware of Arthur's driving will. Arthur's terrible energy made him feel suddenly old. Presently, seated with Harrowby and Torrens at a table covered with papers, and listening to the Duke's voice, he found that, well as he knew him, he could still be surprised by Arthur's amazing capacity for detail. For Arthur had rolled up his maps and was being extremely definite on the subject of the ideal size and nature of camp kettles.

An extraordinary fellow, dear Arthur: really, a most bewildering fellow!

Six

The information imparted to Colonel Audley by Fremantle turned out to be correct, and not, as Audley had more than half suspected, a mild attempt to hoax him. He was to accompany the Duke to Ghent, but not, providentially, until June 8th. He was free therefore to present himself at Lady Vidal's party on the 7th.

The fact of his being engaged to dine at the Duke's table made it unnecessary for him to tell his sister-in-law where he meant to spend the rest of the evening. The Worths were bound for the Opera, where Judith hoped he might perhaps be able to join them.

Lady Barbara, wise in the ways of suitors, expected to see him among the first arrivals, and was piqued when he did not appear until late in the evening. He found her in a maddening mood, flirting with one civilian and two soldiers. She had nothing but a careless wave of the hand for him, and the Colonel, who had no intention of forming one of a court, paused only to exchange a word of greeting with her before passing on to pay his respects to Lady Frances Webster.

That inveterate hero worshipper had found a new object for her affections, a very different personage from Lord Byron, less dangerous but quite as glorious. At the fête at the Hôtel de Ville her eyes had dwelled soulfully upon the Duke of Wellington, and the Duke had lost very little time in becoming acquainted with her. When the Lady Frances discovered from Colonel Audley that there was no likelihood of his Grace's putting in an appearance that evening, she sighed, and seemed to lose interest in the world.

So that's Hookey's latest, is it? thought the Colonel. Too angelic for my taste!

Caro Lamb recognised him, and summoned him to her side. He went at once, and was soon engaged in a light, swift give and take of badinage with her. His manners were too good to allow of his attention wandering, his gaze did not stray from the changeful little face before him; nor, when Caro presently flitted from him to another, did he do more than glance in Barbara's direction. She was lying back in her chair, laughing up into Lavisse's face, bent a little over her. There was a suggestion of possessiveness in Lavisse's pose, and his left hand was resting on Barbara's bare shoulder. Repressing a strong inclination to seize the slim Belgian by the collar and the seat of his elegant kneebreeches and throw him out, the Colonel turned away, and found himself confronting a sandy-haired ensign, who smiled and offered him a glass of wine. 'You're Colonel Audley, aren't you, sir?' he said. 'Bab said you were coming. I'm Harry Alastair.'

'How do you do?' said the Colonel, accepting the glass of wine. 'I believe I once met your brother George.'

'Oh, did you? George is a Bad Man,' said Harry cheerfully. 'I heard today that the Life Guards are under marching orders, so he'll be here pretty soon, I expect. But I say, what's the news, sir? We are going to war, aren't we?'

Colonel Audley did not think there was much doubt of that.

'Well, I'm very glad to hear you say so,' remarked his youthful interlocutor with simple pleasure. 'Only, people talk such stuff that one doesn't known what to believe. I thought you would probably know.' He added in a burst of confidence: 'It's a great thing for me: I've never been in action, you know.'

Colonel Audley expressed a gratifying surprise. 'I had thought you must have been with Graham,' he said.

'No,' confessed Lord Harry. 'As a matter of fact, I was still at Oxford then. Well, to tell you the truth, I only joined in December.'

'How do you like it?' asked the Colonel. 'You're with General Maitland, aren't you?'

'Yes. Oh, it's famous sport! I like it above anything!' said Lord Harry. 'And if only we have the luck to come to grips with Boney himself – all our fellows are mad for the chance of a brush with him, I can tell you! Hallo, what's Bab at now? She's as wild as fire tonight! When George arrives they'll set the whole town in a bustle between them, I daresay.'

A hot rivalry appeared to have sprung up between the men surrounding Barbara for possession of the flower she had been wearing tucked into her corsage. It was in her hand now, and as the Colonel glanced towards her she sprang lightly upon a stool, and held it high above her head.

'No quarrelling, gentlemen!' she called out. 'He who can reach it may take it. Oh, Jack, my poor darling, you will never do it!'

Half a dozen arms reached up; the Lady Barbara, from the advantage of her stool, laughed down in the faces upturned to her. Colonel Audley, taller than any of that striving court, set down his wine glass and walked up behind her, and nipped the flower from her hand.

She turned quickly; a wave of colour rushed into her cheeks. 'Oh! You! Infamous! I did not bargain for a man of your inches!' she said.

'A cheat! Fudged, by Jove!' cried Captain Chambers. 'Give it up, Audley, you dog!'

'Not a bit of it,' responded the Colonel, fitting it in his buttonhole. 'He who could reach it might take it. I abode most strictly by the rules.' He held out his hands to Barbara. 'Come down from your perch! You invited me here tonight and have not vouchsafed me one word.'

She laid her hands in his, but drew them away as soon as she stood on the floor again. 'Oh, you must be content with having won your prize!' she said carelessly. 'I warn you, it came from a hothouse and will soon fade. Dear Jack, I'm devilish thirsty!'

The young man addressed offered his arm; she was borne

away by him into an adjoining salon. With a shade of malice in his voice the Comte de Lavisse said: '*Hélas*! You are set down, *mon Colonel*!'

'I am indeed,' replied Audley, and went off to flirt with one of the Misses Arden.

He was presently singled out by his host, who wanted his opinion of the military situation. Lord Vidal was suffering from what his irreverent younger brother described as a fit of the sullens, but he was pleasant enough to Audley. His wife, her hard sense bent on promoting a match between an improvident sister-in-law and a wealthy (though foreign) nobleman, seized the opportunity to inform the Colonel that her family expected hourly to receive the tidings of Bab's engagement to the Comte de Lavisse. The desired effect of this confidence was a little spoiled by her husband's saying hastily: 'Pooh! nonsense! I don't more than half like it.'

Augusta said with a tinkle of laughter: 'I doubt of Bab's considering that, my dear Vidal, once her affections have been engaged.'

The Marquis reddened, but said: 'The old man wouldn't countenance it. I wish you will not talk such rubbish! Come now, Audley! In my place, would you remove to England?'

'On my honour, no!' said the Colonel. He correctly guessed 'the old man' to be the Duke of Avon, a gentleman of reputedly fiery temper, who was the Lady Barbara's grandfather, and lost very little time in finding Lord Harry Alastair again.

There was no more friendly youth to be found than Lord Harry. He was perfectly ready to tell the Colonel anything the Colonel wanted to know, and it needed only a casual question to set his tongue gaily wagging.

'Devil of a tartar, my grandfather,' said Lord Harry. 'Used to be a dead shot – daresay he still is, but he don't go about picking quarrels with people these days, of course. Killed his man in three duels before he met my grandmother. Those must have been good times to have lived in! But I believe he settled down more or less when he married. George is the living spit of what he used to be, if you can trust the portraits. Bab and Vidal take after my *great*-grandmother. She was red-haired, too, and French into the bargain. And *her* husband – my great-grandfather, that is – was the devil of a fellow!' He tossed off a glass of wine, and added, not without pride: 'We're a shocking bad set, you know. All ride to the devil one way or another. As for Bab, she's as bad as any of us.'

The Lady Barbara seemed, that evening, to be determined to prove the truth of this assertion. No folly was too extravagant for her to throw herself into; her flirtations shocked the respectable; the language she used gave offence to the pure-tongued; and when she crowned an evening of indiscretions by organising a table of hazard, and becoming, as she herself announced, badly dipped at it, it was felt that she had left nothing undone to set the town by the ears.

She was too busy at her hazard table to notice Colonel Audley's departure, nor did he attempt to interrupt her play to take his leave. But seven o'clock next morning found him cantering down the Allée Verte to meet a solitary horse-woman mounted on a grey hunter.

She saw him approaching, and reined in. When he reached her she was seated motionless in the saddle, awaiting him. He raised two fingers to his cocked hat. 'Good morning! Are you in a quarrelsome humour today?' he asked.

She replied abruptly: 'I did not expect to see you.'

'We don't start for Ghent until noon.'

'Ghent?'

'Yes, Ghent,' he repeated, not quite understanding her blank stare.

'Oh, the devil! What are you talking about?' she demanded with a touch of petulance. 'Are you going to Ghent? I did not know it.'

'Didn't you? Then I don't know what the devil I'm talking about,' he said.

A laugh flashed in her eyes. 'I wish I didn't like you, but I do – I do!' she said. 'Do you wonder that I didn't expect to see you here this morning?'

'If it was not because you thought me already on my way to Ghent I most certainly do.'

'Odd creature!' She gave him one of her direct looks, and said: 'I behaved very shabbily to you last night.'

'You did indeed. What had I done? Or were you merely cross?'

'Nothing. Was I cross? I don't know. I think I wanted to show you how damnably I can conduct myself.'

'Thank you,' said the Colonel, bowing in some amusement. 'What will you show me next? How well you can conduct yourself?'

'I never conduct myself well. Don't laugh! I am in earnest. I am odious, do you understand? If you will persist in liking me, I shall make you unhappy.'

'I don't like you,' said the Colonel. 'It was true what I told you the first time I set eyes on you. I love you.'

She looked at him with sombre eyes. 'How can you do so? If you were in a way to loving me did not that turn to dislike when you saw me at my worst?'

'Not a bit!' he replied. 'I will own to a strong inclination to have boxed your ears, but I could not cease to love you, I think, for any imaginable folly on your part.' He swung himself out of the saddle, and let the bridle hang over his horse's head. 'May I lift you down? There is a seat under the trees where we can have our talk out undisturbed.'

She set her hand on his shoulder, but said, half mournfully: '*This* is the greatest imaginable folly, poor soldier.'

'I love you most of all when you are absurd,' said the Colonel, lifting her down from the saddle.

He set her on her feet, but held her for an instant longer, his eyes smiling into hers; then his hands released her waist, and he gathered up both the horses' bridles, and said: 'Let me take you to the secluded nook I have discovered.'

'Innocent!' she said mockingly, falling into step beside him. 'I know all the secluded nooks.'

He laughed. 'You are shameless.'

She looked sideways at him. 'A baggage?'

'Yes, a baggage,' he agreed, lifting her hand to his lips a moment.

'If you know that, I consider you fairly warned, and shall let you run on your fate as fast as you please.'

'*Faute de mieux*,' he remarked. 'Here is my nook. Let me beg your ladyship to be seated!'

'Oh, call me Bab! Everyone does.' She sat down, and began to strip off her gloves. 'Have you still my rose?' she enquired.

He laid his hand upon his heart. 'Can you ask?'

'I began to think you an accomplished flirt. I hope the thorns may not prick you.'

'To be honest with you,' confessed the Colonel, 'the gesture was metaphorical.'

She burst out laughing. 'Your trick! Tell me what it is you want! To flirt with me? I am perfectly willing. To kiss me? You may if you choose.'

'To marry you,' he said.

'Ah, now you are talking nonsense! Has no one warned you what bad blood there is in my family?'

'Yes, your brother Harry. I am much obliged to him, and to you, and must warn you, in my turn, that I had an uncle once who was so much addicted to the bottle that he died of it. Furthermore, my grandfather –'

She put up her hands. 'Stop, stop! Abominable to laugh when I am in earnest! If I married you we should certainly fight.'

'Not a doubt of it,' he agreed.

'You would wish to make me sober and well-behaved, and I –'

'Never! To shake you, perhaps, but I am persuaded your sense of justice would pardon that.'

'My sense of justice might, but not my temper. I should flirt with other men: you would not like that.'

'No, nor permit it.'

'My poor Charles! How would you stop me?'

'By flirting with you myself,' he replied.

'It would lack spice in a husband. I don't care for marriage. It is curst flat. *You* do not know that; but *I* have reason to. Did Gussie tell you I was going to marry Lavisse?'

'Most pointedly. But I think you are not.'

'You may be right,' she said coolly. 'It is more than I can bargain for, though. He is extremely wealthy. I should enjoy the comfort of a large fortune. My debts would ruin you in a year. Have you thought of that?'

'No, but I will, if you like, and devise some means of meeting the difficulty when it arises. Should you object very much to living in a debtors' prison?'

'It might be amusing,' she admitted. 'But it would become tiresome in time. Things do, you know.' She began to play with her riding whip, twisting the lash round her fingers. Watching her, he saw that her eyes had grown dark again, and that she had gripped her lips together in a mulish fashion. He was content to look at her, and presently she glanced up, and said brusquely: 'To be plain with you, Charles, you are a fool! Am I your first love?'

'My dear! No!'

'The more shame to you. Don't you know – ? Good God, can you not see that we should never deal together? We are not suited!'

'No, we are not suited, but I think we might deal together,' he answered.

'I have been spoilt from my cradle!' she flung at him. 'You know nothing of me! You have fallen in love with my face. In fact, you are ridiculous!'

He said rather ruefully: 'Do you think I don't know it? I can discover no reason why you should look with anything but amusement upon my suit. I am a younger son, with no prospects beyond the Army –'

'Gussie said that,' she interrupted, her lip lifting a little.

'She was right.'

She put her whip down; something glowed in her eyes. 'Have you nothing to recommend you to me, then?'

'Nothing at all,' he replied, with a faint smile.

She leaned towards him; sudden tears sparkled on her lashes; her hands went out to him impulsively. 'Nothing at all! Charles, dear fool! Oh, the devil! I'm crying!'

She was in his arms, and raised her face for his kiss. Her hands gripped his shoulders; her mouth was eager, and clung to his for a moment. Then she put her head back, and felt him kiss her wet eyelids.

'Oh, rash,' she murmured. 'I darken 'em Charles – my eye-lashes! Does it come off?'

He said a little unsteadily: 'I don't think so. What odds?'

She disengaged herself. 'My dear, you are certainly mad! Confound it, I never cry! How dared you look at me just so? Charles, if I have black streaks on my face, I swear I'll never forgive you!'

'But you have not, on my honour!' he assured her. He found his handkerchief, and put his hand under her chin. 'Keep still: I will engage to dry them without the least damage being done.' He performed this office for her, and held her chin for an instant longer, looking down into her face.

She let him kiss her again, but when he raised his head, flung off his arms, and sprang up. 'Of all the absurd situations I ever was in! To be made love to before breakfast! Abominable!'

He too rose, and caught and grasped her hands, holding them in a grip that made her grimace. 'Will you marry me?'

'I don't know, I don't know!' Go to Ghent: I won't be swept off my feet!' She gave a gurgle of laughter, and burlesqued herself: 'You must give me time to consider, Colonel Audley! Lord, did you ever hear anything so Bath-missish? Let me go: you don't possess me, you know.'

'Give me an answer!' he said.

'No, and no! Do you think I must marry where I kiss? They don't mean anything, my kisses.'

His grip tightened on her hands. 'Be quiet! You shall not talk so!'

Her mouth mocked him bitterly. 'You've drawn such a pretty picture of me for yourself, and the truth is I'm a rake.'

He turned from her in silence to lead up her horse. With the knowledge that she had hurt him an unaccustomed pain seized her. 'Now you see how odious I can be!' she said in a shaking voice.

He glanced over his shoulder, and said gently: 'My poor dear!'

She gave a twisted smile, but said nothing until he had brought her horse to her. He put her into the saddle, and she bent towards him, and touched his cheek with her gloved hand. 'Go to Ghent. Dear Charles!'

For a moment her eyes were soft with tenderness. He caught her hand and kissed it. 'I must go, of course. I shall be back in a day or two and I shall want my answer.'

She gathered up the bridle. 'I shall give it you – perhaps!' she said, and rode off, leaving him still standing under the elm trees.

He made no attempt to overtake her, but rode back to the town at a sober pace, arriving at his brother's house rather late for breakfast. His sister-in-law, regarding him with a little curiosity, asked him where he had been, and upon his answering briefly, in the Allée Verte, rallied him on such a display on matutinal energy.

'Confess, Charles! You had an assignation with an unknown charmer!'

He smiled, but shook his head. 'Not precisely – no!'

'Don't tell me you rode out for your health's sake! You have not been alone!'

'No,' he replied, 'I had the good fortune to meet Lady Barbara.'

She concealed the dismay she felt, but was for the moment too much nonplussed to say anything. The Earl filled what might have been felt to have been an awkward pause by enquiring in his languid way: 'Is an early morning ride one of her practices? She is an unexpected creature!'

'She is a splendid horsewoman,' said the Colonel evasively.

'Certainly. I have very often seen her at the stag hunting during the winter.'

'Perry calls her a bruising rider!' remarked Judith, with a slight laugh. She poured herself out some coffee, and added in a casual

84

tone: 'Is it true she is about to become engaged to the Comte de Lavisse?'

The Colonel raised his brows. 'What, does gossip say so?'

'Oh yes! That is, his attentions have been so very particular that it is regarded as quite certain. I suppose it would be a good match. He is very wealthy.'

'Very, I believe.'

This response was too unencouraging to allow of Judith's pursing the subject any further. The Colonel started to talk of something else, and as soon as he had finished his breakfast, went away to order his servant to pack his valise. He was soon gone from the house, and although Judith was sorry he was obliged to accompany the Duke of Ghent, she was able to console herself with the reflection that at least he would be out of Barbara Childe's reach.

She might be a little uneasy about his evident admiration for Barbara, but as she had no suspicion of how far matters between them had already gone, she felt no very acute anxiety, and was able to welcome the Colonel home on the following evening without misgiving.

The Earl having an engagement to dine with some officers at the Hôtel d'Angleterre, Judith had invited Miss Devenish to keep her company, and was seated with her in the salon when Colonel Audley walked in.

Both ladies looked up; Judith exclaimed: 'Why, Charles, are you back so soon? This is delightful! I believe I need not introduce you to Miss Devenish.'

'No, indeed: I had the pleasure of meeting Miss Devenish the other evening,' he replied, shaking hands, and drawing up a chair. 'Is Worth out?'

'Yes, at the Hôtel d'Angleterre. Is the Duke back in Brussels? Lord Harrowby and Sir Henry too?'

'No, the visitors are all on their way home to England. The Duke is here, however, but I am afraid you will be obliged to make up your mind to exist without him for a little while,' he said, with a droll look. 'Are you like my sister, Miss Devenish? Do you suffer from nightmares when the Duke is not here to protect you from Boney?'

She smiled, but shook her head. 'Oh no! I am too stupid to understand wars and politics, but I feel sure the Duke would never leave Brussels if there were any danger to be apprehended in his doing so.'

He seemed amused; Judith enquired why she must do without the Duke, and upon being informed of his intention to visit the Army, professed herself very well satisfied with such an arrangement.

The tea tray was brought in a few moments later, and Judith had the satisfaction of hearing her protégée and Colonel Audley chatting with all the ease of old acquaintances over her very choice Orange Pekoe. Nothing could have been more comfortable! she thought. Charles, she knew well, had a sweetness of disposition which made him appear to be pleased with whatever society he found himself in, but she fancied there was more warmth in his manner than was dictated by civility. He was looking at Lucy with interest, taking pains to draw her out; and presently, when the carriage was bespoken to convey her to her uncle's lodging, he insisted on escorting her.

When he returned he found his sister-in-law still sitting in the salon with her embroidery, and the Earl not yet come home from his dinner engagement. He took a seat opposite to Judith, and glanced idly through the pages of the *Cosmopolite*.

'No news more of the Duc d'Angoulême, I see,' he remarked.

'No. There was something in the *Moniteur*, some few days ago, about his having had a success near Montélimart. I believe he has advanced into Valence.'

'I doubt of his enjoying much success. If he favours his brother, I should judge his venture to have been hopeless from the start. You never saw such a set of fellows as the French at Ghent! The worst is that they, most of them, seem to think the war lost before ever it is begun.'

She lowered her embroidery. 'What, even now that the Duke is here?'

'Oh yes! They are quite ready to admit that he did very well in Spain, but now that he is to meet Boney in person they think the result a foregone conclusion.'

'And the King?'

'There's no telling. But whether we can succeed in putting him back on the Throne – However, that's none of my business.'

'What an odd creature he must be! What does he feel about it all, I wonder?'

'I haven't a notion. He seems to care for nothing in the world but comfort and a quiet life. Poor devil! Fitzroy has been making us laugh with some of his tales of what goes on at the Court.'

'Oh, has Lord Fitzroy come back with you? I am glad.'

'So are we all,' said the Colonel, his eyes twinkling. 'Headquarters without Fitzroy are apt to become a trifle sultry. By the by, how in the name of all that's wonderful did that Devenish child come to have such a queer stick of an uncle?'

'He is only her uncle by marriage,' Judith answered. 'Her aunt is perfectly ladylike, you know. And *she* –'

'My dear Judith, I meant nothing against her! I daresay she will make some fortunate fellow a capital wife. An heiress, isn't she?'

She said archly: 'Yes, a considerable heiress. And yet she doesn't squint like a bag of nails!'

He put the *Cosmopolite* down, wrinkling his brow in perplexity. 'Squint like a bag of nails? You're quizzing me, Judith! What is the joke?'

'Have you forgotten my first meeting with you?'

'Good God, I never can have said such a thing of you!'

'Very nearly, I assure you! You came into the room where I was standing with your brother, and demanded: "Where is the heiress? Does she squint like a bag of nails? Is she hideous? They always are!"'

He burst out laughing. 'Did I indeed? No, I will admit that Miss Devenish doesn't squint like a bag of nails. She is a very pretty girl – but I wonder what troubles her?'

'Troubles her?' she repeated in accents of surprise. 'Why, what should trouble her?'

'How should I know? I thought perhaps you might.'

'No, indeed! You have certainly imagined it. She is reserved, I know, and I could wish that that were not so, but I believe it to be due to a shyness very understandable in a girl living in her circumstances. Do you find it objectionable?'

'Not in the least. I merely feel a little curiosity to know what causes it. There is a look in the eye – but you will say I am indulging my fancy!'

'But, Charles, what can you mean? There is a *gravity*, I own. I have found it particularly pleasing in this age of volatile young females.'

'Oh, more than that!' he said. 'I had almost called it a guarded look. I am sure she is not quite happy. But it is infamous of me to be discussing her in this way, after all! It is nothing but nonsense, of course.'

'I hope it may be found so,' replied Judith. '*I* have been told nothing of any secret sorrow, I assure you.'

She said no more, but she was not ill-pleased. Charles seemed to have been studying Lucy closely, and although she could not but be amused at the romantic trend of his reflections, she was glad to find that he had found her young friend of so much interest.

But at seven o'clock next morning Charles was riding down the Allée Verte, no thought of Lucy Devenish in his head. He cantered to the bridge at the end of the Allée without en-countering Barbara, and dismounted there to watch the painted barges drifting up the canal. Fashionable people were not yet abroad, but a couple of Flemish wagons, drawn by teams of fat horses, passed over the bridge. The drivers walked beside him, guiding the horses by means of cord reins passed through haims studded with brass nails. Bright tassels and fringes decorated the horses' harness, and the blue smocks worn by the drivers were embroidered with worsted. They wore red nightcaps on their heads, and wooden sabots on their feet, over striped stockings.

The horses, like all Colonel Audley had seen in the Netherlands, were huge beasts, and very fat. Good forage to be had, he reflected, thinking of the English cavalry and horse artillery on the way to Ostend. From what he had seen of the country it was rich enough to supply forage for several armies. Wherever one rode one found richly cultivated fields, with crops of flax and wheat growing in almost fabulous luxuriance. The Flemish farmers manured their land lavishly; very malodorous it could be, he thought, remembering his journey through the Netherlands the previous year. Except for the woods and copses dotted over the land the whole country seemed to be under cultivation. There should be no difficulty in feeding the Allied Army: but the Flemish were a grasping race, he had been told.

A gendarme in a blue uniform, with white grenades, and high, gleaming boots, rode over the bridge, glancing curiously at the Colonel, who was still leaning his elbows on the parapet and watching the slow canal traffic. He passed on, riding towards Brussels, and for some little time the Colonel's solitude was undisturbed. But presently, glancing down the Allée he saw a horse approaching in the distance, and caught the flutter of a pale blue skirt. He swung himself into the saddle, and rode to meet the Lady Barbara.

She came galloping towards him and reined in. Cheeks and eyes were glowing; she stretched out her hand, and exclaimed: 'I thought you still in Ghent! This is famous!'

He leaned forward in the saddle to take her hand; it grasped his strongly. 'I have been bored to death!' Barbara said. 'Confound you, I have missed you damnably!'

'Excellent! There is only one remedy,' he said.

'To marry you?'

He nodded, still holding her hand.

She said candidly: 'So I feel today. You are haunting me, do you know? But in a week, who knows but that I may have changed my mind?'

'I'll take that risk.'

'Will you?' She considered him, a rather mischievous smile

hovering on her lips. 'You have not kissed me, Charles,' she murmured.

He caught the gleam under her long lashes, and laughed. 'No.'

'Don't you want to – dear Charles?'

'Yes, very much.'

'Oh, this is a pistol held to my head! If I want to be kissed I must also be married. Is that it?' she asked outrageously.

'That is it, in a nutshell.'

Her eyes began to dance. 'Kiss me, Charles: I'll marry you,' she said.

Seven

Colonel Audley was very late for breakfast. He came into the parlour to find his brother standing by the window, glancing through the *Gazette de Bruxelles*, and his sister-in-law with her chair already pushed back from the table. She looked searchingly at him as he entered, for she had heard the front door slam a minute earlier and knew that he had been out riding again. Her heart sank; she had never seen quite that radiant look on his face before. 'Well, Charles,' she said. 'You've been out already?'

'Yes.' He held out his hands to her. 'Wish me joy!' he said.

She let him take her hands, but faltered: 'Wish you joy? What can you mean?'

'Lady Barbara has promised to be my wife,' he answered.

She snatched her hands away. 'Impossible! No, no, you're joking!'

He looked down at her, half laughing, half surprised. 'I assure you I am not!'

'You scarcely know her! You cannot mean it!'

'But, my dear Judith, I do mean it! I am the happiest man on earth!'

The dismay she felt was plainly to be read in her face. He drew back. 'Don't you intend to wish me joy?' he asked.

'Oh, Charles, how could you? She will never make you happy! You don't know –'

'She has made me happy,' he interrupted.

'She is fast – a flirt!'

'You must not say that to me, you know,' he said, quite gently, but with a note that warned her of danger.

The Earl, who had lowered his paper at the Colonel's first announcement, now laid it down, and said in his calm way: 'This is very sudden, Charles.'

'Yes.'

Judith would have spoken again, but Worth engaged her silence by the flicker of a glance in her direction. 'Your mind is, in fact, quite made up?' he said.

'Quite!'

'Then of course I wish you joy,' said Worth. 'When do you mean to be married?'

'Nothing is decided yet. I must see her grandfather. She is her own mistress, but I don't want to – It is not as though I were a very eligible *parti*, you know.'

'You are a great deal too good for her!' exclaimed Judith.

He turned his head, and said with a smile: 'Oh no, Judith! It is she who is a great deal too good for me. When you know her better you will agree.'

She replied as cheerfully as she was able: 'I do wish you very happy, Charles. I will try to know Lady Barbara better.'

He looked at her in rather a troubled way as she went out of the room. But when he had closed the door behind her the trouble vanished from his eyes, and he walked back to the table, and sat down at it, and began to eat his breakfast.

The Earl watched him for some moments in silence. Presently he said: 'Is your engagement to be publicly announced, Charles?'

'Why, I suppose so! There is no secret about it, you know.'

'It is very wonderful,' Worth observed. 'What did she find in you to like so well?'

The Colonel grinned. 'I don't know.'

'You would not, of course,' Worth said dryly. 'Forgive my curiosity, but does Lady Barbara mean to follow the drum?'

'She would, I think, and like it very well. Women do, you know – have you ever met Juana, Harry Smith's wife?'

'I have not met Juana, nor have I met Harry Smith.'

'He's a rifleman: a rattling good fellow, mad as a coot! He went out to America with Pakenham, more's the pity! He married a Spanish child after Badajos: it's too long a story to tell you now, but you never saw such a little heroine in your life! I believe she would go with Harry into action if he would let her. I have seen her fording a river with the water right up to her horse's girths. She will sleep out in the open by a camp fire, wrapped up in a blanket, and never utter a word of complaint. Bab is made of just that high-spirited stuff.'

'I hope you may be right,' said Worth, unable to picture the Lady Barbara in any such situations.

Not very far away, in the Rue Ducale, Lady Vidal shared this mental inability and did not scruple to say so. She had looked narrowly at her sister-in-law when she had come in to breakfast, and had not failed to notice the flame in Barbara's eyes and the colour in her cheeks. 'What have you been doing?' she asked. 'You look quite wild, let me tell you!'

'Oh yes! I am quite wild!' Barbara answered. 'I have taken your advice, Gussie! There! Aren't you pleased?'

'I wish I knew what you meant!'

'Why, that I am engaged to be married, to be sure!'

Her brother's attention was caught by these words. 'What's that? Engaged? Nonsense!'

Lady Vidal exclaimed: 'Bab! Are you serious? It is Lavisse?'

'Lavisse?' repeated Barbara, as though dragging the name up from the recesses of her memory. 'No! Oh no! My staff officer!'

'Are you mad? Charles Audley? You cannot mean it!'

'Yes, I do – today, at least!'

Augusta said bitterly: 'I never reckoned stupidity among your faults. Good God, Bab, how can you be such a fool? With your looks and birth you may marry whom you please: the lord knows you've had chances enough! and you choose a penniless soldier! I will not believe it of you!'

'Charles Audley?' said Vidal. He looked at his sister over frowningly, but not displeased. 'Well, I must say I am surprised. A very good family – perfectly eligible!'

Augusta broke in angrily: 'Eligible! A penniless younger son with no chance of inheriting the title! Pray, how do you propose to live, Bab? Do you see yourself in the tail of an army, sharing all the discomforts of a campaign with your Charles?'

'I might, I think,' said Barbara, considering it. 'It would be something new – exciting!'

'I have no patience with such folly!'

Vidal interposed to say in his heavy fashion: 'It is not a brilliant match – by no means brilliant! I could wish him wealthier, but as for his being penniless – pooh! I daresay he has a very respectable competence.'

'Then Bab will have to learn to live upon a competence,' said Augusta. 'I hope, my dear love, that you have not forgotten the terms of your late husband's will?'

'Oh, who cares! With a handsome fortune I had never enough money, so I may as happily live in debt on a mere competence.'

This ingenious way of looking at the matter had the effect of pulling down the corners of Vidal's mouth. He began to read his sister a homily, but she interrupted him with a little show of temper, and ran out of the room, slamming the door behind her.

Lady Vidal remarked that if one thing were more certain than another it was that the engagement would be of short duration.

'I hope not,' replied Vidal. 'Audley is a very good sort of fellow, very well-liked. If she throws *him* over it will go hard with her in the eyes of the world. What I fear is that a sensible man will never bear with her tantrums. I wish to God she had stayed in England!' He added with an inconsequence Augusta found irritating: 'We must ask him to dine with us. I wish you will write him a civil note.'

'By all means!' she returned. 'The more Bab sees of him the sooner she'll be bored by him. He may dine with us tonight, if he chooses, and accompany us to Madame van der Capellan's party afterwards.'

The civil note was, accordingly sent round by hand to the British Headquarters, where it found Colonel Audley in the company of the Prince of Orange and Lord Fitzroy Somerset.

The Colonel took the note, and tore it open with an eagerness which did not escape the Prince. That young gentleman, observing the elegance of the hot-pressed paper and the unmistakably feminine character of the handwriting, winked at Lord Fitzroy, and said: 'Aha! The affair progresses!'

The Colonel ignored this sally, and moved across to a desk and sat down at it to write an acceptance of the invitation. The Prince strolled after him, and perched on the opposite side of the desk, swinging his thin legs. 'It is certainly an assignation,' he said.

'It is. An invitation to dinner,' replied the Colonel, rejecting one quill and choosing another.

'And it was I who set your feet on the road to ruin! Fitzroy, Charles is in love!'

Lord Fitzroy's small, firm mouth remained grave, but a smile twinkled in his eyes. 'I thought he seemed a little elated. Who is she?'

'The Widow!' answered the Prince.

'What widow?'

The Prince flung up his hands. 'He asks me what widow! *Mon Dieu*, Fitzroy, don't you know there is only one? The Incomparable, the Dashing, the Fatal Barbara!'

'I am not a penny the wiser,' said Lord Fitzroy, his quiet, slightly drawling voice in as great a contrast to the Prince's vivacity as were his fair locks and square, handsome countenance to the Prince's dark hair and erratic features. 'You forget how long it is since I was in England. Charles, that's my pen, and it suits me very well without your mending it. What's more, it's my desk, and I've work to do.'

'I shan't be more than a minute,' replied the Colonel. 'Have you noticed how devilish official he's become lately, Billy? It's from standing in the Great Man's shoes, I suppose.'

'You shall not divert me,' said the Prince. 'I observe the attempt, but it is useless. When do you announce your approaching marriage?'

'Now, if you like,' said the Colonel, dipping his pen in the ink, and drawing a sheet of paper towards him.

The Prince's jaw dropped. He stared at Colonel Audley and then laughed. 'Oh yes, I am very stupid! I shall certainly swallow that *canard*!'

'If he's going to conduct his flirtations on Government paper, I demand to know the identity of the Fatal – what did you say her name was, Billy?'

'Barbara! The disastrous Lady Barbara Childe!' answered the Prince dramatically.

'Barbara Childe? Oh, I know! Bab Alastair that was. Is she accounted fatal?'

'But entirely, Fitzroy! A veritable Circe – and *I* delivered Charles into her power!'

The Colonel looked up. 'Yes, you did, so you shall be the first to know that she is going to become my wife.'

The Prince blinked at him. '*Plaît-il?*'

Colonel Audley sealed his letter, wrote the direction, and got up. 'Quite true,' he assured the Prince, and went out to deliver his note to the waiting servant.

The Prince turned an astonished countenance towards Lord Fitzroy, and said, stammering a little, as he always did when excited 'B – but it's – it's n – not possible! Scores of men have offered for Lady Bab, and she refused them all!'

'Well, she's chosen a very good man in the end,' responded Fitzroy, seating himself at the desk.

'My poor Fitzroy, you do not understand! It is most remarkable – *éclatant*!'

'I see nothing very remarkable in two persons falling in love,' said Fitzroy with unaltered calm. 'Did I happen to mention that I was busy?'

'I am your superior officer,' declared the Prince. 'I command that you attend to me, and immediately treat me with respect.'

Lord Fitzroy promptly stood up, and clicked his heels together. 'I *beg* your Royal Highness's pardon!'

His Royal Highness made a grab at a heavy paperweight on the desk, but Lord Fitzroy was quicker. The entrance into the room of a very junior member of the staff put an end to what promised to be a most undignified scene. Lord Fitzroy at once released the paperweight, and the Prince, acknowledging the newcomer's salute, departed in search of a more appreciative audience.

By the end of the day the news of the engagement had spread all over Brussels. Both parties to it had had to endure congratulation, incredulity, and much raillery. The Colonel bore it with his usual good humour, but he was not surprised, on his arrival in the Rue Ducale, to find his betrothed in a stormy mood. Neither his host nor his hostess was in the salon when he entered it; there was only Lady Barbara, standing by the fireplace with her elbow on the mantelshelf, and one sandalled foot angrily tapping the floor.

The servant announced Colonel Audley, and he walked in to encounter a flashing glance from Barbara's eyes. Her lips parted, not smiling, and he saw her teeth gritted together. He laughed, and went up to her, and took her hands. 'My dear, has it been very bad?' he asked. 'Do you think you can bear it?'

She looked at him; her teeth unclenched: she said: 'Can you?'

'Why yes, but my case is not so hard. They all envy me, of course.'

The white, angry look left her face. She pulled one of his hands up to her mouth, and softly kissed it. 'You're a dear, Charles.'

He took her in his arms. 'You mustn't do that,' he said.

'I wanted to,' she replied, turning her face up to his. 'I always do what I want. Oh, but Charles, how odiously commonplace it is! I wish we had eloped instead!'

'That would have been worse – vulgar!'

'What I do is not vulgar!' she said snappishly.

'Exactly. So you didn't elope.'

She moved away from him to cast herself into a chair by the fire. She thrust one bare foot in its golden sandal forward, and demanded: 'How do you like my gilded toenails?'

'Very well indeed,' he answered. 'Is it a notion of your own?'

'Oh no! It's a trick Parisian harlots have!' she flung at him.

Contrary to her expectation, this made him laugh. She stiffened in her chair. 'Don't you care, then?'

'Not a bit! It's a charming fashion.'

'You will hear it very badly spoke of tonight, I warn you!'

'Oh no, I shan't!' said the Colonel cheerfully. 'Whatever criticisms may be made of you will certainly not be made to me.'

'Do you mean to fight my battles? You will be kept busy!' She opened her reticule, and drew a letter from it and handed it to him. 'Your sister-in-law sent me these felicitations. She doesn't like me, does she?'

'No, I don't think she does,' responded the Colonel, glancing through Judith's civil letter.

An impish look came into her eye. 'I wonder whether she meant you to fall in love with that insipid protégée of hers?' she said. 'I can't recall her name. But an heiress, I believe. Oh, famous! I am sure that was it!'

'But who?' he demanded. 'You do not mean Miss Devenish?'

'Yes, that was the name! Lord, to think I've lost you a fortune, Charles!'

'You must be crazy! I am persuaded Judith could never have entertained such an absurd notion!'

'Flirt with the chit, and see how your sister likes it!'

'No, no, I leave all that sort of thing to you, my sweet!'

'Wretch! Good God, how has this come about? I have talked myself into a good humour. I swear I meant to quarrel with you!' A doubt assailed her; she said challengingly: 'Charles! Was it your doing?'

'Strategy of a staff officer? On my honour, no!'

She jumped up, and almost flung herself into his arms. There was an urgency in the face upturned to his; she said: 'Marry me! Marry me soon – at once – before I change my mind!'

He took her face between his hands, staring down at her. She felt his fingers tremble slightly, and wondered what thoughts chased one another behind the trouble in his eyes. Suddenly his hands dropped to her shoulders, and thrust her away from him. 'No!' he said curtly.

'No?' she repeated. 'Don't you want to, Charles?'

'Want to!' He broke off, and turned from her to the fireplace, and stood looking down at the smouldering logs.

She gave a little laugh. 'This is certainly intriguing. I am rejected, then?'

He looked up. 'Do you think you don't tempt me? To marry you out of hand – to possess you before you had had time to regret! Oh, my love, don't speak of this again! You spoke of changing your mind. If that is to come, you shall not be tied to me.'

'You give me time to consider? Strange! I had never a suitor like you, Charles!'

'I love you too much to snatch you before you know me, before you know your own heart!'

'Ah! You are wiser than I am,' she said, with a faint smile.

They were interrupted by Lady Vidal, who came into the room, followed by her husband. She greeted Colonel Audley with cold civility, but her lack of warmth was atoned for by Vidal's marked display of friendliness. He was able to wish the Colonel joy with blunt cordiality, and even to crack a jest at his sister's expense.

They were soon joined by Lord Harry, who had ridden in from Enghien to attend the evening's party. He seemed to be delighted by the news of the betrothal. He wrung the Colonel's hand with great fervour, prophesied a devilish future for him at Bab's hands, and expressed a strong wish to see how Lavisse would receive the tidings.

'M. de Lavisse, my dear Harry, is quite a matrimonial prize,' said Augusta. 'I fancy your sister cannot boast of an offer from him. He is adroit in flirtation, but it will be a clever woman who persuades him to propose marriage.'

'Dear Gussie! How vulgar!' said Barbara.

'Possibly, but I believe it to be true.'

'Stuff!' said Lord Harry. 'I can tell you this, Gussie, it will be a pretty fool of a woman who lets that fellow persuade her into marrying him!'

'You are a schoolboy, and know nothing of the matter,' responded Augusta coldly.

'Oh, don't I, by Gad?' Lord Harry gave a crack of laughter. 'Don't be such a simpleton!'

Barbara interrupted this dialogue with a good deal of impatience. 'Do not expose yourselves more than you are obliged!' she begged. 'Charles is as yet unacquainted with my family. If he must discover how odious we are, pray let him do so gradually!'

'Very true,' said Augusta. 'We are all of us strangers to him, and he to us. How odd it seems, to be sure!'

Her husband moved restlessly, and said something under his breath. Colonel Audley, however, replied without an instant's hesitation: 'Odd, indeed, but you set me perfectly at my ease, ma'am. You are in a cross humour, and do not scruple to show it. I feel myself one of the family already.'

Barbara's gurgle of laughter broke the astonished silence that followed these words. 'Charles! Superb! Confess, Gussie, you are done up!'

Augusta's stiffened countenance relaxed into a reluctant smile. 'I am certainly taken aback, and must accord Colonel Audley the honours of *that* bout. Come, let us go in to dinner!'

She led the way into the dining parlour, indicated to the Colonel that he should sit at her right hand, and behaved towards him throughout the meal, if not with cordiality, at least with civility.

There was no lack of conversation, the Colonel being too used to maintaining a flow of talk at Headquarters' parties ever to be at a loss, and Lord Harry having an inexhaustible supply of chitchat at his tongue's end. Barbara said little. An attempt by Lord Harry to twit her on her engagement brought the stormy look back into her face. The Colonel intervened swiftly, turning aside the shaft, but not before Barbara had snapped out a snub. Augusta said with a titter: 'I have often thought the betrothed state to be wretchedly commonplace.'

'Very true,' agreed the Colonel. 'Like birth and death.'

She was silenced. Vidal seized the opportunity to advert to the political situation, inaugurating a discussion which lasted until the ladies rose from the table. The gentlemen did not linger for many minutes, and the whole party was soon on its way to Madame van de Capellan's house.

It was an evening of music and dancing, attended by the usual crowd of fashionables. More congratulations had to be endured, until Barbara said savagely under her breath that she felt like a performing animal. Lady Worth, arriving with the Earl and her brother and sister-in-law, was reminded of a captive panther, and though understanding only in part the fret and tangle of Barbara's nerves, felt a good deal of sympathy for her. She presently moved over to her side, saying with a smile: 'I think you dislike all this, so I shall add nothing to what I wrote you this morning.'

'Thank you,' Barbara said. 'The insipidity – the inanity! I could curse with vexation!'

'Indeed, an engagement does draw a disagreeably particular attention to one.'

'Oh the devil! I don't care a fig for that! But this is a milk-and-water affair!' She broke off, as Worth strolled up to them, and extended a careless hand to him. 'How do you do? If you have come to talk to me, let it be of horses, and by no means of my confounded engagement. I think of setting up a phaeton: will you sell me your bays?'

'No,' said Worth. 'I will not.'

'Good! You don't mince matters. I like that. Your wife is a famous whip, I believe. For the sake of our approaching kinship, find me a pair such as you would drive yourself, and I will challenge her to a race.'

'I have yet to see a pair in this town I would drive myself,' replied the Earl.

'Ah! And if you had? I suppose you would not permit Lady Worth to accept my challenge?'

'I am sure he would not,' said Judith. 'I did once engage in something of that nature – in my wild salad days, you know –

and fell under his gravest displeasure. I must decline therefore, for all I should like to accept your challenge.'

'Conciliating!' Barbara said with a harsh little laugh. She saw Judith's eyes kindle, and said impulsively: 'Now I've made you angry! I am glad! You look splendid just so! I could like you very well, I think.'

'I hope you may,' Judith replied formally.

'I will; but you must not be forbearing with me, if you please. There! I am behaving abominably, and I meant to be so good!'

She clasped Judith's hand briefly, allowed her a glimpse of her frank smile, and turned from her to greet Lavisse, who was coming towards her across the room.

He looked pale. He came stalking up to Barbara, and stood over her, not offering to take her hand, not even according her a bow. Their eyes were nearly on a level, hers full of mockery, his blazing with anger. He said under his breath: 'Is it true, then?'

She chuckled. 'This is in the style of a hero of romance, Etienne. It is true!'

'You have engaged yourself to this Colonel Audley? I would not believe!'

'Felicitate me!'

'Never! I do not wish you happy, I! I wish you only regret.'

'That's refreshing, at all events.'

He saw several pairs of eyes fixed upon him, and with a muttered exclamation clasped Barbara round the waist and swept her into the waltz. His left hand gripped her right one; his arm was hard about her, holding her too close for decorum. '*Je t'aime; entends tu, je t'aime!*'

'You are out of time,' she replied.

'Ah, *qu'importe?*' he exclaimed. He moderated his steps, however, and said in a quieter tone: 'You knew I loved you! This Colonel, what can he be to you?'

'Why, don't you know? A husband!'

'And it is I who love you – yes, *en désespére!*'

'But I do not remember that you ever offered for this hand of mine, Etienne.' She tilted her head back to look at him under the sweep of her lashes. 'That gives you to think, eh, my friend? Terrible, that word *marriage*!'

'*Effroyant*! Yet I offer it!'

'Too late!'

'I do not believe! What has he, this colonel, that I have not? It is not money! A great position?'

'No!

'Expectations, perhaps?'

'Not even expectations!'

'In the name of God, what then?'

'Nothing!' she answered.

'You do it to tease me! You are not serious, in fact. Listen, little angel, little fool! I will give you a proud name, I will give you wealth, everything that you desire! I will adore you – ah, but worship you!'

She said judicially: 'A proud name Charles will give me – if I cared for such stuff! Wealth? Yes, I should like that. Worship! So boring, Etienne, so damnably boring!'

'I could break your neck!' he said.

'Fustian!'

He drew in his breath, but did not speak for several turns. When he unclosed his lips again it was to say in a tone of careful nonchalance: 'One becomes dramatic: a pity! *Essayons encore*! When is it to be, this marriage?'

'Oh, confound you, is not a betrothal enough for one day? Are we not agreed that there is something terrible about that word marriage?'

His brows rose. 'So! I am well content. Play the game out, amuse yourself with this so gallant colonel; in the end you will marry me.'

A gleam shot into her eyes. 'A bet! What will you stake – gamester?'

'Nothing! It is sure, and there is no sport in it, therefore.'

The music came to an end; Barbara stood free, smiling and dangerous. 'I thank you, Etienne! If you knew the cross humour I was in! Now! Oh, it is entirely finished!' She turned upon her heel; her gaze swept the room, and found Colonel Audley. She crossed the floor towards him, her draperies hushing about her feet as she walked.

'That's a grand creature!' suddenly remarked Wellington, his attention caught. 'Who is she, Duchess?'

The Duchess of Richmond glanced over her shoulder. 'Barbara Childe,' she answered. 'She is a granddaughter of the Duke of Avon.'

'Barbara Childe, is she? So that's the prize that lucky young dog of mine has won! I must be off to offer my congratulations!' He left her side as he spoke, and made his way to where Colonel Audley and Barbara were standing.

His congratulations, delivered with blunt heartiness, were perfectly well received by the lady. She shook hands, and met that piercing eagle stare with a look of candour, and her most enchanting smile. The Duke stayed talking to her until the quadrille was forming, but as soon as he saw the couples taking up their positions, he said briskly: 'You must take your places, or you will be too late. No need to ask whether you dance the quadrille, Lady Barbara! As for this fellow, Audley, I'll engage for it he won't disgrace you.'

He waved them on to the floor, called a chaffing word to young Lennox on the subject of his celebrated *pas de zéphyr*, and stood back to watch the dance for a few minutes. Lady Worth, only a few paces distant, thought it must surely be impossible for anyone to look more carefree than his lordship. He was smiling, nodding to acquaintances, evidently enjoying himself. She watched him, wondering at him a little, and presently, as though aware of her gaze, he turned his head, recognised her, and said: 'Oh, how d'ye do? A pretty sight, isn't it?'

She agreed to it. 'Yes, indeed. Do all your staff officers perform so creditably, Duke? They put the rest quite in the shade.'

'Yes, I often wonder where would Society be without my boys?' he replied. 'Your brother acquits himself very well, but I believe that young scamp, Lennox, is the best of them. There he goes – but his partner is too heavy on her feet! Audley has the advantage of him in that respect.'

'Yes,' she acknowledged. 'Lady Barbara dances very well.'

'Audley's a fortunate fellow,' said the Duke decidedly. 'Won't thank me for taking him away from Brussels, I daresay. Don't blame him! But it can't be helped.'

'You are leaving us, then?'

'Oh yes – yes! for a few days. No secret about it: I have to visit the Army.'

'Of course. We shall await your return with impatience, I assure you, praying the Ogre may not descend upon us while you are absent!'

He gave one of his sudden whoops of laughter. 'No fear of that! It's all nonsense, this talk about Bonaparte! Ogre! Pooh! Jonathan Wild, that's my name for him!' He saw her look of astonishment, and laughed again, apparently much amused, either by her surprise or by his own words.

She was conscious of disappointment. He had been described to her as unaffected: he seemed to her almost inane.

Eight

*U*pon the following day was published a General Order, directing officers in future to make their reports to the Duke of Wellington. Upon the same day, a noble-browed gentleman with a suave address and great tact, was sent from Brussels to the Prussian Headquarters, there to assume the somewhat arduous duties of military commissioner to the Prussian Army. Sir Henry Hardinge had lately been employed by the Duke in watching Napoleon's movements in France. He accepted his new rôle with his usual equanimity, and commiserated with by his friends on the particularly trying nature of his commission, merely smiled, and said that General von Gneisenau was not likely to be as tiresome as he was painted.

The *Moniteur* of this 11th day of April published gloomy tidings. In the south of France, the Duc d'Angoulême's enterprise had failed. Angoulême had led his mixed force on Lyons, but the arrival from Paris of a competent person of the name of Grouchy had ended Royalist hopes in the south. Angoulême and his masterful wife had both set sail from France, and his army was fast dwindling away.

It was not known what King Louis, in Ghent, made of these tidings, but those who were acquainted with his character doubted whether his nephew's failure would much perturb him. Never was there so lethargic a monarch: one could hardly blame France for welcoming Napoleon back.

The news disturbed others, however. It seemed as though it were all going to start again: victory upon victory for Napoleon;

France overrunning Europe. Shocking to think of the Emperor's progress through France, of the men who flocked to join his little force, of the crowds who welcomed him, hysterical with joy! Shocking to think of Marshal Ney, with his oath to King Louis on his conscience, deserting with his whole force to the Emperor's side! There must be some wizardry in the man, for in all France there had not been found sufficient loyal men to stand by the King and make it possible for him to hold his capital in Napoleon's teeth. He had fled, with his little Court, and his few troops, and if ever he found himself on his throne again it would be once more because foreign soldiers had placed him there.

But how unlikely it seemed that he would find himself there! With Napoleon at large, summoning his Champ de Mai assemblies, issuing his dramatic proclamations, gathering together his colossal armies, only the very optimistic could feel that there was any hope for King Louis.

Even Wellington doubted the ability of the Allies to put King Louis back on the throne, but this doubt sprang more from a just appreciation of the King's character than from any fear of Napoleon. Sceptical people might ascribe the Duke's attitude to the fact of his never having met Napoleon in the field, but the fact remained that his lordship was one of the few generals in Europe who did not prepare to meet Napoleon in a mood of spiritual defeat.

He accorded the news of Angoulême's failure a sardonic laugh, and laid the *Moniteur* aside. He was too busy to waste time over that.

He kept his staff busy too, a circumstance which displeased Barbara Childe. To be loved by a man who sent her brief notes announcing his inability to accompany her on expeditions of her planning was a new experience. When she saw him at the end of a tiring day, she rallied him on his choice of profession. 'For the future I shall be betrothed only to civilians.'

He laughed. He had been all the way to Oudenarde and back, with a message for General Colville, commanding the 4th Division, but he had found time to buy a ring of emeralds and diamonds for Barbara, and although there was a suggestion of weariness about his eyelids, he seemed to desire nothing as much as to dance with her the night through.

Waltzing with him, she said abruptly: 'Are you tired?'

'Tired! Do I dance as though I were tired?'

'No, but you've been in the saddle nearly all day.'

'Oh, that's nothing! In Spain I have been used to ride fifteen or twenty miles to a ball, and be at work again by ten o'clock the next day.'

'Wellington trains admirable suitors,' she remarked. 'How fortunate it is that you dance so well, Charles!'

'I know. You would not otherwise have accepted me.'

'Yes, I think perhaps I should. But I should not dance with you so much. I wish you need not leave Brussels just now.'

'So do I. What will you do while I am away? Flirt with your Belgian admirer?'

She looked up at him. 'Don't go!'

He smiled, but shook his head.

'Apply to the Duke for leave, Charles!'

He looked startled. As his imagination played with the scene her words evoked, his eyes began to dance. 'Unthinkable!'

'Why? You might well ask the Duke!'

'Believe me, I might not!'

She jerked up a shoulder. 'Perhaps you don't wish for leave?'

'I don't,' he said frankly. 'Why, what a fellow I should be if I did!'

'Don't I come first with you?'

He glanced down at her. 'You don't understand, Bab.'

'Oh, you mean to talk to me of your duty!' she said impatiently. 'Tedious stuff!'

'Very. Tell me what you will do while I am away.'

'Flirt with Etienne. You have already said so. Have I your permission?'

'If you need it. It's very lucky: I leave Brussels on the 16th, and Lavisse will surely arrive on the 15th for the dinner in honour of the Prince of Orange. I daresay he'll remain a day or two, and so be at your disposal.'

'Not jealous, Charles?'

'How should I be? You wear my ring, not his.'

His guess was correct. The Comte de Lavisse appeared in Brussels four days later to attend the Belgian dinner at the Hôtel d'Angleterre. He lost no time in calling in the Rue Ducale, and on learning that Lady Barbara was out, betook himself to the Park, and very soon came upon her ladyship, in company with Colonel Audley, Lady Worth and her offspring, Sir Peregrine Taverner, and Miss Devenish.

The party seemed to be a merry one, Judith being in spirits and Barbara in a melting mood. It was she who held Lord Temperley's leading strings, and directed his attention to a bed of flowers. 'Pretty lady!' Lord Temperley called her, with weighty approval.

'Famous!' she said. She glanced up at Judith, and said with a touch of archness: 'I count your son one of my admirers, you see!'

'You are so kind to him I am sure it is no wonder,' Judith responded, liking her in this humour.

'Thank you! Charles, set him on your shoulder, and let us take him to see the swans on the water. Lady Worth, you permit?'

'Yes indeed, but I don't wish you to be teased by him!'

'No such thing!' She swooped upon the child, and lifted him up in her arms. 'There! I declare I could carry you myself!'

'He's too heavy for you!'

'He will crush your pelisse!'

She shrugged as these objections were uttered, and relinquished the child. Colonel Audley tossed him up on to his shoulder, and the whole party was about to walk in the direction of the pavilion when Lavisse, who had been watching from a little distance, came forward, and clicked his heels together in one of his flourishing salutes.

Lady Worth bowed with distant civility; Barbara looked as though she did not care to be discovered in such a situation; only the Colonel said with easy good humour: 'Hallo! You know my sister, I believe. And Miss Devenish – Sir Peregrine Taverner?'

'Ah, I have not previously had the honour! Mademoiselle! Monsieur!' Two bows were executed; the Count looked slyly towards Barbara, and waved a hand to include the whole group. 'You must permit me to compliment you upon the pretty *tableau* you make; I am perhaps *de trop*, but shall beg leave to join the party.'

'By all means,' said the Colonel. 'We are taking my nephew to see the swans.'

'You cannot want to carry him, Charles,' said Judith in a low voice.

'Fiddle!' he replied. 'Why should I not want to carry him?'

She thought that the picture he made with the child on his shoulder was too domestic to be romantic, but could scarcely say so. He set off towards the pavilion with Miss Devenish beside him; Barbara imperiously demanded Sir Peregrine's arm; and as the path was not broad enough to allow of four persons walking abreast, Judith was left to bring up the rear with Lavisse.

This arrangement was accepted by the Count with all the outward complaisance of good manners. Though his eyes might follow Barbara, his tongue uttered every civil inanity required of him. He was ready to discuss the political situation, the weather, or mutual acquaintances, and, in fact, touched upon all these topics with the easy address of a fashionable man.

Upon their arrival at the sheet of water by the pavilion his air of fashion left him. Judith was convinced that nothing could have been further from his inclination than to throw bread to a pair of swans, but he clapped his hands together, declaring that the swans must and should be fed, and ran off to the pavilion to procure crumbs for the purpose.

He came back presently with some cakes, a circumstance which shocked Miss Devenish into exclaiming against such extravagance.

'Oh, such delicious little cakes, and all for the swans! Some stale bread would have been better!'

The Count said gaily: 'They have no stale bread, mademoiselle; they were offended at the very suggestion. So what would you?'

'I am sure the swans will much prefer your cakes, Etienne,' said Barbara, smiling at him for the first time.

'If only you may not corrupt their tastes!' remarked Audley, holding on to his nephew's skirts.

'Ah, true! A swan with an unalterable *penchant* for cake: I fear he would inevitably starve!'

'He might certainly despair of finding another patron with your lavish notions of largess,' observed Barbara.

She stepped away from the group, in the endeavour to coax one of the swans to feed from her hand; after a few moments the Count joined her, while Colonel Audley still knelt, holding his nephew on the brink of the lake, and directing his erratic aim in crumb throwing.

Judith made haste to relieve him of his charge, saying in an undervoice as she bent over her son: 'Pray, let me take Julian. You do not want to be engaged with him.'

'Don't disturb yourself, my dear sister. Julian and I are doing very well, I assure you.'

She replied with some tartness: 'I hope you will not be stupid enough to allow that man to take your place beside Barbara! There, get up! I have Julian fast.'

He rose, but said with a smile: 'Do you think me a great fool? Now *I* was preening myself on being a wise man!'

He moved away before she could answer him, and joined Miss Devenish, who was sitting on a rustic bench, drawing diagrams in the gravel with the ferrule of her sunshade. In repose her face had a wistful look, but at the Colonel's approach she raised her eyes, and smiled, making room for him to sit beside her.

'Of all the questions in the world I believe *What are you thinking about?* to be the most impertinent,' he said lightly.

She laughed, but with a touch of constraint. 'Oh – I don't know what I was thinking about! The swans – the dear little boy – Lady Worth – how I envy her!'

These last words were uttered almost involuntarily. The Colonel said: 'Envy her? Why should you do so?'

She coloured, and looked down. 'I don't know how I came to say that. Pray do not regard it!' She added in a stumbling way: 'One does take such fancies! It is only that she is so happy, and good . . .'

'Are you not happy?' he asked. 'I am sure you are good.'

She gave her head a quick shake. 'Oh no! At least, I mean, of course I am happy. Please do not heed me! I am in a nonsensical mood today. How beautiful Lady Barbara looks in her bronze bonnet and pelisse.' She glanced shyly at him. 'You must be very proud. I hope you will be very happy too.'

'Thank you. I wonder how long it will be before I shall be wishing you happy in the same style?' he said, with a quizzical smile.

She looked started. A blush suffused her cheeks, and her eyes brightened all at once with a spring of tears. 'Oh no! Impossible! Please do not speak of it!'

He said in a tone of concern: 'My dear Miss Devenish, forgive me! I had no notion of distressing you, upon my honour!'

'You must think me very foolish!'

'Well,' he said, in a rallying tone, 'do you know, I do think you a little foolish to speak of your marriage as impossible! Now you will write me down a very saucy fellow!'

'Oh no! But you don't understand! Here is Lady Barbara coming towards you: please forget this folly!'

She got up, still in some agitation of spirit, and walked quickly away to Judith's side.

'Good God! did my approach frighten the heiress away?' asked Barbara, in a tone of lively amusement. 'Or was it your gallantry, Charles? Confess! You have been trifling with her!'

'What, in such a public place as this?' protested the Colonel. 'You wrong me, Bab!'

She said with a gleam of fun: 'I thought you liked public places, indeed I did! Parks – or Allées!'

'Allées!' ejaculated Lavisse. 'Do not mention that word, I beg! I shall not easily forgive Colonel Audley for discovering, with the guile of all staff officers (an accursed race!), that you ride there every morning.'

The Colonel laughed. Barbara took his arm saying: 'I have made such a delightful plan, Charles. I am quite tired of the Allée Verte. I am going further afield, with Etienne.'

'Are you?' said the Colonel. 'A picnic? I don't advise it in this changeable weather, but you won't care for that. Where do you go?'

It was Lavisse who answered. 'Do you know the Château de Hougoumont, Colonel? Ah, no! How should you, in effect? It is a little country seat which belongs to a relative of mine, a M. de Lunéville.'

'I know the Château,' interrupted the Colonel. 'It is near the village of Merbe Braine, is it not, on the Nivelles road?'

The Count's brows rose. 'You are exact! One would say you knew it well.'

'I had occasion to travel over that country last year,' the Colonel responded briefly. 'Do you mean to make your expedition there? It must be quite twelve or thirteen miles away.'

'What of that?' said Barbara. 'You don't know me if you think I am so soon tired. We shall ride through the Forest, and take luncheon at the Château. It will be capital sport!'

'Of whom is this party to consist?' he enquired.

'Of Etienne and myself, to be sure.'

He returned no answer, but she saw a grave look in his face, which provoked her into saying: 'I assure you Etienne is very well able to take care of me.'

'I don't doubt it,' he replied.

Lady Worth had joined them by this time, and was listening to the interchange in silence, but with a puckered brow. The whole party began to walk away from the lake, and Judith, resigning her son into Peregrine's charge, caught up with Barbara, and said in a low voice: 'Forgive me, but you are not in earnest?'

'Very seldom, I believe.'

'This expedition with the Count: you cannot have considered what a singular appearance it will give you!'

'On the contrary: I delight in singularity.'

Judith felt her temper rising; she managed to control it, and to say in a quiet tone: 'You will think me impertinent, I daresay, but I do most earnestly counsel you to give up the scheme. I can have no expectation of *my* words weighing with you, but I cannot suppose you to be equally indifferent to my brother's wishes. He must dislike this scheme excessively.'

'Indeed! Are you his envoy, Lady Worth?'

Judith was obliged to deny it. She was spared having to listen to the mocking rejoinder, which, she was sure, hovered on the tip of Barbara's tongue, by Colonel Audley's coming up to them at that moment. He stepped between them, offering each an arm, and having glanced at both their faces, said: 'I conclude that I have interrupted a duel. My guess is that Judith has been preaching propriety, and Bab announcing herself a confirmed rake.'

'I have certainly been preaching propriety,' replied Judith. 'It sounds odious, and I fear Lady Barbara has found it so.'

'No! Confoundedly boring!' said Barbara. 'I am informed, Charles, that you will dislike my picnic scheme excessively. Shall you?'

'Good God no! Go, by all means, if you wish to – and can stand the gossip.'

'I am quite accustomed to it,' she said indifferently.

Judith felt so much indignation at the lack of feeling shown by this remark that she drew her hand away from the Colonel's arm, and dropped behind to walk with her brother. This left Miss Devenish to the Count's escort, an arrangement which continued until Barbara left the party. The Count then requested the honour of being allowed to conduct her home; Colonel Audley, who was obliged to call at Headquarters, made no objection, and Miss Devenish found herself once more in the company of Sir Peregrine, Lady Worth and Colonel Audley walking ahead of them.

After a few moments, Judith said in a vexed tone: 'You will surely not permit her to behave with such impropriety!'

'I see no impropriety,' he replied.

'To be alone with that man the whole day!'

'An indiscretion, certainly.'

She walked on beside him in silence for some way, but presently said: 'Why do you permit it?'

'I have no power to stop her even if I would.'

'Even if you would? What can you mean?'

'She must be the only judge of her own actions. I won't become a mentor.'

'Charles, how nonsensical! Do you mean to let yourself be ridden over roughshod?'

'Neither to be ridden over nor to ride roughshod,' he answered. 'To manage my own affairs in my own way, however.'

'I beg your pardon,' she said, in a mortified voice.

He pressed her hand, but after a slight pause began to talk of something else. She attempted no further discussion with him on the subject of the picnic, but to Worth, later, spoke her mind with great freedom. He listened calmly to all she had to say, but when she demanded to know his opinion, replied that he thought her intervention to have been ill-judged.

'I had no notion of vexing her! I tried only to advise her!'

'You made a great mistake in doing so. Advice is seldom palatable.'

'I think she is perfectly heartless!'

'I hope you may be found to be wrong.'

'And, what is more, she is a flirt. I am sure there can be nothing more odious!' She paused, but as Worth showed no sign of wishing to avail himself of the opportunity of answering her, continued: 'Nothing could be more unfortunate than such an entanglement! I wonder you can sit there so placidly while Charles goes the quickest way to work to ruin his life! She has nothing to recommend her. She has not even the advantages of fortune; she is wild to a fault; indulges every extravagant folly; and in general shows such a want of delicacy that it quite sinks my spirits to think of Charles forming such a connection!' She again paused, and as Worth remained silent, said: 'Well? Can you find anything to admire in her, beyond a beautiful face and a well-turned ankle?'

'Certainly,' he replied. 'She has a great deal of natural quickness, and although her vivacity often betrays her into unbecoming behaviour, I believe she wants neither sense nor feeling.'

'You will tell me next that you are pleased with the engagement!'

'On the contrary, I am sorry for it. But depend upon it, a man of thirty-five is capable of judging for himself what will best suit him.'

'Oh, Julian, I know she will make him unhappy!'

'I think it extremely probable,' he replied. 'But as neither of us has the power to prevent such a contingency we should be extremely foolish to interfere in the matter.'

She sighed, and picked up her embroidery. After a period of reflection, she said in a mollified tone: 'I don't wish to be censorious, and I must say she is extremely kind to little Julian.'

The entrance of the Colonel put an end to the conversation. He had been dining at the Duke's table, and seemed to be more concerned with the difficulties of the military situation than with Barbara's volatility. He sat down with a sigh of relief before the fire, and said: 'Well! we depart (I need hardly say) at daybreak. It will be a relief to leave these Headquarters behind us. If his temper is to survive this campaign Old Hookey must have a respite from the letters they keep sending from the Horse Guards.'

'Crusty, is he?' said Worth.

'Damned crusty. I don't blame him: I wouldn't be in his shoes for a thousand pounds. What is needed is good troops, and all we hear of is general officers. Added to that, the staff which has been employed here is preposterous. One is for ever tumbling over deputy-assistants who are nothing more than subaltern officers, and no more fit for staff duty than your son would be. They are all being turned off, of course, but even so we shall have too many novices still left on the staff.'

'If I know anything of the matter, you will have more – if Wellington pays any heed to the recommendations he will receive,' remarked Worth.

'He don't, thank the lord! Though, between ourselves, some of those recommendations come from very exalted quarters.' He stood up. 'I am off to bed. Have you made up your mind whether you come along with us, or not, Worth?'

'Yes, as far as to Ghent. Where do you go from there?'

'Oh, Tournay – Mons! All the fortifications. We shall be away for about a week, I suppose.'

Both men had left the house when Judith came down to breakfast next morning. She sat down at the table, with only *The British and Continental Herald* to bear her company, and was engaged in perusing the columns of Births, Marriages, and Deaths, when the butler came in to announce the Lady Barbara Childe.

Judith looked up in surprise; she supposed Lady Barbara to be in the salon, but before she could speak that tempestuous beauty had brushed past the butler into the room.

She was dressed in a walking costume, and carried a huge chinchilla muff. She looked pale, and her eyes seemed over-bright to Judith. She glanced round the room, and said abruptly: 'Charles! I want to see him!'

Judith rose, and came forward. 'How do you do?' she said. 'I am sorry, but my brother has already left for Ghent. I hope it is nothing urgent?'

Barbara exclaimed: 'Oh, confound it! I wanted to see him! I overslept – it's those curst drops!'

Her petulance, the violence of the language she used, did nothing to advance her claims to Judith's kindness. 'I am sorry. Pray will you not be seated?'

'Oh no! There's no use in my staying!' Barbara replied dejectedly. Her mouth drooped; her eyes were emptied of light; she stood swinging her muff, apparently lost in her own brooding thoughts. Suddenly she looked at Judith, and laughed. 'Oh, heavens! what did I say? You are certainly offended!'

Judith at once disclaimed. Barbara said, with her air of disarming candour: 'I am sorry! Only I did wish to see Charles before he left, and I am always cross when I don't get what I want.'

'I hope it was not a matter of great importance.'

'No. That is, I behaved odiously to him yesterday – oh, to you, too, but I don't care for that! Oh, the devil, *now* what have I said?'

She looked so rueful, yet had such an imp of mischief dancing behind her solemnity that Judith was obliged to laugh. 'I wish you will sit down! Have you breakfasted?'

Barbara dropped into a chair. 'No. I don't, you know.' She sighed. 'Life is using me very hardly today. You will say that is my own fault, but it is nevertheless monstrous that when I do mean to be good, to make amends, I must needs oversleep.'

After a moment's hesitation, Judith said: 'You refer, I collect, to your picnic scheme?'

'Of course. I wanted to tell Charles I was only funning.'

'You do not mean to go, then!'

'No.'

'I am so glad! I was completely taken in, I confess.'

'Oh no! I did mean to go – yesterday! But Gussie –' She broke off, grinding her teeth together.

'Your sister-in-law advised you against the scheme?'

'On the contrary!' said Barbara, with an angry little laugh.

'I don't think I quite understand?'

'I daresay you might not. She had the infernal impudence to approve of it. She will be a famous matchmaking mama for her daughters one of these days.'

'Can you mean that she wishes you to marry the Comte de Lavisse?' gasped Judith.

'Most earnestly. Ah, you are astonished. You are not acquainted with my family.'

'But your engagement to my brother! She could not wish to see that broken!'

'Why not?'

'A solemn promise – the scandal!'

Barbara burst out laughing. 'Oh, you're enchanting when you're shocked! An outraged goddess, no less! But you must learn to know my family better. We don't care for scandal.'

'Then why do you forgo your picnic?' demanded Judith.

'I don't know. To spite Gussie – to please Charles! Both, perhaps.'

This answer was not encouraging. Judith was silent for a moment. She stole a glance at Barbara's face, and of impulse said: 'Do you love him?' The words were no sooner uttered than regretted. Such a question was an impertinence; she was not on terms of sufficient intimacy with Barbara to allow of its having been asked.

Flushing, she awaited the snub she felt herself to have earned. But Barbara replied merely: 'Yes.'

'I should not have asked you,' Judith apologised.

'It's of no consequence. I daresay you wish that Charles had never met me. I should, in your place. I'm horrid, you know. I told him so, but he wouldn't listen to me. I never loved anyone before, I think.'

This remark accorded so ill with her reputation that Judith looked rather taken aback.

Barbara gave a gurgle of irrepressible amusement. 'Are you recalling my flirtations? They don't signify, you know. I flirt to amuse myself, but the truth is that I never fancied myself in love with anyone but Charles.'

'I beg your pardon, but to fancy yourself in love could surely be the only justification for flirting!'

'Oh, stuff!' Barbara said. 'Flirtation is delightful; being in love, quite disagreeable.'

'*I* never found it so!'

'Truly?'

Judith considered for a moment. 'No. At least – yes, I suppose sometimes it can be disagreeable. There is a certain pain – for foolish causes.'

'Ah, you are not so stupid after all! I hate pain. Yes, and I hate to submit, as I am doing now, over this tiresome picnic!'

'That I understand perfectly!' Judith said. 'But you do not submit to Charles; *he* made no such demand! Your submission is to your own judgment.'

'Oh no! I don't go because Charles does not wish it. How

tame! Don't talk of it! It makes me cross! I want to go. I am bored to death!'

'Well, why should you not?' Judith said, as an idea presented itself to her. 'A party of pleasure – there could be no objection! If you will accept of my company, I will go with you.'

'Go with me?' said Barbara. 'In Lavisse's place?'

'No such thing! *You* may ride with the Count; *I* shall drive with my sister, Lady Taverner. I am persuaded she would delight in the expedition. I daresay my brother will join us as well.'

The green eyes looked blankly for a moment, then grew vivid with laughter. 'Thus turning a *tête-à-tête* into the most sedate of family parties! Oh, I must do it, if only for the fun of seeing Etienne's dismay!'

'Would you not care for it?' said Judith, a little dashed.

'Of all things!' Barbara sprang up. 'It's for tomorrow. We start early, and lunch at this Château Etienne talks of. It will be charming! Thank you a thousand times!'

Nine

The weather remaining fine, and the Taverners declaring themselves to be very ready to join the picnic, the whole party assembled in the Rue Ducale the next morning. As Lady Taverner's situation made riding ineligible for her, Judith, who would have preferred to have gone on horseback, was obliged to drive with her in an open barouche. Sir Peregrine bestrode a showy chestnut, and Barbara, as usual, rode the Count's Coup de Grâce.

Upon her first setting out Judith had felt perfectly satisfied with her own appearance. She was wearing a round robe, under a velvet pelisse of Sardinian blue. A high-crowned bonnet, lined with silk and ornamented with a frilled border of lace, gloves of French kid, a sealskin muff, and half boots of jean, completed a very becoming toilet. Beside her sister-in-law, who had chosen to wear drab merino cloth over olive-brown muslin, she looked elegant indeed, but from the moment of Barbara's descending the steps of the house in the Rue Ducale she felt herself to have been cast quite in the shade.

Barbara was wearing a habit of pale green, resembling the dress of a hussar. Her coat was ornamented with row upon row of frogs and braiding; silver epaulettes set off her shoulders; and silver braiding stretched half way up her arms. Under the habit, she wore a cambric shirt with a high-standing collar trimmed with lace; a cravat of worked muslin was tied round her throat; and there were narrow ruffles at her wrists. Set jauntily on her flaming head was a tall hat, like a shako, with a plume of feathers adding the final touch of audacity to a preposterous but undeniably striking costume.

Lady Taverner was shocked; Judith, who considered the dress too daring for propriety, yet could not suppress a slight feeling of envy. She could fancy herself in such a habit.

'How can she? Such a quiz of a hat!' whispered Lady Taverner.

However much she might agree with these sentiments, Judith had no notion of spoiling the day's pleasure by letting her disapproval appear. She leaned out of the carriage to shake hands with Barbara, saying with the utmost amiability: 'How delightfully you look! You put me quite out of conceit with myself.'

'Yes, I'm setting a fashion,' replied Barbara. 'You will see: it will be the established mode in a month's time.'

Lady Vidal, who had come out of the house with her husband, merely bowed to Judith from the top of the stone steps, but Vidal put himself to the trouble of coming up to the barouche to thank Judith for her kindness in joining the expedition. He said in a low voice: 'Bab is a sad romp! One of these days her crotchets will be the ruin of her. But *your* presence makes everything as it should be! I shan't conceal from you that I don't above half like that fellow Lavisse.'

Not wishing to join in any animadversions on one who was for this day in some sort her host, Judith passed it off with a smile and a trivial remark. Her dislike of Lavisse was as great as Vidal's, but she was forced to acknowledge the very gentleman-like way in which he had received the news of the augmentation of his party. Not by as much as the flicker of an eyelid did he betray the mortification he must feel. His civility towards the ladies in the barouche was most flattering; he was all smiles and complaisance, prophesying fine weather, and displaying a proper solicitude for their comfort.

'Don't you wish you were coming, Gussie?' Barbara called.

'My dear Bab, you must know that of all insipidities I most detest a family party,' returned Augusta.

Barbara bit her lip, glancing towards the barouche as though she saw it with new eyes. Suddenly impatient, she said: 'Well, why do we wait? Let us, for God's sake, start!'

The Count, who was giving some directions to Judith's coachman, looked over his shoulder with a smile of perfect comprehension. '*En avant*, then!' he said, reining his horse back to allow the barouche to pass. When it had moved forward with Peregrine riding close behind it, he fell in beside Barbara, and said with some amusement: 'You repent already, and are asking yourself what you do in this *galère.*'

'Oh, by God, I must have been mad!' she said.

'Little fool! I admire the guard set about you by your staff officer. It is most formidable!'

'It was not his doing. The notion was Lady Worth's, and I fell in with it.'

'*Impayable!* Why, for example?'

She laughed. 'Oh, to make you angry, of course!'

'But I am not at all angry; I am entirely amused,' he said.

They were making their way down the Rue de la Pépinière in the direction of the Namur Gate. Once outside the walls of the town, the road led through some neat suburbs to the Forest of Soignes, a huge beechwood stretching for some miles to the south of Brussels, and intersected by the main Charleroi Chaussée. The Forest was almost entirely composed of beech trees, their massive trunks rising up out of the ground with scarcely any underwood to hide their smooth, silvery outlines.

Judith had often ridden in this direction, but this was her first visit to the Forest in springtime. She was enchanted with it, and even Lady Taverner, whose spirits were always low during the first months of pregnancy, was moved to exclaim at the grandeur of the scene. Sir Peregrine, in spite of already having got his uppers splashed by the mud of the unpaved portion of the road, seemed pleased also, though he would not allow the vista to be comparable to an English scene.

For the first mile or two the party remained together, Barbara and Lavisse riding at a little distance behind the barouche, but from time to time pressing forward to exchange remarks with its occupants. Shortly after the Forest had been entered, however, Barbara announced herself to be tired of riding tamely along the road. She waved her whip in a rather naughty gesture of farewell, and set her horse scrambling up the bank of the wood. The Count lingered only to assure Judith of the impossibility of her coachman's missing the way, saluted, and followed Barbara.

'I do think her the most unaccountable creature!' exclaimed Lady Taverner. 'It is very uncivil of her to make off like that, besides being so indiscreet!'

Judith, herself disappointed in this fresh evidence of flightiness in Barbara, endeavoured to give her sister-in-law's thoughts another direction.

It was inconceivable to Lady Taverner that any female who was betrothed to one gentleman could desire a *tête-à-tête* with another, and for some time she continued to marvel at Barbara's conduct. Judith did not attend very closely to her remarks; she was lost in her own reflections. She could appreciate the cause of Barbara's perversity, but although she might sympathise with that wildness of disposition which made convention abhorrent to Barbara, she could not but be sorry for it. She was more than ever convinced that this spoiled, fashionable beauty would make Colonel Audley a wretched wife. Her imagination dwelled pitifully upon his future, which must of necessity be a stormy affair, made up of whims and tantrums and debts; and she could not forbear to contrast this melancholy prospect with the less exciting but infinitely more comfortable life he would enjoy if he would but change Barbara for Lucy.

She was roused from these musings by hearing Peregrine announce a village to have come into view. She looked up; the trees flanking the road dwindled ahead in perspective to the village of Waterloo. A round building, standing on the edge of the Forest, half bathed in sunlight, presented a picture charming enough to make her long for her sketchbook and water colours.

They had by this time covered some nine and a half miles, and were glad to be leaving the shade of the Forest. In a few minutes the village was reached, and Lady Taverner was exclaiming at the size and style of the church, a strange edifice with a domed roof, standing on one side of the chaussée. Opposite, among a huddle of brick and stone-built cottages, was a small inn, with a painted signboard bearing the legend, Jean de Nivelles. There was little to detain sightseers, and after pausing for a short while to look at the church, they drove on, up a gentle acclivity leading to the village of Mont St Jean, three miles farther on.

Here the chaussée diverged, one fork continuing over the brow of a hill, and crossing, a little over half a mile beyond Mont St Jean, an unpaved hollow road running from Wavre to Braine l'Alleud, towards Charleroi; and the other running in a south-westerly direction towards Nivelles. The Nivelles road, which the coachman had been instructed to follow, was straight and uninteresting, bordered by straggling hedges, and proceeding over undulating ground until it descended presently between high banks into a ravine extending from the village of Merbe Braine to Hougoumont.

The Château was situated to the south of the hollow road from Wavre, which here, having taken a turn to the south-west, crossed the Nivelles chaussée; and to the east of the chaussée, from which it was approached by an avenue of fine elm trees. The Count's directions had been exact; the coachman turned into the avenue without hesitation; and the carriage bowled along under the spreading branches, and soon passed through the northern gateway of the Châeau. The travellers found themselves in a paved courtyard, surrounded by a motley collection of buildings.

The Château was one of the many such residences to be found in the Netherlands, a semi-fortified house, half manor, half farm. The Château itself, built of stone and brick, was a pretty house, with shuttered windows; there was a small chapel at the southern end of the courtyard; and opposite the Château, on the western side, were some picturesque barns. A gardener's cottage and a cowshed made up the rest of the buildings, which were all clustered together in a friendly fashion, and bathed, at this moment, in pale spring sunlight.

As the barouche drew up outside the door of the Château, Barbara strolled out, with the tail of her habit caught up over one arm, and a glass of wine in her hand. She had taken off her hat, and her short red curls were clustering over her head in not unpleasing disorder. She looked rather mannish, and neither her eyes nor her glancing smile held a hint of the softness which Judith had seen in both the day before.

'Have you had a pleasant drive?' she called out. 'We beat you, you observe.'

'Yes, a delightful drive,' replied Judith, stepping out of the carriage. 'And I have now fallen quite in love with this pretty little Château! How cosy it is! There is nothing stiff, nothing at all formal about these Flemish country houses.'

Lavisse came out of the house at this moment, and while he welcomed the ladies, and directed the coachman where to stable his horses, Barbara stood leaning negligently against the door-post, sipping her wine and blinking, catlike, at the sunshine.

The owner of the house was away, but Lavisse, who appeared to be quite at home, had advised the housekeeper of his advent, and a light luncheon had been prepared for the party. A *fille de chambre* conducted the ladies upstairs to a bedroom where they could leave their pelisses and bonnets, and when they were ready led them down again to a parlour overlooking a walled garden with an orchard beyond.

A table had been laid in the middle of the room, and a fire burned in the hearth. Barbara was lounging in the window, leaning her shoulders against the lintel. As Judith and Harriet came in, a burst of laughter from the two men indicated that she was in funning humour.

The Count at once came forward. He drew Harriet to a chair by the fire, declaring that she must be chilled from the long drive, and insisted on her taking a glass of wine. She accepted, and he stayed by her, engaging her in conversation, while Judith went to the window to admire the garden.

It was laid out in neat walks, much of it under cultivation for vegetables, but there were some flowerbeds as well, and the tops of the fruit trees beyond the mellow brick wall were heavy with blossom. From the window could be seen rose bushes, some fine fig trees, and several orange trees. Judith thought the garden must be enchanting in summer.

'I daresay it is,' agreed Barbara. 'We might arrange another expedition here, perhaps in June.'

'June! Who knows what may have happened by then?'

'Oh, you are thinking of the war, are you? I am tired of it: we have heard too much of it, and nothing ever happens.'

'It certainly seems out of place in this peaceful little Château,' Judith remarked. 'You must have had a delightful ride through the Forest. Such noble trees! I do not think there can be any tree to compare with the beech.'

'Beech trees, are they? To tell you the truth, I did not notice them particularly,' said Barbara. 'Etienne, fill my glass, if you please!'

'Ah, allow *me*!' Peregrine said, hurrying to the table for the decanter that stood on it.

She held out her glass, smiling at him. He filled it, and his own, saying audaciously: 'To your green eyes, Lady Bab!'

She laughed. 'To your blue ones, Sir Peregrine!'

Luncheon was brought in at this moment, and soon the whole party was seated round the table, partaking of minced chicken and scalloped oysters.

Lady Barbara was in spirits, the Count scarcely less so, and everything might have gone off merrily enough had not Lady Taverner taken one of her rare dislikes to Barbara. Like many shy women, she had some strong prejudices. She had never liked Barbara. Until today, she had known her merely by sight and by repute, and, being a just little creature, had refused to condemn her. But from the moment of seeing Barbara come down the steps of her home in her hussar dress she had felt that gossip had not lied. Barbara was fast, and, since she chose deliberately to ride off alone with a dreadful rake, unprincipled into the bargain. She offended every canon of good taste: lounged like a man, tossed off her wine like a man, and (thought Harriet, in her innocence) swore like a trooper. Listening to her conversation at the luncheon table, Harriet decided that some of her sallies were a trifle warm. Shocked, and with a very prim expression on her face, she tried to give the conversation a more decorous turn. It was too pointed an attempt; Barbara looked at her, blankly at first, and then in frank amusement. She addressed an idle remark to Harriet, received the chilliest of monosyllables in reply, and openly laughed.

Judith intervened, and the awkward moment passed. But as Harriet, mortified by the laugh, remained for the rest of the meal apparently oblivious of Barbara's presence, she began to wish that she had never hit upon the idea of arranging this pleasure party. The task of talking to Harriet without ignoring Barbara taxed her powers to the utmost, and by the time they rose from the table she would have been hard put to it to say which of the two ladies she most blamed.

Luncheon at an end, a walk in the orchard and wood was proposed. Harriet declined it, but when she had been comfortably settled with a book by the fire, the rest of the party strolled out into the garden, and after wandering about its paths for a little while, made their way into the orchard. Daffodils were growing under the fruit trees in great profusion. Judith could not resist the temptation of picking some. The Count gave instant permission: his cousin would be only too happy! had, in fact, written to beg that the visitors would consider the Château their own. She soon had an armful; he very considerately ran back to the house with them, to save her the trouble of carrying them; and returned to find her waiting for him under a gnarled old apple tree, Barbara having gone off to explore the wood with Peregrine.

Judith believed Peregrine to be too devoted to his Harriet to be in danger of succumbing to Barbara's charms, but the light raillery that had been going on between them made her feel a little uneasy. Courtesy had obliged her to wait for Lavisse's return, but when he joined her it was she, and not he, who suggested catching up with the others.

They made their way into the wood, but after they had been walking about for a time without seeing anything of the truants, the Count suggested that they should follow the track which led from the Château, through the wood, and over a slight hill to the Charleroi road.

'I mentioned to Bab that there is a view to be obtained from the top of the hill. Without doubt they have gone there,' he said. 'You will not be too tired? It is perhaps a kilometre's distance.'

'I should enjoy it of all things. This spring weather is invigorating, don't you agree?'

'Certainly. But I fear my poor country must disappoint one accustomed to the varied scene in England.'

'By no means. Perhaps there is a variety in England not elsewhere to be found: I myself am a native of Yorkshire, where, we flatter ourselves, we have unsurpassed grandeur. But there is something very taking about this country of yours. If you have none of the rugged beauty I could show you in Yorkshire, you have instead a homely, thriving scene which must inevitably please. So many rivers, so many neat farmsteads, shady copses, and rich fields!'

'This is unexpected praise, madame. Bab declares my country to be too tame. Nothing can happen here, she says.'

'She speaks lightly,' Judith replied. '*My* knowledge of history, though not at all profound, reminds me that, in spite of every appearance to the contrary, stirring events have happened here.'

'You are thinking of your Duke of Marlborough. It is true: this poor land of mine has been often the battlefield of Europe, and may be so yet again – perhaps many times: who knows?'

'Oh, do not think of such a thing! There must be no more wars: we seem to have been fighting ever since I can remember! We shall defeat Bonaparte, and win a lasting peace. Can you doubt it?'

'Be sure I do not desire to doubt it, madame,' he replied.

They were climbing a slight hill, and were soon rewarded by the sight of Barbara and Peregrine, resting on the top. Barbara had found shelter from the wind in the lee of a hedge, and was sitting on the bank. She waved, and called out: 'It is all a hum! Nothing to be seen but a plain sprinkled with hillocks, and a great many fields of green corn.'

Country-bred Peregrine corrected her. 'No, no, you under-state, Lady Bab! There are fields of rye as well, and at least two of clover. What a height the crops must grow to here! I never saw anything to equal it, so early in the year!'

'Oh, now you go beyond me! I find myself at one with Dr Johnson, who declared – did he not? – that one green field was just like another!'

'Horrid old man!' said Judith, who had come up to them by this time. She looked around her. 'Why, how could you libel the view so perversely? How pretty the grey stone walls look through the trees! Is that the Charleroi road?'

'Yes, madame,' said Lavisse. 'The little farm you are looking at is La Belle Alliance.'

'Delightful!' said Judith. 'So many of the villages and the farms here have pretty names, I find. Can we see the place where you are quartered from here?'

'No, it is too far. I ride to it by the Nivelles road, until I am tired of that way, which is, in effect, quite straight and not very amusing. If you should ever honour Nivelles with a visit, I recommend you to come by the Charleroi road. It is a little longer, but you would be pleased, I think, with the village of Vieux-Genappe which one passes through. There is an old stone bridge, and many of the quaint cottages you admire.'

'I know the way you mean,' said Peregrine. 'I went to Nivelles one day last autumn, with a party of friends, and I believe we turned off the chaussée about four miles beyond Genappe.'

'That would be Quatre-Bras,' said the Count.

'Another pretty name for you, Lady Worth,' said Barbara. 'What is that monument I can see in the distance, Etienne?'

He glanced southwards, following the direction of her pointing finger. 'Merely the Observatory. There is nothing here of interest, no monuments, no famous scenes.'

'Very true; it is infamously tame!' she said, with one of her flickering smiles. 'And yet I don't know! Had you taken us to Malplaquet, or Oudenarde, you would have dragged us through hedges and over muddy fields to look at an old battlefield, I daresay. Nothing is more tedious, for there is never anything to be seen but what you may as well look at anywhere else! My late husband plagued my life out with such expeditions. I have seen Sedgemoor, and Naseby, and Newbury – *two* battlefields there, as I remember – and I give you my word there was nothing to choose between any of them, except that one was not so far from the road as another.'

Peregrine, who had been gazing abstractedly to the south, said: 'Well, I suppose for all we know there might be a battle fought hereabouts, might there not? Isn't the Charleroi road one of the main ways into France?'

'Oh, don't, Perry!' said his sister. 'This is too peaceful a spot for battles. There are other ways into France, are there not, Count?'

'Assuredly, madame. There is, for instance, the road through Mons. But Sir Peregrine has reason. It is to guard this highway that my division is quartered about Nivelles.'

'Oh, you don't frighten us, Etienne!' said Barbara. 'When Boney comes – *if* he comes, which I am beginning to doubt – you will meet him at the frontier, and send him about his business. Or he may send you about yours. I shall certainly remain in Brussels. How exciting to be besieged!'

'How can you talk so?' Judith said, vexed at the flippancy of these remarks. 'You do not know what you are saying! Come, it is time we were returning to the Château!'

But at this Barbara began to take a perverse interest in her surroundings, desiring Lavisse to name all the hamlets she could perceive, and wishing that she could explore the dark belt of woods some miles to the east of them. From where they stood, half a mile to the west of La Belle Alliance, a good view of the undulating country towards Brussels could be obtained, and not until Lavisse had pointed out insignificant farmsteads such as La Hay Sainte, north of La Belle Alliance, on the chaussée; and obscure villages such as Papelotte, and Smohain, away to the east, could she be induced to quit the spot. But at last, when she had satisfied herself that the rising ground beyond the hollow crossroad that intersected the chaussée made it impossible for her to see Mont St Jean, and that the wood she wished to explore was quite three miles away, she consented to go back to the Château.

Lady Taverner had been dozing by the fire, and woke with a guilty start when the others rejoined her. A glance at the clock on the mantelpiece made her exclaim that she had no notion that the afternoon could be so far advanced. She began to think of her children, of course inconsolable without her, and begged Judith to order the horses to be put to.

This was soon done, and in a very short time Harriet was seated in the barouche, warmly tucked up in a rug, with her hands buried deep in her muff.

Barbara was standing in the doorway when Judith came out of the house, and said: 'I wonder where Charles is now?'

'In Ghent, I suppose,' Judith replied.

'I wish he had been with us,' Barbara said, with a faint sigh.

'I wish it too.'

'Oh! you are disliking me again? Well, I am sorry for it, but the truth is that respectable females and I don't deal together. I should be grateful to you for getting this party together. Shall I thank you? Confess that it has been an odious day!'

'Yes, odious,' Judith said.

She directed a somewhat chilly look at Barbara as she spoke, and for an instant thought that she saw the glitter of tears on the ends of her lashes. But before she could be sure of it Barbara had turned from her, and was preparing to mount her horse. The next glimpse she had of her face made the very idea of tears seem absurd. She was laughing, exchanging jests with Peregrine, once more in reckless spirits.

Any plan that Peregrine might have formed of deserting the barouche was nipped in the bud by his sister, who said so pointedly that she was glad to have the escort of one gentleman at least that there was nothing for him to do but jog along beside the carriage with the best grace he could muster.

Lavisse and Barbara soon allowed their horses to drop into a walk; the barouche outstripped them, and was presently lost to sight over the brow of a slight hill. Lavisse studied Barbara's profile with a faint smile, and said softly: 'Little fool! Little adorable fool!'

'Don't tease me! I could weep with vexation!'

'I know well that you could. But why?'

'Oh, because I'm bored – tired – anything that you please!'

'It does not please me that you should be bored or tired. I do not wonder at it, however. For me, these saintly Englishwomen are the devil.'

'I don't dislike Lady Worth, if only she would not look so disapproving.'

'Consider, my Bab, she will do so all your life.'

'Oh, confound her, I'll take care she don't get the chance!'

'*Ma pauvre*, I see you surrounded by prim relatives, growing staid – or mad!'

'Wretch! Be quiet!'

'But no, I will not be quiet. Figure to yourself the difference were you to marry me!'

An irrepressible laugh broke from her. 'I do. I should then be surrounded by your light-o'-loves. I have seen enough of that in my own family to be cured of wanting to marry a rake.'

'You have in England a saying that a reformed rake –'

'My dear Etienne, if you were reformed you would be as dull as the next man. You are wasting your eloquence. I do not love you more than a very little. You are an admirable flirt, I grant, and I find you capital company.'

'Do you find your colonel – capital company?'

She turned her head, regarding him with one of her clear looks. 'Do you know, I have never thought of that: it has not occurred to me. It is the oddest thing, but if you were to ask me, what does he look like? how does he speak? I couldn't tell you. I think he is handsome; I suppose him to be good company, because it doesn't bore me to be with him. But I can't particularise him. I can't say, he is handsome, he is witty, or he is clever. I can only say, he is Charles.'

The smile had quite faded from his face; his horse leapt suddenly under a spur driven cruelly home: 'Ah, *parbleu*, you are serious then!' he exclaimed. 'You are lovesick – besotted! I wish you a speedy recovery, *ma belle*!'

Ten

Judith saw nothing of Barbara on the following day, but heard of her having gone to a fête at Enghien, given by the Guards. She was present in the evening at a small party at Lady John Somerset's, surrounded by her usual court, and had nothing more than a nod and a wave of the hand to bestow upon Judith. The Comte de Lavisse had returned to his cantonments, but his place seemed to be admirably filled by Prince Pierre d'Aremberg, whose attentions, though possibly not serious, were extremely marked.

If Barbara missed Colonel Audley during the five days of his absence, she gave no sign of it. She seemed to plunge into a whirl of enjoyment; flitted from party to party; put in an appearance at the Opera; left before the end to attend a ball; danced into the small hours; rode out before breakfast with a party of younger officers; was off directly after to go to the races at Grammont; reappeared in Brussels in time to grace her sister-in-law's soirée; and enchanted the company by singing *O Lady, twine no wreath for me*, which had just been sent to her from London, along with a setting of Lord Byron's famous lyric, *Farewell, Farewell!*

'How can she do it?' marvelled the Lennox girls. '*We* should be dead with fatigue!'

On April 20th Brussels was fluttered by the arrival of a celebrated personage, none other than Madame Catalani, a cantatrice who had charmed all Europe with her trills and her quavers. Accompanied by her husband, M. de Valbrèque, she descended upon Brussels for the purpose of consenting graciously (and for quite extortionate fees) to sing at a few select parties.

On the same evening Wellington drove into Brussels with his suite, and Colonel Audley, instead of ending a long day by drinking tea quietly at home and going to bed, arrayed himself in his dress uniform and went off to put in a tardy appearance at Sir Charles Stuart's evening party. He found his betrothed in an alcove, having each finger kissed by an adoring young Belgian, and waited perfectly patiently for this ceremony to come to an end. But Barbara saw him before her admirer had got beyond the fourth finger, and pulled her hands away, not in any confusion, but merely to hold them out to the Colonel. 'Oh, Charles! You have come back!' she cried gladly.

The Belgian, very red in the face, and inwardly quaking, stayed just enough for Colonel Audley to challenge him to a duel if he wished to, but when he found that the Colonel was really paying no attention to him, he discreetly withdrew, thanking his gods that the English were a phlegmatic race.

The Colonel took both Barbara's hands in his. Mischief gleamed in her eyes. She said: 'Would you like to finish René's work, dear Charles?'

'No, not at all,' he answered, drawing her closer.

She held up her face. 'Very well! Oh, but I am glad to see you again!'

They sat down together on a small sofa. 'You did not appear to be missing me very much!' said the Colonel.

'Don't be stupid! Tell me what you have been doing!'

'There's nothing to tell. What have *you* been doing? Or daren't you tell me?'

'That's impertinent. I have been forgetting Charles in a whirl of gaiety.'

'Faithless one!'

'I have been to the Races, and was quite out of luck; I went to the Opera, but it was Gluck and detestable; I have danced endless waltzes and cotillions, but no one could dance as well as you; and I went to a macao party, and was dipped; to Enghien, and was kissed –'

'What?'

He had been listening with a smile in his eyes, but this vanished, and he interrupted with enough sharpness in his voice to arrest her attention and make her put up her chin a little.

'Well?'

'Did you mean that?'

'What, that I was kissed at Enghien? My dear Charles!'

'It's no answer to say "My dear Charles", Bab.'

'But can you doubt it? Don't you think I am very kissable?'

'I do, but I prefer that others should not.'

'Oh no! how dull that would be!' she said, sparkling with laughter.

'Don't you agree that there is something a trifle vulgar in permitting Tom, Dick, and Harry to kiss you?'

'That's to say *I'm* vulgar, Charles. Am I, do you think?'

'The wonder is that you are not.'

'The wonder?'

'Yes, since you do vulgar things.'

She flushed, and looking directly into his eyes, said: 'You are not wise to talk like that to me, my friend.'

'My dear, did you suppose I should be so complaisant as to allow other men to kiss you? What an odd notion you must have of me!'

'I warned you I should flirt.'

'And I warned you it would only be with me. To be plain with you, I expect you not to kiss any but myself.'

'Tom, Dick, and Harry!' she flashed, betraying a wound.

'Yes – or, for instance, the Comte de Lavisse.'

There was an edge to the words; she glanced swiftly at him, understanding all at once that he was actuated as much by jealousy as by prudery. The anger left her face; she exclaimed: 'Charles! Dear fool! You're quite out: it wasn't Etienne!'

He said ruefully: 'Wasn't it? Yes, I did think so.'

'And were longing to call him out!'

'Nothing so romantic. Merely to plant him a facer.'

She was amused. 'What the devil's that?'

'Boxing cant. Forget it! If you were to add that to your vocabulary it would be beyond everything!'

'Oh, but I know a deal of boxing cant! My brother George is much addicted to the Fancy – himself *displays to advantage*, so I'm told! No *shifting*, not at all *shy*; in fact *rattles in full of gaiety*!'

'Bab, you incorrigible hussy!'

Their disagreement was forgotten; she began to talk to him of George, who was already on his passage to the Netherlands.

It was evident that George, a year older than his sister, was very near her heart. Colonel Audley was barely acquainted with him, but no one who had once met Lord George could fail to recognise him again. When he arrived in Brussels some days later it was from Liedekerke, in the vicinity of Ninove, where he was quartered. He rode into Brussels with the intention of surprising his family at dinner, but happening to encounter a friend on his way up the Montagne de la Cour, went off instead to join a riotous party at the Hôtel d'Angleterre. When he presented himself in the Rue Ducale some hours later it was to learn from the butler that Lord and Lady Vidal were at the Opera, and his sister at a soirée.

'Well, I won't go to the Opera, that's certain,' said his lordship. 'What's this soirée you talk of?'

'I understand, my lord, a gathering of polite persons, with a little music, a –'

'Sounds devilish,' remarked his lordship. 'Who's holding it?'

'Lord and Lady Worth, my lord.'

'Lady Worth, eh?' His lordship pricked up his ears. 'Oh! Ah! I'll go there. Won't throw me out, will they?'

The butler looked horrified. 'Throw you out, my lord?'

'Haven't been invited: don't know the Worths," explained George. 'I'll risk it. Where do they live?'

Judith's salons were crowded when he arrived, and since the evening was too far advanced for her to expect any more guests, she had left her station by the door and was standing at the other end of the long room, talking to two Belgian ladies. The footman's voice, announcing Lord George, was not audible above the clatter of conversation, and Judith remained unaware of his entrance until Madame van der Capellan directed her attention towards him, desiring to know who *ce beau géant* might be.

She turned her head, and saw his lordship standing on the threshold, looking round him with an air of perfect sangfroid. A handsome giant was a description which exactly hit him off. He stood over six foot, in all the magnificence of a Life Guardsman's dress uniform. He was a blaze of scarlet and gold; a very dark young man with curling black hair, and dashing whiskers, gleaming white teeth, and a pair of bold, fiery eyes.

'It is Lord George Alastair,' said Judith. She moved towards him, by no means pleased at the advent of this uninvited guest.

He came at once to meet her. His bow was perfection: the look that went with it was that of a schoolboy detected in crime. 'Lady Worth?'

'Yes,' she acknowledged. 'You – !'

'I know! I know! You're not acquainted with me – don't know me from Adam – wonder how the deuce I got in!'

She was obliged to smile. 'Indeed, I do know you. You are Lord George Alastair.'

'Oh, come now, that's famous! I daresay you won't have me thrown out after all.'

'I am sure it would be a very difficult task,' she said. 'You have come in search of your sister, I expect? She is here, and your brother too. I think they must both be in the farther salon. Shall we go and find them?'

'Devilish good of you, Lady Worth. But don't put yourself out on my account: I'll find 'em.'

She saw that he was looking beyond her, at someone at the other end of the room. She glanced in the same direction, and discovered that the object of his gaze was none other than Miss Devenish. It was plain that Lucy was aware of being stared at; she was blushing uncomfortably, and had cast down her eyes.

'I will show you the way to your sister,' said Judith firmly.

'Thank you – in a moment!' said his lordship, with cool impudence. 'I have seen a lady I know. Must pay my respects!'

He left her side as he spoke, and bore ruthlessly down upon Miss Devenish. She was seated on a sofa, and cast such a scared look up at George that Judith felt impelled to go to her rescue. George was towering over her – enough to frighten any girl! thought Judith indignantly – and Lucy had half risen from the sofa, and then sunk back again.

By the time Judith, delayed by Mr Creevey in the middle of the room, reached her, George had not only shaken hands, but had seated himself beside her. His eyes were fixed on her downcast face with an ardent expression Judith much disliked, and a teasing smile, as impish as his sister's, curled his lips. When Judith came up he rose. 'I am recalling myself to Miss Devenish's memory,' he said. 'It's my belief she had forgotten me.'

'I was not aware that you were acquainted with Lord George, my dear?' Judith said, a question in her voice.

'Oh!' faltered Lucy. 'We met once – at a ball!'

'If that is all, it is no wonder that you were forgotten, Lord George!' Judith said.

'All! No such thing! Miss Devenish, can you look me in the face and say we met only once, at a ball?'

She did look him in the face, but with such an expression of reproach in her eyes as must have abashed any but an Alastair. She replied in a low voice, and with a good deal of dignity: 'It is true that we have several times met: I do not forget it.'

She got up as she spoke, and with a slight inclination of her head moved away to where her aunt was seated. Lord George looked after her for a moment, and then turned to his hostess, saying briskly: 'Where's Bab? In the other salon? I'll go and find her. Now, don't bother your head about me, Lady Worth, I beg! I shall do very well.'

She was perfectly willing to let him go, and with a nod and a smile he was off, making his way across the crowded room through the double doors leading into the farther salon. These had been thrown open, and as he approached them George saw his brother Harry standing between them in conversation with Lord Hay. He waved casually, but Harry, as soon as he caught sight of him, left Hay and surged forward.

'Hallo, George! When did you arrive? Where are you quartered? I am devilish glad to see you!'

George answered these questions rather in a manner of a man receiving a welcome of a boisterous puppy; twitted Harry on the glory of his brand-new regimentals; and demanded: 'Where's Bab?'

'Oh, with Audley somewhere, I daresay! But what a hand you are, not to have written to tell us you were coming!'

'Who's Audley?' interrupted George, looking over the heads of several people in an attempt to see his sister.

'Why, Worth's brother, to be sure! Lord, don't you know? Bab's going to marry him – or so she says.'

This piece of intelligence seemed to amuse George. 'Poor devil! No, I didn't know. New, is it?'

'Oh, they've been engaged for a fortnight or more! Look, there they both are!'

A moment later Barbara was startled by an arm being put familiarly round her waist. 'Hallo, Bab, my girl!' said his lordship.

She turned quickly in his embrace, an exclamation on her lips. 'George! You wretch, to creep up behind me like that!'

He kissed her cheek, and continued to hold her round the waist. 'What's all this I hear about your engagement?' He glanced at Colonel Audley, and held out his free hand. 'You're Audley, aren't you? How d'ye do? Think we've met before, but can't recall where. What the devil do you mean by getting engaged to my sister? You'll regret it, you know!'

'But you must see that I can't, in honour, draw back now,' returned the Colonel, shaking hands. 'When did you arrive? At Liedekerke, aren't you? We're deuced glad to see you fellows, I can tell. How strong are you?'

'Two squadrons. What are these Dutchmen like, hey? Saw

some of them on our way up from Ostend. They're not so badly mounted, but they can't ride.'

'That's the trouble,' admitted the Colonel. 'A great many of them are shocking bad riders. You know we are not getting Combermere to command the cavalry after all? The Horse Guards are sending Lord Uxbridge out to us.'

'Oh, he's a good fellow! You'll like him. But you've served under him, of course. You were with Moore, weren't you? I say, Audley, you Peninsular fellows have the advantage of us – and by Jove, don't you mean to let us know it! A damned rifleman I met tonight called *my* lot Hyde Park soldiers!'

'So you knocked him down, and poor Vidal will be faced with another scandal!' remarked Barbara.

'No, I didn't. Fellow was my host. But when it comes to fighting we'll show you what Hyde Park soldiers can do!'

Barbara, who was tired of a purely military conversation, changed the subject by asking him how her grandfather did. He confessed that he had not seen that irascible gentleman quite lately, but thought – from the energetic tone of his correspondence – that he was enjoying his customary vigorous health.

'In debt again?' asked Barbara. 'Would he not come to the rescue?'

'Oh lord, no! Wrote that he'd see me to the devil first!' replied George. 'But I daresay if I come out of this little war alive he'll pay up.'

'Return of a hero?' enquired the Colonel. 'You'd better get wounded.'

'Devilish good notion,' agreed his lordship. 'Of course if I'm killed it won't matter to me how many debts I've got. Either way I'm bound to win. What are the Prussians like, Audley?'

'I haven't seen much of them, so far. Old Blücher has arrived at Liége, and says he can put 80,000 men in the field. Some of them pretty raw, of course – like our own.'

'Queer old boy, Blücher,' remarked George. 'Saw him last year, when he was in London with the Emperors and all that crowd. Seemed to take very well – people used to cheer him whenever he showed his face out of doors.'

Lady Barbara moved away; Lord George wandered off, and presently discovered Miss Devenish again. He apparently prevailed upon her to present him to her aunt, for when Judith caught sight of him an hour later he was sitting beside Mrs Fisher, making himself agreeable. Judith could see that Mrs Fisher was pleased with him, and hoped that she would not allow herself to be carried away by a title and a handsome face. She had little dependence, however, on that amiable lady's judgment, and was not much surprised to see her beckon to her niece to come and join in her chat with Lord George. Miss Devenish obeyed the summons, but reluctantly. Lord George jumped up as she approached, and in a few minutes succeeded in detaching her from her aunt and bearing her off in the direction of the parlour, where the refreshments were laid out.

It was not until the end of the evening, when her guests were beginning to disperse, that Judith found an opportunity to speak to Lucy. She said then: 'I hope Lord George did not tease you? He is rather a bold young man, I am afraid.'

Lucy coloured, but replied quietly: 'Oh no! I knew him before, in England.'

'Yes, so you told me. I was surprised: I don't think you ever mentioned the circumstance to me?'

There was a little hesitation, a faltering for words. 'I daresay I might not. The occasion did not arise, our acquaintance was not of such a nature –'

'My dear, why should you? I implied no blame! But I was sorry to see him single you out with such particularity. I could see you were a little discomposed, and did not wonder at it. His manners are a great deal too familiar.'

Miss Devenish opened and shut her fan once or twice, and replied: 'I was discomposed, I own. The surprise of seeing him here – and his singling me out, as you describe, put me out of countenance.'

'The attentions of men of his type are apt to be very

143

disagreeable,' said Judith. 'Happily, the violent fancies they take do not last long. I believe Lord George to be a shocking flirt. You, however, have too much common sense to take him seriously.'

'Oh yes! That is, I know what people say of him. Forgive me, but there are circumstances which make it painful for me to discuss – but it is not in my power to explain.'

'Why, Lucy, what is this?' Judith exclaimed. 'I had not thought your acquaintance to be more than a chance meeting at a ball!'

'It was a little more than that. I became acquainted with him when I was staying in Brighton with my cousins last year. There was a degree of intimacy which – which I could not avoid.'

Her voice failed. Judith suspected that the attentions of a dashing young officer had not been wholly unwelcome. She had no doubt that Lord George had speedily overstepped the bounds of propriety, and understood, with ready sympathy, Lucy's feelings upon being confronted with him again. She said kindly: 'I perfectly understand, and beg you won't think yourself bound to confide in me. There is not the least necessity!'

She was obliged to turn away directly after, to shake hands with a departing guest. Lucy rejoined her aunt, who was making signs to her that it was time to go, and no further talk was held on the subject. Lord George, who was engaged with a dazzling brunette, did not observe her departure. Judith, who knew that at least two other ladies had been the objects of his gallantry that evening, was encouraged to hope that his persecution of Lucy had been nothing more than a piece of Alastair devilry, designed merely to make the poor child uncomfortable.

He soon came up to take his leave. He was escorting his sister, whose head just topped his broad shoulder. In spite of the difference in colouring there was a remarkable likeness between them. Spiritually, too, they seemed to be akin; they delighted in the same mischief, used the same careless, engaging manners, shocked the world like children anxious to attract attention to themselves. Judith, confronting them, admitted their charm, and looked indulgently on such a handsome couple.

'I have spent a capital evening, Lady Worth,' said George. 'When you give your next party I hope you may send me a card. I shall certainly come.'

'Of course,' she replied. 'I am glad you took your courage in your hands and came tonight. It would have been a sad thing not to have seen your sister after riding all that way for the purpose.'

'Did he tell you he had come expressly to see me?' said Barbara. 'George, what a liar you are! Depend upon it, Lady Worth, he had quite another quarry in mind. Shall I see you at the Review tomorrow?'

'At Nivelles? Oh no! It is too far – and only a review of Belgian troops. I shall wait to see our own troops reviewed, I believe.'

'Then we shall not meet. But you will be at the Duke's party, I daresay, on Friday. 'Oh, where is Charles? He must procure an invitation for George!'

She drew her hand from her brother's arm as she spoke, and darted off to find the Colonel. She soon came back with him; he promised that a card should be sent to George, and accompanied them both to the door of the carriage. George shook hands at parting, and said warmly: 'You're a good fellow: I wish you happy – though I don't above half like to find Bab engaged to a damned staff officer, I can tell you!'

'We all have our crosses!' retorted the Colonel. 'Mine is to be saddled with a Hyde Park soldier for a brother-in-law.'

'Oh, the devil! You know, you're so puffed up, you Peninsular men, that there's no bearing with you! Goodnight: I shall see you on Friday, I suppose?'

He got into the carriage beside his sister and settled himself in one corner. 'Well, that makes the tenth since Childe died,' he remarked.

'No! I was only once engaged before!'

'Twice.'

'Oh, you are thinking of Ralph Dashwood! *That* was never announced, and can't signify. I am serious now.'

He gave a hoot of laughter. 'Until the next man drifts by! Has he any money?'

'I suppose him to have a younger son's portion. He is not rich.'

'Well, what the devil made you choose him?' demanded George. 'I see no sense in it!'

'I don't care for money,' she replied pettishly.

'More fool you, then. I never knew you when you weren't dipped. Besides, this fellow Audley: I like him, he's a good man – but he ain't your sort, Bab.'

'True, but I loved him from the first. I don't know how it came about. Isn't it odd that one should keep one's heart intact so many years, only to have it crack for a man no more handsome or wealthy than a hundred others? I can find no reason for it, unless it be the trick his eyes have of smiling while his mouth is grave – and that's nonsensical.'

He said rather gloomily: 'I know what you mean. Take it from me, it's the devil.'

'It *is* the devil. I wish to be good, to behave as I should – and yet I don't! If I had never been married to Childe it would be so different! Damnable to have done that to me! I believe it ruined me.'

He yawned. 'Where's the use in worrying? You were willing, weren't you?'

'At eighteen, and the hoyden that I was! What could I know of the matter? Papa made the match; I married to oblige my family, and wretched work I made of it! Jasper – oh, don't let us talk of him: how I grew to loathe him! I was never more glad of anything than his death, and I swore then that no one – *no one* should ever possess me again! Even though I love Charles, even when I desire most earnestly to please him, there is something in me that revolts – yes, revolts, George! It drives me to commit such acts of folly! I use him damnably, I suppose, and shall end by making us both wretched.'

'Shouldn't be surprised,' said George, with brotherly uncon-cern. 'I know *I* wouldn't be in his shoes for a thousand pounds.'

She underwent one of her lightning changes of mood, break-ing into a gurgle of laughter. 'You, without a feather to fly with! You'd sell your soul for half the sum!'

Eleven

*T*he review of the Dutch–Belgian Army at Nivelles, by King William and the Duke of Wellington, passed off creditably. The Duke found the Nassau troops excellent; the Dutch Militia good, but young; and the Cavalry, though bad riders, remarkably well-mounted. Prince Frederick impressed him as being a fine lad, and he wrote as much to Earl Bathurst, in a private letter.

The pity was that his lordship was not similarly pleased with Prince Frederick's father. He was the most difficult person to deal with his lordship had ever met. '*With professions in his mouth of a desire to do everything I can suggest, he objects to everything I propose; it then comes to be a matter of negotiation for a week, and at last is settled by my desiring him to arrange it as he pleases, and telling him that I will have nothing to say to him.*'

Bathurst, who was well acquainted with the Duke's temper, might smile a little over this letter, but there was no doubt that his lordship was being harassed on all sides. He was hampered by possessing no command over the King's Army; and he was receiving complaints of the conduct of his engineers at Ypres, who were accused of cutting his Majesty's timber for palisades. He believed the complaints to be groundless, and was not quite pleased with the way in which they were made.

But the jealousies of the Dutch and the Belgians were small matters compared with the behaviour of the Horse Guards in London. He was accustomed to meet with annoying hindrances in foreign countries, and could deal with them. The powers at the Horse Guards were irritating him far more, with their mania for sending him out bevies of ineligible young gentlemen to fill staff posts. No sooner had he turned off eight officers from the adjutant-general's staff than he received an official letter from Sir Henry Torrens appointing eight others. He had written pretty sharply to Sir Henry on the subject. They talked glibly at the Horse Guards of all such appointments resting at his nomination, but, in actual fact, this was far from being true. His lordship complained of being wholly without power to name any of the officers recommended by his generals, because every place was filled from London. '*Of the list you and Colonel Shawe have sent, there are only three who have any experience at all,*' wrote his lordship acidly. '*Of those there are two, Colonel Elley and Lord Greenock, who are most fit for their situations, and I am most happy they are selected . . . As for the others, if they had been proposed to me I should have rejected them all.*'

The very same day he was sending off another despatch to Torrens, begging him to let him see more troops before sending any more general officers. '*I have no objection; on the contrary, I wish for Cole and Picton to command divisions,*' wrote his lordship, with every intention of seeming gracious. '*I shall be very happy to have Kempt and Pack, and will do the best I can for them . . .*' Quite an affable despatch, this one, much more conciliatory than the one that was on its way to Lord Bathurst. His lordship was not getting the artillery he had demanded; instead of 150 pieces he was to have only eighty-four, including German artillery. He considered his demand to have been excessively small, and he told Bathurst so. '*You will see by reference to Prince Hardenberg's return of the Prussian Army that they take into the field nearly 80 batteries, manned by 10,000 artillery. Their batteries are of eight guns each, so that they will have 600 pieces. They do not take this number for show or amusement,*' continued his lordship sardonically, '*and although it is impossible to grant my demand, I hope it will be admitted to be small.*'

But in spite of the querulous tone of his despatches to London he was not so ill-pleased, after all. He might complain that in England they were doing nothing, and were unable to send him anything, but before April was out he was writing quite cheerfully to Hardinge, English Commissioner to the Prussians, that he was getting on in strength, and had now 60,000 men in their shoes, of whom at least 10,000 were cavalry.

He was glad when Prince Blücher arrived at the Prussian Headquarters. He liked old Marshal 'Forwards', but he wished he would not write to him in German.

But Blücher, with his dozen words of English, and his execrable French, was a better man to deal with than his chief-of-staff. A jealous fellow, Gneisenau, always making difficulties and suspecting him of duplicity.

However, that was a minor annoyance; on the whole, his lordship was satisfied with his Prussian allies, though the circum-stance of their being continually at loggerheads with King William gave him a good deal of trouble. Poor old Blücher was quite lacking in polish; nor could he be made to realise the value of tact in dealing with a fellow like King William. He was for ever omitting to make just those courteous gestures which would have cost him so little and soothed the King's dignity so much. Rather a difficult yoke-fellow, Blücher, apt to get the bit between his teeth, and, unfortunately, imbued with such a dislike of the French that he could not be brought to tolerate even the Royalists among them. But he was not afraid of meeting Bonaparte in the field, and he was a likeable old man, with his fierce, rosy face and fine white whiskers, his spluttering enthusiasm, and his beaming smile.

His lordship was much more comfortable at Headquarters now, for he had got his military secretary back, and Sir Colin Campbell too. His lordship was fond of Lord Fitzroy Somerset, who had lately married his niece, and had so become his nephew by marriage. Lord Fitzroy exactly suited him; for he did what he was told, never committing the appalling offence of setting up ideas of his own and acting on them. His lordship detested independently-minded subordinates. It was not the business of his officers to think for themselves. 'Have my orders for whatever you do!' he said. It was an inflexible rule; nothing made him angrier than to have it broken.

Lord Fitzroy never broke it. He could be trusted to obey every order punctiliously. He got through an amazing amount of work, too, often in the most unsuitable surroundings, and always with a quiet competence that seemed to make little of the mass of correspondence on his hands. He was not one of those troublesome officers, either, who were for ever wanting to go home on leave to attend to urgent private affairs – which his lordship was convinced could be quite as well settled by correspondence. Nor had he ever discovered (just when he was most needed) that the climate in Spain disagreed with his constitution. You could always be sure of Fitzroy.

His lordship was sure of Colin Campbell, too, who had been with him so many years, and managed his household so admirably, in spite of his inability to speak intelligibly any foreign language.

In fact, his lordship was perfectly happy in his personal staff. As for his general staff, though he complained peevishly of having strangers foisted on to him, and of being unable to entrust the details of the departments to any of the young gentlemen on the staff, he was not (if the truth were told) so very badly off there either. He might write to Toreens that he had no means of naming any of the officers he would prefer to all others, but somehow they began to appear on the general staff; seasoned men like Elley, and Waters, Felton Hervey, Greenock, Woodford, Gomm, Shaw, and any number of others. He had Barnes for his adjutant-general; and was getting De Lancey sent out as quartermaster-general; in place of Sir Hudson Lowe. He wanted Murray, of course: De Lancey was only a deputy: but Murray was still in America, and he could not really blame Torrens for being unable to spirit him back to Europe.

To read his lordship's despatches you might think he had no power at all over the appointments in the Army. In one of his irritable moods, he wrote another barbed letter to Bathurst. '*I might have expected that the Generals and Staff formed by me in the last war would have been allowed to come to me again,*' he complained, and continued in a sweeping style which made Lord Bathurst grin appreciatively: '*But instead of that, I am overloaded with people I have never seen before; and it appears to be purposely intended to keep those out of my way whom I wished to have.*' His lordship felt much better after that explosion of wrath, and added: '*However, I'll do the best I can with the instruments which have been sent to assist me.*'

But gentlemen applying for staff appointments in the Duke's army were told at the Horse Guards that the selection of officers to fill these was left to the Duke; and occasionally his lordship seemed to forget that he had no power to employ gentlemen of his own choosing. He might complain of having his hands tied, but when it came to the point his lordship seemed to do very much what he liked. When he wanted Lieutenant-Colonel Grant to come out to him to be at the head of the Intelligence Department, and Lieutenant-Colonel Scovell to take charge of the Department of Military Communications, he told Lord Fitzroy to write offering the posts to both these gentlemen, and only afterwards informed Torrens of having done so. He hoped, coolly, that it would be approved of, and, in point of fact, had not the least doubt that it would be approved of.

But you could not be surprised at his lordship's being a little testy. He was not a pessimistic man, but he rather liked to have a grievance, and was very apt to grumble that he was obliged to do everyone's work in addition to his own. He had, moreover, an overwhelming amount of work of his own to do, and endless annoyances to deal with. The wonder was not that he was peevish in his office but that he was so cheerful out of it. Quite apart from the all-important task of putting the country and the Army in a state of readiness for war, he was obliged to tackle such problems as the amounts of the subsidies to be granted to the various countries engaged in the campaign. First it was Hanover (a complicated business, that); then Austria; then Russia (shocking people to deal with, the Russians); and next it would be the Duke of Brunswick, already on the march with his troops to join the Army.

Subsidies one moment, wagons for the Hanoverians the next; then some quite trivial matter, such as old Arendtschildt's request for permission for certain of his officers to receive a Russian decoration: there was no end to the business requiring his lordship's attention; yet in the midst of it all he could find time to review troops, pay flying visits to garrisons, attend parties, and even to give a large party himself, and appear as lighthearted at it as though he had not a care in the world.

His lordship had a natural taste for festivities, and during his late spell of office as Ambassador to King Louis, had acquired the habit of planning his own parties on a lavish scale. His first in Brussels was a brilliant affair, comprising a dinner at the Hôtel de Belle Vue to his more important guests, including the King and Queen of the Netherlands, followed by a concert, ball, and supper at the Salle du Grand Concert, in the Rue Ducale.

It quite eclipsed the Court party, held some days previously. Everything went off without the smallest hitch; the Catalani was in her best voice; the Duke was the most affable of hosts; his staff seconded him ably; and the Salle was so crowded with distinguished persons that it became at times quite difficult to move about.

The invitation list was indeed enormous, and had cost the staff many a headache, for besides the English in Brussels all the Belgian and Dutch notables had received elegant, cream-laid, gilt-edged cards requesting the honour of their presence. Nearly all of them had accepted, too: the Duc d'Ursel, with his big nose and tiny chin; cheerful little Baron Hoogvorst, and Madame; competent M. van der Capellan, the Secretary of State; the Duc and Duchesse de Beaufort, and Mademoiselle; bevies of Counts and Countesses and Dowager Countesses, all with their blushing daughters and hopeful sons; and of course the Royals: King William, and his lethargic spouse, with their splendid young son, Frederick, and an extensive suite. The Prince of Orange was present as well, but could hardly be included in the Royal party, since he arrived separately, was dressed in the uniform of the Prince of Wales's Own, talked nothing but English, and consorted almost exclusively with his English friends and fellow-generals. He had quite forgotten his huff at being superseded in the command of the Army. He was going to be given the 1st Corps, Lord Hill having the 2nd; and his dread mentor was treating him with so much confidence that he had nothing left to wish for. '*For ever your most truly devoted and affectionate William, Prince of Orange*,' was how the Prince subscribed himself exuberantly in his letters to the Duke. All he ever received in return was '*Believe me, & etc., Wellington.*' His lordship was never fulsome. '*Je supplie Votre Altesse d'agréer en bonté les sentiments respectueux avec lesquels j'ai l'honneur d'être, Monseigneur, de Votre Altesse le très humble et très obéissant serviteur*,' would write some Prussian general painstakingly. '*Write him that I am very much obliged to him,*' scrawled the Duke at the foot of such despatches.

But the Prince of Orange was too well acquainted with his lordship to be cast down by his chilly letters. In fact, the Prince was in high fettle. His personal staff was composed of just the men he liked best: all English, and including his dear friend the Earl of March. He was very happy, sparkling with gaiety, looking absurdly young, and just a little conscious of the dizzy military heights to which he had risen. Sometimes he felt intoxicatingly important, and was a trifle imperious with the generals under his command; but when he found himself in Lord Hill's presence, and looked into that kindly face, with its twinkling eyes and fatherly smile, his importance fell away from him, and he was all eager deference, just as he was with the Duke, or with the veteran Count Alten of the German Legion, whose bright, stern gaze could always disconcert him. Sir Charles Count von Alten was under the Prince, in command of the 3rd Division, which was formed of one British brigade, under Sir Colin Halkett; one brigade of the German Legion, under Baron Ompteda; and one Hanoverian brigade, under Count Kielmansegg. Count Alten was fifty-one years of age, seasoned in war, and rather grim-faced. He was an extremely competent general – so competent that even the men of the Light Division had approved of him when he had commanded them – and a somewhat alarming person for a young gentleman only twenty-four years old to have under him. He was very polite to the Prince, and they got on really very well together, but his Royal Highness was glad that the rest of the 1st Corps, with the exception of the Guards, was composed of Dutch–Belgian troops under two generals who, though experienced soldiers, naturally had a respect for their Hereditary Prince which the English and the Germans could not be expected to share. His *bête noire*, and late second-in-command, Sir Henry Clinton, was commanding a division in Hill's corps; and that much more alarming person even than Count Alten, Sir Thomas Picton, was destined for the Reserve.

Sir Thomas was not expected to arrive in the Netherlands for quite some time, but it was certain that he was coming sooner or later, for the Duke, although he did not much care for him in a personal way, had made a point of asking for him.

The latest important arrival was Lord Uxbridge. A General Order instructing brigade commanders of cavalry to report in future to him had been issued from the adjutant-general's printing office on the day of the Duke's ball. He was to have command of all the British and German cavalry, and was reputed to be a very dashing leader.

He had arrived in the Netherlands in time to attend the Duke's party, and was present at the preceding dinner. When he appeared in the Salle du Concert he attracted a great deal of attention, for the men were anxious to see what sort of a fellow he was, and the ladies could hardly drag their eyes from his resplendent person.

The Peninsula Army had been accustomed to Stapleton Cotton, now Lord Combermere, but the Earl of Uxbridge was the better cavalry general. He had served with distinction under Sir John Moore, but two circumstances had prevented his being employed under Wellington. He had been senior to the Duke, and had further complicated the situation by absconding with the wife of Wellington's brother Henry. This unfortunate affair put the Pagets and the Wellesleys on the worst of bad terms. Henry had been obliged to divorce Lady Charlotte, and any scheme of sending Lord Uxbridge out to Spain had naturally been felt to have been out of the question. Five years later, in

1815, it was an understood thing that Combermere would again command the Cavalry: the Army wanted him, and it was certain that the Duke had applied for him. But to everyone's surprise the Horse Guards sent Uxbridge instead. It was said they had done so at the instigation of that meddlesome person, the Prince Regent, and it was generally felt that the appointment would not only cause grave scandal in England but must also offend the Duke. But the Duke, like the Regent, was not remarkable for holding the marriage tie in any peculiar degree of sanctity, and upon a friend's saying to him that Lord Uxbridge's appointment would give rise to much scandal, replied, with one of his high-nosed stares: 'Why?'

A little disconcerted, his well-meaning friend stammered: 'Well, but – but your Grace cannot have forgotten the affair of Lady Charlotte!'

'No! I haven't forgotten that.'

'Oh! Well – well, that's not all, you know. They say Uxbridge runs away with everyone he can.'

'I'll take damned good care he don't run away with me!' replied the Duke caustically. 'I don't care about anyone else.'

The Army, like the Duke, did not care a button for Lord Uxbridge's amatory adventures: it merely wanted a good cavalry leader. Lord Uxbridge was said to be a veritable Murat: it remained to be seen whether this was true. He was also said to be very haughty. He did not seem so, at first glance: his manners were most polished, his smile ready, and his handshake freely given. His mouth had, indeed, a slightly disdainful curve, and his brilliant dark eyes were rather heavy-lidded, which made them look a little contemptuous, but he showed no signs of snubbing junior officers (which rumour accused him of doing frequently), and seemed, without being over-conciliatory, or in any way affected, to be bent on getting on good terms with his people.

Like the Prince of Orange, he wore full-dress hussar uniform, but with what a difference! No amount of silver lace, swinging tassels, rich fur, or shining buttons could invest the Prince's meagre form with dignity. In that most splendid of uniforms he looked over-dressed, and rather ridiculous. But Lord Uxbridge, tall and most beautifully proportioned, carried it off to perfection. He was forty-seven years old, but looked younger, and was obviously something of a dandy. His white net pantaloons showed not a single crease; over a jacket fitting tightly to the body and almost obscured by the frogs that adorned it, he wore a furred and braided pelisse, caught round his neck with tasselled cords and flung back to hang negligently over his left shoulder. Under the stiff, silver-encrusted collar of his jacket, a black cravat was knotted, with the points of his shirt collar just protruding above it. Several glittering orders, very neat side-whiskers, and fashionably arranged hair completed his appearance. He had not brought his lady out from England, but whether he had left her behind out of tact or from the circumstance of her being in the expectation of a Happy Event was a matter for conjecture. Two of his aides-de-camp were with him: Major Thornhill, of his own regiment, the 7th Hussars; and Captain Seymour, supposed to be the strongest man in the British Army. He was certainly the largest: he topped even the Life Guardsmen, and had such a gigantic frame that he was a butt to his friends and an object of considerable respect to everyone else.

As usual, the military predominated at the ball. Lord Hill was present, with all three of his brothers; General Maitland and Byng; old Sir John Vandeleur, very bluff and affable; General Adam; Sir Henry Clinton, with Lady Susan on his arm; General Colville, who had come all the way from Oudenarde to attend the function; Sir Hussey Vivian, with his shattered hand in a sling, but still perfectly capable of leading his hussar brigade in any charge; Sir William Ponsonby, newly arrived from England with the Union Brigade of Heavy Dragoons; handsome Colonel Sir Frederick Ponsonby, of another branch of the family, with his sister, Lady Caroline Lamb; both the gallant Halketts, Sir Colin and his brother Hew; the adjutant-general, sharp-faced and fiery-spirited; Colonel Arendtschildt, talking to everyone in his incorrigibly bad English; General Perponcher; and genial Baron

Chassé, whom the French, under whom he had served, called Captain Bayonette; Baron Constant de Rebecque, a favourite with the Peninsular officers; Count Bylandt, from Nivelles; and a cluster of Dutch and Belgian cavalry leaders: Baron Ghigny, a little assertive; Baron van Merlen, a little melancholy; General Trip, a heavy man, like his own carabiniers.

Besides those distinguished personages, there were any number of young officers, all very smart and gallant, and acquitting themselves nobly on the floor of the ballroom under the Duke's indulgent eye. Provided there was no question of neglected duty involved, his lordship liked to see his boys dancing the night through, and always made a point of inviting young officers (of the best families, of course) to his balls. They made a good impression on foreigners: such a nice-looking, well-set up lot as they were! But besides that, his lordship liked the younger men; he kept his eye on the promising ones among them, and would very often single them out above their elders. Colborne had been one of his favoured young men; Harry Smith, that mad boy with the Spanish child-wife; and poor Somers Cocks, who had ended a brilliant career at Burgos. 'The young ones will always beat the old ones,' said his lordship, and those he chose for his patronage certainly seemed to prove the truth of his dictum.

As for his personal staff, he was really fond of those youngsters. The oldest of them was Audley at thirty-five, and the rest were mere lads in their twenties, even Lord Fitzroy, at present engaged in shepherding two Belgian ladies to a couple of seats in the front row.

The Duke's eagle eye swept the concert hall, noting with satisfaction that his family were all present, and all performing their duties as hosts to the throng of guests. A good deal of surprise had been felt in Paris at the youthful aspect of his staff, but his lordship knew what he was about when he chose these young scions of noble houses to live with him. He did not want middle-aged men with distinguished records with him: they could be better employed elsewhere, and would, moreover, have bored him. He wanted polished young men of good families, who were of his own world, who knew how to make themselves pleasant in exalted circles, and could amuse his leisure moments with their adventures, and their fun, and their bubbling energy. On an occasion such as this they were invaluable: nothing awkward about any of them; all well-bred boys who had come to him from Oxford or Cambridge (and not from any new-fangled Military College), accustomed all their lives to moving in the first circles, and consequently assured in their manners, graceful in the ballroom, conversable in the salon.

When he came in with his Royal guests, the rest of the party was already assembled. Everyone stood up, the soldiers to attention, civilian gentlemen deeply bowing, and all the ladies swaying into curtsies like lilies in a high wind. The King and Queen acknowledged their reception, the Duke gave a quick look round, saw that everything was just as it should be, nodded his satisfaction to Colonel Audley, who happened to be standing near him, and escorted the Royals to their places.

The concert began with a Haydn symphony, but although his lordship, who had a great appreciation of good music, enjoyed it, the *pièce de résistance* for most of his guests was the appearance of La Catalani. His lordship described her as being as sharp as a Jew, and Colonel Fremantle had certainly found her so. Nothing could induce her to sing more than two songs, and she had haggled over them. However, when she mounted the platform, she looked as lovely as any angel, and when she opened her mouth and let the golden notes soar heavenwards, even Fremantle felt that he must have misjudged her. She favoured the company first with an aria from Porto-Gullo, and then with an allegro, which showed off the flexibility of her voice to admiration. She was cheered, and encored, but there was no getting another song out of her. She curtsied again and again, blew kisses to the audience, and finally withdrew, apparently exhausted.

The dancing began soon afterwards. The Duke, finding himself standing beside Barbara Childe, said: 'Lovely voice that Catalani women has, don't you agree?'

'Yes, she sings like an angel, or a nightingale, or whatever the creature is that sings better than all others. She has put me quite out of temper, I can tell you, for *I* had a song for you, Duke, and flattered myself I should have made a hit!'

'What? Are you going to sing for me?' he asked, delighted. 'Capital! I shall enjoy *that*, I assure you! What is your voice? Why have I not heard it before?'

'Oh,' she said saucily, 'it is not my voice which I depended on to make the hit with you, but the song!'

'Ah, now I believe you are quizzing me, Lady Bab! What song is this?'

She looked demurely, under her lashes, and replied: 'I am sure you would have been pleased! I should have sung for you *Ahé Marmont, onde vai, Marmont!*'

He gave his neigh of sudden laughter. 'Oh, that's very good! That's famous! But, hush! Can't have that song nowadays, you know. Who told you about it? That rascal Audley, was it? They used to sing it a lot in Spain. Pretty tune!'

'Charming! Where was he going, poor Marmont?'

'Back to France, of course,' said his lordship. 'Chased out of Spain: rompéd: that's what the song's about.'

'Oh, I see! He was in Brussels last month, I believe. Did you reckon him a great general, Duke?'

'Oh no, no!' he said, shaking his head. 'Masséna was the best man they ever sent against me. I always found him where I least wanted him to be. Marmont used to manœuvre about in the usual French style, nobody knew with what object.'

He caught sight of his niece, and beckoned to her, and patted her hand when she came up to him. 'Not tired, Emily? That's right! Lady Bab, you must let me present my niece, Lady Fitzroy Somerset. But you must not be standing about, my dear!' he added, in a solicitous undervoice. Lady Fitzroy flushed faintly, but replied in her gentle way that she was not at all tired, had no wish to sit down, and was, in point of fact, looking for her mother and sister. The Duke reminded her bluffly that she must take care of herself, and went off to exchange a few words with Sir

Charles Stuart. Lady Frances Webster, who had been watching him, was very glad to see him go. She profoundly mistrusted Barbara Childe, and had suffered quite an agonising pang at the sight of his lordship whooping with laughter at what Barbara had said to him.

Barbara, however, had no desire to steal his lordship's affection. She had begun to waltz with Colonel Ponsonby; passed from his arms to those of Major Thornhill; and found herself at the end of the dance standing close to Lord Uxbridge, who immediately stepped up to her, exclaiming: 'Why, Bab, my lovely one! How do you do? They tell me you're engaged to be married! How has that come about? I thought you were a hardened case!'

She gave him her hand. 'Oh, so did I, but you know how it is! Besides, Gussie tells me I shall soon be quite *passée*. Have you seen her? She is here somewhere.'

'I caught a glimpse, but to tell you the truth I have been the whole evening shaking hands with strangers. Who is the lucky man? I hope he is one of my fellows?'

'In a way I suppose you may say that he is. He's on the Duke's staff, however – Charles Audley. But tell me, Harry: are you glad to be here?'

'Yes,' he replied instantly. 'Oh, I know what you are thinking, but that's old history now!'

She laughed. 'It is an enchanting situation! Do you find it awkward?'

'Not a bit!' he said, with cheerful unconcern. 'I go on very well with Wellington, and shall do the same with the fellows under me, when they get to know me – and I them. What's forming? A quadrille! Now, Bab, you must and you shall dance with me – for old time's sake!'

'How melancholy that sounds! You must settle it with Colonel Audley, who is coming to claim it. I daresay he won't give it up, for I told him that you were my first love, you know. Charles, I must make you known to Lord Uxbridge.'

'How do you do? Bab tells me you should by rights be one of

my people. By the by, you must let me congratulate you: you are a fortunate fellow! I have been Bab's servant any time these ten years – knew her when she had her hair all down her back, and wouldn't sew her sampler. You are to be envied.'

'I envy you, sir. I would give much to have known her then.'

'She was a bad child. Now, if you please, you are to fancy yourself back in your regiment, and under my command. I have to request you, Colonel Audley (but I own it to be a dastardly trick!), to relinquish this dance to me.'

The Colonel smiled. 'You put me in an awkward position, sir. My duty, and all the Service Regulations, oblige me to obey you with alacrity; but how am I to do so without offending Bab?'

'I will make your peace with her, I promise you,' replied Uxbridge.

'Very well, sir: I obey under strong protest.'

'Quite irregular! But I don't blame you! Come, you witch, or it will be too late.'

He led Barbara into the set that was forming. A hand clapped Colonel Audley on the shoulder. 'Hallo, Charles! Slighted, my boy?'

The Colonel turned to confront Lord Robert Manners. 'You, is it? How are you, Bob?'

'Oh, toll-loll!' said Manners, giving his pelisse a hitch. 'I have just been telling Worth all the latest London scandal. You know, you're a paltry fellow to be enjoying yourself on the staff in stirring times like these, upon my word you are! I wish you were back with us.'

'Enjoying myself! You'd better try being one of the Beau's ADCs, my boy! You don't know when you're well off, all snug and comfortable with the Regiment!'

'Pho! A precious lot of comfort we shall have when we go into action. When you trot off in your smart cocked hat, with a message in your pocket, think of us, charging to death or glory!'

'I will,' promised the Colonel. 'And when you're enjoying your nice, packed charge, spare a thought for the lonely and damnably distinctive figure galloping hell for leather with his message, wishing to God every French sharpshooter didn't know by his cocked hat he was a staff officer, and wondering whether his horse is going to hold up under him or come down within easy reach of the French lines: he will very likely be me!'

'Oh, well!' said Lord Robert, abandoning the argument. 'Come and have a drink, anyway. I have a good story to tell you about Brummell!'

The story was told, others followed it; but presently Lord Robert turned to more serious matters, and said, over a glass of champagne: 'But that's enough of London! Between friends, Charles, what's happening here?'

'It's pretty difficult to say. We get intelligence from Paris, of course, and what we don't hear Clarke does: but one's never too sure of one's sources. By what we can discover, the French aren't by any means unanimous over Boney's return. All this enthusiasm you hear of belongs to the Army. It wouldn't surprise me if Boney finds himself with internal troubles brewing. Angoulême failed, of course; but we've heard rumours of something afoot in La Vendée. One thing seems certain: Boney's in no case yet to march on us. We hear of him leaving Paris, and of his troops marching to this frontier – they *are* marching, but he's not with them.'

'What about ourselves? How do we go on?'

'Well, we can put 70,000 men into the field now, which is something.'

'Too many 2nd Battalions,' said Lord Robert. 'Under strength, aren't they?'

'Some of them. You know how it is. We're hoping to get some of the troops back from America. But God knows whether they'll arrive in time! We miss Murray badly – but we hear we're to have De Lancey in his place, which will answer pretty well. By the by, he's married now, isn't he?'

'Yes: charming girl, I believe. What are the Dutch and Belgian troops like? We don't hear very comfortable reports of them. Disaffected, are they?'

'They're thought to be. It wouldn't be surprising: half of them have fought under the Eagles. I suppose the Duke will try to mix them with our own people as much as possible, as he did with the Portuguese. Then there will be the Brunswick Oels Jägers: they ought to do well, though they aren't what they were when we first had them with us.'

'Well, no more is the Legion,' said Lord Robert.

'No: they began to recruit too many foreigners. But they're good troops, for all that, and they've good generals. I don't know what the other Hanoverians are like: there's a large contingent of them, but mostly Landwehr battalions.'

'It sounds to me,' said Lord Robert, draining his glass, 'like a devilish mixed bag. What are the Prussians like?'

'We don't see much of them. Hardinge's with them: says they're a queer set, according to our notions. When Blücher has a plan of campaign, he holds conferences with all his generals, and they discuss it, and argue over it, under his very nose. I should like to see old Hookey inviting Hill, and Alten, and Picton, and the rest, to discuss his plans with him!'

Lord Robert laughed; Mr Creevey peeped into the room, and seeing the two officers, came in, rubbing his hands together, and smiling like one who was sure of his welcome. There might be news to be gleaned from Audley, not the news that was being bandied from lip to lip, but titbits of private information, such as an officer on the Duke's staff would be bound to hear. He had buttonholed the Duke a little earlier in the evening, but had not been able to get anything out of him but nonsense. He talked the same stuff as ever, laughing a great deal, pooh-poohing the gravity of the political situation, giving it as his opinion that Boney's return would come to nothing. Carnot and Lucien Bonaparte would get up a Republic in Paris; there would never be any fighting with the Allies; the Republicans would beat Bonaparte in a very few months. He was in a joking mood, and Mr Creevey had met jest with jest, but thought his lordship cut a sorry figure. He allowed him to be very natural and good humoured, but could not perceive the least indication of him of superior talents. He was not reserved; quite the reverse: he was communicative; but his conversation was not that of a sensible man.

'Well? What's the news?' asked Mr Creevey cheerily. 'How d'ye do, Lord Robert?'

'Oh, come, sir! It's you who always have the latest news,' said Colonel Audley. 'Will you drink a glass of champagne with us?'

'Oho, so that's what you are up to! You're a most complete hand, Colonel! Well, just one then. What's the latest intelligence from France, eh?'

'Why, that Boney's summoning everyone to an assembly, or some such thing, in the Champ du Mars.'

'I know *that*,' said Mr Creevey. 'I have been talking about it to the Duke. We have had quite a chat together, I can tell you, and some capital jokes too. *He* believes it won't answer, this Champ de Mai affair; that there will be an explosion; and the whole house of cards will come tumbling about Boney's ears.'

'Ah, I daresay,' responded the Colonel vaguely. 'Don't know much about these matters, myself.'

Mr Creevey drank up his wine, and went away in search of better company. He found it presently in the group about Barbara Childe. She had gathered a numbered of distinguished persons about her, just the sort of people Mr Creevey liked to be with. He joined the group, noticing with satisfaction that it included General Don Miguel de Alava, a short, sallow-faced Spaniard, with a rather simian cast of countenance, quick-glancing eyes, and a tongue for ever on the wag. Alava had lately become the Spanish Ambassador at The Hague, but was at present acting as military commissioner to the Allied Army. He had been commissar at Wellington's Headquarters in Spain, and was known to be on intimate terms with the Duke. Mr Creevey edged nearer to him his ears on the prick.

'But your wife, Alava! Is she not with you?' Sir William Ponsonby was demanding.

Up went the expressive hands; a droll look came into Alava's face. '*Ah non, par exemple!*' he exclaimed. 'She stays in Spain. *Excellente femme! – mais forte ennuyeuse!*'

Caroline Lamb's voice broke through the shout of laughter. 'General Alava, what's the news? You know it all! Now tell us! Do tell us!'

'*Mais, madame, je n'en sais rien! Rien, rien, rien!*'

Decidedly, Mr Creevey was out of luck tonight.

Twelve

May came in, bringing trouble. There seemed to be no end to the difficulties for ever springing up round his lordship. Now it was Major-General Hinüber, querulously demanding leave to resign his staff, and to retire to some German spa, because he was not to command the Legion as a separate division: he might go with the Duke's goodwill, but it meant more letter writing, more trouble; now it was news from his brother William, in London: the Peace party was attacking his lordship in Parliament, accusing him of being little better than a murderer, because he had set his name to the declaration that made Napoleon *hors la loi*: he did not really care, he had never cared for public opinion, but it annoyed him. To attack a public servant absent on public service seemed to him 'extraordinary and unprecedented'. Then there was the constant fret of being obliged to deal with the Dutch King, a jealous man, continually raising difficulties, or turning obstinate over petty issues. He could be managed, in the end he would generally give way, but it took time to handle him, and time was what his lordship could least spare.

The question of the Hanoverian subsidy had become acute; King William should have shared the payment with Great Britain, but he was wriggling out of that obligation, on the score that he had only been bound to pay it while he had no troops of his own. His lordship had had an interview with the M. de Nagel over the business, but in the end he supposed the whole charge of the Hanoverian subsidy would fall upon Great Britain.

Trouble sprang up in the Prussian camp. The Saxon troops at Liége mutinied over some question of an oath of allegiance to the King of Prussia, and poor old Blücher was obliged to quit the town. The Saxons would have been willing enough to have come over to the British camp, but his lordship did not want such fellows, and knew that the Prussians would never agree to his having them if he did. They would have to be got rid of before they spread disaffection through the Army, but the question was how to get them out of the country. Blücher wanted them to be embarked on British ships, but his lordship had no transports; his troops were sent out to him on hired vessels, which returned to England as soon as their cargoes were landed. If they were to be escorted through the Netherlands, King William's permission must be obtained, but there was no inducing Blücher to realise the propriety of referring to the King. It would fall on his lordship's shoulders to arrange matters, writing to Hardinge, to Blücher, to King William.

And, like a running accompaniment to the rest, the bickering correspondence with Torrens over staff appointments dragged on, until his lordship dashed off one of his hasty, biting notes, requesting that it should cease. '*The Commander-in-Chief has a right to appoint whom he chooses, and those whom he appoints shall be employed,*' he wrote in a stiff rage. '*It cannot be expected that I should declare myself satisfied with these appointments till I shall find the persons as fit for their situations as those whom I should have recommended to his Royal Highness.*'

On May 6th his lordship was able to tell Lord Bathurst that King William had placed the Dutch–Belgian Army under his command. The appointment had been delayed on various unconvincing pretexts, but at last, and when his lordship had reached the end of his patience, it had been made. Things should go better now; he could begin to pull the whole Allied Army into shape, drafting the troops where he thought proper without the hindrance of having to make formal application for permission to His Majesty.

The month wore on; the weather grew warmer; no more friendly logfires in the grates, no more fur-lined pelisses for the ladies. Out came the cambrics and the muslins: lilac, pomona green, and pale puce, made into wispy round dresses figured with rosebuds, with row upon row of frills round the ankles. Knots of jaunty ribbons adorned low corsages, and gauze scarves floated from plump shoulders in a light breeze. The feathered velvet bonnets and the sealskin caps were put up in camphor. Hats were the rage; chip hats, hats of satin straw, of silk, of leghorn, and of willow: high-crowned, flat-crowned, with full-poke fronts, and with curtailed poke fronts: hats trimmed with clusters of flowers, or bunches of bobbing cherries, with puffs of satin ribbons, drapings of thread net, and frills of lace. Winter half boots of orange jean or sober black kid were discarded: the ladies tripped over cobbled streets in sandals and slippers. Red morocco twinkled under rushed skirts; Villager hats and Angoulême bonnets framed faces old or young, pretty or plain; silk openwork mittens covered rounded arms; frivolous little parasols on long beribboned handles shaded delicate complexions from the sun's glare. Denmark Lotion was in constant demand, and Distilled Water of Pineapples; strawberries were wanted for sunburnt cheeks; Chervil Water, for bathing a freckled skin.

The balls, the concerts, the theatres continued, but picnics were added to the gaieties now, charming expeditions, with flowering muslins squired by hot scarlet uniforms; the ladies in open carriages; the gentlemen riding gallantly beside; hampers of cold chicken and champagne on the boxes; everyone lighthearted; flirtation the order of the day. There were reviews to watch, fêtes to attend; day after day slid by in the pursuit of pleasure; days that were not quite real, but belonged to some half-realised dream. Somewhere to the south was a Corsican ogre, who might at any moment break into the dream and shatter it, but distance shrouded him; and, meanwhile, into the Netherlands was streaming an endless procession of British troops, changing the whole face of the country, swarming in every village; lounging outside estaminets, in forage caps, with their jackets unbuttoned; trotting down the rough, dusty roads with plumes flying and accoutrements jingling; haggling with shrewd Flemish farmers in their broken French; making love to giggling girls in starched white caps and huge voluminous skirts; spreading their Flanders tents over the meadows; striding through the streets with clanking spurs and swinging sabretaches. Here might be seen a looped and tasselled infantry shako, narrow-topped and leathern-peaked; there the bell-topped shako of a Light Dragoon, with its short plume and ornamental cord; or the fur cap of a hussar; or the glitter of sunlight on a Heavy Dragoon's brass helmet, with its jutting crest and waving plume.

Like bright colours in a kaleidoscope, merging into everchanging patterns, the troops were being drafted over the countryside. Life Guardsmen in scarlet and gold, mounted on great black chargers, sleek as satin and splendid with polished trappings, woke dozing villages on the Dender; Liedekerke gaped at the Blues, swaggering up the street as though they owned it; Schendelbeke girls came running to see the hussars ride past with tossing pelisses, and crusted jackets; Castre and Lerbeke billet Light Dragoons in blue with silver lace, and facings of every colour; crimson, yellow, buff, scarlet; Brussels fell in love with Highland kilts and jaunty bonnets, and blinked at trim riflemen in their Jack-a-Dandy green uniforms; Enghien and Grammont swarmed with the Footguards, the Gentlemen's Sons, with their hosts of dashing young ensigns and captains, all so smart and gay, riding in point-to-point races, hurrying off to Brussels in their best clothes to dance the night through, or entertaining bevies of lovely ladies at fêtes and picnics. But thundering and clattering along the roads that led from Ostend came the Artillery, grim troops in sombre uniforms and big black helmets, scaring the lighthearted into momentary silence as they passed, for though the Guards danced, and the cavalry made love, and line regiments scattered far and near swarmed over the country like noisy red ants, it was the sight of the guns that made the merrymakers realise how close they stood to war. All through April and the early weeks in May they landed one after another in the Netherlands: Ross, with his Chestnut Troop of 9-pounders; bearded Major Bull, with heavy howitzers; Mercer, with his artist's eye for landscape and his crack troop; Whinyates, with his cherished Rockets; Beane; Gardiner; Webber-Smith; and the beau ideal of every artillery officer, Norman Ramsay, of Fuentes de Oñoro fame. After the troops came the field brigades: Sandham's, Bolton's, Lloyd's, Sinclair's, Rogers'; all armed with five gleaming 9-pounders and one howitzer. They were an imposing sight; ominous enough to give a pause to gaiety.

But the merrymaking went on, uneasy under the surface, sometimes a little hectic, as though while the sun continued to shine and the Ogre to remain in his den, the civilians and the soldiers and the lovely ladies were being driven on to cram into every cloudless day all the fun and the gaiety it could hold. The Duke gave ball after ball; there were Court parties at Laeken; reviews at Vilvorde; excursions to Ath, and Enghien, and Ghent; picnics in the cool Forest of Soignes.

There was a rumour of movement on the frontier; a tremor of fear ran through Brussels. Count d'Erlon was marching on Valenciennes with his whole corps; the French were massing on the Allied front, a hundred thousand strong; the Emperor had left Paris: he was at Condé; he was about to launch an attack. It was false: the Emperor was still in Paris, and had postponed his meeting of the Champ de Mai until the end of the month. The ladies and the civilians, poised for flight, could relax again: there was nothing to fear: the Duke had told Mr Creevey that it would never come to blows; and was holding another ball.

'Pooh! Nonsense!' said the Duke. 'Nothing to be afraid of yet!'

'I never saw a man so unaffected in my life!' said Mr Creevey. 'He is as cheerful as a schoolboy, and talks as though there were no possibility of war!'

'Then he is damned different with you from what he is with me,' said Sir Charles Stuart bluntly.

'*I have got an infamous Army, very weak, and ill-equipped, and a very inexperienced staff,*' wrote the Duke, in the midst of his balls, and his reviews, his visits to Ghent, and his latest charming flirtation.

'Pooh! Nonsense,' said the Duke, but wrote to Hill at Grammont: '*Matters look a little serious on the frontier.*'

The Duke knew as well as any man what was stirring beyond the frontier, for he had got Colonel Grant out in charge of the Intelligence, and no one knew better than Grant how to obtain desired information. More reliable than the data collected by Clarke and his French spies were Grant's brief reports sent in to General Dörnberg at Mons, and forwarded on by him to Brussels. Grant told of bridges and roads being broken up in the Sambre district, as though for defence; of Count d'Erlon's Corps lying between Valenciennes and Maubeuge in four divisions of infantry; of Reille at Avesnes, with five infantry divisions and three cavalry; of Vandamme between Mézières and Rocroi; and of Count Lobau, at Laon. His information was precise and always to be trusted: no flights into the realms of conjecture for Colonel Grant, a dry Scot, dealing only in facts and figures. Oh yes! matters certainly looked serious on the frontier; and his lordship had received, besides, disquieting intelligence of a huge body of cavalry forming. Sixteen thousand heavy cavalry were in readiness to take the field, and all over France horses were being bought, to bring the total up to forty thousand or more. A report was spread of Murat's having fled by sea from Italy; it was supposed that he would be put in command of this mass of cavalry, for who so brilliant as Murat in cavalry manœuvres? More serious still was the news that Soult had accepted the office of Major-General under the Emperor. That would bring many wavering men over to Napoleon, for Soult's was a name that carried weight.

The Duke of Brunswick arrived, with his Black Brunswickers: men in sable uniforms, with a skull and crossbones on their shakos, and the death of the Duke's father at Jéna to avenge. A handsome man, the Duke, gallant in the field and stately in the ballroom, with gentle manners and a grave, sweet smile. His men were quartered at Vilvorde, north of Brussels, but he himself was continually at Headquarters, troubled over the eternal question of subsidies.

The Nassauers were on the way, led by General Kruse, and a hopeful young Prince, whom his lordship had promised to take into his family. Rather an anxiety, these hereditary princelings, but they were all of them agog to fight under his lordship, flatteringly deferential and eager to be of use.

Blücher moved his Headquarters from Liége to Hannut, drawing closer to the Anglo-Allied Army; De Lancey arrived from England with his young bride, taking Sir Hudson Lowe's place. With a deputy-quartermaster-general he knew, and could trust to do his work without for ever wishing to copy Prussian methods, his lordship found his path smoother. He still had General Röder with him, but meant to drop a word in Blücher's ear when he next saw him. The fellow would have to be removed: he could not learn to fit into the pattern, or to get over his anti-British prejudice. The other commissioners gave his lordship no trouble: Alava was an old friend; he had a real value for clever Pozzo di Borgo from Russia; liked Baron Vincent from Austria; and was on pretty good terms with Netherlands Count van Reede.

He had been shifting his troops about all the month, skilfully concentrating them, forming new brigades, extending here, drawing his regiments in there, until he felt himself to be in a position to withstand any attack. The Prince of Orange's Headquarters were fixed at Braine-le-Comte, but his lordship placed Lord Hill, wise in war, farther west, at Grammont, because to the west lay his communication lines, and the great Mons and Tournay roads from France. In addition to Clinton's and Colville's divisions, forming the 2nd Corps under Hill, his lordship transferred Prince Frederick's corps to him, moving it north-west from Soignes and Braine-le-Comte, by way of Hal and Grammont to Sotteghem, like a piece on a chessboard. Prince Frederick, surviving an interview with his lordship, betrayed a flash of unsuspected humour. '*Il ne m'a ni grondé, ni mis aux arrêts,*' he wrote to his brother.

On May 29th, a day of blazing sunshine, the Duke reviewed the British cavalry in a natural theatre of ground on the banks of the Dender, not far from Grammont. It was an event that drew the fashionables from Brussels and Ghent on horseback and in carriages: ladies in their newest gauzes, gentlemen very natty in polished topboots, long-tailed blue coats, and skin-tight pantaloons. Worth drove his Judith there in a curricle; Lady Barbara drove herself in a phaeton, with a tiger perched up behind; the Vidals came sedately in their carriage; the amazing Sir Sydney Smith, newly arrived from Vienna, and looking so like a mountebank that it was almost impossible to see in him the hero of Acre, sat beside his lady in an open barouche; Sir Peregrine Taverner rode out on a mettlesome bay, like a score of others; and a host of French Royalists flocked out from Ghent to gaze, gasp, fling up their hands, and exclaim to see such magnificent troops, such noble horses, such glittering accoutrements!

But the cavalry paid no heed to the early French arrivals. The roads were thick with dust, and as each squadron, each troop, came on to the ground, off went belts, haversacks, and coats, and out came brushes and wisps of hay, and a regular scrubbing and dusting and polishing began, for the Duke was coming, with a galaxy of foreign visitors, headed by Marshal Blücher, and not one speck of dust must dull a shining boot or spoil the smartness of a scarlet coat, and not one hair of a charger's tail or mane must be out of place.

The arena lay on the opposite side of the river from the village of Schendelbeke, whence the Duke's cortège was expected to arrive, and a temporary bridge had been thrown across the Dender. Many were the anxious glances cast towards the riding ground over the river, as the men rubbed down their horses, spat on silver buttons, and polished them till the sweat ran off their bodies; and once an alarm was raised, an agonised cry of: 'The Duke! the Duke!'

It was a full hour before he was expected to arrive, but a group of richly-dressed horsemen with waving plumes could clearly be seen coming down the hill from the village. Brushes and rags were thrust into haversacks, coats were flung on and belts buckled, but it turned out to be a false alarm. It was not

Wellington after all, but the Duc de Berri, and what did the Iron Duke's troops care for him? The brushing and the polishing were renewed, and the Duc, after riding slowly down to the bridge, suddenly set off at a gallop towards the saluting point, and halted there, glaring at the serried ranks before him. A few cursory glances were cast at him, and one or two coarse jokes cut at his expense, but no further notice was paid him, until he sent one of his suite forward to confer with Lord Uxbridge. A short colloquy took place; the word spread through the ranks that his Highness was claiming the reception due to a Prince of the Blood-Royal, and loud guffaws greeted this jest. The troops knew Mounseer; they had seen him drilling them French fellows; proper bully-ragger he was!

Back went the envoy, and off galloped his Royal Highness in a rage, his suite labouring behind him up the slope to Schendelbeke. Lord Uxbridge had evidently refused the required salute: that was the way! hurrah for his lordship!

Not until two o'clock did the Duke arrive, and by that time all the polishing was done, and the cavalry was drawn up in three imposing lines, facing the bridge. Lining the bank of the river were the Hussars, in squadrons, widely spaced, and with batteries of Horse Artillery on each flank; behind them stood the Heavy Dragoons in compact order, with four batteries; and behind them, in the same close formation, the Light Dragoons flanked by troops of 9-pounders. There were six thousand men drawn up, and it was small matter for wonder that Marshal Blücher was impressed by the sight. He rode beside the Duke, his blue eyes staring under bushy white brows, and a beaming smile under his long moustache. '*Mein Gott, mein Gott!*' he said. '*Ja, ja*, it is goot – it is fery goot, mein frient!'

The troops, sweating under a scorching sun, choked by their high, tight collars, sat their chargers like statues, gazing rigidly before them, while the cortège passed slowly along the ranks. They knew the Duke's hook nose and low cocked hat right enough; they knew Lord Uxbridge, in his hussar dress; and Sir George Wood, who commanded the Artillery; they even knew the Duke of Brunswick, and guessed that the stout old gentleman with the white whiskers was Marshal Blücher; but who the rest of the fine gentlemen might be, in their plumed hats and fancy foreign uniforms, they neither knew nor cared. One or two old soldiers recognised General Alava, but Generals Gneisenau, Kleist, and Ziethen, Pozzo di Borgo, and Baron Vincent, Counts van Reede, and d'Aglié, exclaiming in outlandish tongues among themselves, did not concern them. They thought the Marshal Prince von Blücher a rum touch if ever there was one, opening his bone-box to splutter out his *Achs*, and his *Mein Gotts*, and his *Fery Goots!*

But the Marshal Prince was enjoying himself. He had come over from Tirlemont with his chief-of-staff, and several of his generals, for this occasion, and his friend and colleague had given them a very good luncheon, sent on their horses to Ninove and driven them out from Brussels in comfortable carriages. He was on the best of terms with his colleague, and although he spoke very little English, and very bad French, they had a great deal of conversation together, and found themselves perfectly in accord. A hussar himself, he was loud in praise of the hussars drawn up before him; as for the Heavy Dragoons, *quels physiques, quels beaux chevaux*! Indeed, the horses impressed him more than anything. When he came to Mercer's troop, there seemed to be no getting him past it; each subdivision was inspected, every horse exclaimed at. '*Mein Gott*, dere is not von vich is not goot for Veldt-Marshal!' he declared.

The Duke acknowledged it. It was not to be expected that he would share in the Marshal's rapture, but he asked Sir George Wood whose troop it was, and seemed to approve of it. It did not occur to him to speak to Captain Mercer, following him as he made the inspection. He paid no heed to him, but Mercer was not surprised: it was just like the Duke; he had never a good word for the unfortunate Artillery.

The inspection took a long time; some of the spectators grew rather bored with looking at the motionless ranks, and several ladies complained of the heat. Sir Peregrine Taverner, whose

Harriet was in low spirits and had refused to attend the review, edged his way to Barbara's phaeton; and Lady Worth, her head aching a little from the glare of the sun, closed her eyes, with a request to her lord to inform her if anything should begin to happen.

The Duke and the Marshall at last returned to the saluting point; Lord Uxbridge marched the troops past; Judith woke up; and all the wilting ladies revived at the near prospect of being able to move out of the sun and partake of refreshments.

The military cortège began to move about among the civilians before riding back to Ninove. Various persons were presented to the Marshal Prince; and Colonel Audley was able to seize the opportunity of exchanging a few words with Lady Barbara.

'How do you contrive to look so cool?' he asked ruefully.

'I can't think. I'm bored to tears, Charles!'

'I know. Devilish tedious, isn't it?'

'I only came to see George, and I couldn't even pick him out in that dreadful scarlet mass!' she said pettishly.

'He looked very handsome, I assure you.'

She yawned. 'I'll swear he was cursing the heat! I wish you will drive home with me. We will dine outside the town in one of those charmingly vulgar places in the suburbs, and drink our wine at a table by the roadside, just as the burghers do. It will be so amusing!'

'Oh, don't!' he begged. 'It sounds delightful, and I can't do it!'

'Why can't you?' she demanded, lifting her eyebrows. 'Is it beneath the dignity of a staff officer?'

'You know very well it's not beneath my dignity. But I'm dining at Ninove.'

'That stupid cavalry party of Uxbridge's! Oh, nonsense! it can't signify. No one will give a fig for your absence: you won't even be missed, I daresay.'

He laughed, but shook his head. 'My darling, I daren't!'

She hunched a shoulder. 'I am tired of your duty, Charles. It is so tedious!'

'It is indeed.'

'I see nothing of you. George and Harry can get leave when they want it; why should not you?'

'George and Harry are not on the staff,' he replied. 'I'd get leave if I could, but it's impossible.'

'Well!' She closed her parasol with a snap, and laid it on the seat beside her. 'If it is impossible for you I must find someone else to go with me. Ah, the very man! Sir Peregrine, come here!'

A little startled, the Colonel turned to see Peregrine hurriedly obeying the summons. A bewitching smile was bestowed upon him. 'Sir Peregrine, I want to dine in the suburbs, and Charles won't take me! Will you go with me?'

'Oh, by Jove, Lady Bab, I should think I will – anywhere!' replied Peregrine.

'Good. No dressing up, mind! I intend to go just as I am. You may call for me in the Rue Ducale: is it agreed?'

'Lord, yes, a thousand times! It will be capital fun!' A doubt struck him; he looked at the Colonel, and added: 'That is – you don't mind, Audley, do you?'

'My dear Perry, why should I mind? Go by all means: I wish I might join you.'

'Oh, devilish good of you! At about six, then, Lady Bab: I'll be there!'

He raised his hat to her and walked away; the Colonel said: 'What's your game, Bab?'

'I don't understand you. I had thought the fact of Sir Peregrine's being a connection of yours must have made him unexceptionable. Besides, I like him: have you any objection?'

'I'm not jealous of him, if that is what you mean, but I've a strong notion that it would be better for him not to be liked by you.'

'Ah, perhaps you are right!' she said. Her voice was saintly, but two demons danced in her eyes. 'Lavisse comes to Brussels this evening: I will engage him instead.'

'You're a devil in attack, Bab,' he said appreciatively. 'That's a pistol held to my head, and, being a prudent man, I capitulate.'

'Oh, Charles! Craven! And you a soldier!'

'True: but a good soldier knows when to retreat!'

'Shall you come about again?'

'Yes, but I shall be more careful of my ground. Today I rashly left my flank exposed.'

She smiled. 'And I rolled it up! Well, I will be good! Sir Peregrine shall take me, because it would be stupid to cry off now, but I will be very sisterly, I promise you.'

He held up his hand to her. 'Defeat without dishonour! Thank you!'

She leaned down from her high perch, putting her hand in his. His face was upturned; she said, with her gurgle of laughter: 'Don't smile at me, Charles! If you do I must kiss you just *there*!' She drew her hand away, and laid a finger between his brows.

'Do!'

'No, this place is confoundedly public: I should put you to shame. By the by, Charles, that chit whose name I never can remember – the heiress whom your sister-in-law meant you to marry – you know whom I mean?'

'I do, but it's nonsense that Judith intended her for me.'

'Oh no, I'm sure it's not! But it doesn't signify, only that I thought you would like to know that I rather fancy George to be a little *épris* in that direction.'

'I hope he will not give her a heartache!'

'I expect he will, however. The odd thing is that she is not at all the sort of young woman he had been in the habit of deceiving.' She added thoughtfully: 'One comfort is that he is more likely to make a fool of her than she of him.'

'Really, Bab!' he protested.

'Now, don't be shocked! It would never do for George to marry her. He won't, of course. He depends too much upon my grandfather, and wouldn't dare. *She* may be perfectly ladylike, but her connection with that horrid little Cit of an uncle makes her quite ineligible. My grandfather was himself held to have married beneath him, but that does not make him indulgent towards any mésalliance *we* might wish to make! He is pleased, by the way, with my engagement. I have had letters from him and my grandmother by today's post. You never told me you had written to him, Charles!'

'Of course I wrote to him. Have we his blessing?'

'Decidedly! You are unexceptionable. He did not suppose me to have so much good sense. My grandmother, who is quite the most delightful creature imaginable, writes that she is in doubt of her felicitations being still acceptable by the time they reach me. You observe, Charles, you have broken all records!' She gathered up the reins, and signed to her tiger to jump up behind. 'There seems to be nothing to stay for: I shall go. Who is invited to this dinner of Uxbridge's?'

'All commanding cavalry officers, and of course the foreign visitors.'

'Ah, a horrid male party! You will enjoy it excessively, I daresay, get abominably foxed, and come reeling back to Brussels with the dawn.'

'Well! You have drawn no rose-coloured picture of my character, at all events! There can be no disillusionment for you to fear!'

'No, none for *me*,' she said.

He saw that she was ready to give her horses the office to start, but detained her. 'Do you mean to drive alone? Is not Harry with you?'

'Certainly I mean to drive alone. Harry is not here.'

'Don't tell me there are no young gentlemen eager for the chance to escort you?'

'I have sometimes a strong liking for my own company,' she replied. 'But as for being alone, pray observe Matthew, my tiger.'

'Let someone ride back with you, Bab.'

'Are you afraid I may be molested by the brutal soldiery? I don't fear it!'

'You might well meet with unpleasantness. Is not Vidal here?'

'Yes, driving with Gussie. You will not expect me to curb my horses to keep pace with a sober barouche. I shall spring 'em, you know.'

He stepped back. She said saucily: 'Retiring again, Charles?

You're the wisest man of my acquaintance. Goodbye! Don't be anxious: I am a famous whip.'

She began to make her way out of the ranks of carriages; the Colonel mounted his horse again, and rode off to his brother's curricle. He saluted Judith, but without attending to what she had to say of the review, addressed Worth. 'Julian, be a good fellow, will you, and follow Bab? She's alone, and I don't care for her to be driving all the distance without an escort. You need not so proclaim yourself, by the way, but I should be glad if you would keep her in sight.'

'Certainly,' said Worth.

'Thank you: I knew I might depend on you.'

He raised two fingers to his hat, and rode off. Judith said: 'Well, if she's alone it must be for the first time. Poor Charles! I daresay she has done it simply to vex him.'

'Very possibly,' Worth agreed. 'There is a bad streak in the Alastairs.'

'Yes. Lord George, in particular, is not at all the thing. I am so disturbed to see him making Lucy the object of his attentions! It was most marked last night: he danced with her three times.'

'She did not appear to mind.'

'You are wrong: I saw her look distressed when he came up to her the third time. She is not the girl to have her head turned by a handsome Life Guardsman.'

'She is singular, then,' he said in his driest tone.

Thirteen

*M*ay had worn itself out; and looking back over four weeks of pleasure seeking, Judith could not feel that there had been unalloyed gaiety. She was aware of tension; she had herself been carried into the swirl. No one could foretell what the future held; but everyone knew that these weeks might be the last of happiness. Except when news crept through of movement on the frontier, war was not much talked of. Talking of it could not stop its coming; it was better to put the thought of it behind one, and to be merry while the sun still shone.

But Judith had good sense to guide her, nor was she any longer a single beauty with scores of admirers clamouring for her favours. If she grew tired, she could rest; but Barbara, it seemed, could not rest, and appeared not to wish even to draw breath. She was beginning to look a little haggard; that she took laudanum was an open secret. What caprice it was that drove her on Judith could not imagine. The very fact of her being betrothed to Charles should have made it possible for her to have lived more quietly; she ought not to want to be for ever at parties. When he could he accompanied her, but he had very little leisure for picnics, or for spending days at the races. Often he came off duty looking so tired that it put his sister-in-law out of all patience to find him bent on attending some ball or reception. He denied that he felt tired, and the harassed little frown between his eyes would vanish as he laughed at her solicitude. She was not deceived; she could have shaken Barbara for her selfishness.

But Charles, keeping pace with his betrothed, never allowed a hint of languor to appear in his face or manner. Once Barbara said to him: 'Is it wrong of me not to give up the parties and all the fun? I love it so! And when I am married I shall have to be so sober!'

'No, no, never think that!' he said quickly.

'Gussie says it must be so.'

'It shall not be so! Don't listen to Augusta, I beg of you! Do you think I have not known from the start how little she likes our engagement?'

'Gussie!' she said scornfully. 'I never listened to her in my life!'

But even though she scoffed at Augusta she did listen to her, with an unconscious ear.

'Make the most of your freedom, my dear,' said Augusta. 'You won't have the chance when you've married your staff officer. Will you miss your court, do you think? Shall you mind not being crowded round at every ball you go to? And oh, Bab, do you mean to wear a matronly cap, and bear your Charles a quiverful of stout children? How I shall laugh to see you!'

No, one did not set any store by what Gussie said, but nevertheless those barbs found their mark. Gallant young gentlemen, too, would cry imploringly: 'Oh, don't turn into a sober matron, Bab! Only conceive of a world without Bad Bab to set everyone by the ears!'

They all drew the same picture of her, grown grave, and thinking not of her conquests but of her household; perhaps being obliged to languish in some dull garrison town, with nothing to do but visit other officers' wives, and be civil to Charles.

She would see herself like that, and would thrust the picture behind her, and hurry away to be gay while she could. When Charles was with her, the picture faded, for Charles swore he wanted no such wife. Yet some sobriety Charles did want. There had been an incident in May which he had not laughed at. Some of the officers of Lord Edward Somerset's brigade had given one of the moonlight picnics of which the old-fashioned people so much disapproved. Lord George had been at the root of it; he had engaged Miss Devenish to go to it with his sister, laying his careless command upon Barbara to bring the chit with her. The wonder was that Miss Devenish had liked to go, but she did go, and had managed to get lost with Lord George in a coppice for over an hour. It was no concern of Barbara's. 'Good God, Charles, if a chaperon had been wanted *I* was not the one to choose for the part! Everyone contrived to lose themselves. Why, I had the most absurd half hour myself, with an engaging child from George's regiment on one side of me and Captain Clayton of the Blues on the other.'

'It sounds safe and rather stupid,' he said. 'But Miss Devenish's prolonged absence with George has caused a little talk. I can't but blame you, Bab. You should not have allowed it.'

'My dear Charles, I suppose her to know her own business. The truth is that you are like your sister, and disapprove of moonlight picnics.'

He was silent. She thought he looked displeased, and said with a light laugh: 'Do you wish me to give up such frivolous amusements?'

'I shan't ask you to give them up, Bab.'

'Do you think I would not?'

'I don't know,' he replied. 'I only know that if you did so at my request it would be against your will. If you did not care to go without me, well that would be different.'

Her eyes danced; she looked half roguish, half rueful, and murmured coaxingly: 'Oh, confound you, Charles, you make me seem the veriest wretch! Don't look so gravely at me! I swear I would rather stay at home with you than go to the most romantic of picnics. But when you can't be with me, what the devil *am* I to do?'

She peeped at him under her lashes; he was obliged to laugh, even though there was very little laughter in his heart.

Judith, when she heard of the famous picnic, was aghast. She could not understand how Mrs Fisher could have permitted her niece to take part in such an expedition. The reason was not far to seek: Mrs Fisher was dreaming of bridals. Young people, she said, often behaved foolishly, and indeed she had scolded Lucy for her thoughtlessness, but she dared say there was no harm done, after all.

Judith blamed Barbara for the whole, and wondered how long Charles would bear with her capriciousness.

'I have always felt a little sorry for Bab Alastair,' said the Duchess of Richmond once, in her quiet way. 'Her mama died when Harry was born, and that is a very sad thing for a girl, you know. I am afraid the late Lord Vidal was rather dissolute, and Bab grew up without that refining influence which her mama must have exercised. She has never been in the way of being checked, and was unfortunate in being made a pet of by her papa.'

'Oh!' exclaimed Judith. 'Could that have done harm to a daughter's character?'

'The melancholy truth was, my dear, that Lord Vidal's principles were not high, and he did not scruple to instil into Bab his own cynical notions. You will not repeat it, but Lord Vidal's household was apt to include females of whose very existence young girls should be unaware.'

'But her grandparents!'

'Oh yes, but, you see, Lord Vidal was not always upon terms with his father,' said her Grace. 'And the Duchess was not of an age to dance attendance upon a flighty granddaughter. She was most distressed at that wretched marriage, I know. There can never have been a more shocking business! Childe was a man whose reputation, whose whole manner of life – but I am talking of the dead, and indeed have said too much already.'

'I am glad you have told me as much; it may help me to be patient. I own, I cannot like Barbara.'

'I am sorry for it. Yet she is not heartless, as so many people say. I could tell you of a hundred generous actions. She is accounted perfectly selfish, but I have been a good deal touched by her kindness to my boy during his long, painful convale-scence. I believe no one is aware how often she has forgone some pleasure party merely to sit with poor William for a little while, quite taking him out of himself.'

'Ah, that was kind indeed! You are right: it warms one's heart towards her to hear of such conduct. How does poor William go on? He has not left his room?'

'Oh no! It must be weeks yet before he will be able to stand upon his feet. It was a dreadful accident – he was thrown in such a way! But I don't care to think of it, and can only thank God he has been spared to me.'

Nothing more was said of Barbara, but the conversation remained in Judith's memory. She was able to meet Barbara with more cordiality, and even to pardon some of her wildness; and for a little while could almost hope that she might make Charles happy.

The incident of the moonlight picnic, however, brought back all the old disgust; she could hardly forgive Barbara for having lent herself to what she believed to have been nothing less than a trap laid for Lucy Devenish.

Lucy's own distress was evident. She looked so pale and wretched that Judith began to fear that her affections had been seriously engaged. Lord George was as brazen as might have been expected. He had made Lucy the subject of the latest scandal, but when taxed with it by his elder brother, would do nothing but laugh.

'I wish you will consider me!' complained Vidal.

'Consider you? Why the devil should I?' demanded George.

'It is no very pleasant thing for me, I can tell you, to have my brother pointed out as a rake and a libertine on the one hand, and my sister on the other as –'

'Keep your damned tongue off Bab, unless you want your teeth knocked down your throat, Vidal!' said George, looking ugly.

'Pray do not bring your ringside manners into my drawing-room, George,' said Augusta sharply. 'I find your championing of Bab more than a little absurd, let me tell you!'

He turned, looking down at her from his great height with an expression of mocking indifference. 'You do, do you? And what the devil do you think I care for your opinion?'

'Thank you, I am well aware of your habit of disregarding everyone's opinion but your own. However, Bab's conduct has nothing to do with your folly in entangling yourself with that Devenish chit. Depend upon it, her uncle is merely awaiting his opportunity to force you into marrying her. I know what men of his stamp are like, if you do not.'

'Oho, do you really, Gussie? Where did you come by your knowledge, I should like to know?'

She replied coldly: 'Laugh, if you choose, but do not look to me for help when you find yourself trapped. I suppose you have thought how you will break the news to your grandfather. I don't envy you that task!'

He flushed, seemed about to retort, and then turned on his heel and walked away.

Whatever Mr Fisher's plans might be, Miss Devenish at least did not appear to be desirous of encouraging George's attentions. Judith was a witness of a decided rebuff to his lordship, and could only be glad of it, although she felt sorry for the pain it seemed to cause Lucy. Lucy's wan looks began to make Judith feel anxious, and she even cast about in her mind for some eligible young man to take Lord George's place in the girl's affections.

At the review of the cavalry, she thought she had found a gentleman, who might answer the purpose, but before she could put into execution her amiable plan of inviting him and Lucy to dine one evening her anxieties were diverted in quite another direction.

Sir Peregrine, either from a slight feeling of guilt or from mere thoughtlessness, did not inform his Harriet of his assignation in the suburbs. Upon his return to Brussels he had found Harriet far from well, and quite in the dumps. He bounced in, ready to recount all the day's happenings, but she had the headache, was sipping hartshorn and water, and announced her intention of going to bed and having her dinner sent up to her on a tray.

'Well, I am sorry you have the headache, Harry. Shall you mind if I dine from home? If you would like me to stay with you –'

'Oh no! I shall be better tomorrow, I daresay, but my head aches too much to make me pleasant company tonight. Go out, by all means. I am only sorry to be such a stupid creature!'

So Peregrine had sailed forth to call for Barbara, and had spent an entertaining evening with her in one of the cafés beyond the ramparts.

Had Colonel Audley been able to see them he must have acquitted Barbara of any desire to flirt, but he could scarcely have been pleased with the result of her sisterly behaviour. When she chose to treat a man *en camarade*, she was at her most enchanting. She had not the smallest intention of captivating Peregrine, but her candid way of looking at him, her rippling laugh, her boyish speech, and her sense of fun charmed him irresistibly. He was not in love with her, but he had never in his life encountered so dazzling a creature.

Barbara said frankly at the outset: 'This is capital! I shall pretend you are my young brother. I, if you please, am your elder sister – though I fear I am not quite like Lady Worth.'

Peregrine did not think that she was in the least like Judith, except in being able to talk sensibly of horses. He soon found himself describing his yacht to her; discovered that she also was fond of sailing; and from that moment became her slave. Sailing, riding, cocking, prizefighting: they talked of them all. No squeamish nonsense about Lady Bab! Why, it was like talking to a man, only much more exciting.

It was all quite innocent, but as ill-luck would have it they were seen by some people who were driving back to Brussels from Nivelles, and in less time than might have been thought possible the news that Sir Peregrine was Bab's latest victim was not only current but had reached Harriet's ears.

She was thunderstruck, and, in her nervous condition, easily convinced that the woman whom she had detested ever since the fatal expedition to Hougoumont was stealing from her

Peregrine's affections. No doubt he was tired of such a dull, ailing wife: she did not blame him – or, at any rate, not very much – but no words were bad enough to describe Barbara's wicked malice.

She carried the story to Judith, casting herself upon her bosom and sobbing out her woes. Judith heard her with incredulity. She insisted upon her calming herself, obliged her to drink a glass of wine, and to sit down on the sofa, and said with brisk good sense: 'I don't believe a word of it! What has Perry to say for himself?'

Oh, Harriet might be a fool, but she was not such a fool as to attack Perry with his infidelity!

'Infidelity!' said Judith. 'Stuff and nonsense! What a piece of work about nothing! I daresay he may admire Barbara: who does not? But as for the rest of it – why, Harriet, it is the merest irritation of nerves! If you take my advice you'll think no more of it!'

'How can you be so heartless?' wept Harriet. 'I might have guessed this would happen! I mistrusted her from the start. Perry is tired of me, and she has stolen him from me.'

'I have a great affection for Perry,' responded Judith tartly, 'but I doubt very much his having the power to engage Lady Barbara's interest. Depend upon it, you are making a mountain out of a molehill.'

'Oh no! I have been so poorly of late that I have had no spirits to go into society, and so he has looked elsewhere for amusement. I see it all!'

'Well, Harriet, if he had looked elsewhere it would not be surprising. You know how much I have always deprecated your giving way to lowness as you do. If you have a particle of sense you will abandon your sofa and your everlasting hartshorn, give up maudling your inside with tea, and go about a little, and forget your delicate situation. There! That is plain speaking, but good advice. Dry your tears, and do not waste another thought on the matter. You must have forgotten that Lady Barbara is betrothed to Charles. How could she possibly flirt with Perry?'

'There is nothing too base for that creature to do!' Harriet said, roused to a ferocity surprising in one ordinarily so gentle. 'I pity Charles Audley! He may be deceived, but I am not.'

'That must be considered an advantage. With your eyes open to a possible danger you may act with tact and prudence.'

'It is very easy for you to talk in that careless way! Your husband has not been stealing away from you to flirt with a fast, unprincipled female!'

'Come! This is much better,' said Judith, with a smile. 'If flirtation is all you have to worry about, there can be no occasion for such heat. Lady Bab flirts with everyone, but I believe it to be no more than a fashionable diversion, signifying precisely nothing.'

Harriet burst into tears, and while Judith was endeavouring to give her thoughts a more cheerful direction, Colonel Audley strolled into the room with his nephew on his shoulder. He stopped dead on the threshold when he saw what lay before him, hastily begged pardon, and retreated with all a man's horror of becoming mixed up in a scene of feminine vapours. But before he could make good his escape Judith had called to him to stay.

'Charles, for goodness' sake come here and tell Harriet what a goose she is!'

'Oh!' gasped the afflicted lady. '*He* must not know!'

'Fiddle!' said Judith. 'If the tale is all over town, as you say it is, he will know soon enough. Charles, Harriet has taken a notion into her head that Perry has fallen in love with Lady Barbara, and has been seen dining with her in the suburbs. Now, is there one word of truth in it?'

'I hope he has not fallen in love with her, but it is quite true that they dined together in the suburbs,' replied the Colonel. He set his nephew down, and set him back to his nurse with a friendly pat. 'Off with you, monkey! I am afraid you must blame me, Lady Taverner: it was entirely my fault.'

'Oh no, no!'

'On the contrary, it is oh yes, yes!' he said, smiling. 'The case was, that Bab took a fancy into her head to dine by the roadside at one of those cafés outside the Porte de Namur. I could not escort her, and so Perry became my deputy. That is the whole truth in a nutshell.'

'I knew there must be some very ordinary explanation,' exclaimed Judith. 'Now, Harriet, you can be satisfied, I hope. If Charles sees no harm I am sure you need not.'

But Harriet was far from being satisfied. If the affair had been innocent, why had Perry kept it a secret?

'What! did he forget to tell you?' said the Colonel, exchanging a startled glance with his sister-in-law. 'Stupid young rascal! I advise you to take him severely to task: he's a great deal too forgetful!'

It would not do. Harriet dried her tears, but a score of incidents had been recalled to her mind, and she could not convince herself that Peregrine had not from the outset been attracted by Barbara's wiles. The Colonel's presence made it impossible for her to say that it was all Barbara's fault, which she was sure it was, and so she was silent, allowing Judith to talk, but too busy with her own thoughts to lend more than half an ear to all the sensible things that were being said to her.

She presently went away, leaving Judith and Audley to look at one another in some consternation.

'My dear Charles, nothing could be more unfortunate!' Judith said, with a rueful laugh. 'I acquit Lady Barbara of wishing to enslave poor Perry, but I am afraid there may be a grain of truth in Harriet's suspicions. It has sometimes seemed to me that Perry was a trifle smitten with Lady Barbara.

'Yes, I think he is,' admitted the Colonel. 'But really, Judith, I believe it to be Harriet's own fault!'

'Oh, undoubtedly, and so I have told her! It all arose out of that wretched expedition to Hougoumont! I wish I had not meddled!'

He looked at her with arrested expression in his eyes. 'Why?' he asked. 'What occurred at Hougoumont to give rise to this piece of nonsense?'

The colour rushed into her face. Vexed with herself for having allowed such unguarded words to escape her, she said: 'Oh, nothing, nothing! It was only that Harriet took a dislike to Lady Barbara!'

'Indeed! Why should she do that?'

She found herself unable to meet his gaze with composure, and turned away on the pretext of shaking up the sofa cushions. 'Oh! You know what a country mouse Harriet is! She has not been in the way of meeting fashionable people, and is easily shocked. Lady Barbara was in one of her capricious moods, and I daresay that may have set Harriet against her.'

'You may as well tell me the truth, Judith. Did Bab's caprice lead her to flirt with Perry, or what?'

'No, certainly not. Perry was with us the whole time,' she said involuntarily.

'Perry was with you! Where, then, was Bab?'

'She was with us too, of course. But Harriet and I drove in a barouche, the others rode. I only meant that Perry rode beside us, while Lady Barbara and the Count were not unnaturally tempted to leave the road for the Forest. I am sure they were not to be blamed for that: I should have liked to have done so myself.'

'I see,' he replied.

An uncomfortable silence fell; the Colonel was looking abstractedly out of the window, one hand fiddling with the blind-cord. Judith felt herself impelled to say presently: 'There was nothing more, I assure you. Do not be imagining anything foolish!'

He turned and smiled at her. 'My dear Judith, you are looking quite anxious! There is really not the least cause, I promise you. As for this affair of Perry's, I'll speak to Bab.'

'Don't if you had rather not!' she said. 'I daresay it is all nonsense.'

'The scandal, if there is one, had better be scotched, however.'

But Barbara, when she heard of Harriet's suspicions, exclaimed indignantly: 'Oh, that's great deal too bad! Of all the injustices in this wicked world! I treated him as I treat Harry – I did really, Charles!'

'I don't doubt it,' he said. 'The truth is, I suspect, that you were much more enchanting than you knew. Is Perry in danger of losing his heart to you, do you think?'

'I think he might be made to lose it,' she replied candidly. 'But what a fool his wife must be!'

'I believe she is in a delicate situation just at present.'

'Oh, poor creature! Very well, I will make everything right with her. Then she may be comfortable again.'

The occasion offered itself that same day. Walking in the Park with a party of friends, Barbara saw Lady Taverner approaching with her sister-in-law. She left her friends, and went forward to meet Harriet, holding up a frilled parasol in one hand and extending the other in a friendly fashion. 'I have been wanting to meet you, Lady Taverner,' she said, with one of her swift smiles. 'I believe there is a nonsensical story current, and though I have no doubt of your laughing at it, I daresay it may have vexed you a little.'

The hand was ignored. Lady Taverner turned scarlet and, with a glance of contempt, whisked round on her heel and walked away.

Judith, sensible of the generosity that had prompted Barbara to approach Harriet, stood rooted to the ground in dismay. What could possess Harriet to behave with such rudeness? The folly of it passed her comprehension; she could only gaze after her in amazement. The path was full of people; twenty or thirty pairs of eyes must have witnessed the snub. She said in a deeply mortified voice: 'I beg your pardon! My sister-in-law is not quite herself. I do not know what she could be thinking of!'

She glanced at Barbara, and was not surprised to see her green eyes as hard as two bits of glass. A little colour had stolen into her cheeks; her lips were just parted over her clenched teeth. If ever anyone was in a rage she was in one now, thought Judith. She looked ripe for murder, and really one could not blame her.

'That,' said Barbara, 'was neither wise nor wellbred of Lady Taverner. Convey my compliments to her, if you please, and inform her that I shall endeavour not to disappoint her very evident expectations.'

'She is extremely foolish, and I beg you will not notice her rudeness!' said Judith. 'No one regards what you so rightly call the nonsensical story which is current.'

'How simple of you to think so! The story must *now* be implicitly believed. By tomorrow I shall be credited with a sin I haven't committed, which touches my pride, you know. I always give the scandalmongers food for their gossip.'

'To give them food in this case would be to behave as foolishly as my sister-in-law,' said Judith, trying to speak pleasantly.

'Oh, I have my reputation to consider!' Barbara retorted. 'I make trouble wherever I go: haven't you been told so?'

'I have tried not to believe it.'

'A mistake! I am quite as black as I am painted, I assure you. But I am keeping you from Lady Taverner. Go after her – and don't forget my message!'

Fourteen

*J*udith did not go after her sister-in-law. She had very little hope of inducing Harriet to apologise, nor, upon reflection, did she feel inclined to make the attempt. She could not think Barbara blameless in the affair. However well she might have behaved in extending an olive branch, the original fault was one for which Judith could find little excuse. If Barbara wanted to dine in the suburbs (which, in itself, was a foolish whim) she might as well have chosen an evening when Charles would have been free to have escorted her.

Judith acquitted her of wanting to make mischief. It had all been the result of thoughtlessness, and had Harriet behaved like a sensible woman nothing more need have come of it. But Harriet had chosen to do the one thing that would lend colour to whatever gossip was afoot, and had besides made an enemy of a dangerous young woman. It still made Judith blush to think of the scene. In Barbara's place she would, she acknowledged, have been angry enough to have boxed Harriet's ears. But such sudden anger was usually short-lived. She hoped that a period of calm reflection would give Barbara's thoughts a more proper direction, and determined to say nothing of the occurrence to Charles.

She heard her name spoken, and came out of her reverie to find herself confronting Lord Fitzroy Somerset, who, with his elder brother, Lord Edward, and their nephew, Henry Somerset, was strolling along the path down which her unconscious footsteps had taken her.

Greetings and handshakes followed. Judith was acquainted with Lord Edward, but Lieutenant Somerset, who was acting as his uncle's aide-de-camp, had to be presented to her. Lord Edward had only lately arrived from England, to command the brigade of Household Cavalry. He was twelve years Lord Fitzroy's senior, and did not much resemble him. Fitzroy was fair, with an open brow, and very regular features. Lord Edward was harsh-featured and dark, with deep lines running down from the corners of his jutting nose and his close-lipped mouth, and two clefts between his brows. His eyes were rather hard, and he did not look to have that sweetness of disposition which made his brother universally beloved; but he was quite unaffected, laughed and talked a great deal, and seemed perfectly ready to be agreeable. Judith enquired after his wife; he had not brought her to the Netherlands; he thought – saving Lady Worth's presence! – that the seat of an approaching war was not the place for females.

'Your husband is not engaged in the operations, and so the case is different,' he said. 'But I assure you, the women who would persist in following the Army in Spain were at times a real hindrance to us. Nothing would stop them! Very courageous, you will say, and I won't deny it, but they were the devil to deal with on the march, choking the roads with their gear!'

She smiled, and agreed that it must have been so. She had turned to retrace her steps with the Somersets, and as the path was not broad enough to allow of their walking abreast, Lord Fitzroy and his nephew had gone ahead. She indicated Fitzroy with a nod, and remarked that his brother must not speak so in his hearing.

'Oh, Fitzroy knows what I think!' replied Lord Edward. 'However, he is not an old married man like me, so he must be pardoned. Not but what I think it a great piece of folly on his part. Of course, you know Lady Fitzroy has lately been confined?'

'Indeed I do, and I am one of her daughter's chief admirers!'

'I daresay. A nice thing it would have been had she been obliged to remove in a hurry!'

195

'Depend upon it, had there been any fear of that her uncle must have known of it, and she could have retired without the least hurry to Antwerp. *He* does not appear to share your prejudice against us poor females!'

'The Duke! No, that he does not!' replied Lord Edward, laughing. 'But, come, enough of the whole subject, or I can see I shall be quite out of favour with you! I understand I have to congratulate Audley upon his engagement?'

She acknowledged it, but briefly. He said in his downright way: 'I don't know how you may regard the matter, but I should have said Audley was too good a man for Bab Childe.'

She found herself so much in accordance with this opinion that she was unable to forbear giving him a very speaking glance.

'Just so,' he said, with a nod. 'I have known the whole family for years – got one of them in my brigade now: handsome young devil, up to no good – and I shouldn't care to be connected with any of them. As for Audley, he's the last man in the world I should have expected to be caught by Bab's tricks. Great pity, though I shouldn't say so to you, I suppose.'

'Lady Barbara is very beautiful,' Judith replied, with a certain amount of reserve.

He gave a somewhat scornful grunt, and said no more. They had reached one of the gates opening on to the Rue Royale at this time, and Lord Edward, who was on his way to Headquarters, took his leave of Judith, and strode off up the road with his nephew.

Lord Fitzroy gave Judith his arm. He had to pay a call at the Hôtel de Belle Vue, and was thus able to accompany her to her door. They walked in that direction through the Park, talking companionably of Lady Fitzroy's progress, of the infant daughter's first airing, and other such mild topics, until presently they were joined by Sir Alexander Gordon, very smart in a new coat and sash, on which Lord Fitzroy immediately quizzed him.

Judith listened, smiling, to the interchange of friendly raillery, occasionally being appealed to by one of them, to give her support to some outrageous libel on the other.

'Gordon,' Fitzroy informed her, 'is one of our dressier colleagues. He has seventeen pairs of boots. That's called up-holding the honour of the family.'

'One of Fitzroy's grosser lies, Lady Worth. Now, the really dressy member of the family is Charles.'

'He has the excuse of being a hussar. They can't help being dressy, Lady Worth. However, the strain of trying to procure a sufficiency of silver lace in Spain wore the poor fellow out, and in the end he was quite thankful to be taken into the family. I say, Gordon, why didn't you join a hussar regiment? Was it because you were too fat?'

'A dignified silence,' Gordon told Judith, 'is the only weapon to use against vulgar persons.'

'Very true. It is all jealousy, I daresay. I feel sure you would set off a hussar uniform to admiration.'

'Fill it out, don't you mean?' enquired Fitzroy.

Sir Alexander was diverted from his purpose of retaliating in kind by catching sight of Barbara Childe between two riflemen. 'When does that marriage take place, Lady Worth?' he asked.

'The date is not fixed.'

'There's hope yet, then. That's Johnny Kincaid with her – the tall lanky one on her right. Perhaps he'll cut Charles out. Very charming fellow, Kincaid.'

Fitzroy shook his head. 'No chance of that. Kincaid loves Juana Smith – or so I've always fancied.'

Judith said: 'Is that how you feel, Sir Alexander? About Charles's engagement, I mean?'

'I beg pardon! I shouldn't have said it.'

'You may say what you please. I am forced in general to be very discreet, but you are both such particular friends of Charles's that I may be allowed to speak my mind – which is that it would be better if the marriage never took place.'

'Of course it would be better! There was never anything more unfortunate! We laughed at Charles when it began, but it has turned out to be no laughing matter. It was all the Prince's fault for making the introduction in the first place.'

'Nonsense, Gordon! If he had not someone else would have done it. I am afraid Charles is pretty hard hit, Lady Worth.'

'I am afraid so, too. I wish he were not, but what can one do?'

'One can't do anything,' said Gordon. 'That's the sad part of it: to be obliged to watch one of your best friends making a fool of himself.'

'Do you dislike Lady Barbara?'

'No. I like her, but the thing is that I like Charles much more, and I can't see him tied to her for the rest of his life.'

'It may yet come to nothing.'

'That's what I say, but Fitzroy will have it that if Bab throws him over it will be the end of him.'

'No, I didn't say that,' interposed Lord Fitzroy. 'But you can't live with a man for as long as I've lived with Charles, and come through tight places with him, and work with him, day in, day out, without getting to know him pretty well, and I do say that I believe him to be in earnest over this. I expect he knows his own business best – only I do wish he would stop burning the candle at both ends!'

'He can't,' said Gordon. 'You have to run fast if you mean to keep pace with Bab.'

They had reached the Rue du Belle Vue by this time, and no more was said. Lord Fitzroy took his leave, Sir Alexander escorted Lady Worth to her own door, and she went in, feeling despondent and quite out of spirits.

The Duchess of Richmond held an informal party that evening, at her house off the Rue de la Blanchisserie, which was situated in the northern quarter of the town, not far from the Allée Verte. The Duke of Wellington had, from its locality, irreverently named it the Wash-house, but it was, in fact, a charming abode, placed in a large garden extending to the ramparts, and with a smaller house, or cottage, in the grounds which was occupied, whenever he was in Brussels, by Lord March.

The Duchess's parties were always popular. She had a great gift for entertaining, knew everyone, and had such a numerous family of sons and daughters that her house was quite a rendezvous for the younger set. Besides the nursery party, which consisted of several lusty children who did not appear in the drawing-room unless they had prevailed upon some indulgent friend, like the Duke of Wellington, to beg for them to come downstairs, there was a cluster of pretty daughters, and three fine sons: Lord March, Lord George Lennox, and Lord William.

Lord March was not present at the party, being at Braine-le-Comte with the Prince of Orange; and Lord William, who had had such a shocking fall from his horse, was still confined to his room; but Lord George, one of Wellington's aides-de-camp, was there; and of course the four daughters of the house: Lady Mary, Lady Sarah, Lady Jane, and Lady Georgiana.

The Duke of Wellington did not gratify the company by putting in an appearance. The redoubtable Duchesse d'Angoulême had lately arrived in Ghent, and he had gone there to pay his respects to her, taking Colonel Audley with him. But although the party was composed mostly of young people, several major-generals were present with their wives, quite a number of distinguished civilians, and of course Sir Sydney Smith, working his startling brows up and down, flashing his eyes about the room, and drawing a great deal of attention to himself with his theatrical eccentricities.

Lady Worth, who arrived rather late with her husband, was glad to see that Harriet had torn herself from her couch and had come with Peregrine. It was evident that she had entered the lists against Barbara, for she was wearing one of her best gowns, had had her hair dressed in a new style, and had even improved her complexion with a dash of rouge. She seemed to be in spirits, and Judith was just reflection on the beneficial results of a spasm of jealousy when in walked Barbara, ravishing in a white satin slip under a robe of celestial blue crape, caught together down the front with clasps of flowers. Judith's complacency was ended. Peregrine, like nearly everyone else, was gazing at the vision. Who, Judith wondered despairingly, would look twice at Harriet in her figured muslin and her amethysts, when Barbara stood laughing under the great chandelier, flirting a fan of frosted crape which twinkled in the candlelight, the brilliants round her neck no more sparkling than her eyes?

She glanced round the room, blew a kiss to Georgiana, nodded at Judith. Her gaze swept past Peregrine, and Judith found herself heaving a sigh of relief: she was going to be good, then! The next instant her spirit quailed again, for she caught sight of Harriet's face, set in rigid lines of disdain, and heard her say in a clear, hard little voice to the lady standing beside her: 'My dear ma'am, of course it is dyed! I should not have thought it could have deceived a child. Perry, let me remove into the salon: I find this place a little too *hot* for me.'

That her words had reached Barbara's ears was evident to Judith. The green eyes rested enigmatically on Harriet's face for a moment, and then travelled on to Peregrine. A little tantalising smile hovered on the lovely mouth; the eyes unmistakably beckoned.

'In a minute!' said Peregrine. 'I must say how do you do to Lady Bab first.'

He left Harriet's side as he spoke, and walked right across the room to where Barbara stood, waiting for him to come to her. She held out her hand to him; he kissed it; she murmured something, and he laughed, very gallantly offered his arm, and went off with her towards the glass doors thrown open into the garden.

'But what finesse!' said Worth's languid voice, immediately behind Judith. 'I make her my compliments. In its way, perfect!'

'I should like to box her ears, and Harriet's, and Peregrine's, and yours too!' replied Judith in a wrathful whisper.

'In that case, my love, I will remove one temptation at least out of your way.'

She detained him. 'Worth, you must speak to Perry!'

'I shall do no such thing.'

'It is your duty: after all, he is your ward!'

'Oh no, he is not! He *was* my ward. That is a very different matter. Moreover, my heart wouldn't be in it: Harriet offered battle, and has been defeated in one brilliant engagement. I cannot consider it to be any concern of mine – though I shall be interested to see the outcome.'

'If you have taken it into your head to save your brother at the expense of mine, Julian, I tell you now that I won't have it!' said Judith.

He smiled, but returned no answer, merely moving away to join a group of men by the stairs.

The rest of the evening passed wretchedly enough for Judith. It was some time before Peregrine reappeared, and when he did at last come back from the garden he was in high fettle. Harriet, employing new tactics, had joined the younger guests in the ballroom, and was behaving in a manner quite unlike herself, chattering and laughing, and promising more dances than the night could possibly hold. Never remarkable for his perception, Peregrine beamed with pleasure, and told her that he had known all along that she would enjoy herself.

'I am afraid you have come too late, Peregrine!' she said, very bright eyed. 'Every dance is booked!'

'Oh, that's capital!' he replied. 'Don't bother your head over me: I shall do famously!'

After this well-meaning piece of tactlessness, he withdrew from the ballroom, and was next seen in the salon, turning over the leaves of her music for Barbara, who had been persuaded to sing Mr Guest's latest ballad, *The Farewell*.

On the following morning, while she sat at breakfast, a note was brought round to Judith by hand. It was directed in a fist that showed unmistakable signs of agitation, and sealed with a lilac wafer set hopelessly askew.

'Harriet!' said Judith in long-suffering accents. She tore the sheet open, and remarked: 'Blotched with tears! She wants me to go to her immediately.'

'Will you have the carriage ordered at once, or will you delay your departure long enough to pour me out some more coffee?' enquired the Earl.

'I haven't the least intention of going until I have finished my breakfast, spoken with my housekeeper, and seen my son,' replied Judith, stretching out her hand for his cup. 'If Harriet imagines I shall sympathise with her she very much mistakes the matter. Her behaviour was odiously rude, and I am out of all patience with her. Depend upon it, she has crowned her folly by quarrelling with Perry. Well, I wash my hands of it! Do you think Perry is really in love with that horrid creature?'

'Certainly not,' he answered. 'Perry is a trifle intoxicated, and extremely callow. His present conduct reminds me irresistibly of his behaviour when he first discovered in himself an aptitude for sailing. He has not altered in the smallest degree.'

'Oh, Worth, it would be a dreadful thing if this wretched affair were to come between him and Harriet!'

'Very dreadful,' he agreed, picking up the *Gazette*.

'It is all very well for you to say "Very dreadful" in that hateful voice, just as if it didn't signify an atom, but I am extremely anxious! I wonder why Harriet wants me so urgently?'

It appeared, when Judith saw her an hour later, that Harriet wanted to announce the tidings of her imminent demise. 'I wish I were dead!' she moaned, from behind a positive rampart of bottles of smelling salts, hartshorn, and lavender drops. 'I shall die, for Perry has been so wickedly cruel, and my heart is broken, and I feel quite shattered! I hope I never set eyes on either of them again, and if Perry means to dine at home I shall lock myself in my room, and go home to Mama!'

'You might, if you were silly enough, perform one of those actions,' said Judith reasonably, 'but I do not see how you can accomplish both. For heaven's sake, stop crying, and tell me what is the matter.'

'Perry has been out riding before breakfast with That Woman!' announced Harriet in tragic accents.

Judith could not help laughing. 'Dear me, is that all, you goose?'

'In the Allée Verte!'

'Shocking!'

'By appointment with her!'

'No!'

'And alone!'

'My dear, if there is more to come I shall be obliged to borrow your smelling salts, I fear.'

'How can you laugh? Have you no sensibility? He actually told me of it! He was brazen, Judith! He said she was the most stunning creature he had ever laid eyes on! He said that to *me*!'

'If he said it to you it is a sure sign that his affections are not seriously engaged. If I were you I would take him back to Yorkshire and forget the whole affair.'

'He won't go!' said Harriet, burying her face in her hand-kerchief. 'He said so. We have had a terrible quarrel! I told him –'

Judith flung up her hands. 'I can readily imagine what you told him! Perry is nothing but a heedless boy! I daresay he never dreamed of being in love with Lady Barbara. He thought of her as Charles's fiancée, he found her good company, he admired her beauty. And what must you do but put it into his head to fall in love with her! Oh, Harriet, Harriet, what a piece of work you have made of it!'

This was poor comfort for an afflicted lady, and provoked Harriet to renewed floods of tears. It was some time before she was able to regain any degree of calm, and even when her tears were dried Judith saw that no advice would be attended to until she had had time to recover from the ill-effects of her first quarrel with Peregrine. She persuaded her to take the air in an open carriage, and sat beside her during the drive, endeavouring to engage her interest in everyday topics. Nothing would do, however. Harriet sat with her veil down; declined noticing the flowers in the Park, the barges on the canal, or the pigeons on the steps of St Gudule; and was morbidly convinced that she was an object of pity and amusement to every passer-by who bowed a civil greeting. Judith was out of all patience long before the drive came to an end, and when she at last set Harriet down at the door of her lodging her sympathies lay so much with Peregrine that she was able to wave to him, when she caught sight of him presently, with a perfectly good will.

Such feelings were not of long duration. A second note from Harriet, received during the evening, informed her that Peregrine had returned home only to change his dress, and had gone out again without having made the least attempt to see his wife. Harriet declared herself to be in no doubt of his destination, and ended an incoherent and blistered letter by the expression of a strong wish to go home to her mama.

By the following day every suspicion had been confirmed: Peregrine had indeed been in Barbara's company. He had made one of a party bound for the neighbourhood of Hal, and had picnicked there on the banks of the Senne, returning home only with the dawn. To make matters worse, it had been he whom Barbara had chosen to escort her in her phaeton. Every gossiping tongue in Brussels was wagging; Harriet had received no less than five morning calls from thoughtful acquaintances who feared she might not have heard the news; and more than one matron had felt it to be her duty to warn Judith of her young brother's infatuation. Loyalty compelled Judith to make light of the affair, but by noon her patience had become so worn that the only person towards whom her sympathy continued to be extended was Charles Audley.

He had not made one of the picnic party, and from the circumstance of his being employed by the Duke all the following morning it was some time before any echo of the gossip came to his ears. It reached him in the end through the agency of Sir Colin Campbell, the Commandant, who, not supposing him to be within earshot, said in his terse fashion to Gordon: 'The news is all over town that that young woman of Audley's is breaking up the Taverner household.'

'Good God, Sir, you don't meant it? Confound her, why can't she give Charles a little peace?'

Sir Colin grunted. 'He'll be well rid of her,' he said dourly. He turned, and saw Colonel Audley standing perfectly still in the doorway. 'The devil!' he ejaculated. 'Well, you were not meant to hear, but since you have heard there's no helping it now. I'm away to see the Mayor.'

Colonel Audley stood aside to allow him to pass out of the room, and then shut the door, and said quietly: 'What's all this nonsense, Gordon?'

'My dear fellow, I don't know! Some cock-and-bull story old Campbell has picked up – probably from a Belgian, which would account for its being thoroughly garbled. Did I tell you that I found him bewildering the *maître d'hôtel* the other day over the correct way to lay a table? He kept on saying: "*Beefsteak, venez ici! Petty-patties, allez là!*" till the poor man thought he was quite mad.'

'Yes, you told me,' replied Audley. 'What is the news that is all over town?'

A glance at his face convinced Sir Alexander that evasion would not answer. He said, therefore, in a perfectly natural tone: 'Well, you came in before I had time to ask any questions, but according to Campbell there's a rumour afloat that Taverner is making a fool of himself over Lady Bab.'

'That doesn't seem to me any reason for accusing Bab of breaking up his household.'

'None at all. But you know what people are.'

'There's not a word of truth in it, Gordon.'

'No.'

There was a note of constraint in Gordon's voice which Audley was quick to hear. He looked sharply across at his friend, and read concern in his face, and suddenly said: 'Oh, for God's sake –! You needn't look like that! The very notion of such a thing is absurd!'

'Steady!' Gordon said. 'It isn't my scandal.'

'I know. I'm sorry. But I am sick to death of this town, and the gossip that goes on in it!' He sighed, and walked over to the desk, and laid some papers down on it. 'You had much better tell me, Gordon. What is it now? I suppose you've heard talk?'

'Charles, dear boy, if I had I wouldn't bring it to you,' replied Gordon. 'I don't know what's being said, or care.'

Colonel Audley glanced up and suddenly laughed. 'Damn you, don't look so sorry for me! What a set you are! I'm the happiest man on earth!'

'Famous! If you are, stop wearing a worried frown, and try going to bed at night for a change.' He lounged over to where Audley was standing, and gripped his shoulder, slightly shaking him. 'Damned fool! Oh, you damned fool!'

'I daresay. Thank God, I'm not a fat fool, however!' He drove a friendly punch at Gordon's ribs. 'Layers of it! What you need is a nice, hard campaign, my boy, to take some of it off.'

'Not a chance of it! We'll be in Paris a month from now. I'll give you a dinner at a little restaurant I know where they have the best Chambertin in the whole city.'

'I shall hold you to that. Where is it? I thought I knew all the restaurants in Paris.'

'Ah, you don't know this one! It's in the Rue de – Rue de – confound it, I forget the name of the street, but I shall find it quick enough. Hallo, here's the Green Baby!'

Lieutenant the Honourable George Cathcart, lately enrolled as an extra aide-de-camp, had come into the room. He owed his appointment to the Duke's friendship with his father, the British Ambassador at St Petersburg. He was only twenty-one years old, but during the period of Lord Cathcart's office as military commissioner to the Russian Army, he had acted as his aide-de-camp, and was able to reply now with dignity: 'I am *not* a green baby. I have seen eight general actions. And what's more,' he added, as the two elder men laughed, 'Napoleon commanded in them all!'

'One to you, infant,' said Audley. 'You have us on the hip.'

'Do you think Boney knows he's with us?' said Gordon anxiously.

'Oh, not a doubt of it! He has his spies everywhere.'

'Ah, then, that accounts for him holding off so long! He's frightened.'

'Oh, you – you – !' Cathcart sought for a word sufficiently opprobrious to describe Sir Alexander, and could find none.

'Never mind!' said Gordon. 'You won't be the baby much longer. We shall have his Royal Highness the Hereditary Prince of Nassau-Usingen with us soon, and we understand he's only nineteen.'

'He can't be of any use. What the devil do we want him for?'

'We don't want him. We're just having him to lend tone to the family. Charles, are you going to Braine-le-Comte?'

'Yes, I'm waiting for the letters now. Any message?'

'No. Such is my nobility of character that I'll go in your stead. Now, don't overwhelm me with thanks! Sacrifice is a pleasure to me.'

'I shan't. Pure self-interest gleams in your eye. Give my compliments to Slender Billy, and don't outstay your welcome. Is he giving a dinner party?'

'This ingratitude! How can you, Charles?' Gordon said.

'Easily. I shall laugh if you find the Duke has labelled the despatch "Quick".'

'If there's any "Quick" about it, you shall take it,' promised Gordon.

'Not I! You offered to go, and you shall go. Young Mr Cathcart will enlarge his military experience by kicking his heels here; and Colonel Audley will seize a well-earned rest from his arduous duties.' He picked up his hat from a chair as he spoke, and with a wave to Gordon and an encouraging nod to Cathcart, made for the door. There he collided with a very burly young man, whose bulk almost filled the aperture. He recoiled, and said promptly: 'In the very nick of time! Captain Lord Arthur Hill will be in reserve. Don't be shy, Hill! Come in! You know Gordon likes to have you near him: it's the only time he looks thin.'

Lord Arthur, who enjoyed the reputation of being the fattest officer in the Army, received this welcome with his usual placid grin, and remarked as the Colonel disappeared down the stairs: 'You fellows are always funning. What's happened to put Audley in such spirits? I suppose he hasn't heard the latest scandal? They tell me –'

'Oh, never mind what they tell you!' Gordon said, with such unaccustomed sharpness that Lord Arthur blinked in surprise. He added more gently: 'I'm sorry, but Audley's a friend of mine, and I don't propose to discuss his affairs or to listen to the latest scandal about his fiancée. It's probably grossly exaggerated in any case.'

'Oh, quite so!' said Lord Arthur hastily. 'I daresay there's nothing in it at all.'

Fifteen

*L*eaving Wellington's Headquarters, Colonel Audley made his way across the Park to Vidal's house. Barbara was not in, and as the butler was unable to tell Colonel Audley where she was to be found, he went back into the Park, and walked slowly through it in the direction of the Rue de Belle Vue. He was not rewarded by any glimpse of Barbara, but on reaching his brother's house he found Lady Taverner sitting with Judith, and indulging in a fit of weeping. He withdrew, nor did Judith try to detain him. But when Harriet had left the house he went back to the salon, and demanded an explanation of her grief.

Judith was reluctant to tell him the whole, but after listening for some moments to her glib account of nervous spasms, ridiculous fancies, and depression of spirits, he interrupted her with a request to be told the truth. She was obliged to confess that Peregrine's infatuation with Barbara was the cause of Harriet's tears. She described first the incident in the Park, feeling that it was only fair that he should know what had prompted Barbara's outrageous conduct.

He listened to her with a gradually darkening brow. 'Do you expect me to believe that Bab is encouraging Peregrine's advances out of spite?' he asked.

'*I* should not have used that word. Revenge, let us say.'

'Revenge! We need not employ the language of the theatre, I suppose! What more have you to tell me! I imagine there must be more, since I understand that the whole town is talking of the affair.'

'It is very unfortunate. I blame Harriet for the rest. She quarrelled with Perry, and I have no doubt made him angry and defiant. You know what a boy he is!'

He replied sternly: 'He is not such a boy but that he knew very well what he was about when he made advances to my promised wife!'

'It was very bad,' she acknowledged. 'But, though I do not like to say this to you, Charles, I believe it was not all his fault.'

'No! That is evident!' he returned. He walked over to the window and stood staring out. After a slight pause, he said in a quieter voice: 'Well, now for the rest, if you please.'

'I do not like the office of talebearer.'

He gave a short laugh. 'You need not be squeamish, Judith. I suppose I have only to listen to what the gossips are saying to learn the whole of it.'

'You would hear a garbled version, I assure you.'

'Then you had better let me hear the true version.'

'I only know what Harriet has told me. I am persuaded that had it not been for *her* conduct, which, you know, was very bad, the affair would never have gone beyond that one unfortunate evening in the suburbs. But she cut Lady Barbara in the rudest way! That began it. I could see how angry Lady Barbara was: indeed, I didn't blame her. I hoped her anger would cool. I think it might have – I think, in fact, it had cooled. Then came the Duchess of Richmond's party. I saw Lady Barbara look round the hall when she arrived, and I can vouch for her having made no sign to Perry. I don't think she gave him as much as a civil bow. There was a lull in the conversation; everyone was staring at Lady Barbara – you know how they do! – and Harriet made a remark there could be no misunderstanding. It was stupid and ill-bred: I know I felt ready to sink. She then told Perry that she wished to remove into the salon, saying that the hall was too *hot* for her. Lady Barbara could not but hear. It was said, moreover, in such a tone as to leave no room for anyone to mistake its meaning.'

She paused. The Colonel had turned away from the window,

and was attending to her with a look of interest. He was still frowning, but not so heavily, and at the back of his eyes she fancied she could perceive the suspicion of a smile. 'Go on!' he said.

She laughed. 'Worth said that in its way it was perfect. I suppose it was.'

'He did, did he? What happened?'

'Well, Lady Barbara just took Perry away from Harriet. It is of no use to ask me how, for I don't know. It may sound absurd, but I saw it with my own eyes, and I am ready to swear she neither moved nor spoke. She looked at him, and smiled, and he walked right across the room to her side.'

He was now openly laughing. 'Is that all? Of course, it was very bad of Bab, but I think Harriet deserved it. It must have been sublime!'

'Yes,' she agreed, but with rather a sober face.

He regarded her intently. 'Is there more, Judith?'

'I am afraid there is. As I told you, Harriet quarrelled with Perry. You remember, Charles, that you were in Ghent. It seems that Perry rode out with Lady Barbara before breakfast next morning. I believe she is in the habit of riding in the Allée Verte every morning.'

'You need not tell me that,' he interrupted. 'I know. She appointed Perry to ride with her?'

'So I understand. He made no secret of it, which makes me feel that he cannot have intended the least harm. But Harriet was suffering from such an irritation of nerves that she allowed her jealousy to overcome her good sense; they quarrelled; Perry left the house in anger; and, I dare say out of sheer defiance, joined a party Lady Barbara had got together to picnic in the country that evening. The gossip arose out of being the one chosen to drive with her in her phaeton. I am afraid he has done little to allay suspicion since. It is all such a stupid piece of nonsense, but oh, Charles, if you would but use your influence with Lady Barbara! Harriet is in despair, and indeed it is very disagreeable, to say the least of it, to have such a scandal in our midst!'

'Disagreeable!' he exclaimed. 'It is a damnable piece of work!' He checked himself, and continued in a more moderate tone: 'I beg your pardon, but you will agree that I have reason to feel this strongly. Is Peregrine with Bab now?'

'I do not know, but I judge it to be very probable.' She saw him compress his lips, and added: 'I think if you were to speak to Lady Barbara —'

'I shall speak to Barbara in good time, but my present business is with Peregrine.'

She could not help feeling a little alarmed. He spoke in a grim voice which she had never heard before, and when she stole a glance at his face there was nothing in its expression to reassure her. She said falteringly: 'You will do what is right, I am sure.'

He glanced down at her, and seeing how anxiously she was looking at him, said with a faint smile, but with a touch of impatience: 'My dear Judith, do you suppose I am going to run Peregrine through, or what?'

She lowered her eyes in a little confusion. 'Oh! of course not! What an absurd notion! But what do you mean to do?'

'Put an end to this nauseating business,' he replied.

'Oh, if you could! Such affairs may so easily lead to disaster!'

'Very easily.'

She sighed, and said rather doubtfully: 'Do you think that it will answer? I would have spoke to Perry myself, only that I feared to do more harm than good. When he gets these headstrong fits the least hint of opposition seems to make him worse. I begged Worth to intervene, but he declined doing it, and I daresay he was right.'

'Worth!' he said. 'No, it is not for him to speak to Peregrine. I am the one who is concerned in this, and what I have to say to Peregrine I can assure you he will pay heed to!' He glanced at the clock over the fireplace, and added: 'I am going to call at his house now. Don't look so anxious, there is not the least need.'

She stretched out her hand to him. 'If I look anxious it is on your account. Dear Charles, I am so sorry this should have happened! Don't let it vex you: it was all mischief, nothing else!'

He grasped her hand for a moment, and said in a low voice: 'Unpleasant mischief! It is the fault of that wretched up-bringing! Sometimes I fear – But the *heart* is unspoiled. Try to believe that: I know it.!'

She could only press his fingers understandingly. He held her hand an instant longer, then, with a brief smile, let it go and walked out of the room.

Peregrine was not to be found at his house, but Colonel Audley sent up his card to Lady Taverner, and was presently admitted into her salon.

She received him with evident agitation. She looked frightened, and greeted him with nervous breathlessness, trying to seem at ease, but failing miserably.

He shook hands with her, and put her out of her agony of uncertainty by coming straight to the point. 'Lady Taverner, we are old friends,' he said in his pleasant way. 'You need not be afraid to trust me, and I need not, I know, fear to be frank with you. I have come about this nonsensical affair of Peregrine's. Shall we sit down and talk it over sensibly together?'

She said faintly: 'Oh! How can I – You – I do not know how to –'

'You will agree that I am concerned in it as much as you are,' he said. 'Judith has been telling me the whole. What a tangle it is! And all arising out of my stupidity in allowing Peregrine to be my deputy that evening! Can you forgive me?'

She sank down upon the sofa, averting her face. 'I am sure you never dreamed – Judith says it is my own fault, that I brought it on myself by my folly!'

'I think the hardest thing of all is to be wise in our dealings with the people we love,' he said. 'I know I have found it so.'

She ventured to turn her head towards him. 'Perhaps I was a fool. Judith will have told you that I was rude and ill-bred. It is true! I do not know what can have possessed me, only when she came up to me, so beautiful, and – oh, I cannot explain! I am sorry: this is very uncomfortable for you!'

Her utterance became choked by tears; she groped for her

handkerchief among the sofa cushions, and was startled by finding a large one put into her hand. Her drenched eyes flew upwards to the Colonel's face; a sound between a sob and a laugh escaped her, and she said unsteadily: 'Thank you! You are very obliging! Oh dear, how can you be so – so – I am sure I don't know why I am laughing when my heart is broken!'

Colonel Audley watched her dry her cheeks, and said: 'But your heart isn't broken.'

Harriet emerged from his handkerchief to say with a good deal of indignation: 'I don't see how you can know whether my heart is broken or not!'

'Of course I can know, for I know mine is not.'

This seemed unanswerable. Harriet could only look helplessly at him, and wait for more.

He smiled at her, and took his handkerchief back. 'Crying won't mend matters. I rely on you to help me in this business.'

The idea was so novel that she blinked at him in surprise. 'How can I?'

'By behaving like the sensible woman I know you to be. Confess! didn't you mishandle Peregrine shockingly?'

'Yes, perhaps I did, but how could he be so faithless? I thought he loved me!'

'So he does. But he is very young. In general, a boy goes through a number of calf loves before he marries, but in your case it was different. I expect you were his first love.'

'Yes,' whispered Harriet.

'Well, that was charming,' he said cheerfully. 'Only, you see, this was bound to happen.'

'Bound to happen?'

'Yes, certainly. *You* have not been very well; *he* has been left to his own devices, and in circumstances where it would have been wonderful indeed if, at twenty-three, he had kept his head. This life we are all leading in Brussels is ruinous. Are you not conscious of it?'

'Oh yes, a thousand times yes! I wish I were safely at home!'

'I am glad to hear you say so, for that is what, if you will let me, I am going to advise you to do. Go home, and forget all this.'

'He won't go home!'

'Yes, he will. Only you mustn't reproach him just yet. Later, if you like, and still want to, but not now. He will be very much ashamed of himself presently, and wonder how he can have been such a fool.'

'How can you know all this?'

He smiled. 'I have been twenty-three myself. Of course I know. You may believe me when I tell you that this doesn't signify. No, I know you cannot quite see how that may be true, but I pledge you my word it is.'

She sighed. 'How kind you are! You make me feel such a goose! How shall I prevail upon Perry to take me home? What shall I say to him?'

'Nothing. I am going to have a talk with him, and I think you will find him only too ready to take you home.' He rose, and took out his card case, and, extracting a card, wrote something on the back of it with a pencil picked up from Harriet's escritoire. 'I'll leave this with your butler,' he said. 'It is just to inform Peregrine that I am coming to call on him after dinner tonight. You need not mention that you have seen me.'

'Oh no! But he is sure to be going out,' she said mournfully.

'Don't worry! He won't go out,' replied the Colonel.

She looked doubtful, but it seemed that the Colonel knew what he was talking about, for Peregrine, the card with its curt message in his waistcoat pocket, retired after dinner to his study on the ground floor. Dinner had been an uncomfortable meal. When the servants were in the room a civil interchange of conversation had to be maintained; when they left it, Harriet sat with downcast eyes and a heavy heart, while Peregrine, making a pretence of eating what had been put before him, wondered what Colonel Audley was going to say to him, and what he was to reply.

The Colonel, who had dined at the Duke's table, did not arrive until after nine o'clock, and by that time Peregrine had reached a state of acute discomfort. When the knock at last fell on the front door, he got up out of his chair and nervously straightened his cravat. When the Colonel was shown into the room, he was standing with his back to the empty fireplace, looking rather pale and feeling a trifle sick.

One glance at his visitor's face was enough to confirm his worst fears. This was going to be an extremely unpleasant interview. He wondered whether Audley would insist on satisfaction. He was not a coward, but the knowledge of having behaved very shabbily towards Audley set him at a disadvantage, and made him hope very much that the affair was not going to culminate in a meeting outside the ramparts in the chill dawn.

He tried, from sheer nervousness, to carry the thing off with a high hand, advancing with a smile, and saying with as much heartiness as he could muster: 'Well, Charles! How do you do?'

The Colonel ignored both the greeting and the outstretched hand. He laid his hat and gloves down on the table, saying in a voice that reminded Peregrine unpleasantly of Worth's: 'What I have to say to you, Peregrine, will not take me long. I imagine you have a pretty fair notion why I am here.'

'I –' Peregrine stopped, and then said defiantly: 'I suppose I have. Well, say it, then!'

'I'm going to,' said the Colonel grimly.

Peregrine squared his shoulders and set his teeth. At the end of three minutes he was bitterly regretting having invited the Colonel to speak his mind, and at the end of ten he would have been very glad if the ground had miraculously opened and swallowed him. The Colonel spoke with appalling fluency, and in the most biting of voices. What he said was so entirely unanswerable that after two stumbling attempts to defend himself Peregrine relapsed into silence, and listened with a white face to an exposition of his character which robbed him of every ounce of self-esteem.

When the Colonel at last stopped, Peregrine, who for some time had been standing by the window, with his back to him, cleared his throat, and said: 'I am aware how my conduct must strike you. If you want satisfaction, of course I am ready to meet you.'

This handsome offer was not received quite as Peregrine had expected. 'Don't talk to me in that nonsensical fashion!' said the Colonel scathingly. 'Do you imagine that you're a rival of mine?'

Peregrine winced, and muttered: 'No. It isn't – I didn't –'

'You are not,' said the Colonel. 'You are merely an uncon-ditioned cub in need of kicking, and the only satisfaction I could enjoy would be to have you under me for just one month!'

Peregrine resumed his study of the window blinds. It seemed that Colonel Audley had not yet finished. He spoke of Harriet, and Peregrine flushed scarlet, and presently blurted out: 'I know, I know! Oh, damn you, that will do! It's all true – every word of it! But I couldn't help it! I –' He stopped, and sank into a chair by the table, and covered his face with his hands.

Audley said nothing, but walked over to the fireplace, and stood there, leaning his arms on the mantelpiece, and looking down at the fire irons.

After a few minutes, Peregrine raised his head, and said haltingly: 'You think me a low, despicable fellow, and I daresay I am, but on my honour I never meant to – Oh, what's the use of trying to explain?'

'It is quite unnecessary.'

'Yes, but you don't understand! I never realised till it was too late, and even then I didn't think – I mean, I knew it was you she cared for, only when I'm with her I forget everything else! She's so beautiful, Audley!'

'Yes,' said the Colonel. 'I understand all that. The remedy is not to see any more of her.'

'But I shall see her! I must!'

'Oh no, you must not! I imagine you do not expect her to elope with you?'

'No, no! Good God, such an idea never –'

'Very well then. The only thing you can do, Peregrine, since the sight of her is so disastrous, is to leave Brussels.'

A long silence fell. Peregrine said at last, in a dejected tone: 'I suppose it is. But how can I? There's Stuart's ball tomorrow, and the Duke's on the 7th, and –'

'A civil note to Stuart will answer the purpose,' replied the Colonel, with the tremor of a smile. 'Your wife's indisposition is sufficiently well known to provide you with a reasonable excuse. If you need more, you can inform your friends that the recent activities on the frontier have made you realise the propriety of conveying your family back to England.'

'Yes, but – damn it, Charles, I won't dash off at a moment's notice like that!'

'A packet leaves Ostend on Monday,' said the Colonel. 'You may easily settle your affairs here tomorrow, and be off to Ghent on Sunday. That will enable you to reach Ostend in good time on Monday.'

Peregrine looked at him. 'You mean that I'm not to go to Stuart's tomorrow?'

'Yes, I do.'

'I ought at least to take my leave of Lady Barbara.'

'I will convey your apologies to her.'

Another silence fell. Peregrine got up. 'Very well. You are right, of course. I have been a fool. Only – *you* must know – how it is when she smiles at one. It – I never – oh, well!'

The Colonel walked over to the table, and picked up his hat and gloves. 'Yes, I know. But don't begin to think yourself in love with her, Perry. You're not.'

'No. Of course not,' said Peregrine, trying to speak cheerfully.

The Colonel held out his hand. 'I daresay I shan't see you tomorrow, so I'll say goodbye now.'

Peregrine gripped his hand. 'Goodbye. You're a damned good fellow, Charles, and I'm devilish sorry! I – I wish you very happy. She never thought of me, you know.'

'Thank you! Very handsome of you,' said the Colonel, with a smile. 'My compliments to Lady Taverner, by the way. Don't forget to make my excuses for not going up to take leave of her!'

'No. I'll tell her,' said Peregrine, opening the door, and

escorting him out into the hall. 'Goodbye! Come safely through the war, won't you?'

'No fear of that! I always take good care of my skin!' replied the Colonel, and raised his hand in a friendly salute, and ran down the steps into the street.

Peregrine went slowly upstairs to the salon. He had probably never been so unhappy in his life. Harriet was seated by the window, with some sewing in her hands. They looked at one another. Peregrine's lip quivered. He did not know what to say to her, or how to reassure her when his own heart felt like lead in his chest. All that came into his head to say was her name, spoken in an uncertain voice.

She saw suddenly that he was looking ashamed and miserable. The cause receded in her mind; it was not forgotten, it would never, perhaps, be forgotten, but it became a thing of secondary importance before the more pressing need to comfort him. She perceived that he was no older than his own son, as much in need of her reassurance as that younger Perry, when he had been naughty, and was sorry. She got up, throwing her stitchery aside, and went to Peregrine, and put her arms round him. 'Yes, Perry. It's no matter. It doesn't signify. I was silly.'

He clasped her to him; his head went down on her shoulder; he whispered: 'I'm sorry, Harry. I don't know what –'

'Yes.' She stoked his hair caressingly. The thought of Barbara no longer troubled her. A deeper grief, which she would never speak of, was the discovery that Peregrine was not a rock of strength for her to lean on, not a hero to be worshipped, but only a handsome, beloved boy who went swaggering bravely forth, but needed her to pick him up when he fell and hurt himself. She put the knowledge away from her. His abasement made her uncomfortable; even though she knew it to be make-believe he must be set on his pedestal again. She said: 'Yes, we'll go home. But how shall we settle our affairs here? Will it not take some time?'

He raised his head. 'No, I'll see to everything. You have only to pack your trunks. There is a packet leaving Ostend on Monday.'

'This house! Our passages! How shall we manage?'

'Don't worry: I'll do it all!

He was climbing back on to the pedestal; they would not speak of this incident again; they would pretend, each one of them, that it had not happened. In the end, Peregrine would believe that it had not, and Harriet would pretend, even to herself, because there were some truths it was better not to face.

Judith, anxiously awaiting the result of the Colonel's interview with his brother, could scarcely believe him when he told her curtly that the Taverners were leaving Brussels. She exclaimed: 'You don't mean it! I had not though it to be possible! What can you have said to constrain him?'

'There was no other course to follow. He was fully sensible of it.'

He spoke rather harshly. She said in a pleading tone: 'Do not be too angry with him, Charles! He is so young.'

'You are mistaken: I am not angry with him. I am excessively sorry for him, poor devil!'

'I am persuaded he will soon recover.'

'Oh yes! But that one so near to me should have caused this unhappiness –' He checked himself.

'If it had not been Lady Barbara it would have been another, I daresay.'

He was silent, and she did not like to pursue the topic. Worth presently came in, followed by the butler with the tea tray, and Judith was glad to see the Colonel rouse himself from a mood of abstraction, and join with all his usual cheerfulness in the ordinary commonplace talk of every day.

He did not go out again that evening, nor, next morning, was his horse saddled for an early ride. The sky was overcast, and a thin rain was falling. It stopped later, and by noon the sun was shining, but a press of work at Headquarters kept the Colonel busy all the morning.

In the afternoon there was a review in the Allée Verte of the English, Scottish, and Hanoverian troops quartered in and about Brussels. These constituted the reserve of the Army, and included the 5th Division, destined for the command of Sir Thomas Picton. They were crack troops, and the crowd of onlookers, watching them march past, felt that with such men as these to defend them there could be no need for even the most timorous to fly for safety to the coast.

'Some of our best regiments,' said the Duke, as they went past him.

There was good Sir James Kempt's brigade, four proud regiments: the Slashers, the 32nd, the Cameron Highlanders, and the 1st battalion of the 95th Riflemen, in their dark green uniforms and their jaunty caps.

There was fiery Sir Denis Pack, with his choleric eye, and his heavily arched brows, at the head of the Highland brigade. The Belgians began to cheer, for the kilt never lost its fascination for them, and in this 9th brigade was only one English regiment. The Royal Scots went by with pipes playing, followed by Macara, with his 42nd Royal Highlanders, and by handsome John Cameron of Fassiefern, with the 92nd: the Gay Gordons. The cheering broke out again and again; small boys, clinging to their fathers' hands, shouted: '*Jupes! Jupes! Jupes!*' in an ecstasy of delight; hats were waved, handkerchiefs fluttered; and when the last of the kilts and the tall hats with their nodding plumes had gone by, it was felt that the best of the review was over. Colonel von Vincke's Hanoverians excited little enthusiasm, but the Duke, as he watched them march past, said in his terse fashion: 'Those are good troops, too – or they will be, when I get good officers into them.'

The British ambassador's ball had been fixed to take place in the evening, and the Duke was entertaining a party at dinner before attending it. The Prince of Orange rode in from his Headquarters at Braine-le-Comte in high spirits, and full of news from the frontier; several divisional commanders were present, and the usual corps of foreign diplomats attached to the Anglo-Allied Army. The conversation related almost entirely to the approaching war, and was conducted, out of deference to the foreigners, in firm British-French by everyone but Sir Colin

Campbell, who, having, to the Duke's unconcealed amusement, made three *gaffes*, relapsed into defiant English, and relied on Colonel Audley to translate such of his remarks as he wished to be made public.

The evening was considerably advanced when the dinner party broke up, and the Duke and his guests were almost the last to arrive at Sir Charles Stuart's house. A cotillion was being danced; Colonel Audley saw Barbara, partnered by the Comte de Lavisse; and her two brothers: Harry with one of the Lennox girls, and George with Miss Elizabeth Conynghame. Miss Devenish was not dancing, but stood a little way away, beside Lady Worth. The Colonel soon went to them, claimed both their hands for dances, and stood with them for some moments, watching the progress of the cotillion. Catching sight of him Barbara kissed her fan to him. He responded with a smile, and a wave of the hand, and without any appearance of constraint. Judith could not but wonder at it, and was reflecting upon the unfairness of its having been Peregrine who had borne all the blame, when the Duke's voice, speaking directly behind her, made her turn her head involuntarily.

'Oh yes!' he was saying, in his decided way. 'The French Army is without doubt a wonderful machine. Now, I make my campaigns with ropes. If anything goes wrong, I tie a knot, and go on.'

'What is the most difficult thing in war, Duke?' someone asked him idly.

'To know when to retreat, and to dare to do it!' he replied, without hesitation. He saw Judith looking at him, and stepped up to her. 'How d'ye do? I'm very glad to see you. But you are not dancing! That won't do!'

'No, for I arrived when the cotillion was already formed. May I present to your Grace one who has long desired that honour? – Miss Devenish!'

Blushing, and torn between delight and confusion, Lucy made her curtsy. The Duke shook hands with her, saying with a laugh: 'It's a fine thing to be a great man, is it not? Very happy to make Miss Devenish's acquaintance. But what is all this standing-about? Don't tell me that there is no young fellow wishing to lead you out, for I shan't believe you!'

'No indeed, there are a great many!' replied Judith, smiling. 'But the thing is that Miss Devenish, like me, arrived too late to take part in this set. You will not see her standing about again tonight, I assure you.'

'That's right! Always dance while you may.'

'How long will that be, Duke?' enquired Judith.

'Oh, now you are asking me more than I can tell you! For as long as you please, I daresay.'

He nodded, and passed on. The cotillion came to an end soon after, and as Barbara walked off the floor Colonel Audley went forward to meet her.

She held out her hand to him. 'Wretch! Do you know how confoundedly late you are?'

'Yes. Have you kept my waltzes?'

'Oh, I am in a charming humour! You may have as many as you please.'

'All, then. How do you do, Lavisse? How do you go on in your neighbourhood?'

The Count shrugged. 'Oh, *parbleu*! We watch the frontier, and grow excited at the mere changing of an advance guard. And you? What news have you?'

'Very little. We hear of the Russians approaching Frankfort, and of General Kruse being at Maestricht. Hallo, Harry! *More* leave?'

Lord Harry Alastair had come up to them, and replied to this quizzing remark with a grin and a wink. Having decided upon first meeting him that Audley was a very good sort of a fellow, he had lost no time in making him feel one of the family. He had several times borrowed money from him, which, however, he generally remembered to pay back, soon treated him with affectionate respect, and had even asked his advice on the conduct of an alarming affair with a Belgian lady of easy virtue. The Colonel's advice had been so sound that his lordship declared he owed his preservation to it, and opined darkly that

Audley must have learned a thing or two worth knowing in Spain.

Barbara coolly referred to this affair, enquiring: 'How is the opulent Julie, Harry?'

'Lord, didn't I tell you? I got clear away. It was a near thing, I can tell you. All Charles's doing. He's a man of wide experience, Bab, I warn you!'

'Charles, how shocking! Spanish beauties?'

'Dozens of them!' said the Colonel.

'Depraved! What is this they are striking up? A waltz! I am yours, then.'

He led her on to the floor. She gave a sigh as his arm encircled her waist. He heard it, and glanced down at her. 'Why the sigh, Bab?'

'I don't know. I think it was voluptuous.'

He laughed. 'Abominable word!'

'You dance so delightfully!' she murmured. 'Where have you been hiding these last days?'

'At Headquarters, when I was not laming my horses on these shocking roads. By the by, *had* you to create a scandal in my family?'

'It seemed as though I had to,' she admitted. 'Did it come to your ears?'

'Every word of it. You stirred up a great deal of unhappiness, Bab.'

'What, by permitting poor bored Perry to gain a little experience? Nonsense! I behaved charmingly to him. Oh, you are recalling that I said I would be a sister to him! Well, so I was, until his ridiculous wife chose to challenge me. I won that encounter, however, and will sheathe my sword now, if you like.'

'I wish you had never drawn it, Bab. Lady Taverner wasn't a worthy foe.'

'Ah, that's charming of you! Well, I will engage to let him out of my clutches. I don't see him tonight: is he not coming?'

'No. He is going back to England.'

'Going back to England? He told me nothing of this!'

'It has only quite lately been decided. Brussels does not agree

224

with Lady Taverner. I am charged with a message from Peregrine: his apologies for not being able to take his leave of you in person.'

She was staring at him. 'It is your doing, in fact!' He nodded. Her breast heaved. 'Insufferable!' The word burst from her. 'My God, I could hit you!'

'Why, certainly, if you like, but I don't recommend you to do so in such a public place as this.'

She wrenched herself out of his hold, and walked swiftly off the dancing floor. He followed her, and took her hand, and drawing it through his arm held it there firmly. 'Calm yourself, Bab. If you want to quarrel with me you shall. I daresay Sir Charles would be pleased to lend us his morning-room for the purpose.'

'You are right!' she said, in a low, furious voice. 'This quarrel will not keep!'

He led her out of the ballroom and across the hall to a small parlour. There was no one in it, but the candles had been lit in the wall-sconces. The Colonel shut the door, and remained with his back to it, watching Barbara with a grave look in his eyes.

She went with long, hasty steps to the table in the centre of the room, and there faced him. When she spoke it was plain that she was making an effort to control her voice. 'I desire to understand you. Did you think I had fallen in love with that youth?'

'Of course not. It was he who fell in love with you.'

She made a contemptuous gesture. 'An affair of great moment, that!'

'It was an affair of very great moment to him, and to his wife.'

'What are either of them to you?'

'Not very much, perhaps. That does not signify. I wouldn't let you come between any husband and his wife.'

'Unfortunate! It is one of my pastimes!'

He was silent, his mouth shut hard, his arms folded across his chest. She said angrily: 'You have made me ridiculous! You dared – you *dared* to bundle Peregrine out of the country without a word to me! Do you wish me to confess myself in the wrong?

Very well, I behaved after the fashion of my family, badly! But not so badly that it was necessary to set the Channel between Peregrine and my charms! As though I would not have given him up at a word from you!'

'You are unreasonable,' he replied. 'Was there not a word from me? I seem to remember that you promised to set all to rights. I trusted you, but you broke your word to me. Is it for you to reproach me now? You took Perry from his wife out of spite. That makes me feel sick, do you know? If I thought that you knew what unhappiness – but you didn't! It was mischief – thoughtlessness! But, Bab, you cannot undo that kind of mischief merely by growing cool towards the poor devil you've made to fall in love with you! To see you, to hear your voice, is enough to keep that passion alive! The only course for Peregrine to follow was to go away.'

Her lip curled. 'This is decidedly in the tragic manner! Well! It is at least comforting to know that the scandal Peregrine's flight will create will be of your making. But I have an odd liking for creating my own scandals. You will agree that I am sufficiently adept to require no assistance.'

He moved away from the door, and came towards her. 'My God, where are we drifting? Is that the sum of your ambition, to create a scandal?'

'Oh, certainly! Did I not inform you of it, two months ago?'

'You don't mean what you say. Don't try to make me angry too! This wretched business is over. There is no need to discuss it, believe me!'

'You know very well that there is. You have given me a taste of high-handedness which I don't care for. I dare say you would like me to cry meekly on your shoulder, and promise not to offend again.'

'I would like to believe that you had a heart!'

'Oh, I have, and bestow little bits of it here and there in a most generous fashion.'

'Was *I* the recipient of one of those little bits?'

She grew white, and said abruptly: 'There has been enough of this. I warned you – did I not? – that you were making a mistake when you chose to invest me with all the virtues. Let me advise you to try your fortune with Miss Devenish. She would make you an admirable wife. You might be as possessive as you pleased, and she would love you for it. You can no longer persist in thinking me a suitable bride!'

'Every word you say seems designed to convince me that you are not!'

'Capital!' She did not speak quite steadily, but the smile still curled her lips. 'The truth is, my dear Charles, that we have both of us been fools. I at least should have known better, for I had the advantage of you in having been married before. I admit that I was a little carried away. But I am bored now, confoundedly bored!'

'I envy you!' he said harshly. 'Boredom seems a little thing compared with what I have had to suffer at your hands!'

'Your mistake! Boredom is the most damnable of all sufferings!'

'No! The most damnable suffering is to have your faith in one you love slowly killed. But what should you know of that? You don't deal in love!'

'On the contrary, I deal in it most artistically!'

'I have another word for it,' he said.

'The devil you have! There, it is off at last! You may have perceived that I have been tugging at your ring for the last ten minutes. It should, of course, have been cast at your feet some time ago, but the confounded thing was always too tight. Take it!'

He looked at her for a moment, then held out his hand without a word. She dropped the ring into it, turned sharply on her heel, and went out of the room.

It was some time before the Colonel followed her, but he went back into the ballroom presently, and sought out Miss Devenish. 'Forgive me!' he said. 'I have kept you waiting.'

She looked up with a start. 'Oh! I beg your pardon, I was not attending! What did you say?'

'Isn't this our dance?' he asked.

'Our dance – oh yes, of course! How stupid of me!'

She got up, resolutely smiling, but he made no movement to

lead her on to the floor. 'What is it?' he said quietly.

She gave a gasp, and pressed her handkerchief to her lips. 'Nothing! nothing!'

He took her arm. 'Come into the garden. You must not cry here.'

She allowed herself to be propelled towards the long, open window, but when they stood on the terrace she said in a trembling voice: 'You must think me mad! It is the heat: my head aches with it!'

'What is it?' he repeated. 'You are very unhappy, are you not? Can I do anything to help you?'

A deep sob shook her. 'No one can help me! Yes, I am unhappy. Oh, leave me, please leave me!'

'I can't leave you like this. Won't you tell me what the trouble is?'

'Oh no, how could I?'

'If you are unhappy I am in the same case. Does that make a bond?'

She looked up, trying to see his face in the dusk. 'You? No, that cannot be true! You are engaged to the woman you love, you –'

'No, not now.'

She was startled. 'Oh, hush, hush! What can you possibly mean?'

'My engagement is at an end. Never mind that: it is your unhappiness, not mine, that we are concerned with.'

She clasped his hand impulsively. 'I am so sorry! I do not know what to say! If there were anything I could do –'

'There is nothing to be done, or said. Lady Barbara and I are agreed that we should not suit, after all. I have told you my trouble: will you not trust me with yours?'

'If I dared, you would think me – you would turn from me in disgust!'

'I can safely promise that I should not do anything of the sort. Come, let us sit down on this uncomfortably rustic bench! . . . Now, what is it, my poor child?'

Sixteen

The news that Colonel Audley's engagement was at an end afforded curiously little satisfaction to his friends. They had all wanted to see it broken, and the crease smoothed from between the Colonel's brows, but the crease grew deeper, and a hard look seemed to have settled about his month. Occasionally the old, charming smile flashed out, but although he would talk lightly enough, laugh at the Headquarters' jokes, spar sometimes with his fellow-officers, and dance at the balls as willingly as he had ever done, those who knew him found his cheerfulness forced, and realised sadly that the gay hussar had vanished, leaving in his place an older man, who was rather aloof, often abstracted, and had no confidences to make. The young Prince of Nassau, entering shyly upon his very nominal duties on the Duke's staff, was even a little nervous of him, a circumstance which at first astonished Colonel Gordon. 'Stern?' he repeated. 'Audley? I think your Highness has perhaps mistaken the word?'

'*Un peu sévère*,' said the Prince.

'It's quite true,' said Fremantle. 'Damn the wench!' he added, giving his sash a vicious hitch. 'I wish to God she would go back to England and give the poor devil a chance to forget her! If she had a spark of sensibility she would!'

'Perhaps she doesn't want him to forget her,' suggested Gordon. 'Do you think she means to get him back?'

'If she does she ain't going the right way to work. They're saying she'll have that Belgian fellow – what's his name? Bylandt's brigade: all teeth and eyes and black whiskers. Ugh!'

'Lavisse,' said Gordon, apparently recognising the Count from this description without any difficulty.

'That's it. Such a dog with the ladies! Well, they'll make a nicely-matched pair, and I wish them joy of one another.'

'It must hit Charles pretty badly.'

'Of course it does! Look at him! The Prince here says he looks stern. I daresay that's how it would strike anyone who didn't know him. He looks to me as if he were enjoying a taste of hell.'

He had gauged the matter exactly. Colonel Audley, who had known that Peregrine Taverner's only hope of overcoming his infatuation lay in removing immediately from Barbara's neighbourhood, was tied to Brussels, and was obliged, day after day, to endure tantalising glimpses of Barbara, and night after night to see her waltzing with the Comte de Lavisse, looking up into his face with a smile on her lips and a provocative gleam in her eyes.

There were those who said that if Barbara had been quick to find consolation, so too had Audley. Neither was showing a bruised heart to the world. She had her handsome Belgian always at her side, and the Colonel seemed to have turned to little Miss Devenish. Well, said the interested, she would probably make him a good wife.

Judith, wishing to believe that Charles, freed from his siren, had become sensible of Lucy's worth, still could not quite convince herself that it was so. 'Do you think,' she asked her husband hopefully, 'that a man who had fancied himself in love with Lady Barbara might perhaps suffer from a revulsion of feeling, and so turn to her very opposite?'

'I really have no idea,' replied Worth.

'It is quite true that he has been very much in her company since the engagement was broken off. He dances with her frequently, and seems to look at her with a great deal of kindness. Only –'

She broke off. Worth regarded her with a faint smile. 'What profound observation are you about to make?' he enquired.

'I can't believe that if he were falling in love with Lucy he would be so unhappy. For he is, Worth: you can't deny it! There is an expression in his face when he thinks one is not looking at him – I would like to kill that wicked creature! *She* to jilt Charles!'

'This is all very bewildering,' complained Worth. 'I thought your hopes had been centred on her eventually doing so?'

'Yes, I did hope it, but I didn't know it had gone so deep with him. How wretched everything is! Even my spirits are quite oppressed. Lucy, too! She has no appearance of happiness, which makes me fear that Charles only feels towards her as a brother might.'

He raised his brows. 'Is she in love with him?'

'I very much fear it.'

'Now you have gone quite beyond me,' he said. 'I was under the impression that you had made up your mind that she should fall in love with him?'

'So I had, but I never dreamed then that he would become entangled with the horridest woman in Brussels. If he could requite Lucy's love it would be the most delightful thing imaginable, but I don't believe he does.'

'You will admit it to be early days yet for him to be bestowing his affections a second time.'

'Lady Barbara does not seem to find it too early! But Lucy!' She paused, frowning. 'I was afraid that the child was losing her prettiness over Lord George, but nothing could be more resolute than her shunning of his society. It has seemed to me that since Charles has been free, she has been regaining some of her spirits. But I would not for the world encourage *that* attachment, if there is no hope of Charles's affections becoming animated towards her.'

'May I make a suggestion?'

'Of course: what is it?'

'That you cease to worry your head over either of them,' said Worth. 'You will do no good by it, and if you begin to lose *your* prettiness you will find you have me to reckon with.'

She smiled, but shook her head. 'I cannot help but worry over them. If only Lady Barbara had had enough good feeling to go away from here! It must be painful beyond words for Charles to find himself continually in her company. My only dependence is on his being at last disgusted by her conduct.'

'We will hope for that agreeable end. Meanwhile, Charles can at least consider himself fortunate in being kept busy by the Duke.'

'I suppose so. What does he think of it? Has he made any comment?'

'None to me.'

'I daresay he might not care. I do not consider him a man of much sensibility. He is very amiable and unaffected, but there is a coldness, a lack of feeling for others, which, I confess, repels me at times.'

'He's a hard man, no doubt, but it is just possible, my dear, that he has matters of more moment to occupy him than the love affairs of his staff,' said Worth, somewhat ironically.

The Duke, however, did comment on the broken engagement, though not perhaps in a manner which would have raised Judith's opinion of his character, had she been able to hear him. 'By the by, Fitzroy,' he said, looking up from the latest missive from General Decken on the vexed question of the Hanoverian subsidy, 'what's this I hear about Audley?'

'The engagement is at an end, sir, that's all I've been told.'

'By God, I'm very glad to hear it!' said his lordship, dipping his pen in the standish. 'She was doing him no good, and I'm damned if I'll have my officers ruined for their duties by her tricks!'

That was all his lordship had to say about it, but, as Worth had correctly surmised, he was too busy to have any time to waste on the love affairs of his staff.

He had got his Army together, but spoke of it in the most disparaging terms, and was continually being chafed by the want of horses and equipment. General Decken's demands were rapacious: he could do nothing with the fellow, and would be obliged to refer the whole question of the Hanoverian subsidy to the Government. King William had taken some nonsense into his head over the junction of the Nassau contingent, under General Kruse, with the Dutch–Belgian troops, and was in one of his huffs. It was very difficult to know what went on in that froggish head, but his lordship believed the trouble to have arisen largely out of the Duke of Nassau's failure to write formally to His Majesty on the subject of these troops. Well, if the King would not have them his lordship would be obliged to make some other arrangement.

He had had an exasperating letter from his Royal Highness the Duke of Cambridge, putting a scheme before him for the augment-ation of the German Legion by volunteers from the Hanoverian line regiments. If the Royal Dukes would be a little less busy his lordship would be the better pleased. A nice feeling of dissatis-faction there would be if any such measures were put into action!

'*Both the Legion and the line would be disorganised exactly at the moment I should require their services,*' he wrote, and enclosed for his Royal Highness's digestion a copy of the objections to the precious scheme which he had sent to Lord Bathurst.

In polite circles he was still being flippant about the chances of war, but occasionally he dropped the pretence now. When Georgiana Lennox mentioned a pleasure party to Lille, or Tournay, which some officers had projected, he said decidedly: 'No, better let that drop.'

He gratified Mr Creevey by talking to him in the most natural way, joining him in the Park one day, where Mr Creevey was walking with his stepdaughters. He spoke quite frankly of the debates in Parliament on the war, and Mr Creevey, finding him so accessible, asked with one of his twinkling, penetrating glances: 'Now then, will you let me ask you, Duke, what you think you will make of it?'

'By God!' said his lordship, standing still. 'I think Blücher and myself can do the thing!'

'Do you calculate upon any desertion in Bonaparte's army!' enquired Creevey.

No, his lordship did not reckon upon a man. 'We may pick up a marshal or two,' he added, 'but not worth a damn.'

Mr Creevey mentioned the French King's troops at Alost, but that made his lordship give one of his whoops of laughter. 'Oh! Don't mention such fellows!' he said. 'No, no! I think Blücher and I can do the business!' He saw a British soldier strolling along at some little distance, and pointed to him. 'There,' he said. 'It all depends on that article whether we do the business or not. Give me enough of it, and I am sure.'

This was good news to take home to Mrs Creevey. It gave Creevey a better opinion of the Duke's understanding, too, and made him feel that in spite of every disquieting rumour from the frontier there was no need to fly for safety yet.

There were plenty of rumours, of course, but people had been alarmed so many times to no purpose that they were beginning to take only a fleeting interest in the news that came from France. It was said that everywhere on the road from Paris to the frontier preparations were being made for the movements of troops in carriages. It was said that Bonaparte was expected to be at Laon on June 6th; on June 10th report placed him at Maubeuge, but the Duke had certain intelligence of his being still in Paris, and issued invitations for a ball he was giving later in the month.

He was always giving balls, informal little affairs got up on the spur of the moment, but this was to be a splendid function, outdoing all the others which had been held in Brussels. There would be so many Royalties present that the Duchess of Richmond declared that there would be no room for a mere commoner. The Dutch King and Queen were coming; the Prince of Orange, and Prince Frederick; the Duke of Brunswick; the Prince of Nassau; Prince Bernhard of Saxe-Weimar, who commanded the 2nd Dutch–Belgic Brigade under General Perponcher; and of course the Duc de Berri, with his entourage of exalted personages.

There was much laughing rivalry between his lordship and the Duchess of Richmond over this question of balls. The best hostess in Brussels was not to be outdone by his lordship, and whipped in before him with her gilt-edged invitations for the night of June 15th. His lordship acknowledged himself to have been outmanœuvred, and was obliged to postpone his own ball until later in the month. 'Honours are even, however,' said Georgiana. 'For though Mama has the better date, the Duke has the King and Queen!'

'Pooh!' said her Grace. 'They will make the party very stiff and stupid. It will be all pretension, Duke! I promise you, my ball will be the success of the season!'

'No such thing! It will be forgotten in the success of mine.'

'It will be too hot for dancing by that time. Have you thought of that?'

'We will take this young woman's ruling on that point. Is it ever too hot for dancing, Georgy?' demanded his lordship, pinching her chin.

'No, never!' responded Georgiana. 'Mama, consider! If you provoke the Duke, perhaps he won't come to our party, and then we shall be undone!'

'That would be too infamous!' said the Duchess. 'I will not believe him capable of such dastardly behaviour.'

'No, no, I shall be there!' promised his lordship.

It was hard to believe that in the midst of these light-hearted schemes, other and much grimmer plans were revolving in his lordship's head. Foreigners, coming to Brussels, found the Duke's Headquarters a perplexing place, and his staff incurably flippant. No one seemed to take the approaching war seriously; young officers lounged in and out, talking to one another in a careless drawl that had so much annoyed General Röder; Lord Fitzroy could pause in the writing of important letters to exchange a joke with some friend who apparently thought nothing of interrupting his work; in the adjutant-general's teeming office, assistants and deputy-assistants demanded the names of bootmakers, or discussed the chances of competitors in the horse race at Grammont. It had never seemed to poor General Röder that anyone did any work, for work was mentioned in the most offhand fashion; yet the work was done, and the lounging young officers who looked so sleepy, and dressed so carelessly, carried the Duke's message's to the Army at a speed which made the Prussian general blink. They would drag themselves out of their chairs, groaning, twitting each other on the need for exertion, and stroll out with yawns, and lazy demands for their horses. You would see them mount their English hunters: 'Well, if I don't come back you'll know I've lost myself – Where *is* the damned place?' they would say. But long before you would have believed it possible they could have reached their destination, let alone have returned from it, there they were again, with nothing but the dust on their boots to betray that they had ever left Brussels. General Röder, accustomed to officers bustling about their business, clicking their heels together smartly in salute, discussing military matters with zest and enthusiasm, would never be able to understand these English, who, incomprehensibly, considered it bad *ton* to talk about anything but quite childish trivialities.

But General Röder had been relieved at last, thanking God to be going away from such Headquarters, and in his place a very different officer had come to Brussels. General Baron von Müffling brought no prejudices with him, or, if he did, he concealed them. Gneisenau had warned him to be very much on his guard in the English camp, but General Müffling had dealt with Gneisenau for many years, and knew him to be a prey to preconceived ideas. The General came to Brussels with an open mind, and immediately endeared himself to his hosts by confessing with a disarming smile that in his early studies of the English language he had never got beyond *The Vicar of Wakefield* and Thomson's *Seasons*. He made it his business to try to understand the English character, and to earn the Duke's confidence, and succeeded in both aims to admiration. The Duke found him to be a sensible man, given to speaking the plain truth; and the staff, accustomed to the glaring disapproval of General Röder, declared him to be a very good sort of a fellow, and made him welcome in their own easy unceremonious fashion.

He was soon on good terms with everyone. His manners were polished, his address a mixture of tact and dignity. He did not snort at graceless lieutenants, and he never committed the solecism of introducing grim topics of conversation at festive gatherings. He seemed, in fact, to enjoy life in Brussels, and to be amused by the Headquarters' jokes.

'I think you are something of a wizard, Baron,' said Judith. 'Your predecessor was never on such terms with us all, though he had been in Brussels for so long.'

'That is true,' he replied. 'But General Röder's irritability carried him too far. It is unfair for anyone in the midst of a foreign nation to frame his expectations on the ideas he brings with him. He should instead study the habits and customs of his hosts.'

'Do you find our customs very different from your own?'

'Oh yes, certainly! In your Army, for instance, I find some customs better than ours; others perhaps not so good. There is much to bewilder the poor foreigner, I assure you, madame. There are the Duke's aides-de-camp and *galopins*, for example. One is at first astonished to find that these gentlemen are of the best families, and count it an honour to serve the Duke in this manner. Then one is astonished to see them so nonchalant.' A smile crept into his eyes; he said: 'One finds it hard to believe them to be *des hommes sérieux*! But I discover that these so languid young officers make it a point of honour to ride four of your English miles in eighteen minutes, whenever the Duke adds the word *Quick* to his despatch. So then I perceive that I have been misjudging them, and I must reassemble my ideas.'

'How do you go on with the Duke?' asked Worth.

'Very well, I believe. He is agreeable, and in matters of service very short and decided.'

'Excessively short, I understand!' said Judith, with a laugh.

'Perhaps, yes,' he acknowledged. 'He exercises far greater power in the Army he commands than Prince von Blücher does in ours. It is not the custom, I find, to criticise or control your commander-in-chief. With us it is different. On our staff everything is discussed openly, in the hearing of all the officers, which is, I find, not so good, for time is wasted, and there are always what the Marshal calls *Trübsals-Spritzen* – I think you say, *trouble-squirts*?'

'No, you won't find the Duke discussing his plans with his officers,' said Worth. 'He is not held to be over-and-above fond of being asked questions, either.'

The Baron replied in a thoughtful tone: 'He *allows* questions. It would be more correct to say that he dismisses all such as are unnecessary. There is certainly an impatience to be observed sometimes, but his character is distinguished by its openness and rectitude, and must make him universally respected. There should be the utmost harmony between him and the Marshal, and the exertions of myself and of your estimable Colonel Hardinge must be alike directed towards this end.'

'Yes, indeed,' said Judith faintly. 'I am sure – And how do you like being in Brussels, Baron? I hope you do not agree with General von Röder in thinking us very frivolous!'

'Madame, it is not possible!' he said, with a gallant bow. 'Everyone is most amiable! One envies the English officers the beautiful wives who follow them so intrepidly to the seat of war.'

She could not help laughing. 'Oh! Are you married, Baron?'

'Yes,' he replied. 'I am the possessor of a noble-minded wife and three hopeful children.'

'How – how delightful!' said Judith, avoiding her husband's eye.

But in spite of the occasionally paralysing remarks he made, Baron Müffling was a man of considerable shrewdness, and he soon learned not only to adapt himself to his company but to induce the Duke to trust him. He was perfectly frank with his lordship. 'Prince Blücher will never make difficulties when the talk is of advancing and attacking. In retrograde movements his vexation sometimes overpowers him, but he soon recovers himself,' he told the Duke. 'General Gneisenau is chivalrous and strictly just, but he believes that you should always require from men more than they can perform, which is a principle which I consider as dangerous as it is incorrect. As for our infantry, it does not possess the same bodily strength or powers of endurance as yours. The greater mass of our troops are young and inexperienced. We cannot reckon on them obstinately continuing a fight from morning till evening. They will not do it.'

'Oh! I think very little of soldiers running away at times,' said his lordship. 'The steadiest troops will occasionally do so – but it is a serious matter if they do not come back.'

'You may depend upon one thing,' Müffling assured him. 'When the Prince has agreed to any operation in common, he will keep his word.'

Yes, the Duke could be more than ever sure that he and old Blücher would be able to do the business, in spite of his infamous Army, his inexperienced staff, and every obstacle put in his way by the people at home. His personal staff had been augmented by Lieutenant-Colonel Canning, who had served him in the Peninsula, and had had the temerity to beg to be employed again as an aide-de-camp; and by Major the Honourable Henry Percy, whom he had enrolled as an extra. He had nothing to complain of in his own family at least, though he was inclined to think it a great pity that Audley should not have recovered from his affair with Barbara Childe. However, it did not seem to be interfering with his work, which was all that signified.

Colonel Audley had, in fact flung himself into his work with an energy that must have pleased General Röder, had he been there to see it. It did not help him to forget Barbara, but while he was busy he could not be thinking of her, picturing the glimmer of her eyes, the lustre of her hair, the lovely smile that lifted the corners of her mouth; or torturing himself with wondering what she was doing, whether she was happy, or perhaps secretly sad, and, most of all, who was with her.

There was very little room for doubt about that, he knew. She would be with Lavisse, riding with him, or waltzing with him, held too close in his arms for propriety, his black head close to her flaming one, his lips almost brushing her ear as he murmured his expert lovemaking into it. She was behaving outrageously; even those who had grown accustomed to her odd flights were shocked. She had borrowed Harry's clothes, and had gone swaggering through the streets with George for a vulgar bet; she had won a race in her phaeton against a wild young ne'er-do-well in whose company no lady of breeding would have permitted herself to have been seen. She had appeared at the Opera in a classical robe which left one shoulder bare and revealed beneath its diaphanous folds more than even the most daring creature would have cared to show; she had set a roomful of gentlemen in a roar by singing in the demurest way a couple of the most shocking French ballads. The ladies present had been unable to follow the words of the songs, which were extremely idiomatic, but they knew when their husbands were laughing at improper jokes, and there was not a married man there who had not to endure a curtain lecture that night.

Lord Vidal was furious. He threatened to turn his sister out of doors, which made her laugh. He could not do it, of course, for ten to one she would simply install herself at one of the hôtels, and a pretty scandal that would create. There was only one person to whom she might possibly attend, and that was her grandmother. Vidal had written to that wise old lady the very night the engagement was broken off, begging her to exert her influence, but apparently she did not choose to do so, for she had neither answered his letter nor written one to Barbara.

Even Augusta was taken aback by Barbara's behaviour, and remonstrated with her. Barbara turned on her with a white face and blazing eyes. 'Leave me alone!' she said. 'I'll do what I choose, and if I choose to go to the devil it is my business, and not yours!'

'Oh, agreed!' said Augusta, shrugging bored shoulders. 'But I find your conduct very odd, I must say. If you are hankering after your staff officer –'

A harsh little laugh cut her short. 'Pray do not be ridiculous, Gussie! I had almost forgotten his existence!'

'I am happy to hear you say so, but I fail to see the purpose of all this running about. Why can you not be still?'

'Because I can't, because I won't!'

'Do you mean to have Lavisse?'

'Oh, don't talk to me of more engagements. I have had enough of being tied, I can assure you.'

'Take care he does not grow tired of your tricks. In my opinion you are playing a dangerous game.' She added maliciously: 'You are not irresistible, you know. Colonel Audley seems to have had no difficulty in consoling himself elsewhere. How do you like to be supplanted by a little nobody like Lucy Devenish?'

She had the satisfaction of seeing a quiver run over Barbara's face. Barbara replied, however, without hesitation: 'Oh, she'll make him a capital wife! I told him so.'

Lord George received the news of the broken engagement with careless unconcern. 'I daresay you know your own business best,' he said. 'I never thought him our sort.'

But Lord Harry nearly wept over it. 'The nicest fellow that ever was in love with you, and you jilt him for a damned frog!' he exclaimed.

'If you mean Lavisse, he is a Belgian, and not a Frenchman, and I did not jilt Charles Audley. He was perfectly ready to let me go, you know,' replied Barbara candidly.

'I don't believe it! The truth is you played off your tricks till no man worth his salt would stand it! I know you!'

She twisted her hands in her lap, gripping her fingers together. 'If you know me you must admit that we were not suited.'

'No!' he said hotly. 'You are only suited to a fellow like Lavisse! He will do very well for you, and I wish you joy of him!'

'Thank you,' she said, with a crooked smile. 'I have not yet accepted him, however.'

'Why not? He's as rich as Crœsus, and he won't care how you behave as long as you don't interfere with his little pleasures. You'll make a famous pair!'

He slammed out of her presence, and sought Colonel Audley. The interview was rather a trying one for the Colonel, for there was no curbing Harry's impetuous tongue. 'Oh, I say, sir, don't give her up!' he begged. 'She'll marry that Belgian fellow if you do, sure as fate!'

'My dear boy, you don't –'

'No, but only listen, sir! It ain't vice with Bab – really it ain't, She's spoilt, but she don't mean the things she says, and I'm ready to swear she's never gone beyond flirtation. I daresay you're thinking of that Darcy affair, but –'

'I am not thinking of any affair, Harry.'

'Of course I know she has the devil's own temper – gets it from my grandfather: George has it too – but perhaps you don't understand that the things they do when they are in their rages don't mean anything. Of course, George is a shocking fellow, but Bab isn't. People say she's heartless, but myself I'm devilish fond of her, and if she marries a damned rake like Lavisse it'll be just too much to bear!'

'I'm sorry, Harry, but you have it wrong. It wasn't I who broke the engagement.'

'But Charles, if you would only see her!'

'Do you imagine that I am going to crawl to your sister, begging to be taken on the strength again?'

Harry sighed. 'No. No, of course you wouldn't do that.'

'You say that she is going to marry Lavisse. If that is so, there is no possibility of our engagement's being renewed. In any case – No! it will not do. I have been brought to realise that, and upon reflection I think you must realise it too.'

'It's such a damned shame!' Harry burst out. 'I don't want Lavisse for a brother-in-law! I never liked any of the others half as well as you!'

He sounded so disconsolate that in a mood less bleak the Colonel must have been amused. His spirits were too much oppressed, however, for him to be able to bear such a discussion with equanimity. He was glad when Harry at last took himself off.

Harry's artless disclosures left a painful impression: an unacknowledged hope had lingered in the Colonel's mind that Barbara's encouragement of Lavisse might have been the outcome merely of pique. But Harry's words seemed to show that she was indeed serious. Her family looked upon the match as certain; Colonel Audley was forced to recall the many occasions during their engagement when she had seemed to feel a decided partiality for the Count. He had believed her careless flirtations to be only the expression of a certain volatility of mind, which stronger ties of affection would put an end to. It had not been so. The mischief of her upbringing, the hardening effect of a distasteful marriage, had vitiated a character of whose underlying worth he could still entertain no doubt. That the heart was unspoiled, he was sure: could he but have possessed himself of it he was persuaded all would have been different. Her conduct had convinced him that he had failed, and although, even through the anger that had welled up in him at their last meeting, he had been conscious of an almost overpowering impulse to keep her upon any terms, a deeper instinct had held him silent.

He had passed since then through every phase of doubt, sometimes driven so nearly mad by the desire to hold her in his arms that he had fallen asleep at night with the fixed intention of imploring her to let everything be as it had been before their quarrel, only to wake in the morning to a realization of the impossibility of building happiness upon such foundations. Arguments clashed, and nagged in his brain. He blamed himself for lack of tact, for having been too easy, for having been too harsh. Sometimes he was sure that he had handled her wrongly from the start; then a profounder knowledge would possess him, and he would recognise with regret the folly of all such arguments. There could be no question of tact or mishandling where the affections were engaged. He came back wearily to the only thing he knew to be certain: that since the love she had felt for him had been a light emotion, as fleeting as her smile, nothing but misery could attend their marriage.

After prolonged strife the mind becomes a little numb, repeating dully the old arguments, but ceasing to attach a meaning to them. It was so with Colonel Audley. His brain continued to revolve every argument, but he seemed no longer capable of drawing any conclusions from them. He could neither convince himself that the rift was final nor comfort himself with the hope of renewing the engagement. He was aware, chiefly, of an immense lassitude, but beneath it, and underlying his every word and thought, was a pain that had turned from a sharp agony into an ache which was always present, yet often ignored, because familiarity had inured him to it.

The unfortunate circumstance of his being obliged to remain in Brussels, where he must not only see Barbara continually but was forced to live under the eyes of scores of people whom he knew to be watching him, imposed a strain upon him that began very soon to appear in his face. Judith obliged to respect his evident wish that the affair should be forgotten, was goaded into exclaiming to Worth: 'I could even wish the war would break out, if only it would take Charles away from this place!'

Upon the following day, June 14th, it seemed as though her wish would be granted. She was at Lady Conynghame's in the evening, congratulating Lord Hay upon his win at the races at Grammont upon the previous day, when Colonel Audley came in with news of serious movement on the frontier. On June 13th, Sir Hussey Vivian, whose hussar brigade was stationed to the south of Tournay, had discovered that he had opposite him not a cavalry picket, as had previously been the case, but a mere collection of *douaniers*, who, upon being questioned, had readily disclosed the fact of the French army's concentration about Maubeuge. Shortly after the Colonel's entrance some other guests came in with a rumour that the French had actually crossed the frontier. All disbelief was presently put an end to by the Duke's arrival. He was calm, and in good spirits, but replied to the eager questions put to him that he believed the rumour to be true.

Seventeen

On the following morning the only news was of Sir Thomas Picton's arrival in Brussels. He was putting up at the Hôtel d'Angleterre with two of his aides-de-camp, Captain Chambers of the 1st Footguards, and an audacious young gentleman who ought to have been in London with the 1st battalion of that regiment, but who had procured leave, and contrived to get himself enrolled on Sir Thomas Picton's staff as honorary aide-de-camp. It seemed reasonable to Mr Gronow to suppose that he could quite well take part in a battle in Belgium and be back again in London in time to resume his duties at the expiration of his leave.

While Sir Thomas, a burly figure in plain clothes – for the trunks containing his uniforms had not yet arrived in Brussels – was seated at breakfast, Colonel Canning came in to say that the Duke wished to see him immediately. He finished his breakfast, and went off to Headquarters. He met Wellington in the Park, walking with the Duke of Richmond and Lord Fitzroy Somerset. All three were deep in conversation. Sir Thomas strode up to them, accosting his chief with his usual lack of ceremony, and received a chilling welcome.

'I am glad you are come, Sir Thomas,' said his lordship stiffly. He looked down his nose at the coarse, square-jowled face in front of him. He valued old Picton for his qualities as a soldier, but he had never been able to like him. 'As foul-mouthed an old devil as ever lived,' he had once said of him. Picton's familiarity annoyed him; he delivered one of his painful snubs. 'The sooner you get on horseback the better,' he said. 'No time is to be lost. You will take the command of the troops in advance. The Prince of Orange knows by this time that you will go to his assistance.

A slight bow, and it was plain that his lordship considered the interview at an end. Picton was red-faced, and glaring. Richmond, sorry for the rough old man's humiliation, said something civil, but Picton was too hurt and angry to respond. He moved away, muttering under his breath, and his lordship resumed his conversation.

No further news having arrived from the frontier, Brussels continued its normal life. It was generally supposed that the previous night's report had been another false alarm. The usual crowd of fashionables promenaded in the Park; ladies looked over their gowns for the Duchess of Richmond's ball; gentleman hurried off to the market to order posies for their inamoratas.

Colonel Audley had left his brother's house before Judith was up, but he came in about midday for a few minutes. There was no news; he told her briefly that the chances were that the concentration on Maubeuge was the prelude to a feint; and was able to assure her that no alarm was felt at Headquarters. The Duchess of Richmond's ball would certainly take place; the Prince of Orange was coming in from Braine-le-Comte to dine with the Duke about three; Lord Hill was already in Brussels; and Uxbridge and a host of divisional and brigade commanders were expected to arrive during the course of the afternoon, for the purpose of attending the ball. This certainly did not seem as though an outbreak of hostilities was expected; and further confirmation was later received from Georgiana Lennox, who, meeting Judith on a shopping errand during the afternoon, was able to report that Lord Hill had called in the Rue de la Blanchisserie, and had disclaimed any knowledge of movement on the frontier.

The Prince of Orange arrived in Brussels shortly after two o'clock, in his usual spirits, and after changing his dress in his house in the Rue de Brabant, went round to Headquarters. He had heard no further news, set very little store by the previous night's report, and had ridden in light-heartedly to take part in the evening's festivities, leaving Constant de Rebecque in charge at Braine-le-Comte.

'Well, well!' drawled Fremantle, when his Highness had gone off upstairs to pay his respects to the Duke. 'Our Corps Commander! One comfort is that old Constant will do much better without him. Think there's anything brewing, Canning?'

'I don't know. Another hum, I daresay. Müffling has heard nothing: he was in here a few minutes ago.'

The Duke dined early, sitting down to table with the Prince of Orange and the various members of his staff. At three o'clock a despatch was brought in for the Prince, from Braine-le-Comte. It was from Constant, containing a report received from General Behr at Mons, just after the Prince's departure from his headquarters. The 2nd Prussian Brigade of Ziethen's 1st Corps had been attacked early that morning, and alarm guns fired all along the line. The attack seemed to be directed on Charleroi.

The Duke ran his eye over the despatch. 'H'm! Sent off at 9.30, I see. Doesn't tell us much.'

'Behr had it from General Steinmetz, through Van Merlen,' said the Prince. 'That would put the attack in the small hours, for Steinmetz's despatch you see, was sent off from Fontaine-l'Evêque. Sir, do you think –?'

'Don't think anything,' said his lordship. 'I shall hear from Grant presently.'

At four o'clock Müffling came in with a despatch from General Ziethen, which was dated 9 am from Charleroi. It contained the brief information that the Prussians had been engaged since 4 am. Thuin had been captured by the French, and the Prussian outposts driven back. General Ziethen hoped the Duke would concentrate his army on Nivelles, seven miles to the west of the main Charleroi-Brussels chaussée.

The Duke remained for some moments deep in thought. Müffling presently said: 'How will you assemble your army, sir?'

The Duke replied in his decided way: 'I will order all to be ready for instant march, but I must wait for advice from Mons before fixing a rendezvous.'

'Prince Blücher will concentrate on Ligny, if he has not already done so.'

'If all is as General Ziethen supposes,' said the Duke, 'I will concentrate on my left wing the Corps of the Prince of Orange. I shall then be *à portée* to fight in conjunction with the Prussian Army.'

He gave back Ziethen's despatch and turned away. It was evident to Müffling that he had no more to say, but he detained him for a moment with the question. *When* would he concentrate his army? The Duke repeated: 'I must wait for advice from Mons.'

He spoke in a calm voice, but a little while after Müffling had left the house he showed signs of some inward fret, snapping at Canning for not having immediately understood a trivial order. Canning came away with a rueful face, and enquired of Lord Fitzroy what had gone wrong.

'No word from Grant,' replied Fitzroy. 'It's very odd: he's never failed us yet.'

'Looks as though the whole thing's nothing but a feint,' remarked Fremantle. 'Trust Grant to send word if there were anything serious on hand!'

This belief began to spread through the various offices: if Colonel Grant, who was the cleverest intelligence officer the army had ever had, had not communicated with Headquarters, it could only be because he had nothing of sufficient importance to report.

The afternoon wore on, with everyone kept at his post in case of emergency, but a general feeling over all that the affair would turn out to be a false alarm. Previous scares were recalled; someone argued that if Bonaparte had been in Paris on June 10th with the Imperial Guard, it was impossible for him yet to have reached the frontier.

At five o'clock a dragoon arrived from Braine-le-Comte with despatches for Lord Fitzroy. The Duke was in his office with Colonel de Lancey, but be broke off his conversation as Fitzroy came in, and barked out: 'Well?'

'Despatches from Sir George Berkeley, sir, enclosing reports from General Dörnberg, Baron Chassé, and Baron van Merlen.'

'Dörnberg, eh?' His lordship's eye brightened. 'Has he heard from Grant?'

'No, sir,' replied Fitzroy, laying the papers before him. 'General Dörnberg's letter, as your lordship will see, is dated only 9.30 am.'

'Nine-thirty!' An explosion seemed imminent; his lordship picked up the letters and read them with a cold eye and peevishly pursed lips. Dörnberg, at Mons, merely stated that he had found a picket of French Lancers on the Bavay road, and that the troops at Quivrain had been replaced by a handful of National Guards and Gendarmes. All the French troops appeared to be marching towards Beaumont and Philippeville.

The Duke gave the despatch to De Lancey without comment, and picked up Chassé's and Van Merlen's reports. Van Merlen, writing at an early hour of the morning from Saint Symphorien, stated that the Prussians under General Steinmetz were retiring from Binche to Gosselies, and that if pressed the I Corps would concentrate at Fleurus.

De Lancey looked up with a worried frown from the despatch in his hand. He was finding the post of Quartermaster-General arduous; he had brought a young bride with him to Brussels, too, and was beginning to look rather careworn. 'Then it comes to this, sir, that we have no intelligence later than nine this morning.'

'No. All we know is that there has been an attack on the Prussian outposts and that the French have taken Thuin. I can't move on that information.'

His lordship said no more, but both De Lancey and Fitzroy knew what was in his mind. He had always been jealous of his right, for in that direction lay his communication lines. It was his opinion that the French would try to cut him off from the seaports; he was suspicious of the attack on the Prussians: it looked to him like a feint. He would do nothing until he received more certain information.

Between six and seven o'clock he issued his first orders. The Quartermaster-General's staff woke to sudden activity. Twelve messages had to be written and carried to their various destinations. The whole of the English cavalry was to collect at Ninove that night; General Dörnberg's brigade of Light Dragoons of the Legion to march on Vilvorde; the reserve artillery to be ready to move at daybreak; General Colville's 4th Infantry Division, except the troops beyond the Scheldt, to march eastward on Grammont; the 10th Brigade, just arrived from America under General Lambert and stationed at Ghent, to move on Brussels; the 2nd and 5th Divisions to be at Ath in readiness to move at a moment's notice; the 1st and 3rd to concentrate at Enghien and Braine-le-Comte. The Brunswick Corps was to concentrate on Brussels; the Nassau contingent upon the Louvain road; and the 2nd and 3rd Dutch–Belgic divisions under Generals Perponcher and d'Aubremé were ordered to concentrate upon Nivelles. His lordship had received no intelligence from Mons, and was still unwilling to do more than to put his Army in a state of readiness to move at a moment's notice. The Quartermaster-General's office became a busy hive, with De Lancey moving about in it with his sheaf of papers, and frowning over his maps as he worked out the details for the movements of the divisions, sending out his messages, and inwardly resolving to be done with the Army when this campaign was over. He was a good officer, but the responsibility of his post oppressed him. Too much depended on his making no mistakes. The Adjutant-General had to deal with the various duties to be distributed, with morning-states of men and horses, and with the discipline of the Army, but the Quartermaster-General's work was more harassing. On his shoulders rested the task of arranging every detail of equipment, of embarkation, of marching, halting, and quartering the troops. It was not easy to move an army; it would be fatally easy to create chaos in concentrating troops that were spread over a large area. De Lancey checked up his orders again, referred to the maps, remembered that such-and-such a bridge would not bear the passage of heavy cavalry, that this or that road had been reported in a bad state. At the back of his busy mind another and deeper anxiety lurked. He would send Magdalene to Ghent, into safety. He hoped she would consent to go; he would know no peace of mind if she were left in this unfortified and perilously vulnerable town.

The stir in the Quartermaster-General's office, the departure of deputy-assistants charged with the swift delivery of orders to the divisions of the Army, infected the rest of the staff with a feeling of expectation and suppressed excitement. A few moderate spirits continued to maintain their belief in the attack's being nothing more than an affair of outposts; but the general opinion was that the Anglo-Allied Army would shortly be engaged. Colonel Audley went to his brother's house at seven, to dress for the ball, and on his way through the Park encountered a tall rifleman with a pair of laughing eyes, and a general air of devil-may-care. He thrust out his hand. 'Kincaid!'

The rifleman grinned at him. 'A staff officer with a worried frown! What's the news?'

'There's damned little of it. Are you going to the ball tonight?'

'What, the Duchess of Richmond's? Now, Audley, *do* I move in those exalted circles? Of course I'm not! However, several of ours are, so the honour of the regiment will be upheld. They tell me there's going to be a war. A real *guerra al cuchillo*!'

'Where *do* you get your information?' retorted the Colonel.

'Ah, we hear things, you know! Come along, out with it! What's the latest from the frontier?'

'*Nada, nada, nada*!' said the Colonel.

'Yes, you look as though there were nothing. All alike, you staff officers: close as oysters! My people have been singing *Ahé Marmont* all the afternoon.'

'There's been no news sent off later than nine this morning. Are your pack-saddles ready?'

Kincaid cocked an eyebrow. 'More or less. They won't be wanted before tomorrow, at all events, will they?'

'I don't know, but I'll tell you this, Johnny: if you've any preparations to make, I wouldn't, if I were you, delay so long. Goodbye!'

Kincaid gave a low whistle. 'That's the way it is, is it? Thank you, I'll see to it!'

Colonel Audley waved to him and strode on. When he reached Worth's house he found that both Worth and Judith were in their rooms, dressing for the ball. He ran up the stairs to his own apartment, and began to strip off his clothes. He was standing before the mirror in his shirt and gleaming white net pantaloons, brushing his hair, when Worth presently walked in.

'Hallo, Charles! So you go to the ball, do you? Is there any truth in the rumours that are running round the town?'

'The Prussians were attacked this morning. That's all we know. The Great Man's inclined to think it a feint. He doesn't think Boney will advance towards Charleroi: the roads are too bad. It's more likely the real attack will be on our right centre. Throw me over my sash, there's a good fellow!'

Worth gave it him, and watched him swathe the silken folds round his waist, so that the fringed ends fell gracefully down one thigh. The Colonel gave a last touch to the black stock about his neck, and struggled into his embroidered coat.

'Are you dining with us?'

'No, I dined early with the Duke. I don't know when I shall get to the ball: we've orders to remain at Headquarters.'

'That sounds as though something is in the wind.'

'Oh, there is something in the wind,' said the Colonel, flicking one hessian boot with his handkerchief. 'God knows what, though! We're expecting to hear from Mons at any moment.'

He picked up his gloves and cocked hat, charged Worth to make his excuses to Judith, and went back to the Rue Royale.

The Duke was in his dressing-room when, later in the evening, Baron Müffling came round to Headquarters with a despatch from Gneisenau, at Namur, but he called the Baron in to him immediately. The despatch confirmed the earlier tidings sent by Ziethen, and announced that Blücher was concentrating at Sombreffe, near the village of Ligny. General Gneisenau wanted to know what the Duke's intentions were, but the Duke was still obstinately awaiting news from Mons. He stood by the table, in his shirt-sleeves, an odd contrast to the Prussian in his splendid dress-uniform, and said with a note of finality in his voice which the Baron had begun to know well: 'It is impossible for me to resolve on a point of concentration till I shall have received the intelligence from Mons. When it arrives I will immediately advise you.'

There was nothing for Müffling to do but to withdraw. If he chafed at the delay, he gave no sign of it. He was aware of the Duke's obsession that the attack would fall on his right, and though he did not share this belief he was wise enough to perceive that nothing would be gained by argument. He went back to his own quarters to make out his report to Blücher, keeping a courier at his door to be in readiness to ride off as soon as he should have discovered the Duke's intentions.

The long-awaited news from Mons came in soon after he left the Duke. There had been no further intelligence from Ziethen all day: what had occurred before Charleroi was still a matter for conjecture; and the despatch from Mons contained no tidings from Colonel Grant, but had been sent in by General Dörnberg, who reported that he had no enemy in front of him, but believed the entire French Army to be turned toward Charleroi.

It now seemed certain that a concerted move was being made upon Charleroi, but whether the town had fallen or was still in Prussian hands, how far the French had penetrated across the frontier, was still unknown. After a few minutes' reflection, the Duke sent for De Lancey, and dictated his After-Orders. The disposition of the Dutch–Belgic divisions at Nivelles was to remain unchanged; the 1st and 4th British Divisions were ordered to move on Braine-le-Comte and Enghien; Alten's 3rd Division to move from Braine-le-Comte to Nivelles, and all other divisions to march on Mont St Jean.

The Duke gave his directions in his clear, concise way, finished his toilet, and, a little time before midnight, drove round to General Müffling's quarters. Müffling had been watching the clock for the past hour, but he received the Duke without the least appearance of impatience.

'Well! I've got news from Dörnberg,' said his lordship briskly. 'Orders for the concentration of my Army at Nivelles and Quatre-Bras are already despatched. Now, I'll tell you what, Baron: you and I will go to the Duchess's ball, and start for Quatre-Bras in the morning. You know all Bonaparte's friends in this town will be on tiptoe. The well-intentioned will be pacified if we go, and it will stop our people from getting into a panic.'

The ball had been in progress for some time when the Duke's party arrived in the Rue de la Blanchisserie. All the Belgian and Dutch notables were present; the Prince of Orange, the Duke of Brunswick, the British Ambassador, the foreign commissioners, the Earl of Uxbridge, Lord Hill, and such a host of generals with their aides-de-camp, fashionable young Guardsmen, and officers of cavalry regiments, that the lilac crapes and figured muslins were rendered insignificant by the scarlet and gold which so overpoweringly predominated. Jealous eyes dwelled from time to time on Barbara Childe, who, with what Lady Francis Webster almost tearfully described as fiendish cunning, had appeared midway through the evening in a gown of unrelieved white satin, veiled by silver net drapery à l'Ariane. Nobody else had had such forethought; indeed, complained Lady John Somerset, who but Bab Childe would have the audacity to wear a gown like a bridal robe at a ball? The puces swore faintly at the scarlet uniforms; the celestial blues and the pale greens died; but the white satin turned all the gold-encrusted magnificence into a background to set it off.

'One comfort is that that head of hers positively shrieks at the uniforms!' said a lady in a Spanish bodice and petticoat.

Barbara had come with the Vidals, but Lavisse was missing from her usual escort. None of the officers invited from General Perponcher's division had put in an appearance, a circumstance which presently began to cause a little uneasiness. No one knew just what was happening on the frontier, but wild rumours had

254

been current all day, and the news of the Army's having been put in motion had begun to spread.

It was a very hot night, and the young people, overcoming the prudence of their elders, had had the windows opened in the ballroom. But hardly a breath of air stirred the long curtains, and young gentlemen in tight socks and high collars had begun to mop their brows and agonise over the possible wilting of the starched points of shirt-collars, so nattily protruding above the folds of their black cravats.

The ballroom formed a wing of its own to the left of the hall, and had an alcove at one end and a small ante-room at the other. It was prepared with a charming trellis pattern of roses and had several french windows on each side of it. It opened on to a passage that ran the length of the house, bisecting the hall in the middle. At the back of the hall, and immediately opposite the front door, was the entrance to the garden, with the dining-room on one side of it and two smaller apartments, one of which the Duke of Richmond used as a study, on the other. A fine staircase and a billiard-room flanked the front door. The Duke's study was inhospitably closed, but every other room on the ground floor had been flung open. Candles burned everywhere; and banks of roses and lilies, anxiously sprinkled from time to time by the servants, overcame the hot smell of wax with their heavier scent.

Everything that could make the ball the most brilliant of the season had been done. There was no Catalani in Brussels to sing at the party, but the Duchess had a much more original surprise for her guests than the trills of a mere prima donna. She had contrived to get some of the sergeants and privates of the 42nd Royal Highlanders and the 92nd Foot to dance reels and strathspeys to the music of their own pipes. It was a spectacle that enchanted everyone: scarlet, and rifle-green, and the blaze of hussar jackets were at a discount when the weird sound of the pipes began and the Highlanders came marching in with their kilts swinging, tartans swept over their left shoulders, huge white sporrans bobbing, and the red chequered patterns of their stockings twinkling in the quick steps of the reel. A burst of clapping greeted their appearance; the strathspeys and the sword-dances called forth shouts of Bravo! One daring young lady threw the rose she had been wearing at a blushing private; everyone began to laugh, one or two ladies followed her example, and the Highlanders retired presently, almost over-whelmed by the admiration they had evoked.

But when the skirl of the pipes had died away and the orchestra struck up a waltz, the brief period of forgetfulness left the company. The young people thronged on to the floor again, but older guests gathered into little groups, discussing the rumours, and buttonholing every general officer who happened to be passing. None of the generals could give the anxious any news; they all said they had heard nothing fresh – even Uxbridge and Hill, who, it was thought, must have received certain intelligence. Hill wore his habitual placid smile; Uxbridge was debonair, and put all questions aside with a light-heartedness he was far from feeling. He had had, earlier in the evening, a somewhat disconcerting interview with the Duke. He stood next to him in seniority, and would have liked a little information himself. He had been warned not to ask questions of the Duke if he wished to avoid a snub, but he had prevailed upon Alava, whom he knew to be a personal friend of Wellington, to pave the way for him. But it had not been very successful. 'Plans! I have no plans!' had exclaimed his lordship. 'I shall be guided by circumstances.' Uxbridge had stood silent. His lordship using a milder tone, had clapped him on the shoulder, and added: 'One thing is certain: you and I will both do our duty, Uxbridge.'

The Duke's absence from the ball increased the uneasiness that had lurked in everyone's mind all day. When he arrived soon after midnight, Georgiana Lennox darted off the floor towards him, dragging Lord Hay by the hand, and demanded breathlessly: 'Oh, Duke, do pray tell me! Are the rumours true? Is it war?'

He replied gravely: 'Yes, they are true: we are off tomorrow.'

She turned pale; his words, overheard by those standing near, were repeated, and spread quickly round the ballroom. The music went on, and some of the dancing, but the chatter died, only to break out again, voices sharper, and a note of excitement audible in the medley of talk. Officers who had ridden in from a distance to attend the ball hurried away to rejoin their regiments, some with sober faces, some wildly elated, some lingering to exchange touching little keepsakes with girls in flower-like dresses who had stopped laughing, and clung with frail, unconscious hands to a scarlet sleeve, or the fur border of a pelisse. One or two general officers went up to confer with the Duke, and then returned to their partners, saying cheerfully that there was no need for anyone to be alarmed: they were not going to the war yet; time enough to think of that when the ball was over.

From scores of faces the polite company masks seemed to have slipped. People had forgotten that at balls they must smile, and hide whatever care or grief they owned under bright, artificial fronts. Some of the senior officers were looking grave; here and there a rigid, meaningless smile was pinned to a mother's white face, or a girl stood with a fallen mouth, and blank eyes fixed on a scarlet uniform. A queer, almost greedy emotion shone in many countenances. Life had become suddenly an urgent business, racing towards disaster, and the craving for excitement, the breathless moment compound of fear, and grief, and exaltation, when the mind sharpened, and the senses were stretched as taut as the strings of a violin, surged up under the veneer of good manners, and shone behind the dread in shocked young eyes. For all the shrinking from tragedy looming ahead, there was yet an unacknowledged eagerness to hurry to meet whatever horror lurked in the future; if existence were to sink back to the humdrum, there would be disappointment behind the relief, and a sense of frustration.

The ball went on; couples, hesitating at first, drifted back into the waltz; Sir William Ponsonby seized a girl in a sprigged muslin dress round the waist, and said gaily: 'Come along! I can't miss this! It is quite my favourite tune!'

Georgiana felt a tug at her sleeve, and turned to find Hay

stammering with excitement, his eyes blazing. 'Georgy! We're going to war! Going into action again Boney himself! Oh, I say, come back and dance this! Was there ever anything so splendid?'

'How can you, Hay?' she exclaimed. 'You don't know what you are talking about!'

'Don't I, by Jove! Why, we've been living for this moment!'

'I won't listen to you! It's not splendid: it's the most dreadful thing that has ever happened!'

'But, Georgy –!'

'Go and find someone else to dance with you!' she said, almost crying, and turned away from him to seek refuge beside Lady Worth.

Hay stared after her in a good deal of astonishment, but was diverted from his purpose of following her to make his peace by having his arm grasped by a kindred spirit. 'Hay, have you heard?' said Harry Alastair eagerly. 'Ours have been ordered to Braine-le-Comte. I'm off immediately! Are you coming? Oh no, of course! You'll stay for General Maitland. By Jove, won't we give the French a hiding! There's Audley! I must speak to him before I go!'

He darted off to where the Colonel was standing in conversation with Lord Robert Manners, and stood, impatient but decorous, until it should please the Colonel to notice him. This Audley soon did, smiling to see him so obviously fretting to be off.

'Hallo, Harry! You've got your wish, you see!'

'By Gad, haven't I just! I only came up to say goodbye and wish you luck. I'm off to Braine-le-Comte, you know. It's my first engagement! Lord, won't some of the fellows at home be green with envy!'

'Well, mind you capture an Eagle,' said the Colonel, holding out his hand. 'I daresay I shall run up against you sometime or other, but in case I don't, the best of luck to you. Take care of yourself!'

Lord George Alastair came striding out of the ante-room behind them as Harry wrung the Colonel's hand. He merely nodded to the Colonel, but said curtly to his brother: 'Are you off, Harry? I'll go with you as far as the centre of the town. I'm for Ninove. Where are you for?'

'Braine-le-Comte. You don't look very cheerful, I must say. Been bidding someone a tender farewell?'

'That's it: come along, now!'

'Wait a bit, here's Bab!'

Colonel Audley turned his head quickly, and saw Barbara coming across the room towards him. Her eyes were fixed on her brothers, but as though she were conscious of his gaze she glanced in his direction, and flushed.

Colonel Audley thrust a hand which he found to be shaking slightly in Lord Robert's arm, and walked away with him.

The Duke had gone to sit beside Lady Helen Dalrymple on the sofa. She found him perfectly amiable but preoccupied, breaking off his conversation with her every now and then to call some officer to him to receive a brief instruction. The Prince of Orange and the Duke of Brunswick both conferred with him for some minutes, and then left the ball together, the Prince heedless of everything but the excitement of the moment, the Duke calm, bestowing his grave smile on an acquaintance encountered in the doorway, not forgetting to take his punctilious leave of his hostess.

A few minutes later, Colonel Audley went up to Judith and touched her arm, saying quietly: 'I'm off, Judith. Tell Worth, will you? I haven't time to look for him.'

She clasped his hands. 'Oh, Charles! Where?'

'Only to Ath, with a message, but it's urgent. I'm not likely to return to Brussels tonight. Don't be alarmed, will you? You will see what a dressing we shall give Boney!'

The next instant he was gone, slipping out of the ballroom without any other leave-taking than a word to his hostess. Others followed him, but in spite of the many departures there seemed to be no empty places in the dining-room when the guests presently went in to supper. Tables were arranged round the room; the junior officers, under the wing of Lord William

Lennox, with an arm in a sling and bandages and sticking-plaster adorning his head, crowded round the sideboard, and were honoured by Lord Uxbridge's calling out to them, with a brimming glass held in his hand: 'A glass of wine with the side-table!'

The Duke sat with Georgiana beside him, He seemed to be in good spirits; his loud laugh kept breaking out; he had given Georgiana a miniature of himself, done by a Belgian artist, and was protesting jokingly at her showing it to those seated near them.

Supper had hardly begun when the Prince of Orange came into the room, looking very serious. He went straight to the Duke, and bent over him, whispering in his ear.

A despatch had been brought in by one of his aides-de-camp from Baron Constant at Braine-le-Comte. It was dated as late as 10.30 pm, and reported that Charleroi had fallen not two hours after Ziethen's solitary message had been sent off that morning. The French had advanced twenty miles into Belgian territory. The Prussians had been attacked at Sombreffe by Grouchy, with Vandamme's Corps in support, and had fallen back on Fleurus; Ney had pushed forward on the left to Frasnes, south of Quatre-Bras, with an advance guard of cavalry, but had encountered there Prince Bernhard of Saxe-Weimar, who, taking the law courageously into his own hands, had moved forward from Genappe with one Nassau battalion and a battery of horse artillery. A skirmish had taken place, but Ney had apparently had insufficient infantry to risk an engagement. He had made some demonstrations, but the handful of troops opposed to him had held their ground, and at seven o'clock he had bivouacked for the night. Prince Bernhard had reported the affair to General Perponcher, who, wisely ignoring the Duke's positive orders to assemble his division at Nivelles, had directed it instead on the hamlet and crossroads of Quatre-Bras.

The Duke listened to these tidings with an unmoved countenance. He saw that everyone in the room was watching him, and said in a loud voice: 'Very well! I have no fresh orders to give. I advise your Royal Highness to go back to your quarters and to bed.'

The Prince, whose air of suppressed excitement had escaped no one, withdrew; the Duke resumed his conversation. But the impression created by the Prince's reappearance was not to be banished; except among those who had no relatives engaged in the operations, conversation had become subdued, and faces that had worn smiles an hour earlier now looked a little haggard in the glare of the candlelight. No one was surprised when the Duke went up to his host, saying cheerfully: 'I think it's time for me to go to bed likewise.' In the distance could be heard the ominous sound of bugles calling to arms; dancing seemed out of place, the Duke's departure was for most of those present a welcome sign of the party's breaking up. Wives exchanged nods with their husbands; mothers tried to catch heedless daughters' eyes; Georgiana Lennox stole away to help her brother March pack up.

The Duke said under his breath: 'Have you a good map in the house, Richmond?'

Richmond nodded, and led him to his study. The Duke shut the door and said abruptly: 'Napoleon has humbugged me, by God! He has gained twenty-four hours' march on me.'

He walked over to the desk, and bent over the map Richmond had spread out on it, and studied it for a moment or two in silence.

Richmond stood watching him, startled by what he had said and wondering a little that no anxiety should be apparent in his face. 'What do you intend doing?' he asked presently.

'I've ordered the Army to concentrate on Quatre-Bras,' replied his lordship. 'But we shan't stop him there, and if so, I must fight him *here*.' As he spoke he drew his thumbnail across the map below the village of Waterloo, and straightened himself. 'I'll be off now, and get some sleep.'

In the ballroom a few determined couples were still dancing, but with the departure of the officers the zest had gone from the most carefree young female. Ladies were collecting their wraps, carriages were being called for, and a stream of guests were filing past the Duchess of Richmond, returning thanks and taking leave.

Judith, who had gone upstairs to fetch her cloak, was startled, on her way down again, to encounter Barbara, her train caught over her arm, and in her face an expression of the most painful anxiety. She put out her hand impulsively, grasping Judith's wrist, and said in a strangled voice: 'Charles! Where is he?'

'My brother-in-law left the ball before supper,' replied Judith.

'O God!' The hand left Judith's wrist and gripped the banister-rail. 'He is in Brussels? Yes, yes, he is still in Brussels! Tell me, confound you, tell me!'

There was a white agony in her face, but Judith was unmoved by it. She said: 'He is not in Brussels, nor will he return. I wish you goodnight, Lady Barbara.'

She passed on down the stairs to where Worth stood waiting for her. Their carriage was at the door; in another minute they had entered it, and were being driven out of the gates in the direction of the centre of the town.

Judith leaned back in her corner, trying to compose her spirits. Worth took her hand presently, and held it lightly in his own. 'What is it, my dear?'

'That woman!' she said in a low voice. 'Barbara Childe! She dared to ask me where Charles had gone. I could have struck her in the face for her effrontery! She let Charles go like that – unhappy, all his old gaiety quite vanished!' She found that tears were running down her face, and broke off to wipe them away. 'Don't let us speak of it! I am tired, and stupid. I shall be better directly.'

He was silent, but continued to hold her hand. After a minute or two she said in a calmer tone: 'That noise! It seems to thud in my brain. What is it?'

'The drums beating to war,' he replied. 'The Reserve is being put into motion at once.'

She shuddered. As the carriage drew nearer to the Park, the coachman was obliged to curb his horses to a walk, and

sometimes bring them to a complete standstill. There was scarcely a house in Brussels where soldiers were not billeted; the sound of the trumpets and the drums brought them out, knapsacks slung over their shoulders, coats unbuttoned, and shakos crammed on askew. Some had wives running beside them; others had their arms round Belgian sweethearts; one Highlander was carrying a little boy on his shoulder, while the child's parents, who had been his hosts, walked beside with his knapsack and his musket.

In the great Place Royale a scene of indescribable confusion resigned. The sky was already paling towards dawn, and in the ghostly grey light men, horses, wagons, gun-carriages seemed to be inextricably mixed. Wagons were being loaded, and commissariat trains harnessed; the air was full of a medley of noises: the stamp of hooves on the cobbles, the rumble of wheels, the jingle of harness, the sudden neigh of a horse and the indistinguishable chatter of many voices. An officer called sharply; someone was whistling a popular air; a mounted man rode past; a Colour waved. Soldiers were sitting on the pavement, some sleeping on packs of straw, others checking the contents of their knapsacks.

Judith, who had been leaning forward in the carriage, intent upon the scene, turned suddenly towards Worth. 'Let us get out!'

'Do you care to? You are not too tired?'

'No. I want to see.'

He opened the door and stepped down on to the cobbles, and turned to give his hand to her. She stood beside him while he spoke with the coachman, and then took his arm. They made their way slowly across the Place. No one paid any heed to them; occasionally a soldier brushed past them, or they had to draw aside to allow a wagon to go by, or to pick their way through a tangle of ropes, canteens, corn-sacks, bill-hooks, nose-bags, and all the paraphernalia of an army on the move.

They reached the farther side of the Place at length, and stood for some time watching order grow out of the confusion. Regiments were forming one after the other, and marching down the Rue de Namur towards the Namur Gate. The steady tramp of boots made an undercurrent of sound audible through the shrill blare of the trumpets and the ceaseless beat of the drums. Some of the men sang; some whistled; the riflemen began to form up, and a voice from their ranks shouted: 'The first in the field and the last out of it: the bloody, Fighting Ninety-fifth!' A roar went up; hundreds of voices chanted the slogan. Indifferent-eyed Flemish women, driving market-carts full of vegetables into Brussels from the neighbouring countryside, stared incuriously; an order rang out; another regiment moved forward.

Once Worth bent over Judith, asking: 'Are you not tired? Shall we go home?'

She shook her head.

At four o'clock the sun was shining. In the Park, the pipes were playing *Hieland Laddie*. The sound of them drew nearer, the tread of feet grew to a rhythmic thunder. The Highland Brigade came marching through the Place in the first rays of the sunlight, pipe-majors strutting ahead, ribbons fluttering from the bagpipes, huge fur headdresses nodding, and kilts swinging.

'Were they some of those men who danced for us tonight?' Judith asked, recognising a tartan.

'Yes.'

She was silent, watching them pass through the Place and out of sight. When the music of the pipes was faint in the distance, she said, with a sigh: 'Let us go home now, Julian. I shall remember this night as long as I live, I think.'

Eighteen

*B*y eight o'clock in the morning the last of the regiments had marched out of Brussels. A little later the Duke followed, accompanied by his staff, and a profound silence descended on the city. Judith had fallen asleep some hours before, with the sound of the trumpets and the tread of many feet in her ears. When she awoke the morning was considerably advanced. Her first feeling was of surprise to-find everything quiet, for the shouting and the drumming and the bugle-calls had seemed to run through her dreams. She got up, and looked out between the blinds upon a sun-baked street. A cat curled on the steps of a house opposite was the only living thing in sight. No uniforms swaggered down the street, no ladies in muslins and chip hats floated along to pay their morning calls or to promenade in the Park.

She dressed, and went down to the salon on the first floor. Worth had gone out, but he came in presently with the newspapers. It was being reported in the cafés that the Duke had ridden out in high spirits, saying that Blücher would most likely have settled the business himself by that time and that he would probably be back in Brussels for dinner. The general opinion seemed to be that no action would be fought that day. It was thought that the bulk of the British troops could not be brought up in time. Judith did not know whether to be glad or sorry; the suspense would be as hard to bear as the sound of cannon, she thought.

'Quite a number of people are leaving for Antwerp,' Worth

observed. 'Lady Fitzroy has gone, and I met De Lancey just before he went off to join the Army, who told me that he had prevailed upon that poor young wife of his to go, too.' He paused, but she made no comment. He smiled. 'Well, Judith?'

'*You* would not wish to go if *I* were not here.'

'Very true, but that can hardly be said to have a bearing on the case.'

'I don't want to run away, if you think it would not be wrong in me to stay. I hope you don't mean to talk to me of defeat, for I won't listen if you do.'

'Like you, I'm of a sanguine disposition. But young Julian's nurse beat us both in that respect. She has taken him out into the Park for an airing, and the only emotion roused in her breast by all the racket that went on during the night was a strong indignation at having a child's rest disturbed.'

'Ah, she is a phlegmatic Scot! I have no fear of her losing her head.'

They were interrupted by the butler's coming into the room with the announcement that Lady Barbara Childe was below and wished to speak to the Earl.

Judith was astounded. She had not thought that after their encounter on the previous night Lady Barbara would dare to accost her again, let alone call at her residence. She looked at Worth, but he merely raised his eyebrows, and said: 'Well, I am at home, and perfectly ready to receive visitors. I don't understand why they are left in the hall. Beg her ladyship to come up.'

'Yes, my lord,' said the butler, his bosom swelling at the reproof. 'I should have done so in the first place but that her ladyship desired me to carry the message.'

He withdrew, stately and outraged. The door had scarcely shut behind him when Judith's feelings got the better of her. She exclaimed: 'I wish you had sent her about her business! I do not see why I should be obliged to receive her in my house! And that you should be willing to do so gives me a very poor opinion of your loyalty to Charles!'

'I cannot think that Charles would thank me for turning Lady

Barbara away from my door,' he replied.

There was no time for more; the butler opened the door and announced Barbara; and she came into the room with her long, mannish stride.

Judith rose, but before she had time to speak she was forestalled.

'I didn't mean to force myself into your presence,' Barbara said. 'I am sorry. My business is with your husband.' She paused, and a wintry, rueful smile flashed across her face. 'Oh, the devil! My curst tongue again! Don't look so stiff: I have not come to wreck *your* marriage.' This was said with a good deal of bitterness. She forced herself to speak more lightly, and added, looking in her clear way at Worth: 'I couldn't could I? You at least have never succumbed to my famous charms.'

'No, never,' he replied imperturbably. 'Will you not sit down?'

'No; I do not mean to stay above a minute. The case is that I am in the devil of a quandary over my horses. Would you be so obliging as to house them for me in your stables? There is the pair I drive in my phaeton, and my mare as well.'

'Willingly,' he said. 'But – forgive me – why?'

'My brother and his wife are leaving Brussels this morning. They are gone by this time, I daresay. The house in the Rue Ducale is given up. My own groom is not to be trusted alone, and I do not care to stable the horses at the hôtel. They tell me there is already such a demand for horses to carry people to Antwerp that by nightfall it will be a case of stealing what can't be hired.'

'Lord and Lady Vidal gone!' Judith exclaimed, surprised into breaking her silence.

'Oh yes!' Barbara replied indifferently. 'Gussie has been in one of her confounded takings ever since the news was brought in last night, and Vidal is very little better.'

'But you do not mean to remain here alone, surely?'

'Why not?'

'It is not fit!'

'Ah, you doubt the propriety of it! I don't care for that.' Her mouth quivered, but she controlled it. Judith noticed that she had twisted the end of her scarf tightly between her fingers and was gripping it so hard that her gloves seemed in danger of splitting. 'Both my brothers are engaged in this war,' she said. 'And Charles.'

'I had not supposed that Charles's fate was any longer a concern of yours,' Judith said.

'I am aware of that. But it is my concern, nevertheless.' She stared at Judith with haunted eyes. 'Perhaps I may never see him again. But if he comes back I shall be here.' She drew a sobbing breath, and continued in a hard voice: 'That, however, is my affair. Lord Worth, you are very obliging. My groom shall bring the horses round during the course of the day. Goodbye!' She held out her hand, but drew it back, flushing a little. 'Oh –! You would rather not shake hands with me, I daresay!'

'I have not the least objection to shaking hands with you,' he replied, 'But I should be grateful to you if you could contrive to stop being foolish. Now sit down and try to believe that your differences with my brother leave me supremely indifferent.'

She smiled faintly, and after a brief hesitation sat down in the chair by the table. 'Well, what now?' she asked.

'Are you staying with friends? May I have your direction?'

'I am at the Hôtel de Belle Vue.'

'Indeed! Alone?'

'Yes, alone, if you discount my maid.'

'It will not do,' he said. 'If you mean to remain in Brussels you must stay here.'

She looked at him rather blankly. 'You must be mad!'

'I am quite sane, I assure you. It can never be thought desirable for a young and unprotected female to be staying in a public hotel. In a foreign capital, and in such unsettled times as these, it would be the height of folly.'

She gave a short laugh. 'My dear man, you forget that I am not an inexperienced miss just out of the schoolroom! I am a widow, and if it comes to *folly*, why, I make a practice of behaving foolishly!'

'Just so, but that is no reason why you should not mend your ways.'

She got up. 'This is to no purpose. It is unthinkable that I should stay in your house. You are extremely kind, but –'

'Not at all,' he interrupted. 'I am merely protecting myself from the very just anger I am persuaded my brother would feel were he to find you putting up at an hotel when he returns to Brussels.'

She said unsteadily: 'Please –! We will not speak of Charles. You don't wish me to make a fool of myself, I imagine.'

He did not answer; he was looking at Judith. She was obliged to recognise the propriety of his invitation. She did not like it, but good breeding compelled her to say: 'My husband is right. I will have a room prepared at once, Lady Barbara. I hope you will not find it very disagreeable: we shall do our best to make your stay comfortable.'

'Thank you. It is not I who would find such a visit disagreeable. You dislike me cordially: I do not blame you. I dislike myself.'

Judith coloured, and replied in a cool voice: 'I have not always done so. There have been times when I have liked you very well.'

'You hated me for what I did to Charles.'

'Yes.'

'O God, if I could undo – if I could have it back, all this past month! It is useless! I behaved like the devil I am. That wretched quarrel! The very knowledge that I was in the wrong drove me to worse conduct! I have never been answerable to anyone for my misdeeds: there is a fiendish quality in me that revolts at the veriest hint of – but how should you understand? It is not worthy of being understood!'

She covered her face with her hands. Worth walked across the room to the door, and went out.

Judith said in a kinder tone: 'I do understand in part. *I* was not always so docile as you think me. But Charles! There is such a sweetness of temper, such nobility of mind –'

'Stop!' Barbara cried fiercely. 'Do you think I don't know it? I knew it when he first came up to me, and I looked into his eyes, and loved him. I knew myself to be unworthy! The only thing I

269

did that I am not ashamed of now was to try not to let him persuade me into becoming engaged to him. That impulse was the noblest *I* have ever felt. Though I knew I should not, I yielded. I wanted him, and all my life I have taken what I wanted, without thought or compunction!' She gave a wild laugh. 'You despise me, but you should also pity me, for I have enough heart to wish I had more.'

'I do pity you,' Judith said, considerably moved. 'But having yielded –'

'Yes! Having yielded, why could I not submit? I do not know, unless it be that from the day I married Jasper Childe I swore I would never do so, never allow myself to be possessed, or governed, or even guided. Don't misunderstand me! I am not trying to find excuses for myself. The fault lies deeper: it is in my curst nature!'

'I have sometimes thought,' Judith said, after a short pause, 'that the circumstances of your engagement made it particularly trying for you. In this little town we are obliged to live in a crowded circle from which there can be no escape. One's every action is remarked, and discussed. It is as though your engagement to Charles was acted upon a stage, in all the glare of footlights, for the amusement of your acquaintances.'

'Oh, if you but knew!' Barbara exclaimed. 'You do, in part, realise the evils of my situation but you cannot know what a demon was roused in me by finding myself the object of every form of cheap wit on the one hand, and of benign approval upon the other! It was said that I had met my match, that I was tamed at last, that I should soon settle down to a life of humdrum propriety! *You* would have had the strength to disregard such nonsense: I had not. When I was with Charles it did not signify. Every annoyance was forgotten in his presence; even my damnable restlessness left me. But he was busy; he could not be always at my side; and when he was away from me I was bored. If he had married me when I begged him to! But no! It would not have answered. There must still have been temptation.'

'Yes, I am very sensible of that. You are so much admired: it

must have been hard indeed to give up your –' She hesitated.

'My flirtations,' said Barbara, with a melancholy smile. 'It was hard. You know that I did not give them up. When I look back upon the past month it is with loathing, believe me! It was as though I was swept into a whirlpool! I could not be still.'

'Oh, do no speak of it! I myself have been conscious of what you describe. There has been no time for reflection, no time for anything but pleasure! It was as though we were all a little mad. But I believe Charles understood how it was. He said once to me that the life we were leading was ruinous. It was very true! I do not deny that your wildness made him anxious; indeed, I have blamed you bitterly for it. But all that was nothing!'

'You are thinking of my having made your brother fall in love with me. It was very bad of me.'

'The provocation was severe. I honoured you for coming up to Harriet so handsomely that day. There can be no excuse for her behaviour. It vexed me when you made him go to you at the Richmond's party, but I did not blame you entirely. But afterwards! How could you have let it go on? Forgive me ! I did not mean to advert to this subject. It is over, and should be forgotten. I do not know what passed between you and Charles.'

'Everything of the most damnable on my part!' Barbara said.

'I daresay you might lose your temper. But your conduct since that night! You left nothing undone that could hurt him.'

'Nothing!' Barbara said. 'Nothing that could drive him mad enough to come back to me! I would not go to him: he was to come to me – upon my own terms! Folly! He would not do it, nor did I wish him to. The news that war had broken out brought me to my senses. There was no room then for pride. Even if his affections had been turned in another direction – but I could not believe it could be so, for mine were unaltered! He turned from me in the ballroom, but I thought I saw, in his eyes, a look –'

Her voice was suspended; she struggled to regain her composure, and after a moment continued: 'I tried to find him. Nothing signified but that I should see him before he went away. But he had gone. Perhaps I shall never see him again.'

271

She ended in a tone of such dejection that Judith was impelled to say, with more cheerfulness than she felt: 'We shall not think of that, if you please! Recollect that his employment on the Duke's staff is to his advantage. He will not be in the line. Why, how absurd this is! He has survived too many engagements for us to have the least reason to suppose that he will not survive this one. Indeed, all the Duke's aides-de-camp have been with him for a long time now. Depend upon it, they will come riding back in the best of health and spirits. Meanwhile, I do earnestly beg of you to remain with us!'

'Thank you. I will do so, and try not to disgrace you. You won't be plagued with me too much, I hope. I shall be busy. Indeed, I ought not to be here now. I have promised to go to Madame de Ribaucourt's. She has made herself responsible for the preparation for the wounded, and needs help.'

'Oh, that is the very thing!' Judith cried. 'To be able to be of use! Stay till I fetch my bonnet and gloves! I would like, of all things, to go along with you.'

A few minutes later they left the house together, and set out on foot for their destination. They met few acquaintances on the way; streets which the day before had been full of officers and ladies were now only lined with the tilt-carts designed for the transport of the wounded, and with baggage-wagons, in perfect order, ready to move off at a moment's notice. Flemish drivers were dozing in the carts; a few sentinels were posted to guard the wagons. The Place Royale, strangely quiet after the confusion of the night, had been cleared of all the litter of equipment. There were more wagons and carts there, with a little crowd of citizens standing about, silently staring at them. Horses were picketed in the Park, but a fair number of people were strolling about there, much as usual, except for the gravity of their countenances and the lowered tones of their voices.

At the Comtesse de Ribaucourt's all was bustle and business. Many of Judith's friends were there, scraping lint and preparing cherry-water.

The feeling of being able to do something which would be of

use in this crisis did much to relieve the oppression of everyone's spirits. Dr Brügmans, the Inspector-General of Health, came in at noon for a few moments, and told of the tents to be erected at the Namur and Louvain Gates for the accommodation of the wounded. Various equipments were needed for them, in particular blankets and pillows. Judith willingly undertook the responsibility of procuring all that could be had from her numerous acquaintances in the town, and lost no time in setting out on a house-to-house visitation.

The hours sped by; she was astonished on returning to Madame Ribaucourt's to find that it was already three o'clock; she was conscious neither of fatigue nor of hunger. She sat down at a table to transcribe the list of equipments she had cajoled from her friends, but was arrested in the middle of this task by a sound that made her look up quickly, her pen held in mid-air.

All conversation was stopped short; every head was raised. The sound was heard again, a dull rumble far away in the distance.

Someone said in an urgent voice: 'Listen!' Lady Barbara walked over to the window, and stood there, her head a little bent, as though to hear more plainly.

The sound was repeated. 'It's the guns!' said Georgiana Lennox, dropping the lint she was holding.

'No, no, it's only thunder! Everyone says there can be no action until tomorrow!'

'It is the guns,' said Barbara. She came away from the window, and quite coolly resumed her work of scraping lint.

The distant cannonading had been heard by others besides themselves. All over the town the greatest consternation was felt. People came running out of their houses to stand listening in the street; crowds flocked to the ramparts; and a number of men set out on horseback in the direction of Waterloo to try to get news.

They brought back such conflicting accounts that it was soon seen that very little dependence could be placed on what they said. They had seen nothing; their only information came from peasants encountered on the road; all that was certain was that an action was being fought somewhere to the south of Brussels.

When Judith and Barbara reached home at five o'clock the cannonading was still audible. Everyone they met was asking the same questions: were the Allied troops separately engaged? Had they joined the Prussians? Where was the action being fought? Could the cavalry have reached the spot? Could the outlying divisions have come up? There could be no answer to such questions; none, in fact, was expected.

Worth was at home when the ladies came in. He had seen Barbara's trunks brought round from the Hôtel de Belle Vue, and had installed her frightened maid in the house. He had driven out, afterwards, a little way down the Charleroi road, but, like everyone else, had been unable to procure any intelligence. The baggage-wagons lined the chaussée for miles, he said, but none of the men in charge of them knew more than himself.

They sat down to dinner presently in the same state of anxious expectation. The sound of the guns seemed every moment to be growing more distinct. Judith found it impossible not to speculate upon the chances of defeat. The thought of her child, sleeping in his cot above stairs, made her dread the more acute. She should have sent him to England with Peregrine's children; her selfishness had made her keep them in Brussels; she had exposed him to a terrible danger.

She managed to check such useless reflections, and to join with an assumption of ease in the conversation Worth and Barbara were maintaining.

Some time after dinner, when the two ladies were seated alone in the salon, Worth having gone out to see whether any news had been received from the Army, a knock sounded on the front door, and in a few minutes they were astonished by the butler's announcing Colonel Canning.

Only one visitor could have been more welcome. Judith almost sprang out of her chair, and started forward to meet him. 'Colonel Canning! Oh, how glad I am to see you!'

He shook her warmly by the hand. 'I have only dropped in a for a few moments to tell you that Charles was well when I saw him last. I have been on a mission to the French King, at Alost, and am on my way back now to Quatre-Bras.'

'Quatre-Bras! Is that where the action is being fought? Oh, stay just for a few minutes! We have been without news the whole day, and the suspense is dreadful. Sit down: I will ring for the tea tray to be brought in directly. But have you dined?'

'Yes, yes, thank you! I dined at Greathed's, in the Park. Seeing me pass by his house, he very kindly called to me to come up and join him. Creevey was there too. I can't tell you much, you know. I was sent off just before 5.00, so I don't know how it has been going. However, by the time I left the Brunswickers and the Nassau contingent had arrived, and Van Merlen's Light Cavalry besides, so you may be sure everything is doing famously.'

Barbara said, with a smile: 'Confound you, Colonel, you begin at the end! Let us have the start, if you please!'

'By God!' he said seriously, 'we have had an escape! You won't blab it about the town, but the fact is Boney took us by surprise, and if Ney had pushed on last night, or even this morning, there's no saying what might not have happened. Prince Bernhard had only a battalion of Nassauers and one horse battery at Quatre-Bras.' He gave a chuckle. 'We can guess why Ney didn't, of course. The French know the trick the Duke has of concealing the better part of his troops from sight. No doubt Ney was afraid he'd come up against the whole Army, and dared not risk an attack without more infantry. But God knows why he delayed so long today! They say the French weren't even under arms at ten o'clock this morning. We arrived at half-past to find Orange there with two of his divisions, and nothing of a force in front of him. Charles arrived from Ath a little while after – still in his ball dress! He had no time to waste changing it last night, so there he is, in all his splendour. However, he is not the only one. Where was I?'

'You had arrived at Quatre-Bras to find no very startling force opposing you.'

'Oh yes! Well, so it was. The Duke inspected the position, saw that Ney was making no move, and rode over with Gordon and Müffling to confer with old Blücher, at Ligny.'

'We have not joined the Prussians, then?'

'Oh lord, no! They're seven miles to the east of us, and pretty badly placed, too. I don't know how it has gone with them: they've been engaged all day against Boney himself, but we've had no news. It appears that General Bourmont deserted to Blücher with all his staff yesterday morning, but the old man would have nothing to do with him! I haven't heard of any other desertions. As for the Prussians today, Gordon told me Blücher had his men exposed on the slope of the hill, and that the Duke told Hardinge pretty bluntly that he thought they would be damnably mauled. I daresay they have been. Gneisenau was anxious for the Duke to move to his support, which, I understand from Gordon, he said he would do, if he were not attacked himself. But we were attacked, and there was no question of going to help the Prussians. By the time the Duke got back to our position, somewhere between two and three in the afternoon, the French were in force in a wood in front of us. They started shouting *Vive l'Empereur!* and then we heard Ney go down the line, calling out: "*L'Empereur recompensera celui s'avancera!*" We've heard *that* before, and we knew we were in for it. I can tell you, it was a nice situation to be in, with only a handful of Dutch–Belgic troops to hold the position, and no sign of old Picton with the reserve.'

'But how is it possible?' Judith exclaimed. 'We saw the regiments march out of Brussels in the small hours!'

'There was some muddle over the orders: they were halted at Waterloo, and only reached Quatre-Bras at about half past three. By God, we were glad to see them! The French opened the attack on a farm on the main road. I should think Ney had about fifteen or sixteen thousand men opposed to our seven thousand – but that's a guess. The fields are so deep in rye you can't make out the exact positions of anyone, friend or foe. In some places it's above one's head – or it was, till it got trampled down.'

He paused, for the tea tray was just then brought in. Judith handed him a cup, and he gulped some of the tea down. 'Thank you. Well, the Dutch were driven out of Bossu Wood, and there was a general advance of the French. I needn't tell you the Duke remained as cool as a cucumber throughout. There never was such a man! He was always in the hottest part of the fight – no one knows better than he how to put heart into the men! They may not worship him, as they say the French worship Boney, but by God, they trust him!'

Judith smiled. 'I know how much *you* value him, Colonel. But go on!'

'Well, we couldn't hold the position against such odds, of course. Things were beginning to look devilish black, but Picton came up in the nick of time, which pretty well doubled our strength. But even so it was a ticklish business. The Highland Brigade were cut to pieces, poor devils, but they didn't yield an inch. However, as I told you the Brunswickers came up from Nivelles, then the Nassauers, and Van Merlen's cavalry. That was when I left.' He glanced at the clock on the mantelpiece, swallowed the rest of his tea, and jumped up. 'I must get back. You'll be hearing more news, I daresay: someone is sure to be sent in. Goodbye – don't be alarmed! All's well, you know.'

He hurried away, and not long after he had gone the noise of the firing, which had sounded closer in the stillness of the evening grew more desultory, and by ten o'clock had ceased. Worth came in, saying that the population of Brussels was still wandering about the ramparts and the Park. Great anxiety was being felt on all sides to know the result of the action. No news had as yet come in; some stout-hearted persons were maintaining that the Allies must have held their ground; others, in a state of growing uneasiness, were preparing to remove instantly to Antwerp.

The ladies gave him an account of Canning's visit, recalling as well as they were able his description of the battlefield. Worth listened intently, exclaiming when Barbara spoke of the arrival of the Brunswick and Nassau contingent: 'Then none of our cavalry are engaged!'

'No. Colonel Canning mentioned only General Picton's division.'

He looked serious, and said briefly: 'It is an ill-managed business!'

'The Colonel said the French had taken us by surprise.'

'It may well have been so. From what De Lancey told me this morning, it is plain that Wellington, as late as then, was expecting the attack to be directed on his right. Do you say the Prussians have also been engaged?'

'Yes, at Ligny, but he could not tell us how the day had gone with them. He said Napoleon himself was opposed to them.'

'I would not give a penny for their chances of success!' he said. 'The question will be, can Wellington maintain his communications with Blücher? It is plain Bonaparte has struck this blow in the endeavour to get between our forces. By God, it should be a lesson to those who have been saying he had lost his old genius! It is masterly! The rapidity of his march from Paris, his strategy in launching the attack at our point of junction with Blücher – it is something quite in his old style: one cannot but admire him! If he can succeed in defeating the Prussians, and Ney in carrying our position, it will be a serious business.' He observed Judith's pallor, and dropped his hand on her shoulder, saying more quietly: 'There is no need for alarm. If the day has gone against us we are bound to hear of it in time for me to drive you and the boy to safety. I have given orders in the stables: you need be under no apprehension.'

Barbara, who had walked over to the window, turned, and said in her lively way: 'Confound you, are you one of the croakers? I'll tell you what: I have a very good mind to put my horses up for sale, and so burn my boats!'

'I admire your spirit,' he said, with a slight smile.

'You need not,' she replied. 'I have merely a shocking love of excitement. Consider! In spite of all my adventures I was never till now in danger of falling into the hands of the French. It is something quite out of the common way, and therefore enchanting!'

Judith was obliged to smile at her nonsense, but said protestingly: 'How can you talk so?'

'The devil! How else should I talk? You know, if the French should come I fancy we shall make a hit with them. There is no denying that we are a handsome pair. Neither of us, I am persuaded, need look lower than a Marshal at the very least.'

Such raillery, though it might bring a blush to Judith's cheeks, had the effect of relieving the oppression of her spirits. Nothing more was said of the chances of defeat, and presently Worth went out again to see if any further news had arrived from Quatre-Bras.

He came back a little after eleven, and found that Judith and Barbara were still up. 'I called at Creevey's,' he said. 'Hamilton had been in during the evening on an errand for General Barnes, and of course dropped in on Creevey, to see Miss Ord. The result was still uncertain when he left the field, but Creevey got the impression from him that it was going in our favour. Charles was safe when he left the field: he saw him trying to rally the Belgians, who had had enough, just as he came away. Hamilton reports them as having done well at the start, but they won't stand like our own men. The worst, so far, is that the Duke of Brunswick has fallen. He was killed by a ball passing through his hand to his heart. Hamilton did not mention many of the casualties. The Highlanders have suffered most. Fassiefern and Macara have both fallen; young Hay has gone, too; but I heard of no one else whom we know.'

'Hay!' Barbara lifted her hand to shade her eyes for a moment. 'That boy! Ah, how wanton, how damnable! But go on! If Hay was present, Maitland's brigade must have come up. Could you get no news of Harry?'

'No; Creevey was positive Hamilton mentioned only Hay, and one other, whose name I forget.'

Judith said: 'Depend upon it, he would have told Mr Creevey had your brother been killed.'

'He might not know. But never mind that! What else could you discover, Lord Worth? Shall we hold our ground?'

'I see no reason why we should not. It appears that reinforcements have been arriving ever since five o'clock. The most serious part of the business is that we have no cavalry there worth mentioning. The infantry has done magnificently, however: Hamilton told Creevey that nothing could equal their endurance. Only their steadiness under the onslaughts of Kellermann's cuirassiers saved the day for us at one point. The Belgian and Brunswick cavalry were scattered; our whole position was completely turned, and might have been carried but for the Highlanders – I think he said the 92nd, but I might mistake. The Duke directed them in person, charging them not to fire until he gave the word. They obeyed him implicitly, though he allowed the cuirassiers to come within thirty paces before giving the order for a volley. The attack was completely repulsed, Kellermann drawing off in a good deal of disorder. Hamilton seems to have been full of enthusiasm for the Duke's coolness. It appears he has been everywhere at once, exposing himself in the most reckless fashion.'

'Surely he should not do so.'

'So I think, but you will not get his officers to agree. Even those who dislike him will tell you that the sight of his long nose among them does more to steady the troops than the arrival of a division to support them. He seems to bear a charmed life. What do you think of his being nearly taken by a party of Lancers when the Brunswick Hussars broke under the musketry-fire? He was forced to gallop for his life, made for a ditch lined by the Gordon Highlanders, sang out to them to lie still, and cleared the fence, bayonets and all!'

They remained for some time discussing the news, but the clock striking midnight soon recalled them to a sense of the lateness of the hour. All sound of firing had died away at ten o'clock; nothing had been heard of since; and they could not but believe that if a defeat had been suffered news of it must have reached them. Judith and Barbara went up to their rooms, but they had scarcely begun to undress when the noise of heavy carriages rumbling over the cobbles reached their ears. Nothing could be seen from the windows but people running out of doors to find out what was going on. Shouts and cries seemed to come from all parts of the town; and Judith, pausing only to fling a wrap round her shoulders, hurried to find Worth. He had not yet come upstairs, and called to her from the ground-floor to do nothing until he had discovered what was happening. He went out; Barbara joined Judith in the salon, and they sat in a state of apprehension that made it impossible for either to utter anything but a few occasional, disjointed sentences.

They were soon roused from this condition by the necessity of calming the servants, some of whom were hysterical with fright. Barbara went out into the hall among them, and very soon restored order. While Judith occupied herself with reassuring those whose alarm had had the effect of bereaving them of all power of speech or of action, she dealt in a more drastic manner with the rest, swearing at the butler, and emptying jugs of water over any *fille de chambre* unwise enough to fall into a fit of hysterics.

By the time Worth returned, the household was quiet, and Barbara had gone back into the salon with Judith, who had temporarily forgotten her own fears in amusement at her guest's ruthless methods.

Worth brought reassuring tidings. The noise they had heard had been caused by a long train of artillery, passing through the town on its way to the battlefield. The panic had arisen from a false notion having got about that the train was in retreat. People had rushed out of their houses in every stage of undress; a rumour that the French were coming had spread like wildfire; and the greatest confusion reigned until it became evident, even to the most foolish in the crowd, that the artillery was moving, not away from the field of action but towards it.

'Is that all?' exclaimed Barbara. 'Well, if there is no immediate need for us to become heroines we may as well go to bed. I, at any rate, shall do so.'

'Oh,' said Judith, with a little show of playfulness, 'you need not think that I shall be behind you in sangfroid: you have put me quite on my mettle!'

Goodnights were exchanged; both ladies retired again to their rooms, each with a much better opinion of the other than she had had at the beginning of what, in retrospect, seemed to have been the longest day of her life.

Nineteen

The night was disturbed. Many of the Bruxellois seemed to be afraid to go to bed, and spent the hours sitting in their houses with ears on the prick, ready to run out into the streets at the smallest alarm. Just before dawn a melancholy cortège entered the town, bearing the Duke of Brunswick's body. Numbers of spectators saw it pass through the streets. The sable uniforms of the Black Brunswickers, the grim skull-and-crossbones device upon their caps and the grief in their faces, awed the thin crowds into silence. A feeling of dismay was created; when the sad procession had passed, people dispersed slowly, some to wander about in an aimless fashion till daylight, others returning to their houses to lie down fully clothed upon their beds or to drop uneasily asleep in chairs.

Between five and six in the morning, after an interval of quiet, commotion broke out again. A troop of Belgian cavalry, entering by the Namur Gate, galloped through the town in the wildest disorder, overturning market-carts, thundering over the cobbles, their smart green uniforms white with dust and their horses foaming. They had all the appearance of men hotly pursued, and scarcely drew rein in their race through the town to the Ninove Gate. All was panic; they were shouting: '*Les Français sont ici!*' and the words were immediately taken up by the terrified crowds who saw them pass. The French were said to be only a few miles outside the town, the Allied Army in full retreat before them. Distracted Belgians ran to collect their more precious belongings, and then wandered about, carrying the oddest collection of goods, not knowing where to go, or what to do. Women became hysterical, *filles de chambre* rushing into hotel bedrooms to rouse sleepy visitors with the news that the French were at the gates; mothers clasping their children in their arms and screaming at their husbands to transport them instantly to safety. The drivers of the carts and the wagons drawn up in the Place Royale caught the infection; no sooner had the cavalry flashed through the great square than they set off down every street, rocking and lurching over the pavé in their gallop for the Ninove Gate. In a few minutes the Place was deserted, except for the people who still drifted about, spreading the dreadful news, or begging complete strangers for the hire of a pair of horses; and for a few market-carts driven into the town by stolid peasants in sabots and red night-caps, who seemed scarcely to understand what all the pandemonium was about.

Many of the English visitors behaved little better. Some of those who, on the night of the 15th, had stoutly declared their intention of remaining in Brussels, now ordered their carriages, or, if they possessed none, hurried about the town trying to engage horses to procure passages on the canal track-boats. For the most part, however, the flight of a troop of Belgic cavalry did not rouse much feeling of alarm in British breasts. Ladies busied themselves, as they had done the previous day, with preparations for the wounded, and if there were some who thought the cessation of all gun-fire ominous, there were others who considered it to be a sure sign that all must be well.

Judith and Barbara again went to the Comtesse de Ribaucourt's. On entering the house Judith encountered Georgiana Lennox, who came up to her with a white face and trembling lips, trying to speak calmly on some matter of a consignment of blankets. She was scarcely able to control her voice, and broke off to say: 'Forgive me, this is foolish! Only it is so dreadful – I don't seem able to stop crying.'

Judith took her hand, saying with a good deal of concern: 'Oh, my poor child! Your brothers – ?'

'Oh no, no!' Georgiana replied quickly. 'But Hay has been

killed!' She made an effort to control herself. 'He was almost like one of my brothers. It is stupid – I know he would not care for that, but I can't get it out of my head how cross I was with him for being so glad to be going into action.' She tried to smile. 'I scolded him. I wouldn't dance with him any more, and then I never saw him again. He went away so excited, and now he's been killed, and I didn't even say goodbye to him.'

Judith could only press her hand. Georgiana said rather tightly: 'I can't believe he's dead, you know. He said: "Georgy! We're going to war! Was there ever anything so splendid?" And I was cross.'

'Dearest Georgy, you mustn't think of that. I am sure he did not.'

'Oh no! I know I'm being silly. Only I wish I had not scolded him.' She brushed her hand across her eyes. 'He was General Maitland's aide-de-camp, you know. Now that he has been killed William feels that he must rejoin Maitland, and he is not fit to do so.'

'Your brother! Oh, he cannot do so. His arm is still in a sling, and he looks so ill!'

'That is what Mama feels, but my father agrees that it is William's duty to go to General Maitland. I do not know what will come of it.' Her lips quivered again; she said inconsequently: 'Do you remember how beautifully the Highlanders danced at our ball? They are all dead.'

'Oh, hush, my dear, don't think of such things! Not all!'

'Most of them. They were cut to pieces by the cuirassiers. They say the losses in the Highland brigade are terrible.'

Judith could not speak. She had seen the Highlanders march out of Brussels in the first sunlight, striding to war to the music of their own fifes, and the memory of that proud march brought a lump into her throat. She pressed Georgiana's hand again, and released it, turning away to hide the sudden rush of tears to her own eyes.

She and Barbara returned home a little after noon, to find that Worth had just come back from visiting Sir Charles Stuart. He was able to tell them that an aide-de-camp had ridden in during the morning, having left the field at 4 am. He reported that after a very sanguinary battle the Allied Army had remained in possession of the ground. Towards the close of the action the cavalry had come up, having been delayed by mistaken orders. It had not been engaged on the 16th, but would certainly be in the thick of it today, if the French attack were renewed, as the Duke was confident it would be.

The ladies had hardly taken off their hats when the sound of cheering reached the house; they ran out to the end of the street, where a crowd had collected, and were in time to see a number of French prisoners being marched under guard towards the barracks of Petit Château.

But the heartening effect of this sight was not of long duration. The next news that reached Brussels was that the Prussians had been defeated at Ligny, and were in full retreat. The intelligence brought a fresh feeling of dismay, which was made the more profound by the arrival, a little later, of the first wagon-loads of wounded. In a short time the streets were full of the most pitiable sights. Men who were able to walk had dragged themselves to Brussels on foot all through the night, some managing to reach the town, many collapsing on the way, and dying by the roadside from the effects of their wounds.

Except among those whom panic had rendered incapable of any rational action, the arrival of the wounded made people forget their own alarms in the more pressing need to do what they could to alleviate the sufferings of the soldiers. Ladies who had never encountered more unnerving sights than a pricked finger or the graze on a child's knee, went out into the streets with flasks of brandy and water, and the shreds of petticoats torn up to provide bandages; and stayed until they dropped from fatigue, stanching the blood that oozed from ghastly wounds; providing men who were dying on the pavements with water to bring relief to their last moments; rolling blankets to form pillows for heads that lolled on the cobbles; collecting straw to make beds for those who, unable to reach their own billets, had sunk down on the road; and accepting sad, last tokens from dying men who thought of wives, and mothers, and sweethearts at home, and handed to them a ring, a crumpled diary, or a laboriously scrawled letter.

Judith and Barbara were among the first to engage on this work. Neither had ever come into anything but the most remote contact with the results of war; Judith was turned sick by the sight of blood congealed over ugly contusions, of the scraps of gold lace embedded in gaping wounds, of dusty rags twisted round shattered joints, and of grey, pain-racked faces lying upturned upon the pavement at her feet. There was so little that could be accomplished by inexpert hands; the patient gratitude for a few sips of water of men whose injuries were beyond her power to alleviate brought the tears to her eyes. She brushed them away, spoke soothing words to a boy crumpled on the steps of a house, and sobbing dryly, with his head against the railings; bound fresh linen round a case-shot wound; spent all the Hungary Water she owned in reviving men who had covered the weary miles from Quatre-Bras only to fall exhausted in the gutters of Brussels.

Occasionally she caught sight of Barbara, her flowered muslin dusty round the hem with brushing the cobbles, and a red stain on her skirt where an injured head had lain in her lap. Once they met but neither spoke of the horrors around them. Barbara said briefly: 'I'm going for more water. The chemists have opened their shops and will supply whatever is needed.'

'For God's sake, take my purse and get more lint – as much of it as you can procure!' Judith said, on her knees beside a lanky Highlander, who was sitting against the wall with his head dropped on his shoulder.

'No need; they are charging nothing,' Barbara replied. 'I'll get it.'

She passed on, making her way swiftly down the street. A figure in a scarlet coat lay across the pavement; she bent over it, saying gently: 'Where are you hurt? Will you let me help you?' Then she saw that the man was dead, and straightened herself, feeling her knees shaking, and nausea rising in her throat. She choked it down, and walked on. A Highlander, limping along the road, with a bandage round his head and one arm pinned up by the sleeve across his breast, grinned weakly at her. She stopped, and offered him the little water that remained in her flask. He shook his head: 'Na, na, I'm awa' to my billet. I shall do verra weel, ma'am.'

'Are you badly hurt? Will you lean on my shoulder?'

'Och, I got a wee skelp wi' a bit of a shell, that's all. Gi'e your watter to the puir red-coat yonder: *we* are aye well respected in this toon! We ha' but to show our *petticoat*, as they ca' it, and the Belgians will ay gi'e us what we need!'

She smiled at the twinkle of humour in his eye, but said: 'You've hurt your leg. Take my arm, and don't be afraid to lean on me.'

He thanked her, and accepted the help. She asked him how the day had gone, and he replied, gasping a little from the pain of walking: 'It's a bluidy business, and there's no saying what may be the end on't. Oor regiment was nigh clean swept off, and oor Colonel kilt as I cam' awa'. But I doot all's weel.'

She supported him to the end of the street, but was relieved of her charge there by a burgher in a sad-coloured suit of broadcloth, who darted up with exclamations of solicitude, and cries to his wife to come at once to the assistance of '*notre brave Écossais*.' He turned out to be the owner of the Highlander's billet, and it was plain that Barbara could relinquish the wounded man to his care without misgiving. He was borne off between the burgher and his comfortable wife, throwing a nod and a wink over his shoulder to Barbara; and she hurried on to fight her way into the crowded chemist's shop.

Nothing could have exceeded the humanity of the citizens. There was hardly a house in the town whose doors were not thrown open to the wounded, whether Dutch, or Belgian, German, Scotch or English. The Belgian doctors were working in their shirt-sleeves with the sweat dripping off their bodies; children, who stared with uncomprehending, vaguely shocked eyes, were bidden by their brisk, shrill mothers to hold umbrellas over men huddled groaning on the pavement under the scorching sun; stout burgomasters and grim gendarmes were busy clearing the wounded off the streets, carrying those who could not walk into neighbouring houses, and directing others with more superficial injuries to places of shelter. Sisters of Mercy were moving about, their black robes and great starched white head-dresses in odd contrast to the frivolous chip hats and delicate muslin dresses of ladies of fashion who had forgotten their complexions and their nerves, and in all the heat of the noonday sun, and the stench of blood, and dirt, and human sweat, toiled as their scullery-maids had never done.

In one short hour Judith felt her senses to have become numb; the nausea that she had first felt had left her; in the urgent need to give help there was no time for personal shrinking. A Belgian doctor, kneeling beside an infantryman on a truss of straw in the road, had called to her to aid him; he had told her to hold a man's leg while he dug out a musket-ball from his knee, and roughly bound up the wound. He spoke to her brusquely, and she obeyed him without flinching. A few minutes later she was herself slitting up a coat-sleeve, and binding lint round a flesh-wound that ordinarily would have turned her sick.

At about half past two, when the news came from the Namur and Louvain Gates that the promised tents were at last ready for the wounded, the sky became suddenly overcast. The relief from the sun's glare was felt by everyone, but in a few minutes the fear of a storm was making it necessary to get all who could be moved under shelter. The blackness overhead was presently shot through with a fork of lightning; almost simultaneously the thunder crashed across the sky, rolling and reverberating in an ominous rumble that died away only an instant before a second flash, and a second clap broke out. By three o'clock the lightning seemed continuous, and the thunder so deafening that the fear of the elements overcame in nearly every breast the lesser fear of a French advance. The lurid light, the flickering flashes in a cloud like a huge pall, the clatter in the sky as of a giant's crockery being smashed, made even the boldest quail, and sent many flying to their homes. Rain began to fall in torrents; in a few minutes the gutters were rushing rivers, and those still out in the streets were soaked to the skin. Rain bounced on the cobbles, and poured off the steep gabled roofs; it took the starch out of the nuns' stiff caps, made the pale muslins cling to their owner's bodies, and turned modish straw hats into sodden wrecks.

Barbara, helping a man with a shattered ankle to hop up the steps into a house already containing two wounded Belgians, felt her shoulder touched, and looked round to find Worth behind her. He was drenched, and dishevelled; he said curtly: 'I'll take him. Go home now.'

'Your wife?' she said, her voice husky with fatigue.

'I've sent her home. You have done enough. Go back now.'

She nodded, for she was indeed so exhausted that her head felt light, and it was an effort to move her limbs. Worth slipped his arm round the young Scot she had been supporting, and she clung to the railings for a moment to get her breath.

When she reached home she found that Judith had arrived a few moments before her, and had already gone up to strip off her wet and soiled garments. She came out of her bedroom in a wrapper as Barbara reached the top of the stairs. 'Barbara!' she said. 'Thank God you have come in! Oh, how wet you are! I'll send my woman to you immediately! Yours is in hysterics.'

A weary smile touched Barbara's lips. 'The confounded wench hasn't ceased having hysterics since the guns were first heard. Is there any news?'

'I don't think so. I've had no time to ask. But don't stand there in those wet clothes!'

'Indecent, aren't they?' said Barbara, with the ghost of a chuckle.

'Shocking, but I'm thinking of the cold you will take. I've ordered coffee to be sent up to the salon. Do hurry!'

Twenty minutes later they confronted one another across a table laid out with cakes and coffee. Judith lifted the silver pot, and found that her hand, which had been so steady, was shaking. She managed to pour out the coffee, and handed the cup to

Barbara, saying: 'I'm sorry. I've spilled a little in the saucer. You must be very hungry; eat one of those cakes.'

Barbara took one, raised it to her mouth, and then put it down. 'I don't think I can,' she said in rather a strained voice. 'I beg your pardon, but I feel damnably sick. Or faint – I'm not sure which.'

Judith jumped up. 'No, no, you are not going to faint, and if you are sick, I'll never forgive you! Wait, I'll get my smelling-salts directly!' She stopped, and said: 'No. I forgot. I gave them to that boy whose ear had been shot off. He – oh God, Bab, don't, don't!' With the tears pouring down her own face she flung her arms round Barbara, who had broken into a fit of gasping sobs.

They clung together for a few moments, their torn nerves finding relief in this burst of weeping. But presently each made an effort towards self-control; the sobs were resolutely swallowed, and two noses defiantly blown.

'The devil!' Barbara said faintly. 'Where's that coffee?'

They smiled mistily at each other. 'We're tired,' said Judith. 'Crying like a couple of vapourish idiots!'

Her teeth chattered on the rim of her cup, but she gulped down a little of the coffee and felt better. Outside, the thunder still crashed and rumbled, and the rain streamed down the window-panes. The butler had lit the candles in the room, and presently, seeing how the flashes of lightning made Judith wince, Barbara got up, and drew the blinds together.

'The troops in this awful storm!' Judith said. 'Will the rain never stop?'

'I wonder where they are?'

'The report this morning said that a renewal of the attack was expected.'

'I am not afraid. We remained masters of the field last night, and now all the Army is concentrated there.'

'Very true: we may hear of a victory at any moment now, I daresay.'

They relapsed into silence. The sound of carriage wheels in the street below roused them. The carriage drew up apparently at the house, and while Judith and Barbara were still looking at each other with a sudden question in their eyes, a double knock fell on the front door. Judith found that she was trembling, and saw that Barbara was gripping the arms of her chair with clenched fingers. Neither seemed capable of moving; each was paper white, staring at the other. But in another minute the butler had opened the door and announced Miss Devenish and Mr Fisher.

Judith got up with a shudder of relief, and turned to receive these unexpected guests. Miss Devenish, who was muffled in a long cloak, ran forward, and caught both her friend's arms in a tight clasp. 'Oh, have you news?' she panted. 'I could bear it no longer! All yesterday and today in this terrible uncertainty! I thought you might have heard something, that Colonel Audley might have been here!'

Barbara's hands unclenched. She rose, and walked over to the window under pretext of rearranging the blinds.

'No. We have not seen Charles since he left the ball,' Judith replied. 'Colonel Canning was in last night, and told us then that up till five o'clock Charles was alive and unhurt. We have had no later tidings.'

She disengaged one hand, and held it out to Mr Fisher, who shook it warmly, and embarked on a speech of apology for having intruded on her at such a time. She cut him short assuring him that no apology could be thought necessary, and he said, in his unpolished yet kindly way: 'That's it: I told my girl here you would be glad to see her. For my part, I'm a plain Englishman, and what I say is, let the Belgians run if they will, for it won't make a ha'porth of odds to our fellows! But the silly miss has been in such a taking, covering her ears every time the cannon sounded, and jumping to the window whenever anyone passed in the street, that in the end I said to her: "Lucy, my pet," I said, "rain or no rain, you'll pop on your cloak and we'll drive straight round to your good friend, Lady Worth, and see what she may be able to tell us."'

'Indeed, you did quite right. I am only sorry that I am unable to give you any news. Since hearing of the Prussian defeat, no tidings of any kind have reached us, except such scraps we might pick up from the men who have got back from the battlefield.'

Lucy, who had sunk into a chair, with her hands kneading one another in her lap, raised her head, and asked in an amazed tone: 'You have been out in the streets?'

'Yes, Lady Barbara and I have been doing what we could for the wounded.'

Lucy shuddered. 'Oh, how I admire you! I could not! The sight of the blood – the wounds – I cannot bear to think of it!'

Judith looked at her for an instant, in a kind of detached wonder. Raising her eyes, she encountered Barbara's across the room. A faint smile passed between them; in that moment of wordless understanding each was aware of the bond which, no matter what might come, could never be quite broken between them.

Mr Fisher said: 'Well, I am sure you are a pair of heroines, no less! But I wonder his lordship would permit it, I do indeed! A lady's delicate sensibilities –'

'This is not a time for thinking of one's sensibilities,' Judith interrupted. 'But will you not be seated? I am glad to see you have not fled the town, like some of our compatriots.'

He said heartily: 'No need to do that, I'll be bound! Why, if the Duke can't account for Boney and all his Froggies, he's not the man I take him for, and so I tell my foolish girl here.'

'Such sentiments do you credit,' said Judith, with mechanical civility. She glanced at Miss Devenish, and added: 'Do not be unnecessarily alarmed, Lucy. I believe we must by this time have heard had anything happened to my brother-in-law.'

Miss Devenish replied in a numb voice: 'Oh yes! It must be so, of course. Only I hoped he might perhaps have been sent in with a message. It is of no consequence.'

Judith could not resist glancing in Barbara's direction. She was standing back against the dark curtains, her eyes fixed on Lucy's face with an expression in them of curious intentness.

Judith looked away quickly, and repeated: 'I have not seen Charles since the ball.'

'No.' Miss Devenish looked at Barbara; a little colour crept into her cheeks; she said, stumbling over the words: 'And you, Lady Barbara – I do not like to ask you – but you have heard nothing?'

'Nothing at all,' Barbara replied.

'No; I quite realise – you must wonder at my asking you, but there are circumstances which –' Her voice failed entirely: indeed, her last words had been almost inaudible. She got up, flushing, and reminded her uncle that they had promised not to leave Mrs Fisher for more than half an hour.

He agreed that they must be going, and said in a rallying tone, as he shook hands with Judith: 'Your ladyship will bear me out in assuring this little puss that there is no need for all this alarm. Ah, you may shake your head as much as you please, Missy, but you won't make your old uncle believe that you haven't lost that soft heart of yours to some handsome officer!'

No answer was vouchsafed; Lucy pressed Judith's hand, bowed slightly to Barbara, and hurried out of the room. Mr Fisher begged Judith not to think of accompanying them to the door, again thanked her for receiving him, became aware that the butler was holding open the door for him, and bowed himself out.

A long, painful silence fell in the salon. Barbara had parted the curtains and was looking out into the street. 'It is still raining,' she remarked presently.

'The thunder is less violent, I believe.'

'Yes.'

Judith sat down, smoothing a crease from her dress. She said, without raising her eyes from her skirt: 'I do not believe he cares for her.'

It was a moment before Barbara answered. She said then, in a level tone: 'If he does, I have come by my deserts.'

There could be no gainsaying it. Judith said with a wry smile: 'I wanted him to, you know.'

'Don't you still?'

'No. These days seem to have altered everything. I did not want to receive you in my house, but your strength has supported me as I would not have believed it could. Whatever happened in the past, or whatever is to happen in the future, I can never forget the comfort your presence is to me now.'

Barbara turned her head. 'You are generous!' she said, a note of mockery in her voice. 'But the other side of my character is true, too. Don't set me up on a pedestal! I should certainly tumble down from it.'

At that moment Worth came into the room. He had changed into dry clothes, and said, in answer to Judith's surprised exclamation, that he had come in while Mr Fisher and Miss Devenish were sitting with her. The next question was inevitable: 'Is there any news?'

'Yes, there is news,' he replied. 'It is disquieting, but I believe it may be accounted for by the Prussian defeat. The Allied Army is said to be retreating.'

Judith gazed at him in horror. Barbara said: 'The devil it is! Confound you, I don't believe it!'

'It is a pity your sanguine temperament is not shared by others,' he said dryly. 'The whole town is in an uproar. I am informed on credible authority that as much as a hundred napoleons have been offered for a pair of horses to go to Antwerp.' He flicked open his snuff box and added in a languid tone: 'My opinion of the human race has never been high, but the antics that are being performed at this moment exceed every expectation of folly with which I had previously indulged my fancy.'

'I hope you observe that we at least are preserving our dignity!' retorted Barbara.

'I do, and I am grateful to you.'

'But, Worth! A retreat!' Judith cried.

'Don't disturb yourself, my love. Recollect that Wellington is a master in retreat. If the Prussians have fallen back, we must be obliged to do the same to maintain our communications with them. Until we hear that the retreat is a rout, I must – regretfully, of course – decline to join the rabble on the road to Antwerp.'

Judith could not help laughing, but said with a good deal of spirit: 'Nothing, indeed, could be more odious. We certainly shall not talk of flight yet awhile.'

They dined at an early hour, but although both ladies were very tired from the exertions and the nervous stress they had undergone, neither could think of retiring to bed until further news had been received from the Army. They sat in the salon, trying to occupy themselves with ordinary sewing tasks, until Worth, with a glance at the clock, got up, saying that he would walk round to Stuart's to discover if anything more had been heard. He left the room, and went downstairs to the hall. At the same moment, the ladies heard a knock on the street door, followed an instant later by the confused murmur of voices in the hall.

Twenty

*J*udith ran out to the head of the stairs. Worth called up to her: 'It is Charles, Judith. All is well!'

'Oh, bring him up! Bring him up!' she begged. 'Charles, I am so thankful! Come up at once!'

'I'm in no fit state to enter your drawing-room, you know,' Colonel Audley replied in a tired but cheerful voice.

'Good God, what does that signify?' She caught sight of him as she spoke, and exclaimed: 'You are drenched to the skin! You must change your clothes immediately or Heaven knows what will become of you!'

He mounted the stairs, and as he came into the light cast by a sconce of candles Judith saw that his face was grey with fatigue, and his embroidered ball dress, which he still wore, saturated with rain and mud, a tear in one sleeve and the wristband of his shirt stained with blood.

'You are hurt!' she said quickly.

'No, I assure you I am not. Nothing but a cut from a bayonet: it scarcely broke the skin. I am only sleepy, and very hungry, upon my honour!'

'You shall have dinner the instant you are out of those wet clothes,' she promised, taking his hand between both of hers and clasping it for a moment. 'You are worn out! Oh, dear Charles, the relief of knowing you to be safe!'

She could say no more; he smiled, but seemed to have no energy to waste in answering her. Worth took him by the arm and led him towards the second pair of stairs. 'Come along!' he said. 'The appearance you present is quite appalling, believe me!'

Judith ran back into the salon and tugged at the bell pull. Barbara was standing just inside the door, watching Colonel Audley as he mounted the stairs to his bedroom. She said with a shaky laugh: 'His beautiful ball dress quite ruined! When I think how smart he was, only two nights ago, it makes me want to weep! Was there ever anything so confoundedly silly?'

Upstairs, Worth rang the bell for his valet, and began to help the Colonel to peel off his sodden coat. Through the torn sleeve of a shirt that was clinging to his body could be seen a strip of sticking-plaster, covering a slash upon the upper arm. The blood had dried upon the shirtsleeve, and Audley winced a little as he stripped the shirt off.

'I take it that's not serious?' said Worth.

'Good God, no! A scratch.'

'How did you come by it?'

'Trying to rally those damned Dutch–Belgians!' replied the Colonel bitterly. He added, with the flash of a smile: 'I don't know that I blame them, though, poor devils! They got the brunt of it at the start, and then, to add to their troubles, what must some of our fellows do but mistake a party of them for the French, and open fire on them! It's all the fault of their accursed uniforms, and those bell-topped shakos of theirs.'

'Where's the Army?'

'Before Mont St Jean, rather more than a couple of miles south of Waterloo, bivouacking for the night.'

Worth raised his brows. 'That seems somewhat close to Brussels.'

'No help for it. Old Blücher's gone eighteen miles to his rear, to Wavre. We had to do likewise, of course. But don't worry! We're in a better case than at Quatre-Bras: the ground there was damnable for cavalry.'

The valet came into the room just then, and conversation was suspended while the Colonel's mud-caked Hessians were pulled off, his pantaloons peeled from his legs, and warm water fetched to wash away the dirt, and the sweat and the bloodstains from his tired body. By the time he came downstairs again, in his service uniform, a tray had been brought to the salon and a table spread. He walked into the room just ahead of his brother, smiled rather wearily at Judith, and then saw Barbara standing by the fireplace. A frown creased his brow; his eyes, heavy and bloodshot, blinked at her in a puzzled way. His brain felt clogged; he did not know how she came to be there, and felt too tired to speculate much about the circumstance. A nightmare of estrangement lay between them, but he had been in the saddle almost continuously for two days, had taken part in a fierce battle against superior odds, and knew that perhaps the most serious engagement of his life was ahead of him. His mind refused to grapple with personal considerations; he merely held out his hand, and said: 'I didn't know you were here, Bab. How do you do?'

Judith, who had expected some show at least of surprise, and had been prepared to whisk herself and Worth out of the room, felt that this calm greeting must affect Barbara like a douche of cold water. But Barbara just took the Colonel's hand, and answered: 'Yes, Charles. I am here. Never mind that now. You are hungry and tired.'

'I don't know when I have been more so,' he admitted, turning from her, and seating himself at the table. He accepted a plate of cold beef from Judith, and added: 'Both your brothers are safe. I think George got a scratch or two today, but nothing serious. I suppose Canning gave you an account of our engagement at Quatre-Bras, Julian?'

'Yes, and I heard more later from Creevey, who had seen Hamilton, of Barnes's staff.'

'Oh, did you?' said Colonel, his mouth rather full of beef. 'Then I expect you know all that happened.'

'Very briefly. Hamilton left the field before the engagement ended.'

'The Guards settled it. Cooke's division came up at about half past six, I suppose. Maitland sent Lord Saltoun in with the Light Infantry of the brigade to clear Bossu wood of the French, which he did. I don't really know where Byng's brigade was placed. It was almost impossible to make out anyone's position. One of Halkett's fellows told me they had seen the French actually sending a man galloping ahead to plant a flag as a point for their troops to charge on. You've no idea what the crops are like there. I've never seen rye grown to such a height.'

'When did Halkett arrive? I collect you mean Sir Colin, not his brother?'

'Yes, of course. Hew Halkett's Hanoverians weren't at Quatre-Bras at all. Alten brought up the 3rd Division some-where between four and five in the afternoon, and, by God! They were not a moment too soon. Picton's division was pretty well crippled. I don't know which of the brigades suffered the most, Kempt's or Pack's. To make matters worse, Brunswick had been carried off the field, and his men were badly shaken. Olferman couldn't hold them, and they were retreating in a good deal of haste when old Halkett came up. You know Halkett! – or rather you don't, but he told Olferman without mincing matters what he thought of the retreat, and brought the Brunswickers up under cover of a ditch, like the famous old fighter he is!'

'And the Dutch–Belgians?'

The Colonel shrugged. 'Well, there's no doubt Perponcher saved the situation by moving on Quatre-Bras as he did, and Prince Bernhard's Nassauers behaved splendidly. They had one horse battery with them – Stevenart's, I think – and by Jove, those fellows were heroes! Bylandt's brigade suffered rather severely at the start, and as for the rest – it's a case of the least said the soonest mended.'

'How did the Prince of Orange do?'

'Ask Halkett,' replied the Colonel, with a wry smile. 'Poor Slender Billy! He will get so excited!'

Worth refilled his glass. 'At his age that was to be expected. What has he been up to?'

The Colonel drank some of the wine, and picked up his knife and fork again. 'Oh, Halkett galloped forward to the front with one of his ADCs, saw a corps of cavalry forming, and of course returned at once to his brigade, and gave the order to form squares. The 69th – that's Colonel Morice's regiment – were in the act of doing so when up came Slender Billy, and wanted to know what the devil they were about. "Preparing to meet cavalry" – "Oh, cavalry be damned!" says Billy. "There's none within five miles of you! Form column, and deploy into line at once!" Morice had no choice but to obey, of course. The regiment was actually engaged on the movement when about eight hundred cuirassiers came charging down on the brigade. The 30th and the 33rd were firmly in square, but the cuirassiers rode right through the unfortunate 60th, scattered the Belgian and Brunswick cavalry, got as far as Quatre-Bras itself, and completely turned our position. If it hadn't been for the Duke's directing the 92nd Highlanders himself, God knows what might not have happened!'

'Yes, we heard about that, but not about the Prince's folly!'

'You might not. Don't spread the story! I happened to have been sent with a message to Halkett just before the charge, and was in one of the squares beside him. Poor Morice was killed, and scores of others.'

'Then you had no cavalry at all to withstand the French attacks?'

'No, that was the devil of it. The Lancers cut up Pack's Highlanders horribly. But you can't shake the Fighting Division. When Picton retired at last, it was in perfect order. But the loss has been shocking in his whole division. By nine o'clock we outnumbered the French. I saw Ney myself, several times. He kept on rallying his infantry and hurling it against us – behaving more like a madman than a corps commander, *we* thought. In the end he gave it up, and drew off, and we bivouacked for the night.' He pushed his plate aside, and reached out a hand for the cheese. 'The Duke spent the night at Genappe. We had no news from the Prussians: Hardinge was badly wounded at Ligny, and is *hors de combat*. It turned out that Blücher did send an officer to us overnight, but he got wounded and never reached us. Gordon was sent off down the Namur road with a half squadron of the

10th the first thing this morning, to see what intelligence he could gain. He got as far as a place called Tilly, found that the whole Prussian Army was retreating on Wavre, and that the French were in force about two miles distant. He got back somewhere about eight o'clock, and that was the first news we had of the Prussian corps, and must have been about 40,000 strong. What happened to that corps yesterday we can't make out. We saw it going off towards Ligny, but it doesn't seem to have been engaged at all. As for us, we had only 25,000, after the flight of the Dutch; but instead of renewing the attack Ney did nothing. At ten o'clock the Duke ordered the infantry to retire in successive brigades through the defile of Genappe, to the position of Mont St Jean. They did this in perfect order, all except two battalions of the 95th Rifles, which the Duke kept at Quatre-Bras, with all the cavalry.' He gave a grin, swallowed a mouthful of bread and cheese, and said: 'Old Hookey sat down to read the letters and newspapers from England which had arrived, and then went to sleep by the side of the road, with a paper spread over his face. When he woke up, he had another look at the enemy through his glass, and found them still not under arms. We began to think they might possibly be retreating. However, about two o'clock, Vivian, who was with the Duke, saw a glitter of steel in the sunlight in the direction of Ligny, and we found that it was caused by huge masses of cavalry moving towards us. At the same time, Ney began to show himself on our front. By the by, it was the most curious effect I ever saw in my life. There was an enormous storm cloud blowing up from the north. We were all in a sort of twilight, but the sun was still shining on the French. Queerest thing I ever saw. The Duke ordered the cavalry, and the horse artillery, and the rifles, to fall back steadily, and went on ahead to dine at Genappe, leaving Uxbridge to do the business, which he did beautifully, withdrawing the cavalry in three columns, and keeping Norman Ramsay's troop to guard the rear. We heard the guns in Genappe just about the time the storm burst, and I went back to see what was happening. Apparently the French opened fire on us, but without doing much damage. They seemed to be concentrating their attacks on our centre column – Somerset's and Ponsonby's heavy brigades, and a rearguard of the 7th Hussars and the 23rd Light Dragoons. By the time they were drawn up on the high ground beyond Genappe, the French lancers were in the town. Uxbridge sent in the 7th to clear them out; they were driven back, rallied, went in again gallantly, time after time, but suffered pretty severely. Uxbridge withdrew them at last, and ordered the light dragoons to advance, but as they didn't seem to relish the task, he snapped out: "The Life Guards shall have this honour!" and ordered them up. Of course they asked nothing better than to show us what Hyde Park soldiers could do. Uxbridge sent a couple of squadrons into the town. They rode in like thunder-bolts – magnificent to watch – and completely overthrew the lancers.'

'George?' Barbara said.

He turned his head, as though suddenly recollecting her presence. 'Yes, he took part in it. He was not hurt, merely plastered with mud!' He smiled, and said, looking at Worth again: 'That was the funniest part of the business, the Life Guards getting tumbled in the mud. I never remember such a storm. Within half an hour the horses were sinking to their knees, and some of the fields looked like lakes. The 95th were watching the Life Guards from beyond the town – you know what the riflemen are! Kincaid swore that every time one of them suffered a fall he got up covered in mud, and retired to the rear, as though no longer fit to appear on parade! I can tell you, they had to bear a good deal of roasting! Some of the fellows of the 95th shouted to them: "The uglier, the better the solider!" which is one of our Peninsular sayings. However, even if they did look absurdly ashamed of their dirt they did famously.'

'There was no serious engagement?'

'No, nothing but very pretty manœuvres and skirmishing. Uxbridge is a good man, and, what's more, his work today has given his men faith in him. While all the skirmishing was going on, Whinyates began firing off his beloved rockets, with the idea of amusing our cavalry, drawn up beyond Genappe. The main thing was that it didn't amuse the French at all: they hate rockets.'

'What *are* rockets?' asked Judith, who was sitting with her chin in her hands, listening to him.

'Well, they're just *rockets*,' replied the Colonel vaguely. 'No use asking me: I'm not an artillery man. All I know is that they're fired from a small iron triangle, which is set up wherever you want it. Port-fire is applied, the horrid thing begins to spit sparks, and wriggle its tail as though it were alive, and then suddenly darts off. I'm frightened to death of the things: you never know where they will go! Even Whinyates admits that no two of them ever follow the same course. They go whizzing off, and if you are lucky the shells in their heads burst among the French. But they have been known to turn back on themselves, and one fellow swears one chased him about like a squib, and nearly was the end of him.' He pushed back his chair from the table, and stood up, and went to the window, drawing back the curtains a little way. The rain still beat against the panes. 'A Wellington night!' he said, and let the curtain fall back into place. He looked over his shoulder at Worth. 'I want one of your horses, Julian. My poor brute could scarcely stand up under me when I brought him in.'

'You had better take the bay: he's a stayer.'

'You may not see him again,' said the Colonel, with the flicker of a smile.

'I daresay I shan't. How many have you lost so far?'

'Only one. Judith, will you let me raid the larder? We're devilish short of rations.'

'Of course: take what you want,' she answered readily. 'But must you go back yet? Is it not possible for you to rest for a while?'

He shook his head. 'No; I must be back at Headquarters by midnight, you know. It's nearly ten now, and in this wet and darkness it will take me two hours, or more.'

'Where are the Duke's Headquarters?' asked Worth.

'At Waterloo.' He picked up his cloak from the chair on which he had laid it, and clasped it round his neck. His cocked hat in its oilskin cover lay ready to his hand; he tucked it under his arm, and said, with a little hesitation: 'Judith, if you should see Miss Devenish –' He paused, as though he did not know how to continue.

'I shall, I expect,' she replied. 'Do you desire some message to her?'

'No – only that I wish you will tell her that you have seen me tonight, and that all is well.'

'Certainly,' she said.

'Thank you. Don't forget, will you?' He kissed her cheek in a brotherly fashion, and said, with something of his old gaiety: 'You are a capital creature, you know' You understand how important it is to feed a man well!'

'Cold beef!' she protested.

'Nothing could have been better, I assure you. Don't be alarmed if you hear some cannonading tomorrow! We shall have at least one Prussian corps with us, and we don't mean to lose this war, I promise you.' He gave her shoulder a pat, and turned towards Barbara. She was looking pale, but perfectly composed, and held out her hand. He took it. 'I don't know why you are here, but I'm glad you are,' he said. 'Forgive me if I seem dull and stupid. There is so much to say, but I've not time, and this is not the moment. I believe your friend Lavisse to be unhurt. I should have told you before.'

'I am glad, but he is not so much my friend that it can concern me.'

'Tired of him, Bab?' he said.

She winced. He said at once: 'I'm sorry! That was shockingly rude of me.' His hand gripped hers more tightly. 'Goodbye, my dear. Now, Worth, if you please.'

He released her hand, and turned from her to his brother. The corner of his heavy cloak just brushed her dress as he swung round on a spurred heel; he took Worth's arm, and walked to the door with him. 'I'll take a couple of bottles of your champagne, Julian,' he said, and the next instant was gone from Barbara's sight. She heard his voice on the stairs, as he went down with Worth. 'By the by, the 10th did damned well today. They might have been on the parade ground. However, the rain put an end to the skirmishing.'

Judith walked quickly to the door and shut it. 'Skirmishing! Champagne!' she said with a strong indignation. 'How could he? As though he had not a thought in his head but of divisions, and brigades, and regiments!'

'He hasn't,' said Barbara.

'When I think of the suspense you have been in, what you have suffered from the circumstance of – And he behaved as though nothing were of the least consequence but this dreadful war!'

Barbara gave a laugh. 'Is anything else of consequence? I like him for that!'

'You are made to be a soldier's wife! I was put out of all patience! Oh, Bab, that message! What can he have meant by it?'

Barbara looked at her with glinting eyes, and the lifting smile that meant danger. 'I could take him away from that chit in a week. Less! A day!'

'I daresay you might: indeed, I've no doubt of it. But I wish you would not talk so.'

'Do not alarm yourself. I shan't do it. If only he comes safe back he may have her – yes, and I'll smile and be glad!' Her face broke up; she cried out: 'No, not that! but I won't make mischief – I promise I won't make mischief!'

Twenty minutes later Worth re-entered the room to find both ladies seated on the sofa, in companionable silence. He said in his calm way: 'Take my advice, and go to bed. There is no danger tonight, but I may be obliged to convey you to the coast tomorrow. So get what rest you can now.'

'Has Charles gone?' Judith asked.

'Yes – and your Sunday dinner with him.'

'Oh dear! But it does not signify. I wish it would stop raining! I do not like to think of him riding all that way in this downpour!'

'He will do very well, I assure you. If you wish to be pitying

305

anyone, pity the poor devils who are bivouacking out in the open tonight.'

She rose. 'I do pity them. Come, Bab! he is right; we should go to bed.'

The words were hardly spoken when they heard a knock on the street door. Even Worth looked a little surprised, and raised his brows. The butler had not yet retired to bed; they heard him go to the door and open it; and a moment later the stairs creaked under his heavy tread. He entered the salon, but before he could announce the visitor, Lucy Devenish had rushed past him into the room.

A wet cloak and hood enveloped her; she was pale, and evidently in great agitation. She looked wildly round the room, and then, fixing her eyes on Judith's astonished countenance, faltered: 'My uncle heard that Colonel Audley had been at Sir Charles Stuart's!'

'He has been there, and here, too, but I am afraid he has this moment gone,' said Judith. 'My dear child, surely you did not come alone, and in this shocking storm? Let me take your cloak! How imprudent this is of you!'

'Oh, I know, I know! But I could not sleep without trying to get news! No one knows that I am not in my bed – it is wrong of me, but indeed, indeed I had to come!'

Judith removed the dripping cloak from her shoulders. 'Hush, Lucy! There is no need for this alarm. Charles is safe, and all is well, upon my honour!'

Miss Devenish pushed the hair from her brow with one distracted hand. 'I ran the whole way! I hoped to see him – but it is no matter!' She made an effort to be calm, and sank down upon a chair, saying: 'I am so glad he is safe! Did he tell you what had been happening? Was there any news? What did he say?'

'Yes, indeed; he has been describing to us how our Army has been obliged to retreat to Mont St Jean. It appears there has been no very serious fighting today: nothing but some cavalry skirmishes, which he said were extremely *pretty*, if you please!'

'Oh –! Please tell me! I – we have heard so little all day, you see,' Lucy said, with a forced laugh.

'There was nothing of any consequence, my dear. Indeed, from what he said I gathered that only some hussars and the Life Guards have been actually engaged with the enemy. Charles himself –'

She stopped, for Lucy had sprung up, her face so ghastly and her manner so distraught that for a moment Judith almost feared that she had taken leave of her senses. 'Charles? What is *he* to me?' Lucy said hoarsely. 'It is George – George! Was there no word? No message for me? Lady Barbara, for God's sake tell me, or I shall go mad with this suspense!'

'*George*?' gasped Judith, grasping a chairback for support.

'Yes, George!' Lucy cried fiercely. 'I can bear no more! I must know what has become of him, I tell you!'

'He is perfectly safe,' said Barbara coolly.

Lucy gave a long sigh and dropped on to the sofa. 'Oh, thank God, thank God!' she sobbed. 'What I have undergone – The torture! The suspense!'

Across the room, Barbara's eyes met Judith's for a moment; then she glanced down at Lucy's bowed head, and said: 'Oh, confound you, must you cry because he is safe?'

Judith stepped up to the sofa and laid her hand on Lucy's shoulder. 'Lucy, what is this folly?' she asked. 'What can Lord George be to you?'

Lucy lifted her face from her hands. 'He is my husband!' she said.

A dumbfounded silence fell. Barbara was staring at her with narrowed eyes, Judith in utter incredulity. With deliberation, the Earl polished his quizzing glass, and raised it, and gazed at Lucy in a dispassionately considering fashion.

'George actually married you?' said Barbara slowly. 'When?'

'Last year – in England!' Lucy replied, covering her face with her hands.

'Then all these months –!' Judith ejaculated. 'Good God, how is this possible?'

'It is true. I am aware of what your feelings must be, but oh, if you knew how bitterly I have been punished, you would pity me!'

'I do not know what to say! It is not for me to reproach you! But what can have prompted you to commit such an act of folly? Why this long secrecy? I am utterly at a loss!'

'Ah, you are not acquainted with my grandfather!' said Barbara. 'The secrecy is easily explained. What, however, passes my comprehension is how the devil you persuaded George into marriage!'

'He loves me!' Lucy said, rearing up her head.

'He must indeed do so. Odd! I should not have thought you the girl to catch his fancy.'

'Oh, Bab, pray hush!' besought Judith.

'Nonsense! If Miss Devenish – I beg pardon! – if Lady George has become my sister the sooner she grows accustomed to the language I use the better it will be. So George was afraid to confess the whole to my grandfather, was he?'

'Yes. I cannot tell you all, but you must not blame him! Mine was the fault. I allowed myself to be swept off my feet. The marriage took place in Sussex. George was in the expectation of gaining his promotion –'

'Ah, I begin to understand you! My grandfather was to have given him the purchase money, eh? Instead he was obliged to spend in hushing up the Carroway affair, and was disinclined to assist George further.'

'Yes,' said Lucy. 'Everything went awry! That scandal – but all that is over now! Indeed, indeed, George loves me, and there can be no more such affairs!'

'My poor innocent! But continue!'

'He said we must wait. His circumstances were awkward: there were debts; and I was unhappily aware of my uncle's dislike of him. I feared nothing but anger could be met with in that quarter. My uncle thinks him a spendthrift, and that, in his eyes, outweighs every consideration of birth or title. To have declared our marriage would have meant George's ruin. But the misery of my position, the necessity of deceiving my uncle and my aunt, the wretchedness of stolen meetings with George – all these led to lowness of spirits in me, and in him the natural irritation of a man tied in such a way to one who –' Her utterance was choked by sobs; she overcame them, and continued: 'Misunderstandings, even quarrels, arose between us. I began to believe that he regretted a union entered into so wrongly. When my uncle and aunt decided to come to Brussels in January, I accompanied them willingly, feeling that nothing could be worse than the life I was then leading. But the separation seemed to draw us closer together! When George arrived in this country all the love which I thought had waned seemed in an instant to reanimate towards me! *He* would have declared our marriage then: it was I who insisted on the secret still being kept! Think me what you will! I deserve your censure, but my courage failed. Situated as I was, in the midst of this restricted society, believed by all to be a single woman, I could not face the scandal that such a declaration would have caused! I was even afraid to be seen in his company lest anyone should suspect an attachment to exist between us. All the old wretchedness returned! George – oh, only to tease me into yielding! – began to devote himself to other and more beautiful females. I have come near to putting an end to my existence, even! Then the war broke out. I saw George at the Duchess's ball. Every misunderstanding seemed to vanish, but we had so little time together! He was forced to leave me: had it not been for Colonel Audley's promising to send me word if he could, I must have become demented!'

'Then Charles knew?' Judith exclaimed.

'Yes! On the very night that his engagement was put an end to he found me in great distress, and persuaded me to confide in him. His nature, so frank and upright, must have revolted from the duplicity of mine, but he uttered no word of blame. His sympathy for my situation, the awkwardness of which he understood immediately, his kindness – I cannot speak of it! I had engaged his silence as the price of my confidence. His promise was given, and implicitly kept.'

'Good God!' said Judith blankly. She raised her eyes from

Lucy's face, and looked at Barbara. She gave an uncertain laugh. 'Oh, Bab, the fools we have been!'

'Yes! And the wretch Charles has been! Infamous!' Barbara walked up to the sofa, and laid her hand on Lucy's shoulder. 'Dry your tears! Your marriage is in the best tradition of *my* family, I assure you.'

Lucy clasped her hand. 'Can you ever forgive me?'

'What the devil has my forgiveness to do with it? You have not injured me. I wish you extremely happy.'

'How kind you are! I do not deserve to be happy!'

'You are very unlikely to be,' said Barbara, somewhat dryly. 'George will make you a damnable husband.'

'Oh no, no! If only he is not killed!' Lucy shuddered.

It was some time before she could regain her composure, and nearly an hour before she left the house. Worth had ordered the horses to be put to, and undertook to escort her to her uncle's lodgings. Judith and Barbara found themselves alone at last.

'Well!' Barbara said. 'You will allow that at least I never contracted a secret marriage!'

'I have never been so deceived in anyone in my life!' Judith replied, in a shocked tone.

Twenty-One

Colonel Audley reached the village of Waterloo a few minutes before midnight. The road through the Forest of Soignes, though roughly paved down the centre, was in a bad state, the heavy rainfall having turned the uncobbled portions on either side of the pavé into bogs which in places were impassable. Wagons and tilt cars were some of them deeply embedded in mud, and some overturned after coming into collision with the Belgian cavalry in their flight earlier in the day. In the darkness it was necessary for a horseman to pick his way carefully. The contents of the wagons in some cases strewed the road; here and there a cart, with two of its wheels in the air, lay across the pavé; and several horses which had fallen in one of the mad rushes for safety had been shot, and now sprawled in the mud at the sides of the chaussée. The rain dripped ceaselessly from the leaves of the beech trees; the moonlight was obscured by heavy clouds; and only by the glimmer of lantern slung on the wagons lining the road was it possible to discern the way.

At Waterloo, lights burned in many of the cottage windows, for there was not a dwelling-place in the village, or in any of the hamlets nearby, which did not house a general and his staff, or senior officers who had been fortunate enough to secure a bed or a mattress under cover. The tiny inn owned by Veuve Bedonghien, opposite the church, was occupied by the Duke, and here the Colonel dismounted. A figure loomed up to meet him. 'Is it yourself, sir?' his groom enquired anxiously, holding up a lantern. 'Eh, if that's not his lordship's Rufus!'

The Colonel gave up the bridle. 'Yes. Rub him down well, Cherry!' The faint crackle of musketry fire in the distance came to his ears. 'What's all this popping?'

Cherry gave a grunt. 'Proper spiteful they've been all evening. Pickets, they tell me. "Well," I said, "we didn't do such in Spain, that's all I know."'

The Colonel turned away and entered the inn. An orderly informed him that the Duke was still up, and he went into a room in the front of the house to make his report.

The Duke was seated at a table, with De Lancey at his elbow, looking over a map of the country. Lord Fitzroy occupied a chair on one side of the fire, and was placidly writing on his knee. He looked up as the Colonel came in, and smiled.

'Hallo, Audley!' said his lordship. 'What's the news in Brussels?'

'There's been a good deal of panic, sir. The news of our retreat sent hundreds off to Antwerp,' replied the Colonel, handing over the letters he had brought.

'Ah, I daresay! Road bad?'

'Yes, sir, and needs clearing. In places it's choked with baggage and overturned carts. I spoke to one of our own drivers, and it seems the Belgian cavalry upset everything in their way when they galloped to Brussels.'

'I'll have it cleared first thing,' De Lancey said. 'It's the fault of these rascally Flemish drivers! There's no depending on them.'

Sir Colin Campbell came into the room, and upon seeing Audley remarked that there was some cold pie to be had; the Duke nodded dismissal, and the Colonel went off to a room upstairs which was occupied by Gordon and Colonel Canning. A fire had been lit in the grate, and several wet garments were drying in front of it. Occasionally it belched forth a puff of acrid woodsmoke, which mingled with the blue smoke of the two officers' cigars, and made the atmosphere in the small apartment extremely thick. Gordon was lying on a mattress in his shirt-sleeves, with his hands linked behind his head; and Canning was sprawling in an ancient armchair by the fire, critically inspecting a crumpled coat which was hung over a chair back to dry.

'Welcome to our humble quarters!' said Canning. 'Don't be afraid! You'll soon get used to the smoke.'

'What a reek!' said Audley. 'Why the devil don't you open the window?'

'A careful reconnaissance,' Gordon informed him, 'has revealed the fact that the window is not made to open. What are you concealing under your cloak?'

The Colonel grinned, and produced his bottles of champagne, which he set down on the table.

'Canning, tell the orderly downstairs to get hold of some glasses!' said Gordon, sitting up. 'Hi, Charles, don't put that wet cloak of yours anywhere near my coat!'

Canning hitched the coat off the chair back, and tossed it to its owner. 'It's dry. We have a very nice billet here, Charles. Try this chair! I daren't sit in it any longer for fear of being too sore to sit in the saddle tomorrow.'

Colonel Audley spread his cloak over the chair back, sat down on the edge of the truckle bed against the wall, and began to pull off his muddied boots. 'I'm going to sleep,' he replied. 'In fact, I rather think that I'm asleep already. Where's Slender Billy?'

'At Abeiche. Horses at L'Espinettes.'

The Colonel wiped his hands on a large handkerchief, took off his coat, and stretched himself full length on the patchwork quilt. 'What do they stuff their mattresses with here?' he enquired. 'Turnips?'

'We rather suspect mangel-worzels,' replied Canning. 'Did you hear the pickets enjoying themselves when you came in?'

'Damned fools!' said Audley. 'What's the sense of it?'

'There ain't any, but if the feeling in our lines and the French lines tonight is anything to go by we're in for a nasty affair tomorrow.'

'Well, I don't approve of it,' said Gordon, raising himself on his elbow to throw the stub of his cigar into the fire. 'We used to manage things much better in Spain. Do you remember those fellows of ours who used to leave a bowl out with a piece of money in it every night for the French vedettes to take in exchange for cognac? Now, that's what I call a proper, friendly way of conducting a war.'

'There wasn't anything very friendly about our fellows the night the French took the money without filling the bowl,' Audley remarked. 'Have the French all come up?'

'Can't say,' replied Canning. 'There's been a good deal of artillery arriving on their side, judging from the rumbling I heard when I was on the field half an hour ago. Queer thing: our fellows have lit campfires, as usual, but there isn't one to be seen in the French lines.'

'Poor devils!' said Audley, and shut his eyes.

Downstairs, the Duke was also stretched on his bed, having dropped asleep with that faculty he possessed of snatching rest anywhere and at any time. At three o'clock Lord Fitzroy woke him with the intelligence that Baron Müffling had come over from his quarters with a despatch from Marshal Blücher at Wavre.

The Duke sat up, and swung his legs to the ground. 'What's the time? Three o'clock? Time to get up. How's the weather?'

'Clearing a little, sir.'

'Good!' His lordship pulled on his hessians, shrugged himself into his coat, and strode into the adjoining room, where Müffling awaited him. 'Hallo, Baron! Fitzroy tells me the weather's beginning to clear.'

'It is very bad still, however, and the ground in many places a morass.'

'My people call this sort of thing "Wellington weather",' observed his lordship. 'It always rains before my battles. What's the news from the Marshal? Hope he's no worse?'

The Marshal Prince had been last heard of as prostrate from the results of having been twice ridden over by cavalry when his horse was shot under him at Ligny. It would not have been surprising had an old gentleman of over seventy years of age succumbed to this rough usage, but Marshal Forwards was made of stern stuff. He was dosing himself with a concoction of his own, in which garlic figured largely, and had every intention of leading his army in person again. He had ordered General Bülow to march at daybreak, through Wavre, on Chapelle St Lambert, with the Second Army Corps in support; and wrote asking for information, and promising support.

After a short conference with the Duke, Müffling went back to his own quarters to send off the intelligence that was wanted, and to represent to General Gneisenau in the plainest language the propriety of moving to the support of the Allied Army without any loss of time.

The Duke, apparently quite refreshed by his short nap, sat down to write letters. '*Pray keep the English quiet if you can,*' he wrote to Sir Charles Stuart. '*Let them all be prepared to move, but neither be in a hurry nor a fright, as all will yet turn out well.*'

But his lordship had not forgotten the bugbear of his right wing. Only a few hours earlier, he had sent orders to General Colville, at Braine-le-Comte, to retire upon Hal, and had instructed Prince Frederick to defend the position between Hal and Enghien for as long as possible. It was his opinion that Bonaparte's best strategy would be to outflank him, and seize Brussels by a *coup de main*. '*Il se peut que l'ennemi nous tourne par Hal,*' he wrote to the Duc de Berri. '*Si cela arrive, je prie votre Altesse Royale de marcher sur Anvers et de vous cantonner dans le voisinage.*'

His lordship found time to send a note to his Brussels flirt, too. His indefatigable pen warned that her family ought to make preparations to leave Brussels, but added: '*I will give you the earliest intimation of any danger that may come to my knowledge. At present I know of none.*'

His letters all written and despatched, his final dispositions checked, the Duke sent for his shaving water; and Thornhill, his phlegmatic cook, began to prepare breakfast. His lordship was notoriously indifferent to the food he ate (he had, in fact, once consumed a bad egg at breakfast before one of his battles in Spain, merely remarking in a preoccupied tone, when he had finished it: 'By the by, Fitzroy, is that egg of yours fresh? for mine was quite rotten'), but Thornhill had his pride to consider, and might be trusted to concoct a palatable meal out of the most unpromising materials.

Just before the Duke left his Headquarters, a lieutenant of hussars rode into Waterloo at a gallop, and flung himself out of the saddle at the door of the little inn. His gay dress was generously splattered with mud, but Colonel Audley, leaning against the doorpost, had no difficulty in recognising an officer of his own regiment, and hailed him immediately: 'Hallo! Where are you from?'

The lieutenant saluted. 'Lindsay, sir, of Captain Taylor's squadron on picket duty at Smohain. Message for his lordship from General Bülow!'

'Come in, then. What's the news at the front?'

'Nothing much our way, sir. It's stopped raining, but there's a heavy mist lying on the ground. Captain Taylor saw two corps of French cavalry, in close column, dismounted, within a carbine shot of our vedettes, and a patrol of heavy cavalry moving off to the east: to feel for the Prussians, he supposed. Captain Taylor had just moved our squadron into Smohain village when a Prussian officer with a patrol arrived with the news that General Bülow's corps was advancing and was three-quarters of a league distant. Captain Taylor sent me off at once with the intelligence.'

'You'll be welcome,' said the Colonel, and handed him over to Lord Fitzroy.

The Duke set out to join the Army at an early hour, and was accompanied by a numerous suite. In addition to his aides-de-camp a brilliant *corps diplomatique* rode with him, in all the splendour of their various uniforms. Prussia, Austria, Spain, the Netherlands, and little Sardinia were represented in the persons of Barons Müffling and Vincent, Generals Pozzo di Borgo and Alava, Counts van Reede and D'Aglié, and their satellites. Orders and gold lace glittered and plumes waved about his lordship, a neat plain figure, mounted on a hollow-backed horse of little beauty and few manners.

The Duke whom his troops had christened Beau Douro, was

dressed, with his usual care and complete absence of ostentation, in a blue frock, short blue cloak, white pantaloons, and tasselled hessians. The only touch of dandyism he affected was a white cravat instead of a black stock. His low-crowned cocked hat had no plume, but bore beside the black cockade of England, three smaller ones in the colours of Portugal, Spain, and the Netherlands. He held his telescope in his hand, and sat an ugly horse with no particular grace.

His lordship cared nothing for the appearance of his horse. 'There may be faster horses, no doubt many handsomer,' he said, 'but for bottom and endurance I never saw his fellow.' Indeed, he had paid a long price for Copenhagen, and had used him continually in Spain. He was an unpleasant brute to ride, but he seemed to delight in going into action, and evinced far more delight at the sight of troops than the troops felt at his too near approach. 'Take care of that there 'orse! We know him!' said the Peninsular veterans, keeping wary eyes on his powerful hindquarters. ''E kicks out!'

The position which the Allied Army had taken up on the previous night was some two miles south of Waterloo, before the village of Mont St Jean, and immediately in rear of the hollow road which led westward from Wavre to the village of Braine-l'Alleud. The ground had been surveyed the preceding year, and a map drawn of it, and although it was not perhaps ideal, it possessed one feature at least which commended it to the Duke. It fell away in a gentle declivity to the north, which enabled his lordship to keep all but the front lines of his troops out of sight of the enemy. The hollow road, which dipped in some places between steep, hedge-crowned banks, was intersected by the caussée leading from Brussels to Charleroi, and, farther west, by the main road from Nivelles, which joined the chaussée at Mont St Jean. In itself it nearly everywhere constituted the front line of the position, but there were several outposts, like bastions, dotted along the position. On the extreme left there were the farm of Ter La Haye, and the village of Papelotte, occupied by Prince Bernhard of Saxe-Weimar's Nassau troops. On the left centre, situated three hundred yards south of the hollow road, upon the western side of the Charleroi chaussée, was La Haye Sainte, a semi-fortified farm, with a garden and orchard attached; and on the right, where the hollow road took a southerly bend before crossing the Nivelles highway, was the château and wood of Hougoumont, whose main gate gave on to the short avenue leading to the Nivelles road, down which, so short a time before, Lady Worth had driven in an open barouche, on an expedition of pleasure.

The country was undulating, and to the east of the Charleroi road a valley separated the Allied front line from the ridge, where, as soon as day broke, French troops could be seen assembling. To the west of the chaussée, the banks of the hollow road became less steep; behind Hougoumont, and overlooking it, was a high plateau, bounded on the right by the ravine through which the Nivelles road ran. Across this road, another plateau was occupied by Lord Hill's Corps, drawn back *en potence*, and occupying the villages of Braine-l'Alleud and Merbe Braine.

The Army, retreating to this position through the storm of the previous afternoon, had spent a miserable night, exposed to a downpour that turned the ground into a bog, saturated coats and blankets, and streamed through the canvas tents. Straw, bean-stalks, sheaves or rye and barley had been collected by the men to form mattresses, but nothing could keep the wet out. Gunners sought shelter under the gun carriages; infantrymen huddled together under the lee of hedges, and many, abandoning all attempt to sleep, sat round the campfires, deriving what comfort they could from their pipes, and a comparison of these condi-tions with those endured in Spain. Peninsular veterans assured the Johnny Newcomes that the miseries they were undergoing were as nothing to the sufferings met with in the Pyrenees. One or two recalled the retreat of Sir John Moore's army upon Corunna, till the raw recruits, listening wide-eyed to the description of forced marches, barefoot over mountain passes deep in snow, began to feel that they were not so very badly off after all. No rations had been served out overnight, but quite a number of skinny fowls had been looted by seasoned campaigners, and were broiled in kettles over the campfires.

The rain ceased shortly before daybreak, but the atmosphere was vapoury, and heavy with damp. Men got up from their sodden beds shaking as though with ague, their garments clammy over their numb bodies, and their teeth rattling in their heads with a chill that seemed to have penetrated into their very bones. A double allowance of gin served out at dawn helped to bring a little warmth to them, but there were some who, lying down exhausted the night before, did not wake in the morning.

The vicious spitting of musketry had sounded up and down the line of pickets at intervals during the night, but with the daylight a general popping began, as the men fired their pieces in the air to clean the barrels of rust. The vedettes and the sentries were withdrawn; optimists declared the weather to be fairing up; old soldiers became busy drying their clothes and cleaning their arms; young soldiers stared over the dense mist in the valley to the ridge where the French were beginning to show themselves.

At five o'clock, drums, bugles, and trumpets all along the two-mile front sounded the Assembly. Staff officers were seen galloping in every direction; brigades began to move into their positions: here a regiment of Light Dragoons changed ground; there a battalion of blue-coated Dutch–Belgians marched along the hollow road with their quick, swinging step; or a troop of horse artillery thundered over the ground to a position in the front line. A breakfast of stir-about was served to the men; a detachment of riflemen, posted in a sandpit on the left side of the Charleroi road, immediately south of its junction with the hollow road, began to make an *abattis* across the chaussée with branches of trees.

A tumbledown cottage on the main road, between Mont St Jean and the hollow way, had been occupied during the night by the Colonel of the 95th Rifles, and some of his officers and men had kindled a fire against one of its walls, and had boiled a huge camp kettle full of tea, milk, and sugar over it. The Duke stopped there for a cup of this sticky beverage on his way from Waterloo; and Colonel Audley, standing beside his horse, and also sipping tea from a pannikin, found himself accosted by Captain Kincaid, whose invincible gaiety did not seem to have been in the least impaired by a night spent in the pouring rain. He had slept soundly, waking to find his clothes drenched and his horse, which he had tethered to a sword stuck in the ground, gone.

'Just drew his sword, and marched off!' he said. 'Did you ever hear of an adjutant going into action without his horse? You might as well go without your arms.'

'Johnny, you crazy coot!' the Colonel exclaimed, laughing.

'How was I to know the brute had no proper feeling towards me? He's a low fellow: I found him hobnobbing half a mile off with a couple of artillery horses.'

'You know, you have the luck of the devil!' the Colonel told him.

'I have, haven't I? You'd have said I might as well have looked for a needle in a haystack as for one horse in this mob. Have some more tea? That kettle of ours ought to get its brevet for devotion to duty. It has supplied everyone of the bigwigs with tea, from the Duke downwards.'

'No, I won't have any more. Where are you stationed?'

'Oh, right in the forefront! Our 2nd and 3rd Battalions have been drafted to General Adam, and I believe are over there, on the right wing,' replied Kincaid, with an airy gesture to the west. 'But the rest of us are going to occupy a snug sandpit, and the knoll behind it, on the chaussée, opposite to La Haye Sainte. I've had a look at the position: we shall have our right resting on the chaussée and as far as I can see we ought to get the brunt of whatever the French mean to give us.'

'Well, that'll give you something to brag about,' said the Colonel, handing over his empty pannikin. 'Good luck to you, Johnny!'

At nine o'clock, the Duke rode from end to end of the position, inspecting the disposition of the troops and making final alterations. There being as yet no sign of the Prussians advancing from the east, two brigades of light cavalry, Sir Hussey Vivian's hussars and Sir John Vandeleur's dragoons, had been posted to guard the left flank until the Prussians should arrive to relieve them. On Vandeleur's right, Prince Bernhard of Saxe-Weimar's brigade of Nassau and Orange-Nassau troops held the advance posts of Papelotte and Ter La Haye. Behind him, Vincke's and Best's Hanoverians were ranged. Next came Pack's Highlanders, a skeleton of the brigade which had marched out of Brussels on June 15th; and Kempt's almost equally depleted 8th Brigade. These troops, with Vincke's Landwehr battalions, made up the 5th Division under Sir Thomas Picton, and occupied the left centre of the line. In support, some way behind the line, on the downward slope of the ground to the rear, Sir William Ponsonby's Union Brigade of English, Scots, and Irish dragoons was drawn up, with Ghigny's brigade of light cavalry some little way behind them. The hollow road, at this point, dipped between steep banks, crowned on the northern side by straggling hedges which afforded cover for the division. On the southern slope of the bank, closing the interval between Pack's right and Kempt's left, was placed Count Bylandt's brigade of Dutch–Belgians, in an uncomfortably exposed position, looking across the valley to the ridge occupied by the French. Kempt's right lay in the angle formed by the chaussée and the hollow road from Wavre. The 1st Battalion of the 95th Rifles was attached to the brigade, and their light troops were posted in a sandpit almost opposite La Haye Sainte, and on the knoll behind it, considerably in advance of the line.

La Haye Sainte itself, situated three hundred yards south of the crossroad, abutted directly on to the chaussée and was occupied by the 2nd Light Battalion of Ompteda's Germans, under Major Baring. Beyond its white walls and blue-tiled roof, the main Charleroi road descended into the valley, and rose again to where, on the southern ridge, the farm of La Belle Alliance could be seen from the Allied line.

The chaussée, cutting through the centre of the Allied line, separated Picton's division from Sir Charles Alten's, drawn up to the west of it. Colonel von Ompteda's brigade of the King's German Legion lay with its left against the chaussée, and with La Haye Sainte in its immediate front; next came Count Kielmansegg's Hanoverian line battalions; and, west of them, where the hollow road began to curve southwards, was Sir Colin Halkett's brigade of one Highland and three English regiments. From Halkett's right, to where the Nivelles road crossed the hollow way, the ground was strongly held by Cooke's division of British Guards occupying the high ground behind and over-looking the château of Hougoumont. Seven companies of the Coldstream, under Sir James Macdonnell, had been thrown into the château, and had been busy all night strengthening the fortifications; while the four light companies of the division, under Lord Saltoun, were spent forward as skirmishers into the wood and orchard.

In the triangle of ground formed by the junction, at Mont St Jean, of the two great highways from Charleroi and Nivelles, a number of cavalry brigades were massed behind the infantry, and out of sight of the enemy. In rear of Ompteda, and separated from the Union Brigade of heavy cavalry only by the chaussée, was Lord Edward Somerset's heavy brigade of Household Cavalry: Life Guards, Dragoons and Blues, in magnificent array. Behind them, in reserve, was Baron Collaert's Dutch–Belgic cavalry division, comprising a brigade of carabiniers, under General Trip; and a brigade of light cavalry under Baron van Merlen. Immediately to the rear of Kielmansegg were General Kruse's Nassau troops, in reserve, with Colonel Arentschildt's light dragoons and hussars of the legion supporting them; and, lying against the Nivelles road, considerably withdrawn from the front, was the Brunswick contingent. Upon the plateau behind the Guards' division were posted Major-General Dörnberg's light dragoons; a Hanoverian regiment known as the Cumberland Hussars; and Major-General Grant's hussar brigade, which lay directly behind Byng's Guards, against the Nivelles road, overlooking the ravine running north of Merbe Braine, and the plateau beyond.

On this plateau, drawn back *en potence* to guard the right flank of the line, was Lord Hill's Second Army Corps. Of this corps, Sir Henry Clinton's division occupied the ground nearest to the highway, Adam's brigade being drawn up immediately to the west of it. The village of Merbe Braine, nestling to the north behind a belt of trees, was occupied by Hew Halkett's brigade of Hanoverian militia, and Colonel Du Plat's line battalions of the legion. Some way to the west, Baron Chassé's Dutch–Belgic division was stationed round Braine-l'Alleud, Colonel Detmer's brigade occupying the village itself and Count d'Aubremé's brigade being posted to the south-west, round the farm of Vieux Foriez, as an observation corps. Of General Colville's 4th Division, eight miles away at Hal with Prince Frederick's corps, only one brigade was present, Colonel Mitchell's which was formed on the west of the Nivelles road, covering the avenue which led to the great north gate of Hougoumont.

Attached to the divisions and the cavalry brigades were brigades and troops of artillery, those in front line being placed in the intervals of the infantry brigades, and slightly in advance of them. Rogers's brigade and Ross's Chestnut Troop guarded the Charleroi chaussée; Whinyates was attached to the Union Brigade with his rockets; Gardiner was Vivian's hussars; Stevenart's heroic battery with Prince Bernhard's Nassauers; Rettberg before Best; Byleveld with Count Bylandt's brigade; while, west of the chaussée, in front of Alten's and Cooke's divisions, were ranged Cleeve's and Kuhlmann's German batteries, Bean's, Webber-Smith's, Ramsay's and Bull's brigades and troops, each with six guns, manned by eighty or more gunners and drivers, half a dozen bombardiers, and the usual complement of sergeants, corporals, farriers, and trumpeters. Each troops came up in sub-divisions, an impressive cavalcade with two hundred horses, and a train of forge carts, spare-wheel carriages and extra-ammunition wagons. Every horse was brought on to the field in the pink of condition, his flanks plumped out with plundered forage. A hard life, the artillery officer's, for while, on the one hand, plundering was strictly forbidden by the Duke, on the other, the allowance of forage was insufficient to put the fat on the horses which his lordship demanded. 'Either way you quake in your shoes,' declared Captain Mercer bitterly. 'Bring your troop on to the ground with your beasts a shade thinner than the next man's, and that damned cold eye of the Duke's will see the difference in a flash. You won't be asked questions about it, and if you try to defend yourself you won't be attended to. You'll be judged out of hand as unfit for your command, and very likely removed from the Army as well. But if you plunder the poor foreigner's fields, and he reports you to the Duke – whew!'

While the Duke, accompanied by his military secretary, his aides-de-camp, the Prince of Orange, Lord Uxbridge, the diplomatic corps, and their train, was inspecting his position, the French columns were mustering upon the opposite heights. The weather was clearing fast, the mist in the hollows curling away in wreaths; and occasionally a pale shaft of sunlight would pierce through the clouds for a moment or two. The ground, intersected by hedges of beech and hornbeam, was nearly all of it under cultivation, crops of rye, wheat, barley, oats and clover standing shoulder-high, with here and there a ploughed field showing dark between the stretches of waving grain.

The bulk of the French army had bivouacked about Genappe, but at nine o'clock, just as the Duke started to ride down his lines, the heads of the columns began to appear above the ridge to the south. Drums and trumpets were first heard, and then the music of the bands, playing a medley of martial tunes. Strains of the *Marseillaise*, mingled with *Veillons au Salut de l'Empire*, floated across the valley to the Allied lines. Four columns, destined to form the first line, came marching over the hill, and deployed in perfect order, just as seven others appeared descending the slope. From the Allied lines the whole magnificent spectacle was watched by thousands of pairs of eyes. Knowledgeable gentlemen exclaimed at intervals: 'That's Reille's corps, moving off to their left! . . . that's D'Erlon! . . . those are Kellermann's cuirassiers!'

The mist still lay white in the valley, but beyond it, less than a mile distant, the ground was gradually becoming covered with dark masses of infantry. As the divisions deployed, the cavalry began to appear. Squadron after squadron of cuirassiers galloped over the brow of the hill, their steel breastplates and copper crests occasionally caught by the feeble rays of sunlight trying to pierce through the clouds. The slope was soon vivid with bright, shifting colours, as Chasseurs à Cheval, blazing with green and gold, giant carabiniers in white, brass-casqued dragoons, hussars in every colour, Grenadiers à Cheval in imperial blue with bearskin shakos, and red lancers with towering white plumes and swallow-tailed pennons fluttering on the ends of their lances, cantered into their positions.

It was an hour and a half before the movement which brought the French Army into six formidable lines, forming six double W's, was completed, and during that time the Duke of Wellington was employed in inspecting his own position. Sir Thomas Picton, still in his frockcoat and round hat, grimly concealing even from his aides-de-camp that an ugly wound, roughly bandaged by his servant after Quatre-Bras, lay beneath his shabby coat, had also inspected it very early in the morning, and had told Sir John Colborne, of Adam's brigade, that he considered it to be the most damnable place for fighting he had ever seen.

Lord Uxbridge, tall and handsome in his magnificent hussar dress, preferred the position to that of Quatre-Bras, but was fretted by the impossibility, owing to the suddenness of the order to advance on June 16th, of forming his cavalry into divisions; and by the circumstance of having been formed by the Duke, at the eleventh hour, that the Prince of Orange desired him to take over the command of all the Dutch–Belgic cavalry. Uxbridge accepted the charge, but was forced to observe that he thought it unfortunate that he should have had no opportunity of making himself acquainted with any of the officers, or their regiments. He was anxiously awaiting the arrival of the Prussian corps to relieve Vivian's and Vandeleur's much needed brigades on the left flank, and more than once adverted to its non-appearance. The Duke, whose irritability fell away from him the moment he set foot on a battlefield, replied calmly that they would be up presently: the roads were in a bad state, which would account for their delay.

Baron Müffling, knowing the Prussian chief of staff's mistrust of the Duke, was also anxious, and had already despatched one of his Jägers to try to get news of Bülow's advance. He knew that the Duke had placed the weakened 5th Division on the left centre in the expectation of its being immediately strengthened by Prussian infantry: and having by this time identified himself far more with the British than with the Prussian Army, Bülow's delay caused him a good deal of inward perturbation. Being a sensible man, he refused to permit his anxiety to oppress him, but fixed his mind instead on the problems immediately before him. He rode beside the Duke, acquainting himself with the disposition of the Allied troops, and occasionally proffering a suggestion. When he went with him into the château of Hougoumont, he felt considerable doubts of the possibility of the post's being held by a mere detachment of British Guards. But the Duke seemed perfectly satisfied. He rode into the courtyard through the great north gate, and was met by Lieutenant-Colonel Sir James Macdonnell, a huge Highlander with narrowed, humorous eyes, a square jowl, and the frame of an ox, whom he greeted in a cheerful tone, and with marked friendliness. Macdonnell took him round the fortifications, showing him the work which the garrison had been engaged on during the night. The brick walls of the garden had been pierced for loopholes; wooden platforms erected to enable a second firing line to shoot over the walls; and flagstones, timbers, and broken wagons used as barricades to the various entrances. The Duke gave the whole a hasty survey, and, as he prepared to mount his horse again, nodded to Müffling, and said: 'They call me a Sepoy General. Well! Napoleon shall see today how a Sepoy General can defend a position!'

Müffling bowed, but thought the chances of holding the

château so small that he felt obliged to express his doubts. 'It is not, in my opinion, sir, a strong post. I confess, I find it hard to believe that it can be held against a determined assault.'

The Duke swinging himself into the saddle, gave a short laugh, and pointed at the impassive Highlander. 'Ah! You do not know Macdonnell!' he said.

Those of his staff who stood near him laughed; the Duke raised two fingers to his hat, and rode off.

The Baron caught him up on the avenue leading to the Nivelles road, and began to urge the propriety of strengthening the post. His trained eye had instantly perceived that it was of paramount importance, for the possession of it by the French would enable them to enfilade the Allied lines from its shelter. 'Even supposing that the garrison should be able to hold it against assault, Duke, how will it be if the enemy advances up the Nivelles road?' he argued.

'We shall see,' responded his lordship. 'Let us take a look at the ground.'

An inspection of the Nivelles road, and the country to the south of it, resulted in his lordship's drawing in his right wing a little, raising a battery to swept the road, and posting some infantry in the rear. Several aides-de-camp went galloping off with brief messages scrawled on leaves torn from his lordship's pocketbook, and the Duke turned his attention to the wood to the south of the château, which was occupied by Saltoun's light companies of the Guards. His lordship altered this arrangement, withdrawing the Guards into the garden and orchard, and desiring the Prince of Orange to send orders to Prince Bernhard to despatch a battalion of his Nassau troops to occupy the wood. Colonel Audley was sent at the same time to bring up a detachment of Hanoverians, and rode off in a spatter of mud kicked up by his horse's hooves.

Upon his return to the Duke, who had moved towards the centre of the position, he passed by the 1st Guards, and caught a glimpse of Lord Harry Alastair, looking rather tired, but apparently in good spirits. He called a greeting to him, and Lord

Harry came up, and stood for a moment with his hand on the Colonel's saddlebow. 'Enjoying yourself Harry?' asked Audley.

'Lord, yes! You know we were engaged at Quatre-Bras, don't you? By Jove, there was never anything like it, was there? If only poor Hay – but never mind that!' he added hastily, blinking his sandy lashes. 'It's just that he was rather a friend of mine. I say, though, what do you think? I'm damned if William Lennox didn't present himself for duty this morning! Nothing of him to be seen for bandages, and of course General Maitland sent him packing. He's just gone off, he and his father. Devilish sportsmanlike of him to come, I thought!' He detained the Colonel a moment longer, saying: 'Have you seen anything of George, sir? They say the Life Guards were engaged at Genappe yesterday.'

'Yes, I saw George in the thick of it, but he came out with nothing but a scratch or two!'

'Oh, good! Give him my love, if you should happen to run into him at any time, and tell him I'm in famous shape. Goodbye! the best of luck, Charles!'

'Thanks: the same to you!' said the Colonel, and waved and rode on.

By ten o'clock, the Duke had completed his inspection, but the French Army was still deploying on the opposite heights, and guns, their wheels up to the naves in mud, were being dragged into position along the ridge. A little before eleven o'clock, a Prussian *galopin* arrived with a despatch for General Müffling, who had only a few minutes before rejoined the Duke, after making an examination of the ground beyond Papelotte, on the left wing. He had been driven back by a French patrol coming up from the village of Plancenoit, to the south, but not before he had satisfied himself that a Prussian advance by the plateau of St Lambert would not only be possible but extremely beneficial. He wrote down his views, read them to the Duke, who said, in his decided way: 'I quite agree!' and was in the act of sending an aide-de-camp to Wavre, with the despatch, when the Prussian *galopin* found him.

The despatch he had brought was from Marshal Blücher, and

was dated 9.30 am from Wavre. '*Your Excellency will assure the Duke of Wellington from me,*' wrote the Marshal Prince, '*that, ill as I am, I shall place myself at the head of my troops, and attack the right of the French, in case they undertake anything against him.*'

There was a postscript subjoined to this missive by another and more cautious hand. General Count von Gneisenau, still convinced that his English ally's early service in India had made him a master in the art of duplicity, entreated the Baron '*to ascertain most particularly whether the Duke of Wellington has really adopted the decided resolution of fighting in his present position: or whether he only intends some demonstration, which might become very dangerous to our Army.*'

To Müffling, who profoundly respected the openness of the Duke's character, and knew how serious the coming engagement was likely to be, this postscript was exasperating. He neither mentioned it to the Duke nor made enquiries of him which he knew to be superfluous. The despatch which he had already written must convince Gneisenau of the seriousness of his lordship's intentions. He gave it to his aide-de-camp, telling him to be sure to let General Bülow read it, if, on his way to Wavre, he should encounter him. He could do nothing more to hasten the march of the Prussian 4th Corps, and having seen the aide-de-camp off, had little else to do but wait, in steadily growing impatience, for news of his compatriots' approach.

The deploying movements of the French had been completed by half past ten. The music and the trumpet calls ceased, and the columns stood in a silence that seemed the more absolute from its marked contrast to the medley of martial noises that had been resounding on all sides for the past hour. As the village clocks in the distance struck eleven, the Duke took up position with all his staff, near Hougoumont, and looked through his glass at the French lines. A very dark, wiry young officer, with a thin, energetic face in which a pair of deep-set eyes laughed upon the world, came riding up to the Duke, and saluted smartly. The Duke called out: 'Hallo, Smith! Where are you from?'

'From General Lambert's brigade, my lord, and they from

329

America!' responded Brigade-Major Harry Smith, with the flash of an impudent grin.

'What have you got?'

'The 4th, the 27th, and the 40th. The 81st remain in Brussels.'

'Ah, I know! But the others: are they in good order?'

'Excellent, my lord, and very strong,' declared the Major.

'That's all right,' said his lordship, 'for I shall soon want every man.'

'I don't think they will attack today,' remarked one of his staff, frowning across the valley.

'Nonsense!' said his lordship, with a snap. 'The columns of attack are already forming, and I think I have seen where the weight of the attack will fall. I shall be attacked before an hour. Do you know anything of my position, Smith?'

'Nothing, my lord, beyond what I see – the general line, and the right and left.'

'Go back and half Lambert's brigade at the junction of the two great roads from Charleroi and Nivelles. I'll tell you what I want of you fellows.'

He rode a little way with Smith, apprising him of his intentions. The Major, who was one of his lordship's promising young favourites, listened, saluted, and rode off at a canter to the rear. He cut across the slope behind Alten's division, leapt a hedge, and came down on to the chaussée almost on top of Colonel Audley, who, having been sent on an errand to Mont St Jean, was riding back to the front.

'God damn your – Harry Smith, by all that's wonderful! I might have known it! When did you arrive? Where's your brigade?'

'At Waterloo. We were held up by the wagons and baggage upset all over the road from Brussels, and when we got to Waterloo we met Scovell, who had been sent by the Duke to see if the rear was clear – which, by God, it was not! He requested us to sweep up the litter before moving on! What's the news with you, old fellow?'

'Oh, famous! How's Juana? You haven't brought her out with you, I suppose?'

'Haven't brought her out with me?' exclaimed the Major. 'She was sitting down to dinner with Lambert at some village just the other side of the Forest last night!'

'Good God, you don't mean to tell me she's with the brigade now?'

'No, I've sent her back to Ghent with her groom,' replied the Major coolly. 'We're in for a hottish day, from the looks of it. I understand my brigade will be wanted to relieve old Picton. Cut up at your little affair at Quatre-Bras, was he?'

'Devilishly. Someone said he himself had been wounded, but he's here today, so I suppose he wasn't. I must be off.'

'By Jove, and so must I! We shall meet again – here or in hell! *Adios! Bienes de fortuna!*'

He cantered off; the Colonel set his horse at the bank on the right of the chaussée, scrambled up, and rode past Lord Edward Somerset's lounging squadrons up the slope to the front line.

By the time he had found the Duke it was just past eleven o'clock. He joined a group of persons gathered about his lordship, and sat with a loose rein, looking along the ridge opposite.

'Heard about Grant?' asked Canning, who was standing next to him.

'No: which Grant?' replied the Colonel absently.

'Oh, not General Grant! Colonel Grant. He did send the information of the French massing on Charleroi on the 15th – the very fullest information, down to the last detail. It's just come to hand!'

'Just come to hand?' repeated Audley. 'How the devil did it take three days to reach us?'

'Ask General Dörnberg,' said Canning. 'It was sent to him, at Mons, and he, if you please, coolly sent it back to Grant, saying that it didn't convince him that the French really intended anything serious! Grant then despatched the information direct to the Duke, but of course, by that time, we were on the march. Good story, ain't it?'

'Dörnberg ought to be shot! Who the devil is he to question Grant's Intelligence?'

'My very words,' remarked Gordon, who had come up to them. He glanced towards the French lines, and said, with a yawn: 'Don't seem to be in a hurry to come to grips with us, do they?'

The words had scarcely been uttered when the flash of cannonfire flickered all along the ridge, and the silence that had lain over the field for over an hour was rent by the boom of scores of great guns trained on the Allied position. The scream of a horse, hit by roundshot, sounded from a troop of artillery close at hand; a cannonball buried itself in the soft ground not three paces from where Colonel Audley was standing, and sent up a shower of mud. His horse reared, snorting; he gentled it, shouting to Gordon above the thunder of the guns: 'What do you call this?'

'Damned noisy!' retorted Gordon.

The flashes and the puffs of smoke continued all along the ridge, suddenly a deafening crash, reverberating down the Allied line, answered the challenge of the French cannons, and a cheer went up: the English batteries had come into action.

Twenty-Two

*T*he French, after their usual custom, had opened a cannonade over the whole front. Behind the quick-set hedges the first lines of British infantry remained lying down, while the second lines of cavalry, drawn back on the downward slope to the north, suffered little from shot which for the most part fell short of them. The sodden condition of the ground caused many of the shells to explode harmlessly in deep mud, but there were uncomfortable moments when shells with extra long fuses fell among the troops, hissing and burning for some time before they burnt. Some of the old soldiers lit pipes, and lay smoking and cracking jokes, but every now and then there would be a sob from some man hit by a splinter, or a groan from a boy with a limb shattered by caseshot. In front line, in the intervals between the brigades, the gunners were busy, loading the 9-pounders with round shot with a case over it, the tubes in vents, portfires glaring and spitting behind the wheels.

The Duke was standing by Maitland's brigade on the right, critically observing the effect of the French cannonade. The shots tore up the ground beside him, and hissed over his head, but he merely remarked: 'That's good practice. I think they fire better than in Spain.'

The cannonade continued until twenty minutes past eleven without any movement of infantry attack being made by the enemy. The hottest fire was being directed upon Hougoumont, but the wood on the southern side of the château to a large extent protected it. At twenty minutes past eleven, Prince Jérôme

Bonaparte's division of infantry, belonging to Reille's corps, on the French left, began to advance in column towards the wood, with a cloud of skirmishers thrown out in front. These were met by a blaze of musketry fire from the Hanoverian and Nassau troops posted among the trees. The Duke shut his telescope with a snap, and galloped down the line, with his staff streaming behind him, to where Byng's brigade was drawn up on the high ground behind the château. An order was rapped out; Colonel Canning wheeled his horse, and made for the spot where Captain Sandham's field battery was stationed. 'Captain Sandham! You are wanted immediately in front! Left limber up, and as far as you can!'

The order was swiftly repeated: 'Left limber up! At a gallop, march!'

The horses strained at their collars; the mud gave up its hold on the wheels with a sucking sound; the train moved forward, lurching and clanking over the ground, and came up in grand style, guns loaded with powder, priming wires in the vents to prevent the cartridges slipping forward, slow matches lighted. The leading gun, a howitzer, was quickly unlimbered, and its first shell burst over the head of the French column moving upon the wood of Hougoumont. The other guns followed suit one after the other, as they came into position and unlimbered; and in a few minutes an additional and destructive fire was being directed on the column by Captain Cleeve's battery of the legion, in front of Alten's division.

The column shuddered under the fire, and checked. In the wood, the skirmishers were already engaged with the Hanoverian and Nassau defenders. Twelve pieces of horse artillery of Reille's corps were pushed forward, and a heavy counter-cannonade was begun. The column of infantry recovered, and pressed on, leaving its dead and wounded lying on the field. A well-directed fire from Sandham's and Cleeve's batteries again threw it into disorder, but it reformed, and reached the wood, driving the defenders, back from tree to tree. The popping of musketry now mingled with the rear of the cannons; and a steady trickle of wounded men began to make their way to the shelter of the British line.

Colonel Audley, who had been sent off to the left wing with instructions to Sir Hussey Vivian not to fire on any troops advancing from the west, did not see the start of the fight in Hougoumont Wood. By the time he returned to the Duke, it had been in progress for half an hour, and the Nassauers, after contesting the ground with a good deal of courage, were giving way. More of Reille's corps had moved to Jérôme's support, and the skirmishers of the Guards, pressed back through the Great Orchard, were being driven into an alley of holly and yew trees separating it from the smaller orchard surrounding the garden.

The Nassauers, retreating in disorder, poured out on to a sunken lane forming the northern boundary of the Hougoumont enclosure. When Colonel Audley rode up, the Duke, spurring forward from his position in front of Byng's brigade, was trying to rally them. But his presence, so invigorating to his own men, had very little effect upon the Nassauers, some of whom, in the panic of the moment, actually fired after him as he rode through their ranks. 'Pretty scamps to win a battle with!' he said, with a bark of laughter; and wasting no more time on them, he galloped off to where, a few yards from where the Nivelles highway crossed the hollow road to Braine-l'Alleud, Major Bull's howitzer troop was drawn up. He brought the troop up in person, explaining in a few incisive sentences what he wanted done. Major Bull, ordered to clear the wood with shell fire, considered the position calmly for a moment, and gave his gunners their directions. It was a ticklish business, for the château, with its defenders, lay between his troop and the enemy, and a shell falling short must inevitably drop among the British Guards, desperately fighting in the alleys south of the garden wall. The first shell shot up, clearing the enclosures, and exploded over the wood.

'That's right!' said his lordship. 'That's good shooting. Well, Audley, any news of the Prussians yet?'

'No, sir. A patrol of French cavalry came up to Colonel Best's people. He formed the brigade in squares, but the cavalry seemed only to be reconnoitring, and drew off again. The French are massing their guns in the centre of the line.'

'Oh yes! This is nothing but a diversion,' said the Duke, nodding towards Hougoumont. He found that several officers from Byng's brigade had come up to watch the struggle, and told them curtly to get back to the brigade. 'You will have the devil's own fire on you immediately!' he said, and, as though to prove the truth of his words, a hurricane of grape and round shot began to whistle about the position, as Reille's gunners found their range.

The howitzer shells, falling thick in the wood, drove Jérôme back. The swarms of French infantry rallied, and came on again; the Hanoverians were forced back and back, through sheer weight of numbers, into the orchard. A glimpse of red showed through the trees; Jérôme's troops hurled themselves forward at what they believed to be a line of British soldiers, and were brought up short by the brick wall enclosing the garden. They tried to scale it, but the Coldstream Guards, posted on the inner platforms and at the loopholes, poured in such a murderous fire that the blue-coated infantry recoiled. The ditches lining the alley separating the wood from the orchard became choked with dead; in the orchard, Saltoun's light companies began to press back the invaders; but the 1st Léger Regiment succeeded in setting fire to a haystack, and, under cover of the black smoke, crept round the western side of the château. A British battery, raking the Nivelles road, was assailed by a storm of *tirailleurs*, and suffered such loss of men and horses that it was forced to retire. A horse battery attached to Piré's lancers, who had come up as an observation corps to the south-west, opened fire on Bull's troop; and the Guards posted on the avenue leading from the high road to the north gate of the château saw, through the smothering whorls of smoke, hundreds of Jérôme's men advancing on them.

The north gate was open, and it was down the avenue of elm trees that reinforcements of men and ammunition were being passed into the château. The Hanoverians defending the approach to the avenue were overwhelmed and flung back in confusion. The Guards, attacked on all sides, stood shoulder to shoulder, fighting off the waves of the French that broke over them, and retreating, step by step, to the gateway. The French saw Hougoumont almost within their grasp; one of their generals spurred forward, shouting to his men to prevent the closing of the gates. They surged after him, but a sergeant of the Coldstream dashed forward, right into the mass of the enemy, and hurled himself at General Cubières. Before the French had had time to realise what was happening, the general had been dragged from his horse, and Sergeant Fraser, brandishing a blood-stained halberd, was up in the saddle, and riding hell-for-leather towards the gate. The momentary check caused by this diversion enabled the handful of Guards to reach the courtyard, but a party of sapeurs, recovering from their astonishment at Fraser's daring, rushed after him, led by a young sous-lieutenant of ferocious mien. The Guards, fighting their way backwards through the gateway, heard above the rattle of musketry and the thunder of artillery a yell of: '*En avant, l'Enfonceur!*' and saw the sapeurs coming charging through the smother of black smoke. They made a desperate attempt to shut the gates, but with a roar of rage and triumph the sapeurs flung themselves against the heavy doors. The Guards, reduced in numbers, suffocated by the smoke, could not hold them. Amid the crash of timbers and crumbling masonry, the French burst through into the courtyard and fought for possession of the gatehouse.

The noise reached the ears of Macdonnell, directing the defence of the garden wall. Shouting to three of his officers who stood nearest him, he raced, drawn sword in hand, to the inner yard, and across it to the wicket leading to the main courtyard. There the most appalling sight met his eyes. The courtyard was full of Frenchmen; some of the Guards were fighting to defend the cowshed, where their own wounded lay; from every ambush of shed, or window, or cellar, a steady musketry fire was holding the surge of men through the gateway in check; while in the château, the Guards besieged on the staircase had hacked away the lower steps, and were firing down upon the French trying to storm up to them. By the gate, the pavingstones were slippery with blood, and cumbered by the dead and wounded who lay there; a heroic little band, under the command of two sergeants, was still fighting to prevent the gatehouse from falling, but in the gateway itself the French were massed, and outside reinforcements were advancing down the avenue.

Roaring at his officers to follow him, Macdonnell launched himself across the courtyard. Hatless, with nothing but a sword in his hand, he fell upon the French in the gateway, and with such force that they broke involuntarily, as they would have broken before the charge of a mad bull. His officers and a few sergeants rushed to his support. For an instant the French were scattered; and while a couple of ensigns and two sergeants held them at bay, Macdonnell and Sergeant Graham set their shoulders to the double doors, and forced them together, the sweat pouring down their faces and the muscles standing out like corrugations down their powerful thighs.

Yells of fury sounded outside, as Graham, while his colonel held the doors together against every effort of the sapeurs to force them open, slammed the great iron crossbar into position. Bayonets and hatchets beat upon the unyielding timbers; and the French trapped in the courtyard tried to set fire to the barns before being shot or bayoneted by the Guards who were round them.

A few brave men managed to scale the wall, but were shot before they could even leap down into the courtyard. Fresh columns were being moved down by Jérôme, and had carried the avenue. Colonel Audley, his right sleeve torn by a musketball, was sent flying to bring up two guns from Bolton's battery, and arrived above the north alley enclosing the orchard just as Colonel Woodford led forward four companies of the Guards to the relief of the garrison.

'There, my lads: in with you! Let me see no more of you!' the Duke called out to them.

The Guards gave him a cheer, and went in at the charge. They drove the French before them at the point of the bayonet, sweeping them away from the château walls; and Woodford managed to reinforce the garrison through a side door leading into the alley. The light companies reoccupied the ground they had lost, and Jérôme drew off to re-form his mutilated battalions.

Several officers of the staff corps had galloped up with messages for the Duke from time to time; of his personal staff, Lord Arthur Hill and young Cathcart were both mounted on troopers, their horses having been shot under them; and Colonel Audley had suffered a contusion on his right arm from a glancing musketball. Fremantle, returning from the left wing, found him trying to tie his handkerchief round the flesh wound with one hand and his teeth, and pushed up to him, saying: 'Here, let me do that!'

'Any news of Blücher?' asked Audley.

'Not so much as a sniff of those damned Prussians! My God, you've got a pretty shambles here! What's been going on?'

'We all but lost Hougoumont, that's all. Bull's had to retire. He's been enfiladed by a troop of horse artillery belonging to the lancers over there.' He jerked his head towards the Nivelle's road. 'Jérôme's bringing up reserve after reserve. Looks as though he means to take Hougoumont or perish in the attempt. Anything happening anywhere else?'

'Not yet, but we'll be in for it soon, or I'm a Dutchman. Never saw so many guns massed in my life at the batteries they're bringing up in the centre. There you are – all right and tight!'

It was now nearly one o'clock, and for an hour and a half the most bitter struggle had been raging for the possession of Hougoumont. The Duke, who seemed to have been everywhere at once, cantered back to the centre of the position, to where an elm tree stood on the highest point of the ground, to the west of the Charleroi chaussée. He had no sooner arrived there than an artillery officer came up to him in a great state of excitement, stating that he could clearly perceive Bonaparte and all his staff before the farm of La Belle Alliance, and had no doubt of being able to direct his guns on to them.

This suggestion was met by a frosty stare, and a hasty: 'No, no, I won't have it! It is not the business of general officers to be firing upon each other!'

'Just retire quietly,' said Gordon, in the chagrined officer's ear. 'Forget that you were born! You had better not have been, you know.'

Colonel Fremantle's description of the guns being assembled upon the opposite ridge had not been exaggerated. During the struggle about Hougoumont, battery after battery had been brought up on the French side, covering the whole of the Allied centre, from Colin Halkett's brigade on the right of Alten's division to Prince Bernhard's Nassauers at Papelotte. Nearly eighty guns had been massed upon the ridge, and at one o'clock the most infernal cannonade broke out. Shells screamed through the air, ploughing long furrows in the ground as they fell, blowing the legs off horses, exploding in the Allied lines, and scattering limbs and brains over men crouching behind the meagre shelter of the quick-set hedges. The infantry set its teeth and endured. Young soldiers, determined not to lag behind their elders in courage, gulped and smiled waveringly as the blood of fallen comrades spattered in their faces; veterans declared that this was nothing, and went on grimly cracking their jokes. On the high ground under the elm tree balls hummed and whistled round the Duke and his brilliant staff, until he said in his cool way: 'Better separate, gentlemen: we are a little too thick here.'

Shortly after one o'clock, Reille's guns, away to the right, succeeded in setting fire to the haystack in the yard of Hougoumont. In the centre of the line, smoke was beginning to lie thickly in the valley between the opposing ridges. The air was hot and acrid; and a curious noise, like the hum of a gigantic swarm of bees, was making novices ask anxiously: 'What's that? What's that buzzing noise?'

Baron Müffling, after a short colloquy with the Duke, rode away to take up his position with the cavalry brigades on the left flank. Messenger after messenger went galloping off to try to gain some intelligence of the Prussian advance, for it was plain that the cannonade was a prelude to an attack upon the Allied centre, which, held by Picton's and Alten's divisions on either side of the chaussée, was the weakest part of the line.

At half past one, the cannonade slackened, and above the diminishing thunder could be heard the French drums beating the *pas de charge*.

'Here comes Old Trousers at last!' sang out a veteran, uncorking his muzzle stopper and slipping off his lock cap. 'Now for it, you Johnny Newcomes!'

On the ridge of La Belle Alliance, a huge mass of infantry was forming, flanked by squadrons of cuirassiers. Sharp-eyed men on the Allied front swore they could discern Bonaparte himself; that he was there was evident from the shouts of '*Vive l'Empereur!*' and the dipping of colours, as the regiments filed past the group beside the chaussée. The rub-a-dub of drums and the blare of trumpets now mingled with the roar of artillery. Four divisions of infantry, led by Count D'Erlon, began to advance down the slope to the hollow road, in ponderous columns at 400 pace intervals, showing fronts from 160 to 200 files. The battalions of each division were deployed, and placed one behind the other, except on the French left, where Allix's division was formed into two brigades side by side, under Quiot and Bourgeois. These moved forward to encircle the farm of La Haye Sainte, Quiot branching off to the west of the chaussée and Bourgeois advancing to the east of it. A determined musketry fire from the orchard and the windows of the farm met them, but Baring's Germans were soon driven from the orchard and gardens into the building itself. While the other divisions moved in three columns down the slope towards the Allied left centre, the Lüneberg field battalion was detached from Count Kielmansegg's brigade, and sent forward to try to reinforce Baring. These young troops advanced boldly down the slope, but wavered under the French fire. The sight of their own skirmishers falling back took the heart out of them. They began to retreat; the cuirassiers, covering Quiot's left flank, swept down upon them, and in their disordered state killed and rode over many of them, driving the rest back with great loss to their own lines.

Upon the eastern side of the chaussée the three other columns, led by Donzelot, Marcognet, and Durutte, moved steadily down upon the Allied line. As each column cleared its own guns on the ridge behind it, and descended the slope into the valley, these began firing again, until the thunder and crash of artillery drowned the roll of the drums and the shrill blare of the trumpets.

To the eyes that watched this tidal advance, it seemed as though the whole slope was covered with men. European armies had seen these columns, and had broken and fled before them, appalled by the sheer weight of infantry opposed to them. The British had time and again proved the superiority of line over column, but Count Bylandt's Dutch–Belgic brigade, badly placed on the slope confronting the French position, already demoralised by the heavy cannonading, could not stand the relentless march of the columns towards them. They had suffered considerably at Quatre-Bras, had had no rations served out to them since the morning of the previous day, and had seen Count Bylandt carried off the field. The men in their gay uniforms and white-topped shakos began to waver, and before the head of the column immediately in their front had reached the valley below them, they fled. The exertions of their officers, frantically trying to check the rout, were of no avail. The men, some of them flinging down their arms, broke through the hedge in their rear, and retreated in the wildest confusion through the interval between Kempt's and Pack's brigades. Byleveld's battery was swept back in the rush, and a great gap yawned in the Allied line.

The Dutch–Belgians were met by derisive calls from Pack's Highlanders. Not a man in the 5th Division caught the infection of that mad panic; instead, the Scots helped the terrified foreigners to the rear with sly bayonet thrusts, while the men of Kempt's left, until called to order by their officers, fired musket-balls into the retreating mass.

In the confusion, Colonel Audley, desperately trying with a handful of others to stem the rush, came upon Lavisse, livid and cursing, laying about him with the flat of his sword. 'That's no use, man!' he shouted. 'Christ, can't you fellows get your men together? Form them up in the rear, and bring them on again, for God's sake! We can't afford this gap!'

'Damn you, do I not know?' Lavisse gasped.

'Och, sir, let the puir bodies gang!' shouted a sergeant of the Gordons. '*We* dinna want furriners hired to fight for us!'

The three companies of the 95th Rifles, posted on the knoll and in the sandpit in front of Kempt's right, were firing steadily into Bourgeois' and Donzelot's columns, advancing on either side of them; and two of Ross's 9-pounders, guarding the chaussée, caused Bourgeois' brigade to swerve away from La Haye Sainte to its right, where it was thrown against Donzelot's division, and advanced with it in one unwieldy mass. The riflemen stood their ground until almost hemmed in by the sea of French, but were forced at last to abandon the sandpit and retreat to the main position.

Bylandt's men had forced their way right to the rear, and although Byleveld's troop had extricated itself from the mêlée and was in the front line again, firing into the head of the column already starting to deploy in the valley, over two thousand Dutch–Belgians had deserted from the line, leaving three thousand men of Picton's decimated division to face the charge of thirteen thousand Frenchmen.

Picton, wasting no time in trying to bring Bylandt's men to the front again, deployed Kempt's brigade into an attenuated two-deep line, to fill the breach. Below, in the hollow road and the cornfields beyond it, the French columns were also trying to deploy in the constricted space afforded for such a movement. The whole valley swarmed with blue-coated infantry, struggling in the press of their own numbers to get into line. The front ranks charged up the banks of the hedge concealing the British troops, shouting and cheering, confident that the flight of the large body of troops in their front had left the field open to them through the Allied centre. Picton's voice blared above the roar of cannon: 'Rise up!'

343

The men of Kempt's brigade, crouched behind the hedge, leaped to their feet; the French saw the bank crowned by a long line of red, overlapping their column on either side. Every musket was at the present; a volley riddled the advancing mass; and as the French recoiled momentarily under it, Picton roared: 'Charge! Hurrah!' and Kempt's warriors, with the British cheer the French had learned to dread, charged with bayonets levelled.

To the east of Donzelot, Marcognet's column was surging up the bank to where Pack's Highlanders waited, a little drawn back from the crest. 'Ninety-second! Everything has given way in front of you!' Pack shouted. 'You must charge!'

A yell of 'Scotland ever!' answered him. The skirl of pipes soared above the din, and the men of the Black Watch, the Royals, and the Gordons, all with the deaths of comrades to avenge, hurled themselves through the hedge at the advancing column.

In Kempt's brigade, the Camerons, attacked by a devastating crossfire from Bourgeois' column on their right, began to give way. Picton shouted to one of Uxbridge's aides-de-camp: 'Rally the Highlanders!' The next instant he fell, shot through the right temple. Captain Seymour rode forward to obey this last command, but it was the Duke, watching the crash of the two armies from the high ground in the centre, who galloped before him into the thick of the fight, and succeeded in rallying the Camerons and the hard-pressed riflemen.

'Stand fast, Ninety-fifth! We must not be beaten!' he shouted. 'What will they say in England?'

A ragged cheer answered him; he re-formed the 79th himself, and directed them to fire upon the column that had driven them back, only withdrawing out of the heat of the battle when he saw that they stood firm.

The guns on both sides had ceased fire as the French and the British troops met, but in the valley smoke lay thick, and muskets spat and crackled. The French were hampered by the size of their own columns, but although the men of Picton's depleted division had checked their advance by the sheer ferocity of their charge, they could not hope to hold such overwhelming numbers at bay. West of the chaussée, the cuirassiers, having routed the Lüneberg battalion, re-formed under the crest of the Allied position. Ignorant of what the reverse slope of the ground concealed, they charged up the bank, straight at Ompteda's men, hidden behind it. But the Germans had opened their ranks to permit the passage of cavalry through them. Before the cuirassiers had reached the crest, they heard the thunder of hooves above them, and the next instant the Household Brigade was upon them, led by Uxbridge himself, at the head of the 1st Life Guards.

With white crests, and horses' manes flying, the Life Guards came up at full gallop and crashed upon the cuirassiers in flank. The earth seemed to shudder beneath the shock. The Hyde Park soldiers never drew rein, but swept the cuirassiers from the bank, and across the hollow road in the irresistible impetus of their charge. Swords rang against the cuirasses; someone yelled above the turmoil: 'Strike at the neck!' and the cuirassiers, already a little disorganised by their encounter with the German infantry, were flung back in fighting confusion. The Life Guards and the 1st Dragoon Guards hurled their left flank past the walls of La Haye Sainte in complete disorder, and scattered Quiot's brigade of infantry assailing the farm. The right flank of the cuirassiers swerved sharply to the east, and plunged down on to the chaussée to escape from the fury of six-foot men on huge horses, who seemed to have no idea of charging at anything slower than a full gallop. Not more than half their number had crossed the chaussée to the valley where Donzelot was driving his congested ranks against Kempt's brigade, when the rest of the Household Cavalry, coming up on the left of the Life Guards, fell upon them in hard-riding squadrons, and crumpled them up. The *abattis*, so painstakingly built up by the riflemen, was scattered in an instant; the cuirassiers were cut down in hundreds, and the Dragoon Guards rode over them to charge full tilt into the column of French infantry pressing Kempt's men back.

At the same moment, an aide-de-camp rode up from the rear

to the hedge beyond which Pack's Highlanders were fighting fiercely with the men of Marcognet's division. For one moment he stood there, closely observing the state of the battle raging in the valley; then he took off his cocked hat and waved it forwards.

There was yell of: 'Now then, Scots Greys!' and the next instant the whole of the Union Brigade came thundering up the reverse slope. The French, disordered through their inability to deploy their enormous column before the Highlanders charged them, appalled hardly more by the fury of the kilted devils who rushed on them than by the unearthly music of the pipes playing *Scots, Wha' Hae* in the hell of blood and smoke and clashing arms that filled the valley, heard the cavalry thundering towards them, and looked up to see great grey horses clearing the hedge above them.

They fell back. In the valley, officers were shouting to the Gordons to wheel back by sections to let the cavalry pass through. The Scots Greys tightened their grips, and came slipping and scrambling down the bank shouting: 'Hurrah, Ninety-second! Scotland for ever!' as they caught sight of the red-feathered bonnets in the press and the smoke below.

Greys, Royals, and Inniskillings, riding almost abreast, poured over the hedge and down into the seething valley. The Gordons were yelling: 'Go at them, the Greys! Scotland for ever!' and snatching at stirrup-leathers as the Greys rode through them, so that they too were borne forwards in this terrific charge. Somewhere, lost in the smoke, a pipe-major was coolly playing, *Hey, Johnny Cope, are ye waukin' yet?* while all around sounded screams, shouts, musketry fire, and the clash of steel.

Many of the horses and their riders were brought down by musketballs or the desperate thrust of bayonets, but the cavalry charge had caught Marcognet's column unawares and in confusion. The Union Brigade rode over the column, lopping off heads with their sabres, while the Gordons, who had been carried forward with them, did deadly work with the bayonet. To the right, where Donzelot's men had fought their way through Kempt's thin lines to the crest of the position, the Royal

Dragoons, unchecked by the frontal fire that met them, charged straight for the leading column of the division. The column faced about and tried to retreat over the hedge, but there was no time to get to safety before the Royals were in their midst, their sabres busy and their horses squealing, biting, and striking out with their iron-shod forefeet. Between the Greys and the Royals, the Inniskillings, with their blood-curdling howl, broke through Donzelot's rear brigades. As the Royals, capturing the Eagle, charged on over the slaughtered leading column to the supporting ones behind it, and the Greys rode down Marcognet's men, the French, utterly demoralised, began throwing down their arms and crying for quarter.

The Household Brigade, having broken the cuirassiers and smashed their way through Bourgeois' rear column, dashed on, deaf to the trumpets sounding the Rally and to the voices of Uxbridge and Lord Edward trying to recall them, up the slope towards the great French battery on the ridge. The Union Brigade, leaving behind them a plain strewn with dead and wounded, and prisoners being herded to the rear, charged after the Household troops, and galloped up the slope to within half-carbine shot of where Napoleon himself was standing, by the farm of La Belle Alliance.

A colonel of the Greys shouted: 'Charge! Charge the guns!' and his men dashed after him, through a storm of shot, laming the horses, cutting the traces, and sabring the gunners.

The cavalry charge had put almost all Count D'Erlon's Corps d'Armée to rout, but it had been carried too far. Ahead, solid columns of infantry were advancing from the French rear; and behind, from either flank, lancers and cuirassiers were riding to cut off the retreat.

A voice cried: 'Royals, form on me!' The Greys and the Inniskillings on the ridge, their horses blown, themselves badly mauled, looked round in vain for their officers, and tried to re-form to meet the onset of the French cavalry. The Colonel who had led them in the charge towards the battery had been seen riding among the guns like a maniac, with both hands lopped off at the wrists, and his reins held between his teeth; but he had fallen, and a dozen others with him. A sergeant called out: 'Come on, lads! That's the road home!' and the gallant little band rode straight for the oncoming cavalry that separated it from its own lines.

A pitiful remnant broke through. On the Allied left wing, Vandeleur flung forward his light dragoons to cover the retreat. They cheered the heavies as they passed them, caught the lancers in flank, and drove them back in disorder. The survivors of the Union Brigade reached the shelter of their own lines, having pierced three columns, captured two Eagles, wrecked fifteen guns, put twenty-five more temporarily out of action, and taken nearly three thousand prisoners.

Twenty-Three

The great infantry attack on the Allied left centre had failed. The Household Brigade had repulsed Quiot from La Haye Sainte; Bourgeois and Donzelot had been forced to retreat with heavy loss; and Marcognet's division was shattered. The remaining column, led by Durutte, had had more success, but was forced to retire in the general retreat. Durutte had advanced against Papelotte, and had driven Prince Bernhard's Nassauers out of the village. These re-formed, and in their turn drove out the French. Vandeleur's brigade of light cavalry charged the column, and it drew off, but in good order.

On the Allied side the losses were enormous. Kempt and Pack could no longer hope to hold the line, and Lambert's brigade was ordered up from Mont St Jean to reinforce them. The Union Brigade had been cut to pieces; the Household troops were reduced to a few squadrons. Of the generals, Picton had been killed outright in the first charge; Sir William Ponsonby, leading the Union Brigade on a hack horse, was lying dead on the field with his aide-de-camp beside him; and Pack and Kempt, on whom the command of the 5th Division had devolved, were wounded. Lord Edward Somerset, unhorsed, his hat gone, the lap of his coat torn off, got to his own lines miraculously unscathed.

Lord Uxbridge, who, when the Life Guards and the Dragoon Guards ignored the Rally, had ridden back to bring up the Blues in support, only to find that they had galloped into first line before ever they had passed La Haye Sainte, listened in contemptuous silence to the congratulations of the Duke's suite upon the brilliant success of his charge. He turned away, remarking to Seymour, with a disdainful curve to the mouth: 'That *Troupe dorée* seems to think the battle is over. But had I, when I sounded the Rally, found only four well-formed squadrons coming on at an easy trot we should have captured a score of guns and avoided these shocking losses. Well! I deviated from my own principle: the *carrière* once begun the leader is no better than any other man. I should have placed myself at the head of the second line.'

During D'Erlon's attack, the cannonading had been kept up on the other parts of the line, while, round Hougoumont, the struggle still raged with unabated fury, more and more men of Reille's Corps being employed in the attempt to capture the château. The stubborn resistance of the Guards inside the château and garden, and of Saltoun's light companies, holding the orchard and the alley to the north in the teeth of all opposition, awoke a corresponding determination in the French generals. No attempt was made to mask the post; Jérôme, Foy, and Bachelu were all sent against it; and a howitzer troop was summoned up to drop shells upon the buildings. At a quarter to three, the roof of the château was blazing, and the Duke, observing it, scrawled one of his brief messages in his pocket-book: '*I see that the fire has communicated from the Haystack to the roof of the Château. You must, however, still keep your men in those parts to which the fire does not reach. Take care that no men are lost by the falling in of the roof or floors. After they will have fallen in, occupy the ruined walls inside the gardens; particularly if it should be possible for the Enemy to pass through the Embers in the inside of the house.*'

He tore out the leaves, and folded them, and handed them to Colonel Audley, with a curt instruction.

The Colonel made his way to the right, behind Alten's division. The going was hard, the ground being heavy from the recent storm, and the smoke from the shells bursting all round making it difficult to see the way. He caught a glimpse of some squadrons of Dutch carabiniers, drawn up considerably to the rear, with their left against the chaussée, out of range of the cannonshots; passed by General Kruse's Nassauers, held in reserve; and arrived at length on the plateau overlooking Hougoumont. Skirting a regiment of dragoons of the legion, who announced themselves to belong to General Dörnberg's brigade, the Colonel took a deep breath, gave his horse a pat on the neck saying: 'Now for it, my lad!' and plunged forward into the region of shot and shell bursts. As he rode past Maitland's Guards, lying down in line four-deep above the bend of the hollow road to the south, a cannonball screamed past his head, and made him duck involuntarily. An officer commanding a troop of horse artillery, a little to the west of the 1st Guards, saw him, and laughed, shouting: 'Whither away, Audley?'

'To Hougoumont. Ramsay, where the devil has Byng's brigade got to?'

'In there, most of 'em,' replied Ramsay, pointing to the Hougoumont enclosures. 'They tell me the ditches are piled up with the dead: don't add to their number, if you can avoid it!'

'Damn you, I'm shaking with fright already!' called Audley over his shoulder.

Ramsay laughed, and waved him on. The last sight Colonel Audley had of him was sitting his horse beside his guns, as cool as though engaged on field manœuvres, waving his hand, and laughing.

He set spurs to his horse, and galloped forward into the smoke and the heat of the fight round Hougoumont. He found himself soon among what seemed to be a steady stream of wounded, making their painful way to the rear. The lane behind the château, which was flanked by ditches and elm trees, was lined with some of the light companies of the Guards regiments, and in the orchard beyond a never-ending skirmish was going on. From the cover of the tree trunks, and the ditches, the Guards, stepping over their own dead, were upholding their proud reputation. The carnage was appalling, but Colonel Audley, making his way to the northern wicket leading into the château, could see no signs of dismay in even the youngest face. When a man fell, with a queer little grunt as the ball struck him, those near him would do no more than glance at him in the intervals of reloading their muskets. They were intent on their marksmanship, their strained eyes staring ahead through the drifting smoke, their muskets at the ready.

Except for a shot which carried away his horse's ear, and caused the poor beast to rear up, snorting and squealing, the Colonel reached the wicket gate without sustaining any injury, and penetrated into the courtyard.

The scene outside in the enclosures faded to insignificance before the inferno within the walls. The haystack was still blazing, and not only the roof of the château but also a cowshed where the wounded had been lying, had caught fire. The heat was overpowering; shells were falling on the buildings; horses, caught in flaming stables, were screaming; a few men, unrecognizable in torn and blackened uniforms, were working desperately to drag the last of the wounded out of the cowshed, while others, forming a chain, were pouring bucketful after bucketful of water on the smoking walls. On every side sounded the crash of falling timbers, the bursting of shells, and the groans of men, who, unable to move for shattered legs or ghastly stomach wounds, were scorched by the fire and driven mad by pain and thirst. A sergeant of the Coldstream shouted to Audley above the din that Colonel Macdonnell was in the garden, and thither Audley made his way, out of the heat and the fire, into what seemed an oasis set in the middle of hell.

Reille's guns were all trained on the courtyard and the surrounding buildings, and scarcely any shells had fallen in the neat garden which Barbara Childe had planned to visit again in the summer. Roses were blooming in the formal beds; the long turf walks between were shaded by fruit trees, and perfectly smooth. The Colonel had no time to waste in gazing on this refreshing scene; but its contrast with the horror of the courtyard most forcibly struck him as he strode towards the high brick wall on the southern side. Here the defenders were for the most part gathered, some firing through the rough loopholes, other mounted on the wooden platforms, and firing over the top of the wall into the infantry in the orchard and the fringe of the wood beyond. Colonel Audley soon found Macdonnell, and delivered the Duke's message. The big Scot read it, and gave a short laugh. 'He need not worry: we can hold the place. But send more ammunition down to us, Audley, if you can: we're running damned short. How is it going along the rest of the line?'

'The 5th Division and the heavy brigades have repulsed an infantry attack on the left centre, sir. No one has it as hot as you, so far.'

'Ah! Well, no one has troops like my fellows. Tell the Duke there's no talk of surrender here.'

Making his way back again through the house and the courtyard, Colonel Audley once more reached the wicket gate, and found his horse, which he had tethered there, apparently not much troubled by the loss of his ear. He mounted, and galloped back to the main position, crossing the hollow road just below the spot where the few companies of Byng's brigade not engaged in the struggle about Hougoumont were posted. He did not see Byng himself, but gave Macdonnell's message to a senior officer, who begged him to carry it further, to the Prince of Orange's staff. He rode on towards Maitland's brigade, where he was informed the Prince was to be found, but was told there by Maitland himself that the Prince had moved to the left, towards Alten's division.

'I'll send one of my family, if you like,' Maitland said. 'The trouble is to get the carts through to Hougoumont.'

'You have enough on your hands, sir, by the look of it. I must pass Alten's division in any case.'

Maitland had his glass to his eye, and replied in a preoccupied tone: 'Very well. I don't like the look of those fellows moving up round the eastern side of Hougoumont. I wonder – no, never mind: off with you!'

The Colonel left him still watching the stealthy advance of a large body of French light troops who were creeping along the eastern hedge of the Hougoumont enclosure with the evident intention of turning Saltoun's left flank, and galloped on towards the centre of the line.

The Prince of Orange, who was surrounded by numerous staff, was not difficult to pick out. He was wearing his English hussar dress, with an orange cockade in his hat, and was standing beside Halkett's bridge on the right flank of the division, his glass, like Maitland's trained on the advancing French skirmishers. The Colonel rode towards him, but arrived in his presence in a precipitate fashion which he did not intend. A shell, bursting within a few yards of him, brought his horse down in mid-gallop; the Colonel was shot over his head, feeling at the same moment something like a red-hot knife sear his left thigh, and fell almost at the feet of Lord March.

The explosion, and the heavy fall, knocked him senseless for a moment or two, but he soon came to himself, to find March's face bent over him. He blinked at it, recollected his surroundings, and tried to laugh. 'Good God, what a way to arrive!'

'Are you hurt, Charles?'

'No, merely dazed,' replied the Colonel, grasping his friend's hand, and pulling himself up. 'My horse killed?'

'One of the men shot him. His fore legs were blown off at the knees. We thought you were gone. You are hurt! I'll get you to the rear.'

'You'll do no such thing!' said the Colonel, feeling his leg through his blood-stained breeches. 'I think a splinter must have caught me. I'll get one of Halkett's sawbones to tie it up. I was looking for you fellows. I've been charged by Colonel Macdonnell to see that more ammunition is sent down to him.'

'I'll pass the message. Things are looking rather black at the moment.' He pointed towards the hedge of the Hougoumont.

At that moment the Prince cantered up, looking pale and rather excited. 'March! I've ordered the light troops not to stir from their position! They were forming to move against those skirmishers who are trying to turn Saltoun's left flank, but I'm sure the Duke will have seen that movement, and will make his own dispositions. You agree?'

'Yes, sir.'

'Eh, *mon Dieu*, if one knew what were best to do – but no, I'm right! Charles, go at once to the rear: you are bleeding like a pig! My dear fellow, I have so much on my hands – ah, I was right! I knew it! See there, March! The Guards are moving down to cut off his attempt! All is well then, and it is a mercy I would not permit the light troops to go. March, take Charles to the rear, and find him a horse – no, a surgeon! *Au revoir*, Charles. I wish – but you see how it is: I have not a moment!'

He flew off again; Audley's eyes twinkled; he said: 'Has he been like this all day?'

March smiled. 'This is nothing. But you mustn't laugh at him; he's doing well – quite well, if only he wouldn't get excited. Good, there's one of the assistant-surgeons! Finlayson! Patch Colonel Audley up, will you? I'll get you a trooper from somewhere, Charles. Take care of yourself!'

The Colonel's wound was found to have been caused, as he suspected, by a splinter. This was speedily, if somewhat painfully, extracted, and his leg bound up, by which time one of the sergeants of the 30th Regiment had come up, leading a trooper. The Colonel mounted, declaring himself to be in splendid shape, and rode off as fast as his heavy steed would bear him.

The Duke was standing on Alten's right flank, on the highest part of the position. The time was a little after three o'clock, and Colonel Audley rejoined his lordship just as the sadly diminished Household Brigade was returning from a charge led by Uxbridge against a French force once more attacking the farm of La Haye Sainte. Baring had been reinforced by two companies after the overthrow of D'Erlon's columns, and the little garrison, in spite of having lost possession of the orchard and garden, was stoutly defending the buildings. The second attack, which was not very rigorously pressed, had been repulsed, and the charge of the Household Cavalry seemed to have succeeded. The French infantry had drawn off again, and except for the continued but not very severe cannonade against the whole Allied front, and the bitter fight about Hougoumont, a lull had fallen on the battle. Colonel Audley seized the opportunity to ride to the rear, where, on the chaussée a little below Mont St Jean, his groom was stationed with his remaining horses. He fell in with Gordon on the way, and learned from him that the head of Bülow's crops was reported to have reached St Lambert, five miles to the east of La Belle Alliance.

'Coming along in their own good time, damn them!' said Gordon. 'They say the roads are almost impassable, but I'll tell you what, Charles, if we don't get some reinforcements for our left centre before we're attacked again we shall be rompéd.'

'Where's Lambert?'

'Just come up into the front line, which means we haven't a single man in reserve on the left – unless you count Bylandt's heroes as reserves.'

'I shouldn't care to trust to them,' admitted the Colonel. 'Did their officers ever succeed in re-forming them?'

'I don't know. Pack's fellows have started a tale that they've all gone off for a picnic in the Forest. I never saw such a damnable rout in all my life! It was God's mercy it happened where it did, and not before some of our raw regiments. You were there, weren't you? Is it true that Picton's rascals fired after them?'

'They tried to, but we restrained them. Does anyone know what is going to happen next?'

'I certainly don't. All I do know is that I wish to God we had some of the fellows stationed at Hal here,' replied Gordon candidly.

For over half an hour no sign of a fresh attack was made by enemy. Speculation was rife in the Allied lines; no one could imagine what the next move was going to be, or against what part of the line it would be directed. At Hougoumont, all but two companies of Byng's brigade, which were left to guard the Colours, had been drawn into the fight in the orchards and wood. Colonel Hepburn, whom the Prince of Orange had seen advancing with the remaining companies of the Scots Guards to Lord Saltoun's relief, had taken over the command from him after assisting him to drive Foy's men out of the orchard; and

Saltoun had retired to his brigade, with just one-third of the men of the light companies whom he had led into action.

The gradual absorption of Byng's entire brigade in the defence of the Hougoumont made it imperative to reinforce the right of the line. Shortly before four o'clock, an aide-de-camp was sent off to bring up some young Brunswick troops, held in reserve, to fill the gap. This had hardly been accomplished when the firing on the Allied right centre suddenly became so violent that after a very few minutes of it the Duke withdrew his troops farther back from the crest of the position. Old soldiers with a score of battles behind them admitted, as they lay flat on their bellies under the rain of grape, round shot, and spherical case, that they had never experienced such a cannonading. Occasionally a greater explosion than the rest would roar above the din as an ammunition wagon was struck, and a column of smoke would rise vertically in the air, spreading like an umbrella.

Everyone knew that the cannonade was the prelude to an attack, but when those on the high ground on the right of the Charleroi road saw forming across the valley on the ridge of La Belle Alliance, not infantry divisions but huge masses of cavalry, they were thunderstruck. It soon became evident that the attack was going to be directed against the right centre of the Allied line, for the squadrons, which had first appeared on the east of the Charleroi road, crossed it, obliquing to their left, and advanced slowly but in beautiful order through the fields of deep corn that lay between the advance posts of Hougoumont and Lay Haye Sainte.

Twenty-four squadrons of Milhaud's cuirassiers led the cavalcade in first line, their burnished breastplates and helmets making them look like a wall of steel. They were supported by nineteen squadrons of the light cavalry of the guard: red lancers with high white plumes, gaudy horse trappings, and fluttering pennons, in second line; and, in third line, the Chausseurs à Cheval in green dolmans embroidered richly with gold, black bearskin shakos on their heads, and fur-trimmed pelisses swinging from their shoulders.

It was a formidable array, terrifying to inexperienced troops, but regarded by the staff officers who watched its assembly with a good deal of criticism.

'Good God, this is too premature!' Lord Fitzroy exclaimed. 'They cannot mean to attack unshaken infantry with cavalry alone!'

'Perhaps Ney's gone mad,' suggested Canning hopefully. 'What the devil has he done with his infantry columns?'

'I fancy the Prussians must be at something on the left,' said the Duke, overhearing this interchange.

'I shall believe in the Prussians when I see them,' remarked Canning to Colonel Audley.

There was no opportunity for further speculation. Orders were sent to the brigade to prepare to withstand cavalry attacks; aides-de-camp dashed off through the hail of shot; and the troops lying on the ground beside their arms were quickly formed into two lines of squares, placed chequer-wise behind the crest of the position. In support, all the available cavalry was mustered; the two British heavy brigades, now reduced to a few squadrons, under the command of Lord Edward Somerset; Trip's carabiniers; seven squadrons of Van Merlen's light cavalry; a regiment of Brunswick Hussars; Colonel Arendtschildt's brigade of the legion; and a part of Dörnberg's and Grant's brigades. A demonstration by some French lancers by the Nivelles road had succeeded in drawing off two of Grant's regiments and one of Dörnberg's, so that of Grant's brigade only the 7th Hussars, who had suffered great loss at Genappe, on the previous day, were left to meet the attack of French cavalry; and of Dörnberg's only the 1st and 2nd Light Dragoons of the legion. In all, it was a meagre force to throw against the forty-three squadrons assembling between Hougoumont and La Haye Sainte, and the want of the two British brigades guarding the left flank of the line until the Prussians should arrive to relieve them began to be acutely felt.

The Brunswickers, who had been brought up to fill the gap on Maitland's right, were raw troops, and the Duke wisely strengthened them by sending for a regiment from Colonel Mitchell's brigade, posted west of the Nivelles road, and stationing it between their two squares. Light troops were ordered to fall back upon the squares immediately in their rear, irrespective of nation or brigade; the artillery was instructed to keep up a steady fire upon the advancing cavalry until the last possible moment, and then to run for safety to the infantry squares; guns were double-loaded with shot and canister; and the squares formed four deep, the front ranks kneeling, so that each square presented four faces bristling with bayonets.

The French artillery fire ceased as the squadrons began to advance, at a slow trot. Owing to the Duke's having withdrawn his right centre slightly down the reverse slope of the position to protect it from the cannonading, the French, advancing to the crest, saw no infantry opposing them. They were met by a devastating fire of artillery, but though their front ranks were disordered by the gaps torn in the lines, they pushed on intrepidly. As the leading squadrons breasted the rise, the trumpets sounded the Charge, and the cuirassiers, cheering, and shouting '*En avant!*' spurred forward, and saw ahead of them, not an army in retreat, as they had been led to suppose, but motionless squares, awaiting their charge in grim British silence.

The British gunners, remaining at their posts until almost surrounded by the surge of horsemen, were firing at point-blank range. As the cuirassiers charged up to the batteries, the terrible case shot brought them down in tangled heaps of men and horses together. When the muzzles of their guns almost touched the leading squadrons, the artillery men, some detaching the wheels from their guns and bowling them along with them, rushed to the nearest squares and flung themselves down under the bayonets.

In a cacophony of shouts, trumpets calls, and the discharge of carbines, the cuirassiers charged down upon the silent squares. When they came to within thirty paces, the order to fire upon them was given, and a storm of bullets rattled against the steel breastplates, for all the world like hailstones on a glass roof. Those in the rear ranks of the squares were employed in reloading the muskets, and the repeated volleys caused the advancing columns to split, and to swerve off to right and left, only to receive a still more devastating flank of fire from the sides of the squares. In a very few moments all order was lost, the cuirassiers jostling one another in the spaces between the squares, some riding against the red walls to discharge their carbines and pistols into the set faces upturned behind the gleaming *chevaux de frise* of bayonets; other trotting round and round in an attempt to find a weak spot to break through.

No sooner had the cuirassiers passed the first line of squares then the artillerymen dashed back to their guns, to meet with renewed fire the second columns of lancers and chasseurs, ascending the southern slope in support of the cuirassiers. The same tactics were repeated, with the same results. The squadrons, already thrown in to some disorder by the charges of case shot exploding among them, obliqued before the frontal fire of the squares. Soon the whole plateau was covered with horsemen: lancers, chasseurs and cuirassiers, mixed in inextricable confusion, spreading right up to the second line of squares. Man after man fell in the British ranks, but the gaps were always filled, and the squares remained unbroken. Skirmishers, taking cover behind the carcasses of dead horses, kept up a steady fire on the congested mass of the enemy. Wounded and dead sprawled beneath the hooves; and unhorsed cuirassiers cast off their encumbering breastplates to struggle back through the press to the safety of their own lines. When the confusion was at its height, the Allied cavalry charged up from the rear and drove the French from the plateau.

They retired, leaving the ground littered with horses, men, piles of cuirasses, and accoutrements; but no sooner had the last of them disappeared over the crest than the punishing cannonade burst forth again, while Ney re-formed his muddled squadrons in the valley.

The attack, though it had not broken the squares, had considerably weakened them. The Duke, riding down the line, heartening the troops with the sight of his well-known figure and the sound of his loud, cheerful voice, sent aides-de-camp galloping off to bring up Clinton's division, in reserve on the west of the Nivelles road.

This consisted of General Adam's British Light Brigade, comprising the 1st battalion of Sir John Colborne's Fighting 52nd, the 71st Highland Regiment, and two battalions of the 95th Rifles; Colonel Du Plat's brigade of the legion; and Hew Halkett's Hanoverian Landwehr battalions.

Colonel Audley was one of those sent on this errand, and galloping through the hail of shot, reached the comparative quiet of the ground west of the Nivelles road, to find Lord Hill awaiting the expected instructions to send reinforcements from his corps into the front line. The Colonel, parched with thirst, coughing from the smoke of the shells, his wounded thigh throbbing, and his horse blown, sketched a salute, and thrust the Duke's message into his hand.

'Having a hot time of it in the centre, aren't you?' said Hill. He cast a glance at the Colonel's face, and added in his kindly way. 'You look as though a drink would do you good. Hurt?'

'No sir!' gasped the Colonel, trying to get the smoke out of his lungs. 'But we must have reinforcements before they come on again!'

'Oh yes! you shall have them!' Hill nodded to his younger brother and aide-de-camp. 'Give Audley some of that wine of yours, Clement.'

Audley, gratefully accepting a long-necked bottle, drank deeply, and sat recovering his breath while Lord Hill issued his instructions. It was his task to lead Adam's brigade to a strategic but dangerous position between the north-east angle of Hougoumont and the point on the higher ground behind the hollow road where the Brunswick troops stood huddled in two squares, with one British between. The boys, for they were little more, in their sombre uniforms and death's-head badges, were shaking, kept together only by the exertions of their officers, and the moral support afforded by the sight of the seasoned British regiment separating their squares.

Hew Halkett was brought up in support of the Brunswickers on Maitland's right; Du Plat was formed on the slope behind Hougoumont; and Adam's brigade, forming line four deep, came up to fill the interval between the Brunswickers and Hougoumont. The brigade was met by the Duke in person, who pointed to the cloud of skirmishers assailing the left flank of the Guards defending the orchard, and briefly ordered them to: 'Drive those fellows away!'

The artillery fire, which was mowing the ranks down, ceased, and the men, lying on the ground, were again ordered to form squares. The cavalry came riding over the crest as before, but this time it was seen that a considerable portion of their force was kept in compact order, and took no part in the attempt to break through the infantry squares. These horsemen were evidently formed to attack the Allied cavalry, but no sooner had the previous confusion of squadrons splitting and obliquing to right and left been repeated than the Allied cavalry, not waiting to be attacked, advanced to meet them and again drove them over the crest and down the slope.

The same tactics were repeated time after time, but with the same lack of success. The men forming the squares grew to welcome the cavalry attacks as a relief from the terrible cannonading that filed the intervals between them.

The Duke, who seemed to be everywhere at once, generally riding far ahead of the cortège that still galloped devotedly after him, was pale and abstracted, but gave no other sign of anxiety than the frequent sliding in and out of its socket of his telescope. If he saw a square wavering, he threw himself into it, regardless of all entreaties not to risk his life, and rallied it by the very fact of his presence.

'Never mind! We'll win this battle yet!' he said, and his men believed him, and breathed more freely when they caught a glimpse of that low cocked hat and the cold eyes and bony nose beneath it. They did not love him, for he did not love them, but there was not a man serving under him who had not complete confidence in him.

'Hard pounding, this, gentlemen,' he said, when the cannonade was at its fiercest. 'Let's see who will pound the longest.'

When the foreign diplomats remonstrated with him, he said bluntly: 'My Army and I know each other exactly, gentlemen. The men will do for me what they will do for no one else.'

Lord Uxbridge led two squadrons of the Household Brigade against a large body of cavalry advancing to attack the squares, and although he could not drive it back, he managed to hold it in check. Major Lloyd fell, mortally wounded, beside his battery. Sometimes the cuirassiers succeeded in cutting men off from the angles of the squares, but before they could escape to the rear, staff officers galloped after them and got them back to their positions. At times, the squares, growing smaller as the men fell in them, were lost to sight in the sea of horsemen all round them.

Between four and five o'clock, convinced at last that no flanking attack was contemplated on his right, the Duke sent to order Baron Chassé up from Braine-l'Alleud.

Staff officers were looking anxious; artillerymen, seeing little but masses of enemy cavalry swarming all over the position, waited in momentary expectation of receiving the order to retreat. The heat on the plateau was fast becoming unbearable. Reserves brought up from the rear felt themselves to be marching into a gigantic oven, and young soldiers, hearing for the first time the peculiar hum that filled the air, stared about them fearfully through the smoke, flinching as the shots hissed past their heads, and asked nervously: 'What makes that humming noise like bees?'

Colonel Audley, riding back from an errand to the right wing, had his second horse killed under him close to a troop of horse artillery, drawn up in the interval between two Brunswick squares, in a slight hollow below the brow of the position, north of Hougoumont. He sprang clear, but heard a voice call out: 'Hi! Don't mask my guns! Anything I can do for you, sir?'

'You can give me a horse!' replied the Colonel, trying to recover his breath. He looked into a lean, humorous face, shaded by the jut of a black, crested helmet, and asked: 'Who are you?'

'G Troop – Colonel Dickson's, under the command of Captain Mercer – at your service!'

'Oh yes! I know.' The Colonel's eyes travelled past him to a veritable bank of dead cuirassiers and horses, not twenty paces in front of his guns. He gave an awed whistle. 'Good God!'

'Yes, we're having pretty hot work of it here,' replied Mercer. A shell came whizzing over the crest, and fell in the mud not far from his troop, and lay there, its fuse spitting and hissing. He broke off to admonish his men, some of whom had flung themselves down on the ground. The shell burst at last, without, doing much damage; and the nonchalant Captain turned back to Colonel Audley, resuming, as though only a minor interruption had occurred: '– pretty hot work of it here. We wait till those steel-clad gentry come over the rise, and then we give 'em a dose of roundshot with a case over it. Terrible effect it has. I've seen a whole front rank come down from the effects of the case.'

'Do you mean that you stand by your guns throughout?'

'Take a look at those squares, sir,' recommended Mercer, jerking his head towards the Brunswickers, who were lying on the ground to the right and left of his rear. 'You can't, at the moment, but if you care to wait you'll see them form squares, huddled together like sheep. If we scuttled for safety among them, they'd break and run. They're only children – not one above eighteen, I'll swear. Gives 'em confidence to see us here.'

'You're a damned brave man!' said the Colonel, taking the bridle of the trooper which a driver had led up.

'Oh, we don't give a button for the cavalry!' replied Mercer. 'The worst is this infernal cannonading. It plays the devil with us. We've been pestered by skirmishers, too, which is damned nuisance. Only way I can stop my fellows wasting their charges on them is to parade up and down the bank in front of my guns. That's nervous work, if you like!'

'I imagine it might be,' said the Colonel, with a grin. 'Don't get your troop cut up too much, or his lordship won't be pleased.'

'The artillery won't get any of the credit for this day's work in any case, so what's the odds?' Mercer replied. 'Fraser knows what we're about. He was here a short time ago, very much upset from burying poor Ramsay.'

The Colonel had one foot in the stirrup, but he paused and said sharply: 'Is Ramsay dead?'

'Fraser buried him on the field not half an hour ago. Bolton's gone too, I believe. Was Norman Ramsay a friend of yours, sir? Pride of our service, you know.'

'Yes,' replied Audley curtly, and hoisted himself into the saddle, wincing a little from the pain of his wounded thigh. 'I must push on before your steel-clad gentry come up again. Good luck to you!'

'The same to you, sir, and you'd better hurry. Cannonade's slackening.'

The pause following the third onset of the cavalry was of longer duration than those which had preceded it. Ney had sent for reinforcements, and was reassembling his squadrons. To Milhaud's and Lefebvre-Desnouettes' original forty-three squadrons were now added both Kellermann's divisions and thirteen squadrons of Count Guyot's dragoons and Grenadiers à Cheval, making a grand total of seventy-seven squadrons. Not a foot of the ground, a third of a mile in width, lying between Hougoumont and La Haye Sainte, could be seen for the glittering mass of horsemen that covered it. It was an array to strike terror into the bravest heart. They advanced in columns of squadrons: gigantic carabiniers in white with gold breastplates; dragoons wearing tiger-skin helmets under their brass casques, and carrying long guns at their saddlebows; grenadiers in imperial blue, with towering bearskin shakos; steel-fronted cuirassiers; gay chasseurs; and white-plumed lancers, riding under the flutter of their own pennons. They did not advance with the brilliant dash of the British brigades, but at a purposeful trot. As they approached the Allied position the earth seemed to shake under them, and the sound of the horses' hooves was like dull thunder, swelling in volume. Fifteen thousand of Napoleon's proudest horsemen were sent against the Allied infantry squares, to break through the Duke's hard-held centre. They came over the crest in wave upon wave; riding up in the teeth of the guns until the entire plateau was a turbulent sea of bright, shifting colours, tossing plumes, and gleaming sabres. The fallen men and horses encumbering the ground hampered their advance, and once again the musketry fire from the front faces of the squares caused the squadrons to swerve off to right and left. Lancers, grenadiers, dragoons jostled one another in the press, their formation lost; but the tide swept on up to the second line of squares, and surrounded them. Some of the cavalry pushed right down the slope to the artillery wagons in the rear, and slew the drivers and horses, but though men were dropping all the time in the squares, the gaps were instantly filled, and when a square became disordered, the sharp command: 'Close up!' was obeyed before the Cavalry could take advantage of the momentary confusion. For three-quarters of an hour the squares were almost swamped by the overwhelming hordes that pressed up to them, fell back again before the fire of the muskets, and rode round and round, striking with swords and sabres at the bayonets, discharging carbines, and making isolated dashes at the corners of the squares.

The French were driven off the plateau, when in hopeless confusion, by the charge of the Allied cavalry, but they retreated only to re-form. The cannonading burst forth again, and the sorely tried infantry, deafened by the roar of artillery, many of them wounded and all of them worn out by the grim struggle to keep their ranks closed, lay down on the torn ground, each man wondering in his heart what would be the end.

When the squadrons came over the crest again, Colonel Audley was nearly caught among them. He was mounted on his last horse, the Earl of Worth's Rufus, and owed his preservation to the hunter's pace. He snatched out his sword when he saw the cavalry bearing down upon him, threw off a lance by his right side, and clapping his spurs into Rufus's flanks, galloped for his life. One of Maitland's squares opened its files to receive them, and he rode into the middle of it and the files closed behind him.

'Hallo, Audley!' drawled a tall Major, who was having sticking-plaster put on a sabre cut. 'That was a near thing, wasn't it?'

'Too damned near for my taste!' replied Audley, sliding out of the saddle and looping Rufus's bridge over his arm. He eased his wounded leg, with a grimace. 'See anything of the Duke, Stuart?'

'Not quite lately. He went off towards the Brunswickers, I think. Some of those fellows seem to revel in this sort of thing.'

'The younger ones don't like it.'

The surgeon, having finished his work on the Major's arm, bustled away, and the Major, drawing his tunic on again, said, with a grave look: 'What do you make of it?'

Audley returned the look. 'Pretty black.'

The Major nodded. He buttoned up his coat, and said: 'We don't see much of it here, you know. Nothing but smoke and this damned cavalry. One of the artillery fellows who took cover in our square during the last charge said he thought it was all over with us.'

'Not it! We shall win through!'

'Oh, not a doubt! But damme, if ever I saw anything like this cavalry affair! Look at them, riding round and round! Makes you feel giddy to watch them.' He glanced round the square, and sighed. 'God, my poor regiment!' He saw a slight stir taking place in one of the ranks, and hurried off towards the wall of red shouting: 'Close up, there! Stand fast, my lads! We'll soon have them over the hill!'

The inside of the square was like a hospital, with wounded men lying all over the ground among the ammunition boxes and the débris of accoutrements. Those of the doctors attached to the regiment who had not gone to the rear were busy with bandages and sticking plaster, but there was very little they could do to ease the sufferings of the worse cases. From time to time, a man fell in the ranks, and crawled between the legs of his comrades into the square. The dead lay among the living, some with limbs twisted in a last agony, and sightless eyes glaring up at the chasing clouds; others as though asleep, their eyelids mercifully closed, and their heads pillowed on their arms.

Almost at Audley's feet, a boy lay in a sticky pool of his own blood. He looked very young; there was a faint smile on his dead lips, and one hand lay palm upwards on the ground, the fingers curling inwards in an oddly pathetic gesture. Audley was looking down at him when he heard his name feebly called. He turned his head and saw Lord Harry Alastair not far from him, lying on the ground, propped up by knapsacks.

He stepped over the dead boy at his feet, and went to Harry, and dropped on his knee beside him. 'Harry! Are you badly hurt?'

'I don't know. I don't think I can be,' Harry replied, with the ghost of a smile. 'Only I don't seem able to move my legs. As a matter of fact, I can't feel anything below my waist.'

The Colonel had seen death too many times not recognise it now in Harry's drawn face and clouding eyes. He took one of the boy's hands and held it, saying gently: 'That's famous. We must get you to the rear as soon as these hordes of cavalry have drawn off.'

'I'm so tired!' Harry said, with a long sigh. 'Is George safe?'

'I hope so. I don't really know, old fellow.'

'Give him my love, if you see him.' He closed his eyes, but opened them again after a minute or two, and said: 'It's awful, isn't it?'

'Yes. The worst fight I ever was in.'

'Well, I'm glad I was in it, anyway. To tell you the truth, I haven't liked it as much as I thought I should. It's seeing one's friends go, one after the other, and being so hellish frightened oneself.'

'I know.'

'Do you think we can hold out, Charles?'

'Yes, of course we can, and we will.'

'By Jove, it'll be grand if we beat Boney after all!' Harry said drowsily. A doctor bent over a man lying beside him. The Colonel said urgently: 'Can't you get this boy to the rear when the cavalry draws off again?'

A cursory glance was cast at Harry. 'Waste of time,' said the doctor. 'I'm sorry, but I've enough on my hands with those I *can* save.'

The Colonel said no more. Harry seemed to be dropping asleep. Audley stayed holding his hand, but looked up at a mounted officer of the Royal Staff Corps who was standing close by. 'What's happening?'

'Our cavalry's coming up. By God, in the very nick of time too! I think Grant must have brought back his fellows from the Nivelles road. Yes, by Jove, those are the 13th Light Dragoons! Oh, well done! Go at them, you devils, go at them!'

His excitement seemed to rouse Harry. He opened his eyes, and said faintly: 'Are we winning?'

'Yes, Grant's brigade is driving the French off the plateau.'

'Oh, splendid!' He smiled. 'I say, you won't be able to call me a Johnny Newcome any longer, will you?'

'No, that I shan't.'

Harry relapsed into silence. Outside the dogged square Grant's light dragoons had formed, and charged the confused mass of French cavalry, hurling it back from the plateau and pursuing it right the way down the slope to the low ground near the orchard of Hougoumont. In a short while, the plateau, which had seethed with steel helmets, copper crests, towering white plumes, and heavy bearskin shakos, was swept bare of all but Allied troops, mounds of French dead and wounded, and riderless horses, some of them wandering aimlessly about with blood streaming from their wounds, some neighing piteously from the ground where they lay, others quietly cropping the trampled grass.

The Colonel bent over Lord Harry. 'I must go, Harry.'

'Must you?' Harry's voice was growing fainter. 'I wish you could stay. I don't feel quite the thing, you know.'

'I can't stay. God knows I would, but I must get back to the Duke.'

'Of course. I was forgetting. I shall see you later, I daresay.'

'Yes, later,' the Colonel said, a little unsteadily. 'Goodbye, old fellow!' He pressed Harry's hand, laid it gently down, and rose to his feet. His horse stood waiting, snorting uneasily. He mounted, saluted Harry, who raised a wavering hand in return, and rode away to find the Duke.

Twenty-Four

*T*he cavalry attacks were abating at last, but under cover of them renewed attempts were being made on La Haye Sainte. Again and again Major Baring sent to his brigade demanding more ammunition. One wagon never reached the farm; another was found to contain cartridges belonging to the Baker rifles used by the 95th, which were of the wrong calibre for the German rifles.

Colonel Audley arrived at the centre, immediately west of the Charleroi chaussée, in time to witness Uxbridge leading the gallant remnant of the Household Brigade against a column of French infantry, covered by cavalry, advancing upon the farm. Their numbers were so diminished that they could make little impression, and were forced to retire. Uxbridge, his hussar dress spattered with mud and soaked with sweat, went flying past to bring up Trip's Carabiniers, a powerful body of heavy cavalry, nine squadrons strong, who were drawn up behind Kielmansegg's brigade. He placed himself at their head, gave them the order to charge, and rode forward, only to be stopped by Horace Seymour snatching at his bridle and bellowing: 'They don't follow you, sir!'

Uxbridge checked, and rode back, ordering the reluctant Carabiniers with a flood of eloquence to follow the example of the shattered Household Brigade. Nothing could avail, however: the squadrons would not attend to him, but began to retire, seeping a part of the 3rd Hussars of the legion before them. Old Arendtschildt's voice could be heard above the bursting shells, raised in a fury of invective; the German hussars, scattered by the sheer weight of the Carabiniers, were only restrained from engaging with their Dutch allies by the exertions of their officers, who rode among them, calling them to order, and re-forming them as the Carabiniers passed through to the rear. The stolid Germans, roused to rage by their forced rout, rallied, and charged down upon the French about La Haye Sainte. They were driven back by the cuirassiers supporting the infantry column; and the Hanoverian regiment, the Cumberland Hussars, which had been brought up, began to retire. Captain Seymour, despatched by Uxbridge to stop this retreat, thundered down upon them, a giant of a man on a huge charger, and grabbed at the commanding officer's bridle, roaring at them to get his men together, and bring them up again. The Hanoverian colonel, who seemed dead to all feeling of shame, replied in a confused way that he could not trust his men: they were appalled by the repulse of the Household Troops; their horses were their own property; he did not think they would risk them in a charge against such overwhelming odds. He almost cringed under the menace of the English giant who loomed over him, pouring insults on his head, but he would do nothing to stop the retreat. Seymour abandoning him, appealed to his next in command to supersede him, to any officer who had courage enough to rally his troops and lead them to the charge. It was useless: he galloped back to his chief, reporting failure.

'Tell their colonel to form them up out of range of the guns!' Uxbridge ordered.

But the Cumberland Hussars had no intention of taking part in the fight, and by the time Captain Seymour reached the Colonel again, the whole regiment was in full retreat towards Brussels.

Colonel Audley, finding the Duke at last, was sent off immediately with a scrawled message for Uxbridge. '*We ought to have more Cavalry between the two high roads. That is to say, 3 Brigades at least . . . One heavy and one light Brigade might remain on the left.*'

This note delivered into Uxbridge's hands, Colonel Audley found himself beside Seymour, still seething with rage at the behaviour of the Hanoverians and the Dutch–Belgians. From him he learned that the head of the Prussian column, coming up to the west of Papelotte, had been sighted at about five o'clock, and that Baron Müffling, almost frantic at the delay, had ridden in person to bring up the reinforcements so desperately needed.

The farm of La Haye Sainte had caught fire from the cannonade directed upon it. Two of the French guns had been brought up to the north of it, and were enfilading Kempt's lines on the west of the chaussée. These were speedily silenced by the 95th Rifles, terribly reduced in numbers but still holding their ground in front of Lambert's brigade; but French skirmishers were now all round La Haye Sainte. A message from General Alten reached Baron Ompteda, requesting him, if possible, to deploy a battalion and sent it against these *tirailleurs*. Ompteda, knowing that they were strongly supported by cavalry, sent back this intelligence to his general, but the Prince of Orange, carried away by the excitement of the moment, and forgetful of the disaster attendant upon his interference at Quatre-Bras, impetuously ordered him to advance at once. Ompteda looked at him for one moment; then he turned and gave the command to deploy the 5th Line battalion of the legion. Placing himself at its head, he led it against the French skirmishers, and drove them back. The cuirassiers in support charged down upon him; he fell, and half his men with him, cut to pieces by the cavalry. Arendtschildt, watching from the high ground to the north, flung his hussars into the fray again. They fell upon the cuirassiers in flank and drove them back, enabling the shattered remnant of the 5th Line battalion to reach the main position. Fresh French cavalry advanced and drove the hussars back, but the riflemen, on the knoll above the sandpit across the road, who had been impatiently awaiting their opportunity, no sooner saw the ground cleared of Ompteda's infantry than they poured in such an accurate fire that the French cavalry was thrown into confusion, and the German hussars drew off in good order.

The cavalry attacks on the right had almost ceased; the Duke sent to withdraw Adam's brigade from its exposed position on to the high ground on Maitland's right; and despatched Colonel Fremantle to the left wing, where the Prussians were beginning to come up, with a request for reinforcements of three thousand infantry to strengthen the line. The Colonel returned with a message from General Bülow and Ziethen that their whole Army was coming up, and they could make no detachment. He was delayed on his way back by finding Prince Bernhard's Nassauers, who had behaved with the greatest gallantry all day, being put to rout by a Prussian battery of eight guns which was busily employed in firing on them in the mistaken belief that they were French troops.

'A pretty way to behave after taking the whole day to come up!' he told Lord Fitzroy wrathfully. 'The Prince rallied his fellows a quarter of a mile behind the line, but I had to gallop all the way back to Ziethen to get him to send orders to stop his damned battery!'

'How long before Ziethen can bring his whole force up?' Fitzroy demanded. 'Things are looking pretty black.'

'God knows! Müffling is doing all he can to hasten them, but there's only some advance cavalry arrived so far. They say they had the greatest difficulty to get here, owing to the state of the roads. Wouldn't have come at all if it hadn't been for old Blücher cheering them on. If it weren't so damned serious it would be comical! No sooner did Ziethen's advance guard get within reach of us than they heard we were being forced to retreat, and promptly turned tail and made off. You can imagine old Müffling's wrath! He went after them like one of Whinyates' rockets, and ordered them up at once. The main part of the Prussian Army is already engaged round Plancenoit, if Ziethen is to be believed. If they really are attacking Boney on his right flank, it would account for Ney not bringing infantry up against us. Ten to one, Boney's had to employ most of it against Bülow.'

Uxbridge, seeing the Household Cavalry drawn up in a thin, extended line behind Ompteda's and Kielmansegg's brigades, sent Seymour to tell Lord Edward to withdraw his men to a less exposed position. Seymour came back with a grim answer from

374

Lord Edward, still holding his ground: 'If I were to move, the Dutch in support of me would move off immediately.'

The fire had been extinguished at La Haye Sainte, but the garrison had fired its last cartridge, and was forced, after holding it in the teeth of the French columns all day, to abandon the post. Fighting a hand-to-hand rearguard action against the French breaking in through every entrance, Major Baring got out of the farm, and back to the lines, with forty-two men left of the original four hundred who had occupied the farm.

La Haye Sainte had fallen, and the effects of its loss were at once felt. Quiot, occupying it in force, brought up his guns and opened a crippling fire upon the Allied centre. To the east the smoke hung so thickly that, although not a hundred yards between them, the men of the 95th, reduced to a single line of skirmishers, could only see by the flash of their pieces where the French gunners were situated. Their senior officers had all been carried off the field, and the command of the battalion had fallen upon a captain. Behind the riflemen, Sir John Lambert was standing staunchly in support, in the angle of the chaussée and the hollow road, with three regiments, two living and one lying dead in square. On the west of the chaussée, the shot and the shells from the French batteries were tearing great rents in already depleted ranks. Alten had fallen; and Ompteda was dead. Staff officers from the various brigades galloped up from all sides to beg the Duke for orders. 'There are no orders,' he said. 'My only plan is to stand my ground here to the last man.'

Though his staff fell about him, he continued to ride up and down his lines, rallying failing troops, restraining men who, maddened by the rain of deadly shot, could hardly be kept from launching themselves through the smoke in a desperate charge against their persecutors. 'Wait a little longer, my lads: you shall have at them presently,' he promised.

'By God, I thought I had heard enough of this man, but he far surpasses my expectations!' Uxbridge exclaimed. 'It is not a man, but a god!'

De Lancey, the quartermaster-general, was struck by a spent

cannonball at the Duke's side, and fell, imploring those who hurried to him not to move him, for he was done for. Behind the crumbling ranks of Alten's division was only the extenuated line of Lord Edward's cavalry. The Duke brought up the only remaining Brunswickers in person, and formed them to fill the gap. They marched up bravely, but the sight of the horrors all around them, and the dropping of men in their own ranks, shook them. They broke, and fell back, but shouting to his aide-de-camp to rally them, the Duke spurred after them, rounding them up, heartening them by word and gesture. Gordon and Audley raced after him, and the terrified soldiers were re-formed and led up again.

Uxbridge rode off like the wind, to bring up the cavalry from the left wing. He met Sir Hussey Vivian advancing to the centre of his own initiative, learned from him that the Prussians were at last arriving in force, and despatched a message to Vaneleur to move to the centre in Vivian's wake.

A staff officer met Vivian's brigade on its way to the centre, and exchanged his own wounded hunter for a trooper belonging to the 18th Hussars. 'The Duke has won the battle if only we could get the damned Dutch to advance!' he told one of the officers.

The brigade, coming up behind the infantry lines from their comparatively quiet position on the left flank, could see no sign of victory in the desolation which surrounded them. Dead and dying men lay all over the ground; mutilated horses wandered about in aimless circles; cannonballs were tossing up the trampled earth in great gashes; and a pall of smoke hung over all. Vivian led the brigade over the chaussée, and saw Lord Edward Somerset, in a Life Guardsman's helmet, with a bare couple of squadrons drawn up west of the road. He called out: 'Lord Edward, where is your brigade?'

'Here,' replied Lord Edward.

Audley, engaged in rallying the Brunswickers, heard Gordon's voice raised above the whistle and hum of shot: 'For God's sake, my Lord, don't expose yourself! This is no work for you!'

The next instant Audley saw him fall, but he could neither desert his post to go to him nor discover whether he were dead or alive. Gordon was carried off; Brunswickers, their panic checked, saw Vivian's hussar brigade in support of them, and stood their ground; the Duke rode off to another part of the line.

Colonel Audley, his senses deadened to the iron rain about him, struggled after, saw Lord March, dismounted and kneeling on the ground, supporting a wounded man in his arms, and shouted to him: 'March! March! Is Gordon alive?'

'Oh, my God, not Gordon too?' March cried out in an anguished tone.

The Colonel pushed up to him, saw that the man in his arms was Canning, and almost flung himself out of the saddle.

A musketball had struck Canning in the stomach; he was dying fast, and in agony that made it difficult for him to speak. Some men of the 73rd Regiment had raised him to a sitting position with their knapsacks. He gasped out: 'The Duke – is he safe?'

'Yes, yes, untouched!'

A ghastly smile flickered over Canning's mouth; he tried to clasp Audley's hand; turned his head a little on March's shoulder; managed to speak their names; and so died.

An agitated officer from Ghigny's brigade came riding up while March still held Canning's body in his arms. '*Milord, mon Capitaine, je vous en prie! C'est Son Altesse lui même qui est en ce moment blessé! Il faut venir tout de suite!*'

March, lost in grief, seemed not to hear him. Colonel Audley, hardly less distressed, laid a hand on his shoulder. 'He's gone, March. Lay him down. Slender Billy's hurt.'

March raised his head, dashing the tears from his eyes. 'What's that?' he glanced up at the Dutchman standing over them. The message was repeated: the Prince had been hit in the shoulder while leading some of General Kruse's Nassauers to the charge, and had fallen so heavily from his horse that the sense seemed to have been knocked out of him. March laid Canning's body down, and got up. 'I'll come at once. Where is he?'

He rode away with the Dutch officer; Colonel Audley, consigning Canning's body to the care of an officer of Halkett's brigade, also mounted, and plunged off through the confusion to find the Duke again.

Vandeleur had come up from the left flank with his brigade of light dragoons, and, passing behind Vivian, had formed his squadrons more to the right, immediately in rear of Count D'Aubremé's Dutch–Belgian line battalions, brought up from Vieux Foriez to fill a gap on the right centre. Here they were exposed to a galling fire, but D'Aubremé's men in their front were weakening, and to have withdrawn out of range of the guns would have left the road open to the Dutch–Belgians for retreat. They closed their squadron intervals, and Vivian had done, to prevent the infantry passing through to the rear, and stood their ground, while Vandeleur, with some of his senior officers, bullied and persuaded the Dutch–Belgians into forming their front again.

At seven o'clock things looked very serious along the Allied front. To the west, only some Prussian cavalry had arrived to guard the left flank; Papelotte and the farm of Ter La Haye were held by Durutte, whose skirmishers stretched to the crest of the Allied position; the gunners and the *tirailleurs* at La Haye Sainte were raking the centre with their fire; and although twelve thousand men of Reille's Corps d'Armée had failed all day to dislodge twelve hundred British Guards from the ruins of Hougoumont, all along the Allied line the front was broken, and in some places utterly disorganised.

The Duke remained calm, but kept looking at his watch. Once he said: 'It's night, or Blücher,' but for the most part he was silent. An aide-de-camp rode up to him with a message from his general that his men were being mowed down by the artillery fire, and must be reinforced. 'It is impossible,' he replied. 'Will they stand?'

'Yes, my lord, till they perish!'

'Then tell them that I will stand with them, till the last man.'

Turmoil and confusion, made worse by the smoke that hung

heavily over the centre, and the débris that littered the ground from end to end of the line, seemed to reign everywhere. Staff officers, carrying messages to brigades, asked mechanically: 'Who commands here?' The Prince of Orange had been taken away by March; three generals had been killed; five others carried off the field, too badly wounded to remain; the adjutant-general and the quartermaster-general had both had to retire. Of the Duke's personal staff, Canning was dead; Gordon dying in the inn at Waterloo; and Lord Fitzroy, struck in the right arm while standing with his horse almost touching the Duke's, had left the field in Alava's care. Those that were left had passed beyond feeling. It was no longer a matter for surprise or grief to hear of a friend's death: the only surprise was to find anyone still left alive on that reeking plain. Horse after horse had been shot under them; sooner or later they would probably join the ranks of the slain: meanwhile, there were still orders to carry, and they forced their exhausted mounts through the carnage, indifferent to the heaps of fallen red-coats sprawling under their feet, themselves numb with fatigue, their minds focused upon one object only: to get the messages they carried through to their destinations.

Just before seven o'clock, a deserting colonel of cuirassiers came galloping up to the 52nd Regiment, shouting: '*Vive le Roi!*' He reached Sir John Colborne, and gasped out: '*Napoléon est là avec les Gardes! Voilà l'attaque qui se fait!*'

The warning was unnecessary, for it had been apparent for some minutes that the French were mustering for a grand attack all along the front. D'Erlon's corps was already assailing with a swarm of skirmishers the decimated line of Picton's 5th Division; and to the west of La Haye Sainte, on the undulating plain facing the Allied right, the Imperial Middle Guard was forming in five massive columns.

Colonel Audley was sent on his last errand just after seven. He was mounted on a trooper, and the strained and twisted strapping round his thigh was soaked with blood. He was almost unrecognisable for the smoke that had blackened his face, and was feeling oddly light-headed from the loss of blood he had suffered. He was also very tired, for he had been in the saddle almost continually since the night of June 15th. His mind, ordinarily sensitive to impression, accepted without revulsion the message of his eyes. Death and mutilation had become so common that he who loved horses could look with indifference upon a poor brute with the lower half of its head blown away, or a trooper, with its forelegs shot off at the knees, raising itself on its stumps, and neighing its sad appeal for help. He had seen a friend die in agony, and had wept over him, but all that was long past. He no longer ducked when he heard the shots singing past his head; when his trooper shied away, snorting in terror, from a bursting shell, he cursed it. But there was no sense in courting death unnecessarily; he struck northwards, and rode by all that was left of the two heavy brigades, drawn back since the arrival of Vivian and Vandeleur some three hundred paces behind the front line. An officer in the rags of a Life Guardsman's uniform, his helmet gone, and a blood-stained bandage tied round his head, rode forward, and hailed him.

'Audley! Audley!'

He recognised Lord George Alastair under a mask of mud, and sweat, and bloodstains, and drew rein. 'Hallo!' he said. 'So you're alive still?'

'Oh, I'm well enough! Do you know how it has gone with Harry?'

'Dead,' replied the Colonel.

George's eyelids flickered; under the dirt and the blood his face whitened. 'Thanks. That's all I wanted to know. You saw him?'

'Hours ago. He was dying then, in one of Maitland's squares. He sent you his love.'

George saluted, wheeled his horse, and rode back to his squadron.

The Colonel pushed on to the chaussée. His horse slithered clumsily down the bank on to it; he held it together, and rode across the pavé to the opposite bank and scrambled up, emerging upon the desolation of the slope behind Picton's division. He urged the trooper to a ponderous gallop towards the rear of Best's brigade. A handful of Dutch–Belgians were formed in second line; he supposed them to be some of Count Bylandt's men, but paid little heed to them, wheeling round their right flank, and plunging once more into the region of shot and shell bursts.

He neither saw nor heard the shell that struck him. His horse came crashing down; he was conscious of having been hit; blood was streaming down his left arm, which lay useless on the ground beside him, but there was as yet no feeling in the shattered elbow-joint. His left side hurt him a little; he moved his right hand to it, and found his coat torn, and his shirt sticky with blood. He supposed vaguely that since he seemed to be alive this must be only a flesh wound. He desired nothing better than to lie where he had fallen, but he mastered himself, for he had a message to deliver, and struggled to his knees.

The sound of horse's hooves galloping towards him made him lift his head. An adjutant in the blue uniform and orange facings of the 5th National Militia dismounted beside him, and said in English: 'Adjutant to Count Bylandt, sir! I'm directed by General Perponcher to – *Parbleu*! it is you, then!'

Colonel Audley looked up into a handsome, dark face bent over him, and said weakly: 'Hallo, Lavisse! Get me a horse, there's a good fellow!'

'A horse!' exclaimed Lavisse, going down on one knee, and supporting the Colonel in his arms. 'You need a surgeon, my friend! Be tranquil: my General sends to bear you off the field.' He gave a bitter laugh, and added: 'That is what my brigade exists for – to succour you English wounded!'

'Did you succeed in rallying your fellows?' asked the Colonel.

'Some, not all. Do not disturb yourself, my rival! You have all the honours of this day's encounter. *My* honour is in the dust!'

'Oh, don't talk such damned theatrical rubbish!' said the Colonel irritably. He fumbled with his right hand in his sash, and drew forth a folded and crumpled message. 'This has to go to

General Best. See that it gets to him, will you? – or, if he's been killed, to his next in command.'

A couple of orderlies and a doctor had come up from the rear. Lavisse gave the Colonel into their charge, and said with a twisted smile: 'You trust your precious message to me, my Colonel?'

'Be a good fellow, and don't waste time talking about it!' begged the Colonel.

He was carried off the field as the attack upon the whole Allied line began. On the left, Ziethen's advance guard had reached Smohain, and the Prussian batteries were in action, firing into Durutte's skirmishers; while somewhere to the south-east Bülow's guns could be heard assailing the French right flank. Allix and all that was left of Marcognet's division once more attacked the Allied left; Donzelot led his men against Ompteda's and Kielmansegg's depleted ranks, while the Imperial Guard of Grenadiers and Chasseurs moved up in five columns at rather narrow deploying intervals, in echelon, crossing the undulating plain diagonally from the chaussée to the Nivelles road. Each column showed a front of about seventy men, and in each of the intervals between the battalions two guns were placed. In all, some four thousand five hundred men were advancing upon the Allied right, led by Ney, *le Brave des Braves*, at the head of the leading battalion.

The sun, which all day had been trying to penetrate the clouds, broke through as the attack commenced. Its setting rays bathed the columns of the Imperial Guard in a fiery radiance. Rank upon rank of veterans who had borne the Eagles victorious through a dozen fights advanced to the beat of drums, with bayonets turned to blood-red by the sun's last glow, across the plain into the smoke and heat of the battle.

Owing to their diagonal approach the columns did not come into action simultaneously. Before the battalions marching upon the British Guards had reached the slope leading to the crest of the Allied position, Ney's leading column had struck at Halkett's brigade and the Brunswickers on his left flank.

Over this part of the line the smoke caused by the guns firing from La Haye Sainte lay so thick that the Allied troops heard but could not see the formidable advance upon them. Colin Halkett had fallen, wounded in the mouth, rallying his men round one of the Colours; two of his regiments were operating as one battalion, so heavy had been their losses; and these were thrown into some confusion by their own light troops retreating upon them. Men were carried off their feet in the surge to the rear; the Colonel, on whom the command of the brigade had devolved, seemed distracted, saying repeatedly: 'What am I to do? What would you do?' to the staff officer sent by the Duke to 'See what is wrong there!' The men of the 33rd, fighting against the tide that was sweeping them back, re-formed, and came on, shouting: 'Give them the cold steel, lads! Let 'em have the Brummagum!' A volley was poured in before which the deploying columns recoiled; to the left, the Brunswickers, rallied once more by the Duke himself, followed suit, and the Imperial Guard fell back, carrying with it a part of Donzelot's division.

Those of the batteries on the Allied front which were still in action met the advance with a fire which threw the leading ranks into considerable disorder. Many of the British batteries, however, were useless. Some had been abandoned owing to the lack of ammunition; several guns stood with muzzles bent down, or touch-holes melted from the excessive heat; and more than one troop, its gunners either killed or too exhausted to run the guns up after each recoil, had its guns in a confused heap, the trails crossing each other almost on top of the limbers and the ammunition wagons. Ross's, Sinclair's, and Sandham's were all silent, Lloyd's battery was still firing from in front of Halkett's brigade; so was Napier, commanding Bolton's, in front of Maitland; and a Dutch battery of eight guns, belonging to Detmer's brigade, brought up by Chassé in second line, had been sent forward to a position immediately to the east of the Brunswick squares, and was pouring in a rapid and well-directed fire upon the Grenadiers and the men on Donzelot's left flank.

As the Brunswickers and Halkett's men momentarily repulsed the two leading columns, which, on their march over the uneven ground, had become merged into one unwieldy mass, the Grenadiers and the Chasseurs on the French left advanced up the slope to where Maitland's Guards lay silently awaiting them. The drummers were beating the *pas de charge*, shouts of '*Vive l'Empereur!*' and '*En avant à la baïonette!*' filled the air. The Duke, who had galloped down the line from his position by the Brunswick troops, was standing with Maitland on the left flank of the brigade, not far from General Adam, whose brigade lay to the right of the Guards. Adam had ridden up to watch the advance, and the Duke, observing through his glass the French falling back before Halkett's men exclaimed: 'By God, Adam, I believe we shall beat them yet!'

At ninety paces, the brass 8-pounders between the advancing battalions opened fire upon Maitland's brigade. They were answered by Krahmer de Bichin's Dutch battery, but though the grape shot tore through the ranks of the Guards the Duke withheld the order to open musketry fire. Not a man in the British line was visible to the advancing columns until they halted twenty paces from the crest to deploy.

'Now, Maitland! Now's your time!' the Duke said at last, and called out in his deep, ringing voice: 'Stand up, Guards!'

The Guards leaped to their feet. The crest, which had seemed deserted, was suddenly alive with men, scarlet coats standing in line four-deep, with muskets at the present. Almost at the point of crossing bayonets they fired volley after volley into the Grenadiers. The Grenadiers, in column, had only two hundred muskets able to fire against the fifteen hundred of Halkett's and Maitland's brigades, deployed in line before them. They tried to deploy, but were thrown into confusion by a fire no infantry could withstand.

On Maitland's left, General Chassé had brought up Detmer's brigade of Dutch–Belgians in perfect order. When the word to charge was given, and the sound of the three British cheers was heard as the Guards surged forward, the Dutch came up at the double, and, with a roar of '*Oranje boven!*' drove the French from the crest in their front.

The Guards, scattering the Grenadiers before them, advanced until their flank was threatened by the second attacking column of Chasseurs. The recall was sounded, and the order given to face-about and retire. In the din of clashing arms, crackling musketry, groans, cheers, and trumpet calls, the order was misunderstood. As the Guards regained the crest, an alarm of cavalry was raised. Someone shrieked: 'Square, square, form square!' and the two battalions, trying to obey the order, became intermingled. A dangerous confusion seemed about to spread panic through the ranks, but it was checked in a very few moments. The order to 'Halt! – Front! – Form up!' rang out; the Guards obeyed as one man, formed again four-deep, and told off in companies of forty.

In the immediate rear of Maitland's and Halkett's brigades, D'Aubremé's Dutch–Belgians, formed in three squares, appalled by the slaughter in their front, began to retreat precipitately upon Vandeleur's squadrons. The dragoons closed their ranks until their horses stood shoulder to shoulder; Vandeleur galloped forward to try to stem the rout; and an aide-de-camp went flying to the Duke on a foaming horse, gasping out that the Dutch would not stand, and could not be held.

'That's all right,' answered his lordship coolly. 'Tell them the French are retiring!'

Meanwhile, to the right, where Adam's brigade held the ground above Hougoumont, Sir John Colborne, without waiting for orders, had acted on his own brilliant judgment. As the columns advanced upon Maitland, he moved the 52nd Regiment down to the north-east angle of Hougoumont, and right-shouldered it forward, until it stood in line four-deep parallel to the left flank of the second column of Chasseurs.

Adam, seeing this deliberate movement, galloped up, calling out: 'Colborne! Colborne! What are you meaning to do?'

'To make that column feel our fire,' replied Sir John laconically.

Adam took one look at the Chasseurs, another at the purposeful face beside him, and said: 'Move on, then! The 71st shall follow you,' and rode off to bring up the Highlanders.

The Chasseur column, advancing steadily, was met by a frontal fire of over eighteen hundred muskets from the 95th Rifles and the 71st Highlanders, and as it staggered, the Fighting 52nd, the men in third and fourth line loading and passing muskets forward to the first two lines, riddled its flank. It broke, and fell into hideous disorder, almost decimated by a fire it could not, from its clumsy formation, return. A cry of horror arose, taken up by battalion after battalion down the French lines: '*La Guarde recule!*'

Before the column could deploy, Sir John Colborne swept forward in a charge that carried all before it. The officer carrying the Colour was killed, and a hundred and fifty men on the right wing, but the advance was maintained, right across the ground in front of the Allied line, the Imperial Guard being driven towards the chaussée in inextricable confusion. The 2nd and 3rd battalions of the Rifles, with the 71st Highlanders, followed the 52nd in support; the Imperial Guard, helpless under the musketry fire, cast into terrible disorder through their inability to deploy, lost all semblance of formation, and retreated *pêle-mêle* to the chaussée, till the ground in front of the Allied position was one seething mass of struggling, fighting, fleeing infantry.

Hew Halkett brought up his Hanoverians into the interval between Hougoumont and the hollow road; the 52nd advanced across the uneven plain until checked by encountering some squadrons of Dörnberg's 23rd Light Dragoons, whom, in the dusk, they mistook for French cavalry and fired upon.

The Duke, who had watched the advance from the high ground beside Maitland, galloped up to the rear of the 52nd, where Sir John, having ordered his adjutant to stop the firing, was exchanging his wounded horse for a fresh one.

'It is our own cavalry which has caused this firing!' Colborne told him.

'Never mind! *Go* on, Colborne, *go* on!' replied the Duke, and galloped back to the crest of the position, and stood there, silhouetted against the glowing sky on his hollow-backed charger. He raised his cocked hat high in the air, and swept it forward, towards the enemy's position, in the long-looked-for signal for a General Advance. A cheer broke out on the right, as the Guards charged down the slope. The crippled forces east of the chaussée, away down to their left, heard it growing louder as it swelled all along the line towards them, took it up by instinct, and charged forward out of the intolerable smoke surrounding them, on to a plain strewn with dead and dying, lit by the last rays of a red sun, and covered with men flying in confusion towards the ridge of La Belle Alliance.

Cries of: '*Nous sommes trahis!*' mingled with the dismayed shouts of '*La Garde recule!*' Donzelot's division was carried away in the rush of Grenadiers and Chasseurs; the retreat had become a rout. Ney, on foot, one epaulette torn off, his hat gone, a broken sword in his hand, was fighting like a madman, crying: 'Come and see how a Marshal of France dies!' and, to D'Erlon, borne towards him in the press: 'If we get out of this alive, D'Erlon, we shall both be hanged!'

Far in advance of the charging Allied line, Colborne, having crossed the ground between Hougoumont and La Haye Sainte, had reached the chaussée, and passed it, left-shouldering his regiment forward to ascend the slope towards La Belle Alliance.

To the right, Vivian had advanced his brigade, placing himself at the head of the 18th Hussars. 'Eighteenth! You will, I know, follow me!' he said, and was answered by one of his sergeant-majors: 'Ay, General! to hell, if you'll lead us!'

Taking up his position on the flank of the leading half-squadron, holding his reins in his injured right hand, which, though it seemed reposed in a sling, was just capable of grasping them, he led the whole brigade forward at the trot. As the hussars cleared the front on Maitland's right, the Guards and Vandeleur's light dragoons cheered them on, and they charged down on to the plain, sweeping the French up in their advance past the eastern hedge of Hougoumont towards the chaussée at La Belle Alliance.

Through the dense smoke laying over the ground the Duke galloped down the line. When the Riflemen saw him, they sent up a cheer, but he called out: 'No cheering, my lads, but forward and complete your victory!' and rode on, through the smother, out into the sea of dead, to where Adam's brigade was halted on the ridge of La Belle Alliance, a little way from where some French battalions had managed to re-form.

The Duke, learning from Adam that the brigade had been halted for the purpose of closing the files in, scrutinised the French battalions closely for a moment, and then said decidedly: 'They won't stand: better attack them!'

Baron Müffling, looking along the line from his position on the left flank, saw the General Advance through the lifting smoke. Kielmansegg's, Ompteda's and Pack's shattered brigades remained where they stood all day, but everywhere else the regiments charged forward, leaving behind them an unbroken red line of their own dead, marking the position where, for over eight hours of cannonading, of cavalry charges, and of massed infantry attacks the British and German troops had held their ground.

From Papelotte to Hougoumont the hillocky plain in front was covered with dead and wounded. Near the riddled walls of La Haye Sainte the cuirassiers lay in mounds of men and horses. The corn which had waved shoulder-high in the morning was everywhere trodden down into clay. On the rising ground of La Belle Alliance the Old Guard was making its last stand, fighting off the fugitives, who, trying to find shelter in its squares, threatened to overwhelm them. These three squares, with one formed by Reille, south of Hougoumont, were the only French troops still standing firm in the middle of the rout. With the cessation of artillery fire by the hollow road the smoke was clearing away, but over the ruins of Hougoumont it still rose in a slow, black column. Those of the batteries which had been able to follow the advance were firing into the mass of French on the southern ridge; musketry crackled as the Old Guard, with Napoleon and his staff in the middle of their squares, retreated step by step, fighting a heroic rearguard action against Adam's brigade and Hew Halkett's Hanoverians. Where Vivian, with Vandeleur in support, was sweeping the ground east and south of Hougoumont, fierce cavalry skirmishing was in progress, and the Middle Guard was trying to re-form its squares to hold the hussars at bay.

Müffling, detaching a battery from Ziethen's Corps, led it at a gallop to the centre of the Allied position. He met the Duke by La Haye Sainte. His lordship called triumphantly to him from a distance: 'Well! You see Macdonnell has held Hougoumont!'

Müffling, who found himself unable to think of what the Guards at Hougoumont must have endured without a lump's coming into his throat, knew the Duke well enough to realise that his brief sentence was his lordship's way of expressing his admiration, and nodded.

The sun was sinking fast; in the gathering dusk musket-balls were hissing in every direction. Uxbridge, who had come scatheless through the day, was hit in the knee by a shot passing over Copenhagen's withers, and sang out: 'By God! I've got it at last!'

'Have you, by God?' said his lordship, too intent on the operations of his troops to pay much heed.

Colin Campbell, preparing to support Uxbridge off the field, seized the Duke's bridle, saying roughly: 'This is no place for you! I wish you will move!'

'I will when I have seen these fellows off,' replied his lordship.

To the south-east of La Belle Alliance, the Prussians, driving the Young Guard out of Plancenoit, were advancing on the chaussée, to converge there with the Allied troops. Bülow's infantry were singing the Lutheran hymn, *Now thank we all our God*, but as the columns came abreast of the British Guards, halted by the road, the hymn ceased abruptly. The band struck up *God Save the King*, and as the Prussians marched past they saluted.

It was past nine o'clock when, in the darkness, south of La Belle Alliance, the Duke met Prince Blücher. The Prince, beside himself with exultation, carried beyond coherent speech by his admiration for the gallantry of the British troops and for the generalship of his friend and ally, could find only one thing to say as he embraced the Duke ruthlessly on both cheeks: 'I stink of garlic!'

When his first transports of joy were a little abated, he offered to take on the pursuit of the French through the night. The Duke's battered forces, dog-tired, terribly diminished in numbers, were ordered to bivouac where they stood, on the ground occupied all day by the French; and the Duke, accompanied by a mere skeleton of the brilliant cortège which had gone with him into the field that morning, rode back in clouded moonlight to his Headquarters.

Baron Müffling, drawing abreast of him, said: 'The Field Marshal will call this battle Belle-Alliance, sir.'

His lordship returned no answer. The Baron, casting a shrewd glance at his bony profile, with its frosty eye and pursed mouth, realised that he had no intention of calling the battle by that name. It was his lordship's custom to name his victories after the village or town where he had slept the night before them. The Marshal Prince might call the battle what he liked, but his lordship would head his despatch to Earl Bathurst: 'Waterloo'.

Twenty-Five

For those in Brussels the day had been one of increasing anxiety. Contrary to expectation, no firing was heard, the wind blowing steadily from the north-west. The Duke's despatch to Sir Charles Stuart, written from Waterloo in the small hours, reached him at seven o'clock, and shortly afterwards Baron van de Capellan, the Secretary of State, issued a reassuring proclamation. After that no news of any kind was received in the town for many hours.

Colonel Jones, left in Brussels during the Duke's absence as Military Commander, was besieged all the morning by applications for passports. Every track-boat bound for Antwerp was as full as it could hold of refugees; money could not buy a pair of horses in all Brussels. Scores of people drove off at an early hour, with baggage piled high on the roofs of their carriages; the town seemed strangely quiet and deserted; and the church bells ringing for morning service sounded to sensitive ears like a knell.

Both Judith and Barbara had slept the night through, in utter exhaustion, but neither in the morning looked as though she were refreshed by this deep slumber. Except for discussing in a desultory manner the extraordinary revelation Lucy Devenish had made on the previous evening, they did not talk much. Once Judith said: 'If you knew the comfort it is to me to have you with me!' but Barbara merely smiled rather mockingly, and shook her head.

In the privacy of their own bedroom, Judith had remarked impulsively to Worth: 'I am out of all conceit with myself! I have been deceived alike in Lucy and in Barbara!'

'You might certainly be forgiven for having been deceived in Lucy,' Worth replied. 'I imagine no one could have suspected such a melodramatic story to lie behind that demure appearance.'

'No, indeed! I was never more shocked in my life. Bab says George will make her a very bad husband, and if it were not unchristian I should be much inclined to say that she will have nothing but her just deserts. But Bab! I could not have believed that she had such strength of character, such real goodness of heart! Have not you been surprised?'

'No,' he replied. 'I should have been very much surprised had she not, in this crisis, behaved precisely as she has done. My opinion of her remains unchanged.'

'How can you talk so? You cannot have supposed from her conduct during these past months that she would behave so well now!'

'On the contrary, I never doubted her spirit. She is, moreover, just the kind of young woman who, under the stress of such conditions as these, is elevated for the time above her ordinary self.'

'For the time! You place no dependence on this softened mood continuing, I collect!'

'Very little,' he answered.

'You are unjust, Worth! For my part, I am persuaded that she repents bitterly of all that has passed. Oh, if only Charles is spared, I shall be so glad to see him reunited to her!'

'That is fortunate, since I have little doubt that you will see it.'

'You don't think it will do?'

'I am not a judge of what will suit Charles. It would not do for me. She will certainly lead him a pretty dance.'

'Oh no, no! I am sure you are mistaken!'

He smiled at the distress in her face, and pinched her chin. 'I daresay I may be. I will admit, it you like, that I prefer this match to the one *you* tried to make for Charles, my dear!'

She blushed. 'Oh, don't speak of that! At least there is nothing of that lack of openness in Bab.'

'Nothing at all,' he agreed somewhat dryly.

She saw that she could not talk him round to her way of thinking, and allowed the conversation to drop.

They had scarcely got up from the breakfast table, a little later, when they received a morning call from Mr and Mrs Fisher.

'She has confessed, then!' Judith exclaimed when the visitors' cards were brought to her.

'In floods of tears, I'd lay my last guinea!' said Barbara.

'It is not to be wondered at if she did weep!'

'I abominate weeping females. Do you wish for my support at this interview?'

'Oh yes, they will certainly desire to see you.'

'Very well, but I'll be hanged if I'll be held accountable for George's sins.'

It was as Judith had supposed. Lucy had confessed the whole to her aunt and uncle. They were profoundly shocked, and Mr Fisher seemed almost bewildered. He said that he could not understand how such a thing could have come to pass, and so far from blaming Barbara for her brother's conduct, several times apologised to her for it. Mrs Fisher, torn between a sense of propriety and a love of romance, was inclined to find excuses for the young people, in which occupation Judith gladly assisted her. Mr Fisher agreed, but with a very sober face, that since the marriage had actually taken place there was nothing to do but to forgive Lucy. Barbara's presence prevented him from expressing his opinion of Lord George's character, but it was plain that this was not high. He sighed deeply several times, and shook his head over his poor girl's chances of happiness. Mrs Fisher exclaimed, with the tears springing to her eyes: 'Oh! If only she is not even now, perhaps, a widow!'

This reflection made them all silent. After a moment, her husband said heavily: 'You are very right, Mrs Fisher. Ah, poor child, who knows what this day may not bring upon her? You must know, Lady Worth, that she is already quite overcome by her troubles, and is laid down upon her bed with the hartshorn.'

'I am sure it is no wonder,' Judith responded, avoiding Barbara's eye.

The Fishers soon took their leave, and the rest of the morning was spent by Judith and Barbara in rendering all the assistance in their power to those nursing the wounded in the tent by the Namur Gate. Returning together just before four o'clock they found visitors with Worth in the salon, and walked in to discover these to be none other than the Duke and Duchess of Avon, who had arrived in Brussels scarcely an hour previously.

Barbara stood on the threshold, staring at them. 'What the devil –? Grandmama, how the deuce do you come to be here?'

The Duke, a tall man with grizzled hair and fiery dark eyes, said: 'Don't talk to your grandmother like that! What's this damnable story I hear about that worthless brother of yours?'

Barbara bent to kiss her grandmother, a rather stout lady, with a straight back, and an air of unshakable imperturbability: 'Dear love! Did you come for my sake?'

'No, I came because your grandfather would do so. But this is very surprising, this news of George's marriage. Tell me, shall I like his wife?'

'You'll have nothing to do with her!' snapped his Grace. 'Upon my word, I'm singularly blessed in my grandchildren! One is such a miserable poltroon that he takes to his heels the instant he hears a gun fired; another makes herself the talk of the town; and a third marries a damned Cit's daughter. You may as well tell me what folly Harry has committed, and be done with it. I wash my hands of the pack of you! There is no understanding how I came to have such a set of grandchildren.'

'Vidal's behaviour is certainly very bad,' agreed the Duchess. 'But I find nothing remarkable about George's and Bab's conduct, Dominic. Only I'm sorry George should have married in such a hole-and-corner fashion. It will make it very awkward for his wife. You have not told me if I shall like her, Bab.'

'You will think her very dull, I daresay.'

'You will not receive her at all!' stated his Grace.

The Duchess replied calmly: 'Your mother received me, Dominic.'

'Mary!'

'Well, my dear, but the circumstances were far more disgraceful, weren't they?'

'I suppose you will say that *I* am to blame for George's conduct?'

'At all events, you are scarcely in a position to condemn him,' she said, smiling. 'You made a shocking *mésalliance* yourself. Dear me, how rude we are, to be sure! Here is Lady Worth come in, and not one of us pays the least heed! How do you do, my dear child? You must let me thank you for your kindness to my granddaughter. I am afraid she has not used your family very well.'

'Oh, ma'am, that is all forgotten!' Judith said, taking her hand. 'I cannot find words to express to you what it has meant to me to have her here during this terrible time!' She turned, towards the Duke, saying with a quiver in her voice: 'This is not a moment for reproaches! If you knew what we have seen – what may even now be happening – forgive me, but every consideration but the one seems so trivial, so –' Her voice failed, she averted her face, groping in her reticule for her handkerchief. She recovered her composure with a strong effort, and said in a low tone: 'Excuse me! We have been among the wounded the whole morning, and it has a little upset me.'

Barbara pushed her into a chair, saying: 'Confound you, Judith, if you set me off crying, I'll never forgive you!' She looked at the Duke. 'Well, sir, my compliments! You must be quite the only man to come *into* Brussels today! Did you come because there was a battle being fought, or in despite of it?'

'I came,' replied his Grace, 'on account of the intelligence received by your grandmother from Vidal. So you have jilted Charles Audley, have you? I congratulate you!'

'Your congratulations are out of place. I never did anything more damnable in my life.'

'Why, Bab, my girl!' said his Grace, surprised. He put his arm round her, and said gruffly: 'There, that will do! You are a baggage, but at least you have some spirit in you! When I think of that white-livered cur, Vidal, running for his life –'

'Oh, that was Gussie's doing! Did you meet them on your way here?'

'I? No, nor wish to! We landed at Ostend, and drove here through Ghent. If it had not been for the rabble choking the road we should have been here yesterday.'

'Yes,' said his wife. 'They warned us in Ghent not to proceed farther, as we should certainly be obliged to fly from Brussels, so naturally your grandfather had the horses put to immediately.'

He regarded her with a grim little smile. '*You* were not behindhand, Mary!'

'Certainly not. All this dashing about makes me feel myself a young woman again. Which reminds me that I must call upon my new granddaughter. You will give me her uncle's direction, Bab.'

'Understand me, Mary –'

'I will give it to you, ma'am, but you must know that Mr Fisher regards the match with quite as much dislike as does my grandfather.'

This remark brought a sparkle into the Duke's eye. 'He does, does he? Go on, Miss! Go on! What the devil has he against my grandson?'

'He thinks him a spendthrift, sir.'

'Ha! Damned Cit! He may consider himself lucky to have caught George for his nobody of a niece!'

'As to that, Lucy is his heir. I fancy he was looking higher for her. Her fortune will not be inconsiderable, you know, and in these days –'

'So he was looking higher, was he? An Alastair is not good enough for him! I'll see this greasy merchant!'

The Duchess said in her matter-of-fact way: 'You should certainly do so. It will be much more the thing than that wild notion you had taken into your head of riding out with Lord Worth towards the battlefield.'

'Fisher can wait,' replied his Grace. 'I have every intention of going to see what news can be got the instant I have swallowed my dinner.'

'Dinner!' Judith exclaimed. 'How shocking of me! I had forgotten the time. You must know, Duchess, that here in Brussels we have got into the way of dining at four. I hope you will not mind. You must please stay and join us.'

'You should warn them that Charles bore off our Sunday dinner,' Barbara said, with a wry smile.

'You may be sure my cook will have contrived something.'

The Avons were putting up at the Hôtel de Belle Vue, and the Duchess at once suggested that the whole party should walk round to dine there. It was declined, however; Judith's confidence in her cook was found not to have been misplaced; and in a very few minutes they were all seated round the table in the dining-parlour.

The conversation was mostly of the war. The wildest rumours were current in Ghent, and the Duke was glad to listen to a calm account from Worth of all that had so far passed. When he heard that the Life Guards had driven the French lancers out of Genappe, he looked pleased, but beyond saying that if George did not get his brevet for this he supposed he would be obliged to purchase promotion for him, he made no remark. As soon as they rose from the table, he and Worth took their departure, to ride towards the Forest of Soignes in search of intelligence, and Judith, excusing herself, left Barbara alone with her grandmother.

'I have surpassed myself, ma'am,' Barbara said in a bitter tone. 'Did Vidal write you the whole?'

'Quite enough,' replied the Duchess. 'I wish, dearest, you will try to get the better of this shocking disposition of yours.'

'If Charles comes back to me there is nothing I will not do!'

'We will hope he may do so. Your grandfather was very much pleased with the civil letter Colonel Audley wrote to him. How came you to throw him off as you did, my love?'

'O God, Grandmama!' Barbara whispered, and fell on her knees beside the Duchess, and buried her face in her lap.

It was long before she could be calm. The Duchess listened in understanding silence to the disjointed sentences gasped out, merely saying presently: 'Don't cry, Bab. It will ruin your face, you know.'

'I don't give a damn for my face!'

'I am very sure that you do.'

Barbara sat up, smiling through her tears. 'Confound you, ma'am, you know too much! There, I have done! You don't wish me to remove to the Hôtel de Belle Vue, do you? I cannot leave Judith at this present.'

'By all means stay here, my love. But tell me about this child George has married, if you please!'

'I cannot conceive what possessed George to look twice at her. She is quite insipid.'

'Dear me! I had better go and call upon her aunt.'

She very soon took her leave, setting out on foot to the Fishers' lodging. Her visit did much to sooth Lucy's agitation; and her calm good sense almost reconciled Mr Fisher to an alliance which he had been regarding with the deepest misgiving. Neither his appearance nor the obsequiousness of his manners could be expected to please the Duchess, but she was agreeably surprised in Lucy, and although not placing much dependence upon her being able to hold George's volatile fancy, went back presently to her hôtel feeling that things might have been much worse.

Worth returned at about six o'clock, having parted from the Duke at the end of the street. He had very little news to report. He described meeting Creevey in the suburbs, and their mutual surprise at finding the Sunday population of Brussels drinking beer, and making merry, round little tables, for all the world as though no pitched battle were being fought not more than ten miles to the south of them. It had been found to be impossible to penetrate far into the Forest, on account of the baggage choking the road, but they had met with a number of wounded soldiers making their way back to Brussels, and had had speech with a Life Guardsman, who reported that the French were getting on in such a way that he did not see what was to stop them.

'He had taken part in a charge of the whole Household Brigade, and says that they have lost, in killed, wounded, and prisoners, more than half their number. George, however, was safe when the man left the field. A private soldier's opinion of the battle is not to be depended on, but I don't like the look of things.'

Scarcely an hour later, the town was thrown into an uproar by the Cumberland Hussars galloping in through the Namur Gate, and stampeding through the streets, shouting that all was lost, and the French hard on their heels. They seemed not to have drawn rein in their flight from the battlefield, and went through Brussels scattering the inhabitants before them.

People began once more to run about, crying: '*Les Français sont ici! Ils s'emparent à porte de la ville! Nous sommes tous perdus! Que ferons-nous?*' Many people kept their horses at their doors, but no more troops followed the hussars, and the panic gradually abated. A little later, a large number of French prisoners entered the town under escort, and were marched to the barracks of Petit Château. The sight of two captured Eagles caused complete strangers to shake one another by the hand; more prisoners arrived, and hopes ran high, only to be dashed by the intelligence conveyed by one or two wounded officers that everything had been going as badly as possible when they had left the field. The Adjutant-General's chaise-and-four was seen by Mr Creevey to set out from his house in the Park and bowl away, as fast as the horses could drag it, to the Namur Gate. More and more wounded arrived in town, all telling the same tale: it was the most sanguinary battle they had ever known; men were dropping like flies; there was no saying in the smoke and the carnage who was still alive or who had been killed; no time should be lost by civilians in getting away.

In curious contrast to this scene of agitation, light shone in the Théâtre de la Monnaie, where Mlle Ternaux was playing in *Œdipe à Colonne* before an audience composed of persons who either had no relatives or friends engaged in the battle or who looked forward with pleasure to the entrance of Bonaparte into Brussels.

At half past eight o'clock, Worth, who had gone out some time before in quest of news, came abruptly into the salon where Judith and Barbara were sitting in the most dreadful suspense, and said, with more sharpness in his voice than his wife had ever heard: 'Judith, be so good as to have pillows put immediately into the chaise! I am going at once towards Waterloo: Charles is there, very badly wounded. Cherry has just come to me with the news.'

He did not wait, but strode out to his own room, to make what preparations for the journey were necessary. Both ladies ran after him, imploring him to tell them more.

'I know nothing more than what I have told you. Cherry had no idea how things were going – badly, he thinks. I may be aware some time: the road is almost blocked by the carts overturned by the German cavalry's rout. Have Charles's bed made up – but you will know what to do!'

'I will have the pillows put in the chaise,' Barbara said in a voice of repressed anguish, and left the room.

The chaise was already at the door, and Colonel Audley's groom waiting impatiently beside it. He was too overcome to be able to tell Barbara much, but the little he did say was enough to appal her.

Colonel Audley had been carried to Mont St Jean by some foreigners; he did not know whether Dutch or German.

'It does not signify. Go on!'

Cherry brushed his hand across his eyes. 'I saw them carrying him along the road. Oh, my lady, in all the years I've served the Colonel I never thought to see such a sight as met my eyes! My poor master like one dead, and the blood soaked right through the horse-blanket they had laid him on! He was taken straight to the cottage at Mont St Jean, where those damned sawbones – saving your ladyship's presence! – was busy. I thought my master was gone, but he opened his eyes as they put him down, and said to me: "Hallo, Cherry!" he said, "I've got it, you see."'

He fairly broke down, but Barbara, gripping the open chaise door, merely said harshly: 'Go on!'

'Yes, my lady! But I don't know how to tell your ladyship what they done to my master, Dr Hume, and them others, right there in the garden. Oh, my lady, they've taken his arm off! And he bore it all without a groan!'

She pressed her handkerchief to her lips. In a stifled voice, she said: 'But he will live!'

'You would not say so if you could but see him, my lady. Four horses he's had shot under him this day, and a wound on his leg turning as black as my boot. We got him to the inn at Waterloo, but there's no staying there: they couldn't take in the Prince of Orange himself, for all he had a musketball in his shoulder. Poor Sir Alexander Gordon's laying there, and Lord Fitzroy too. Never till my dying day shall I forget the sound of Sir Alexander's sufferings – him as always was such a merry gentleman, and such a close friend of my master's! Not but what by the time we got my master to the inn he was too far gone to heed. I shouldn't have spoken of it to your ladyship, but I'm that upset I hardly know what I'm saying.'

Worth ran down the steps of the house at that moment, and curtly told Cherry to get up on the box. As he drew on his driving-gloves, Barbara said: 'I have put my smelling-salts inside the chaise, and a roll of lint. I would come with you, but I believe you will do better without me. O God, Worth, bring him safely back!'

'I shall certainly bring him back. Go in to Judith, and do not be imagining anything nonsensical if I'm away some hours. Goodbye! A man doesn't die because he has the misfortune to lose an arm, you know.'

He mounted the box; the grooms let go the wheelers' heads, and as the chaise moved forward one of them jumped up behind.

For the next four hours Judith and Barbara, having made every preparation for the Colonel's arrival, waited, sick with suspense, for Worth's return. The Duke of Avon walked round the Hôtel de Belle Vue at ten o'clock, and, learning of Colonel

Audley's fate from Judith's faltering tongue, said promptly: 'Good God, is that all! One would say he had been blown in pieces by a howitzer shell to look at your faces! Cheer up, Bab! Why, I once shot a man just above the heart, and he recovered!'

'That must have been a mistake, sir, I feel sure.'

'It was,' he admitted. 'Only time I ever missed my mark.'

At any other time both ladies would have wished to hear more of this anecdote, but in the agitation of spirits which they were suffering nothing that did not bear directly upon the present issue had the power to engage their attention. The Duke, after animadverting with peculiar violence upon Mr Fisher's manners and ideals, bade them goodnight, and went back to his hôtel.

Hardly more than an hour later, Creevey called to bring the ladies news. His prospective stepson-in-law, Major Hamilton, had brought the Adjutant-General into Brussels a little after ten o'clock, and had immediately repaired to Mr Creevey's house to warn him that in General Barnes's opinion the battle was lost, and no time should be wasted in getting away from Brussels.

'I could not go to bed without informing you of this,' Creevey said. 'I thought it only right that you should know, and decide for yourselves what were best to do under the circumstances.'

'Thank you,' Judith said. 'It was kind of you, but there is now no question of our leaving Brussels. My brother-in-law is severely wounded. Worth has gone to bring him in.'

He looked genuinely concerned, and pressed her hand in the most speaking way. 'I am excessively sorry to hear of this! But once you have Colonel Audley in your care you will see how quickly he will recover!'

'We hope – Do you and Mrs Creevey mean to go to Antwerp?'

'No, it is out of the question to move Mrs Creevey in her present state of health. I don't scruple to tell you, my dear ma'am, that General Barnes's prognostications do not convince me that all is over. Hamilton tells me he was shot through the body at about five o'clock, and borne off the field. I cannot but feel that if the battle had been lost we must by now have received intelligence of it. Do you know what I judge by? Why, I'll tell you! The baggage-train is still moving *towards* the battlefield! To my mind, that proves that all is well.'

'I had not thought of that. Yes, indeed: you must be right. You put us quite at our ease, Mr Creevey. Thank you again for coming to us!'

He saw that the result of the battle was of less importance to her at the moment than Colonel Audley's fate, and after lingering only for a few moments to express his sympathy, took his leave and went back to the Rue du Musée.

After he had gone, no further interruptions occurred. The evening was mild, with a fitful moonlight shining through the lifting storm-clouds. Barbara had drawn back the blinds and opened one of the windows, and sat by it almost without stirring. In the street below a few people passed, but the sounds that drifted to the salon were muffled, as though Brussels were restless but quiet.

Once Judith said: 'Would you like to lie down upon your bed for a little while? I would wake you the instant he comes.'

'I could not rest. But you –'

'No, nor I.'

The brief conversation died. Another hour crept by. As the church clocks struck the hour of one, the clatter of horses' feet on the cobbles reached the ladies' straining ears. Lanterns, dipping and rocking with the lurch of a chaise, were seen approaching down the street, and in another moment Worth's chaise-and-four had drawn up outside the house.

Barbara picked up the branch of candles from the table. 'Go down. I will light the stairs,' she said.

Judith ran from the room, feeling her knees shaking under her. The butler and Worth's valet were already at the door: there was nothing for her to do, and, almost overpowered by dread, she remained upon the landing, leaning against the wall, fighting against the nervous spasm that turned her sick and faint. She saw Barbara standing straight and tall in her pale dress, at the head of the stairs, holding the branch of candles up in one steady hand. A murmur of voices reached her ears. She heard the butler exclaim, and Worth reply sharply, A groan, and she knew that Charles lived, and found that the tears were pouring down her cheeks. She wiped them away, and, regaining command of herself, ran back into the salon, and snatching up a companion to the chandelier Barbara held, bore it up the second pair of stairs to the Colonel's room. She had scarcely had time to turn back the sheets from the bed before Worth and Cherry carried Colonel Audley into the room.

Judith could not suppress an exclamation of horror. The Colonel had been wrapped in his own cloak, but this fell away as he was lowered on to the bed, revealing a bloodstained shirt hanging in tatters about him. His white buckskins were caked with mud, and had been slit down the right leg to permit of the flesh wound on his thigh being dressed. His curling brown hair clung damply to his brow; his face, under the blackening smoke, was ghastly; but worst of all was the sight of the bandaged stump where so short a time ago his left arm had been. He was groaning, and muttering, but although his pain-racked eyes were open it was plain that he was unconscious of his surroundings.

'Razor!' Worth said to his valet, who had followed him up the stairs with a heavy can of hot water. 'These boots off first!' He glanced across at the two women. 'This is no fit sight for you. You had better go.'

'Fool!' Barbara said, in a low, fierce voice.

'As you please,' he shrugged, and, taking the razor from his valet's hand began to slit the seams of the Colonel's Hessians.

While he got the boots off, Barbara knelt down by the bed and sponged away the dirt from the Colonel's livid face. Judith stood beside her, holding the bowl of warm water. Over Barbara's head, she spoke to Worth: 'Will he live?'

'He is very ill, but I believe so. I have sent for a surgeon to come immediately. The worst is this fever. The jolting of the chaise has been very bad for him. I thought at one time I should never get through to Waterloo: the road is choked – wagons lying all over it, baggage spilt and plundered, and horses shot in their traces. There was never anything so disgraceful!'

'The battle?'

'I know no more than you. I met Charles in a common tilt-wagon half way through the Forest, being brought to Brussels with a dozen others. Everything is turmoil on the road: I could come by no certain intelligence; but I conjecture that all must be well, or the French much by now have penetrated at least to the Forest.'

He moved up to the head of the bed, and while he and his valet stripped the clothes from the Colonel's body, Barbara poured away the tainted water in the bowl and filled it with fresh. She looked so pale that Judith feared she must be going to faint, and begged her to withdraw. She shook her head. 'Do not heed me! I shall not fail.'

By the time an over-driven surgeon had arrived, the Colonel was lying between clean sheets, restlessly trying to twist from side to side. At times it needed all Worth's strength to prevent him from turning on to his injured left side; occasionally he made an effort to wrench himself up; once he said quite clearly: 'The Duke! I've a message to deliver!' But mostly his utterance was indistinct, and interrupted by deep groans.

The surgeon looked grave, and saw nothing for it but to bleed him. Judith could not help saying with a good deal of warmth: 'I should have thought he had lost enough blood!'

She was not attended to; the surgeon had been at work among the wounded since the previous morning, and was himself tired and harassed. He took a pint of blood from the Colonel, and it seemed to relieve him a little. He ceased his restless tossing and fell into a kind of coma. The surgeon gave Worth a few directions, and went away, promising to return later in the morning. It was evident that he did not take a very hopeful view of the Colonel's state. He would not permit of the bandages being removed to enable him to inspect the injuries to the thigh and the left side of the body. 'Better not disturb him!' he said. 'If Hume attended to him, you may depend upon it the wounds have been properly dressed. I will see them later. There is nothing for it now but to keep him quiet and hope for the fever to abate.'

He hurried away. Worth bent over the Colonel, feeling his hand and brow. Over his shoulder, he addressed the two women: 'Settle it between yourselves, but one of you must go and rest. Charles is in no immediate danger.'

'There can be no doubt which of us must go,' said Judith. 'Come, my poor child!'

'Oh no! You go!'

'No, Bab. It is you Charles will want when he comes to himself, and if you sit up now you will drop in the end, and think how shocking that would be! It is of no use to argue; I am quite determined.'

Barbara glanced towards the bed; the Colonel was lying still at last, sunk in a heavy stupor. 'Very well,' she said in a deadened tone. 'I will do as you wish.'

Judith led her away, with an arm round her waist. Barbara went unresistingly, but by the time they had reached her room such a fit of shuddering had seized her that Judith was alarmed. She forced her to sit down in a chair, while she ran to fetch her smelling-salts and the hartshorn. When she came back, the shudders had given place to dry sobs that seemed to convulse Barbara's whole body. She contrived to make her swallow a dose of hartshorn and water, and got her upon the bed, and sat with her till she was a little calmer. Barbara gasped: 'Oh, do not stay! Go back to him! This is nothing!'

'Worth will send if he needs me. Only tell me where I may find your laudanum drops.'

'Never! *He* did not like me to!'

'In such a case as this he could have no objection!'

'No, I tell you! See, I am better; I wish you to go back.'

Judith drew the quilt up over her shoulders. 'I will go, if it will relieve your mind. There, my dear, do not look like that! He will recover, and you will both be so happy together!' She bent, and kissed Barbara, and had the satisfaction of seeing the dreadful pallor grow less deathly. 'I shall come back in a little while to see how you go on,' she promised, and, setting the candle where its tongue of light would not worry Barbara's eyes, went softly back to Colonel Audley's room.

Barbara returned to the sick-room shortly after six o'clock. Judith came forward to meet her, saying in a low tone. 'We think him better. The pulse is not so tumultuous. There has been a good deal of restlessness, but you see he is quiet now. Oh, my dear, such glorious news! Bonaparte has been utterly overthrown and the whole French Army put to rout! Worth sent round to Sir Charles Stuart's an hour ago, and he had just himself heard from General Alten of our complete victory! You must know that Alten was brought in, severely wounded, very late last night, but had left instructions with one of his aides-de-camp to let him know the result of the battle at the earliest opportunity. The news reached him at three o'clock.'

'The French Army routed!' Barbara repeated. 'Good God, is it possible? Oh, if anything can make Charles recover, it must be that news!'

'You shall tell him when he wakes,' Judith said. 'I am going to bed for an hour or so. Worth has gone off to shave and change his clothes, but his man is just outside if you should need any assistance. But indeed, my dear, Charles is better.'

She went away. Barbara took her vacated chair by the bedside, and sat watching the Colonel. He lay quiet, except for the occasional twitching of his hand. She felt it softly, and found it, though still dry and hot, no longer burning to the touch. Satisfied, she folded her own hands in her lap, and sat without moving, waiting for him to awaken.

A few minutes after seven he stirred. A deep sigh broke the long silence; he opened his eyes, clouded with sleep, and gave a stifled groan. His hand moved; Barbara took it in hers and lifted it to her lips. He looked at her, blankly for a moment, then with recognition creeping into his eyes, and, with it, the ghost of his old smile. 'Why Bab!' he said, in a very faint voice. 'You've come back to me!'

Tears hung on her lashes; she slipped to her knees, and laid her cheek against his. '*You* have come back to *me*, Charles. I shall never let you go again.'

He put his arm weakly around her, and turned his head on the pillow to kiss her.

Twenty-Six

or a minute everything was forgotten in the passing away of all bitterness and grief between them. Neither spoke: explanations were not needed; for each all that signified was that they were together again.

Barbara raised her head at last, and taking the Colonel's face between her hands, looked deep into his eyes, her own more beautiful through the mist of tears that filled them than he had ever seen them. 'My darling!' she whispered.

He smiled wearily, but as fuller consciousness returned to him, his thoughts turned from her. 'The battle? They were massing for an attack.'

'It is over. The French have been overthrown: their whole Army is in full retreat.'

A flush of colour came into his drawn face. 'Boney's beat! Hurrah!'

She rose from her knees and moved away to measure out the medicine that the surgeon had left for him. When she came back to the bedside the Colonel was lying with his hand across his eyes, and his lips gripped tightly together. Her heart was wrung, but she said only: 'Here is a horrid potion for you to swallow, dear love.'

He did not answer, but when she slid her arm under him to raise him, he moved his hand from his eyes, and said in a carefully matter-of-fact voice: 'I remember now. I've lost my arm.'

'Yes, dear.'

He drank the dose she was holding to his mouth, leaning against her shoulder. As she lowered him again on to the pillows, he said with an effort : 'It's a lucky thing it was only my left. It has been a most unfortunate member. I was wounded in it once before.'

'In that case, we will say good riddance to it. Oh, my love, my love, does it hurt you very much?'

'Oh no! Nothing to signify,' he answered, lying gallantly.

He seemed as though he would sink back into the half-sleep, half-swoon which had held him for so long, but presently he opened his eyes, and turned them towards Barbara with an expression in them of painful anxiety. 'Gordon? Have you heard?'

'Only that he had been wounded.'

He was obliged to be satisfied, but she saw that although his eyes were closed again he was fully awake. She said, taking his hand between hers: 'We shall know presently.'

'Fitzroy, too,' he said, in a fretting tone. 'You would have heard if the Duke had been hit. But March took Slender Billy away. That was after Canning fell. How many of us are left? They dropped off, man after man – I cannot recall –' He broke off, and drew his hand away, once more covering his eyes with it.

She saw that he was growing agitated, and although she longed to ask for news of her brothers, she remained silent. But after a slight pause, he said abruptly: 'George was alive just before I was struck. I saw him.'

Her pent-up anxiety found relief in a gaping sigh. She waited for a moment, then whispered: 'Harry?'

He shook his head. A sob broke from her; she buried her face in the coverlet to stifle the sound, and presently felt his hand come back to hers, feebly clasping her fingers.

She remained on her knees until she saw that he had dropped into an uneasy sleep. As she rose, Worth came into the room. She laid a finger to her lips, and moved silently to meet him.

'Has he waked?' Worth asked in a low voice.

'Yes. He is quite himself, but I think in a good deal of pain.'

'That was bound to be. Go down to breakfast. Your grand-mother is here. I will send if he should rouse and wish for you.'

She nodded, and slipped away. Judith was asleep on her bed, but breakfast had been laid in the parlour, and the Duchess of Avon was sitting behind the coffee cups.

She greeted her granddaughter with a smile and a tender embrace. 'There, dearest! Such a happy morning for you after all! Sit down, and I will give you some coffee.'

'Harry is dead,' Barbara said.

The Duchess's hand trembled. She set the coffee pot down, and looked at Barbara.

'Charles told me. George was alive when he left the field.'

The Duchess said nothing. Two large tears rolled down her cheeks. She wiped them away, picked up the coffee pot again, poured a cup out rather unsteadily and gave it to Barbara. After a long pause she said: 'Such foolish thoughts keep crossing my mind. One remembers little, forgotten things. He would always call me "The Old Lady", in spite of your grandfather's disliking it so. Such a bad, merry boy!' She stretched out her hand to Barbara, and clasped one of hers. 'Poor child, I wish I could say something to comfort you.'

'It seems as though every joy that comes to one must have a grief to spoil it.'

'It is so, but think instead, dearest, that every grief has joy to lighten it. Nothing in this world is quite perfect, nor quite unbearable.' She patted Barbara's hand, and said in a voice of determined cheerfulness: 'When you have eaten your breakfast, I am going to send you round to see your grandfather. A turn in the fresh air will make you feel better.'

'I could not leave Charles.'

'Nonsense!' said her Grace. 'I am going to sit with your precious Charles, my dear. I know far better than you what to do for a wounded man. I have had a great deal of practice, I assure you.'

So when Colonel Audley opened his eyes again, it was to see a grey-haired lady, with humorous eyes, bending over him. He blinked, and, since she was smiling, weakly smiled back at her.

411

'That is much better!' she said. 'Now you shall take a little gruel, and be quite yourself again. Worth, be so good as to lift your brother slightly, while I put another pillow beneath his shoulders.'

The Colonel turned his head, as Worth came up on the opposite side of the bed, and held out his hand. 'Hallo, Julian!' he said. 'How did I get here?'

'I brought you in. There! Is that comfortable?'

'Bab was here,' said the Colonel, frowning. She said Boney was beat. I didn't dream that.'

'No, certainly you did not. Bab will back directly. Meanwhile, here is her grandmother come to see you.'

'So that is who you are!' said the Colonel, looking up at the Duchess. 'But I don't quite understand – am I being very stupid?'

'Not at all. You cannot imagine how I come to be here. Well, I came to see what Bab was about to have jilted you so shock-ingly, only to find that that was quite forgotten and that you are going to be married after all. So now open your mouth!'

He swallowed the mouthful of gruel put to his lips, but said: 'Am I going to be married?'

'Certainly you are. Open again!'

He obeyed meekly. 'I should like to see Bab,' he said, when the spoon was once more removed.

'So you shall, when you have drunk up all your gruel,' promised the Duchess.

The Colonel thought it over, and then said in a firmer tone: 'I'll be shaved first.'

'My dear fellow, why worry?' Worth said.

'By all means let him be shaved,' said the Duchess, frowning at him. 'He will feel very much more the thing.'

When Barbara came in with her grandfather to be met by the news that Colonel Audley was in the valet's hands, being shaved, she exclaimed: 'Shaved! Good God, how came you to let him disturb himself for such a foolish thing?'

'My love, when a man begins to think of shaving you may take it from me that he is on the road to recovery,' said the Duchess.

She took her husband's hands, and squeezed them. 'Bab has told you, hasn't she, Avon? My dear, we must be very proud of our boys, and try not to grieve.'

He put his arm round her, saying: 'Poor Mary! Depend upon it, we shall soon get news of that scamp George being safe and sound. I have been to Stuart's and learned from him that the Duke is in the town. Our losses have been enormous, by all accounts, but just think of Bonaparte completely overset! By God, it makes up for all!'

The arrival just then of the surgeon put an end to any further conversation. The Duchess and Worth accompanied him upstairs to the Colonel's room. He admitted that he had not expected to find his patient in such good shape, but pulled a long face over the leg wound, which, from having been so roughly bound upon the battlefield, and chafed by continued exertion, was in a bad state. He took Worth aside, and warned him that he should prepare the Colonel's mind for amputation.

Worth said, with such an icy rage in his voice that the surgeon almost recoiled : 'You'll save that leg: do you hear me?'

'Certainly I shall do my utmost,' replied the surgeon stiffly. 'Perhaps you would like one of my colleagues to see it?'

'I should,' said Worth. 'I'll have every doctor this town holds to see it before I'll permit you or any other of your kidney to hack my brother about any more!'

'You are unreasonable, my lord!'

'Unreasonable! Get Hume!'

'Dr Hume has already so much on his hands –'

'Get him!' snapped Worth.

The surgeon bowed, and walked off. The Duchess, who had come out of the Colonel's room, nodded approvingly, and said: 'That's right. Don't pay any heed to him! We will apply fomentations, and say nothing at all to the poor boy about amputation. I wish you will ask my granddaughter to find some flannel and bring it to me.'

'I will,' he said, and went downstairs in search of Barbara.

He met, instead his wife, who informed him that the Comte

413

de Lavisse had that instant entered the house and was with Barbara in the back-parlour.

He looked annoyed, but she said: 'He came, most kindly, to enquire after Charles. Only fancy, Worth! It was he who had Charles carried off the field! I declare, I could almost have embraced him, much as I dislike him!'

'I will see him, and thank him. Will you get the flannel for the fomentations?'

'Yes, immediately,' she replied.

Downstairs, the Count faced Barbara across the small room, and said, gripping a chairback: 'I did not think to find you here! I may know what I am to understand, I suppose!'

She said abstractedly: 'He is better. He has even desired to be shaved.'

'I am delighted to hear it! You perhaps find me irrelevant?'

'Oh no! I am so glad you are safe. Only my mind is so taken up just now –'

'It is seen! By God, I think you are a devil!'

She said rather listlessly: 'Yes, I know. It does no good to say I'm sorry, or I would.'

He struck the chairback with his open palm. 'In fact, you made a fool of me!'

She replied with a flash of spirit: 'Oh, the devil! You at least were fair game!'

He gave a short laugh. '*Touché!* I might have known! I cut an ignoble figure beside your heroic staff officer, do I not? You have doubtless heard that my brigade fled – fled without firing a shot!'

'I hadn't heard,' she replied. 'I am sorry.' There did not seem to be anything more to say. She tried to find something, and added: 'It was not that. I always loved Charles Audley.'

'Thank you! It needs no more! Convey my felicitations to the Colonel: I wish that that shell had blown him to perdition!'

She was spared having to answer him by Worth's entering the room at that moment. The Count, picking up his shako, held out his hand. '*Adieu!* It is unlikely that we meet again.'

She shook hands, and went back to the Colonel. Worth

414

attempted to thank the Count for his kind offices the previous day, but was cut short.

'It is nothing. I was, in fact, ordered by my General to do my possible for the Colonel. I am happy to learn that my poor efforts were not wasted. I am returning immediately to my brigade.'

Worth escorted him to the door, merely remarking: 'You must allow me, however, to tell you that I cannot but consider myself under a deep obligation to you.'

'Oh, *parbleu*! It is quite unnecessary!' He shook hands, but paused half way down the steps, and looked back. 'You will tell the Colonel, if you please, that his message was delivered,' he said, and saluted, and walked quickly away.

Worth had hardly shut the door when another knock fell upon it. He opened it again to find Creevey on the top step, beaming all over his shrewd countenance, and evidently bubbling with news.

He declined coming in: he had called only to see how Colonel Audley did, and would not intrude upon the family at such a time. 'I have just seen the Duke!' he announced. 'I have been to his Headquarters, hearing that he had come in from Waterloo, and found him in the act of writing his despatch. He saw me from his window, and beckoned me up straightway. You may imagine how I put out my hand and congratulated him upon his victory! He said to me in his blunt way: "It has been a damned serious business. Blücher and I have lost thirty thousand men." And then, without the least appearance of joy or triumph, he repeated: "It has been a damned nice thing – the nearest run thing you ever saw in your life." He told me Blücher got so damnably licked on Friday that he could not find him Saturday morning, and had to fall back to keep up his communications with him. Upon my word, I never saw him so grave, not so much moved! He kept on walking about the room, praising the courage of our troops, in particular those Guards who kept Hougoumont against the repeated attacks of the French. "You may depend upon it," he said, "that no troops but the British could have held Hougoumont, and only the best of them at that!" Then he said – not with any vanity, you know, but very seriously: "By God! I don't think it would have done if I had not been there."'

'I can readily believe that,' Worth replied. 'Does he anticipate that there will be any more fighting?'

'No, that is the best of all! He says that every French Corps but one was engaged in the battle, and the whole Army gone off in such a perfect rout and confusion he thinks it quite impossible for them to give battle again before the Allies reach Paris.'

'Excellent news! I am much obliged to you for bringing it to me.'

'I knew you would be glad to hear of it! You'll give my compliments to the ladies, and to poor Audley: I must be off, to catch the mail.'

He bustled away, and Worth went upstairs to convey the tidings to his brother, whom he found lying quietly, with his hand in Barbara's. He told him what had passed, and had the satisfaction of seeing the Colonel's eyes regain a little of their sparkle. Lavisse's parting message evoked only a languid: 'Poor devil! What a piece of work to make of nothing!' Worth, seeing that he was tired, went away, leaving him to the comfort of Barbara's presence.

The Duchess remained in the house all day, and the Duke, after trying in vain to obtain intelligence of George's fate, and calling at the Fishers' lodging to see Lucy (whom he declared to be a poor little dab of a thing, not worth looking at), took up his quarters in Lady Worth's salon. He was permitted to visit Audley for a few minutes before dinner, and took his hand in a strong hold, saying with a softened expression in his rather hard eyes: 'Well, my boy, so you mean to have that vixen of mine, do you? You're deserving of a better fate, but if you're determined you may take her with my blessing.'

'Thank you, sir,' said the Colonel.

'And mind you keep her this time!' said his Grace. 'I won't have her back on my hands again!'

His wife and granddaughter, judging that a very little of his bracing personality was enough for the Colonel in his present condition, then sent him away, and he went off to announce to Judith that, whatever he might think of George's choice, he was very well satisfied with Barbara's.

He bore his wife off to the Hôtel de Belle Vue for dinner, promising, however, to permit of her returning to Worth's house later in the evening, to see how the Colonel went on. The fomentations had afforded some relief; there was no recurrence of the fever which had alarmed the ladies earlier in the day; and although the pulse was unsteady, the Duchess was able to inform her granddaughter before leaving the house that she had every expectation of the Colonel's speedy recovery.

He was too weak to wish to indulge in much conversation, but he seemed to like to have Barbara near him. He lay mostly with closed eyes under a frowning brow, but if she moved from her chair it was seen that he was not asleep, for his eyes would open and follow her about the room. She soon found that her absence from his side made him restless, and so placed her chair close to the bed, and sat there, ready in an instant to bathe his brow with vinegar and water, to change the fomentations, or just to smile at him and take his hand.

It was not such a reunion as she had imagined. Her thoughts were confused. Harry's death lay at the back of them, like a bruise on her spirit. She had been prepared to hear that Charles had been killed, but she had never thought that he might come back to her so shattered that he could not take her in his arms, so weak that the smile, even, was an effort. There was much she had wanted to say to him, but it had not been said, and perhaps never would be. No drama attached to their reconciliation: it was quiet, tempered by sorrow.

Yet in spite of all, as she sat hour after hour beside Charles, a contentment grew in her and the vision of the conquering hero, who should have come riding gallantly back to her, faded from her mind. Reality was less romantic than her imaginings, but not less dear; and his feeble laugh and expostulation when she fed him with her grandmother's prescribed gruel were more precious to her than the most ardent love-making could have been.

Her dinner was sent up to her on a tray, and Judith and Worth sat down in the dining-parlour alone. They had not many minutes risen from the table when a knock fell on the street door, and an instant later George Alastair walked into the salon.

Judith exclaimed at the sight of him, for his appearance was shocking. His baggage not having reached Nivelles, where his brigade was bivouacked, he had not been able to change his tattered jacket and mud-splashed breeches. An epaulette had been shot off; a bandage was bound round his head; and he limped slightly from a sabre-cut on one leg. He looked pale, and his blood-shot eyes were heavy and red-rimmed from fatigue. He cut short Judith's greetings, saying curtly: 'I came to enquire after Audley. Can I see him?'

'He is better, but very weak. But sit down! You look quite worn out, and you are wounded!'

'Oh, this!' He raised his hand to his head. 'That will only spoil my beauty. Don't waste your pity on me, ma'am!'

'Have you dined?' Worth asked.

'Yes: at my wife's!' George replied, flinging the word at him. 'I have also seen my grandparents, and have nothing left to do before rejoining my regiment except to thank Audley for his kind offices towards my wife.'

'I am very sure he does not wish to be thanked. Oh, how relieved your grandparents must be to know you are safe, to have had the comfort of seeing you!'

He replied, with the flash of his sardonic smile: 'Yes, extremely gratifying! It is wonderful what a slash across the brow can do for one. You will be happy to hear, ma'am, that my wife will remain in my grandparents' charge until such time as she may follow me to Paris. May I now see Audley?'

She looked doubtful. He saw it, and said rather harshly: 'Oblige me in this, if you please! What I have to ask him will not take me long.'

'To ask him?' she repeated.

'Yes, ma'am, to ask him! Audley saw my brother die, and I want to know where in that charnel-house to search for his body!'

She put out her hand impulsively. 'Ah, poor boy! Of course you shall see him! Worth will take you up at once.'

'Thank you,' he said with a slight bow, and limped to the door, and opened it for Worth to lead the way out.

Judith was left to her own melancholy reflections, but these were interrupted in a very few minutes by yet another knock on the street door. She paid little heed, expecting merely to have a card brought in to her with kind enquiries after the state of Colonel Audley's health, but to her astonishment the butler very soon opened the door into the salon and announced the Duke of Wellington.

She started up immediately. The Duke came in, dressed in plain clothes, and shook hands, saying: 'How do you do? I have come to see poor Audley. How does he go on?'

She was quite overpowered. She had never imagined that in the midst of the work in which he must be immersed he could find time to visit the Colonel. She had even doubted his sparing as much as a thought for his aide-de-camp. She could only say in a moved voice: 'How kind this is in you! We think him a little better. He will be so happy to receive a visit from you!'

'Better, is he? That's right! Poor fellow, they tell me he has had to lose his arm.'

She nodded, and, recollecting herself a little, began to congratulate him upon his great victory.

He stopped her at once, saying hastily: 'Oh, do not congratulate me! I have lost all my dearest friends!'

She said in a subdued voice: 'You must feel it, indeed!'

'I am quite heart-broken at the loss I have sustained,' he replied, taking a quick turn about the room. 'My friends, my poor soldiers – how many of them have I to regret! I have no feeling for the advantages we have acquired.' He stopped, and said in a serious tone: 'I have never fought such a battle, and I trust I shall never fight such another. War is a terrible evil, Lady Worth.'

She could only throw him a speaking glance; her feelings threatened to overcome her; she was glad to see Worth come back into the room at that moment, and to be relieved of the necessity of answering the Duke. She sank down into a chair while Worth shook hands with his lordship. He, too, offered congratulations and comments on the nature of the engagement. The Duke replied in an animated tone: 'Never did I see such a pounding-match! Both were what you boxers call gluttons. Napoleon did not manœuvre at all. He just moved forward in the old style, in columns, and was driven off in the old style. The only difference was that he mixed cavalry with his infantry, and supported both with an enormous quantity of artillery.'

'From what my brother has said, I collect that the French cavalry was very numerous?'

'By God, it was! I had the infantry for some time in squares, and we had the French cavalry walking about us as if they had been our own. I never saw the British infantry behave so well!'

'It has been a glorious action, sir.'

'Yes, but the glory has been dearly bought. Indeed, the losses I have sustained have quite broken me down. But I must not stay: I have very little time at my disposal, as you may imagine. I came only to see Audley.'

'I will take you to him at once, sir. Nothing, I am persuaded, will do him as much good as a visit from you.'

'Oh, pooh! nonsense!' the Duke said, going with him to the door. 'I shall be in a bad way without him, and the others whom I have lost, I can tell you!'

He followed Worth upstairs to Colonel Audley's room, only to be brought up short on the threshold by the sight of Lord George, standing by the bed. A frosty glare was bent on him; a snap was imminent; but Audley, startled by the sight of his Chief, still kept his wits about him, and said quickly: 'Lord George Alastair, my lord, who has been sent in to have his wounds attended to, and has been kind enough to visit me on his way back to the brigade.'

'Oh!' said his lordship. 'Avon's grandson, are you? I'm glad to see you're alive, but get back to your brigade, sir! There's too much of this going on leave!'

Thankful to have escaped with only this mild reproof, George effaced himself. The Duke stepped up to the bed, and clasped Colonel Audley's hand. 'Well! We have given the French a handsome dressing!' he said heartily. 'But I'm sorry to see you like this, my poor fellow! Never mind! Fitzroy's had the misfortune to lost his right arm, you know. I've just seen him: he's perfectly free from fever, and as well as anybody could be under such circumstances.'

'His right arm!' the Colonel said. 'Oh, poor Fitzroy!'

'There, don't distress yourself! Why, what do you think! He's already learning to write with his left hand, and will be back with me again before I've had time to turn round.'

Audley struggled up on his elbow. 'Sir, what of Gordon?'

A shadow crossed the Duke's face. He said in a broken voice: 'Ah, poor Gordon! He lived long enough to be informed by myself of the glorious success of our actions. They carried him to my Headquarters at Waterloo, you know. Hume called me at three this morning to go to him, but he was dead before I got there.'

The Colonel gave a groan and sank back upon his pillows. 'A little restaurant in Paris!' he whispered. 'O God!'

Barbara moved forward, and slid her hand into his. His fingers gripped it feebly; he lay silent, while the Duke, turning to Worth, asked in his blunt fashion: 'Who has him in charge? Has Hume been here?'

'Not yet,' Worth replied. 'I am extremely anxious to get him, but there seems to be no possibility of securing his services.'

'Nonsense! I'll send him round at once,' said his lordship. 'Can't afford to lose any more of my family.' He bent over Colonel Audley again, and laid his hand on his right shoulder. 'Well, Audley, I must go. You'll be glad to know that we're moving on immediately. Old Blücher took up the pursuit last night, and you may be sure we shan't discontinue our operations till we get to Paris. As for Boney, in my opinion, *il n'a que se pendre*.

But I shall be in a bad way without you fellows: take care that you lose no time in rejoining me!'

'I shall report for duty the instant I can stand on my feet, sir. Who takes the despatch to England?'

'Percy, with three Eagles as well. Goodbye, my boy: now, don't forget! I rely on your following me as soon as you may.'

He pressed the Colonel's shoulder, and went away, with a nod to Barbara and a brief handshake for Worth.

He was as good as his word in sending Dr Hume to see the Colonel. The eminent doctor presented himself before an hour had passed, briskly expressing his regret at being kept by a press of work from coming sooner.

His arrival coincided with that of the surgeon who had taken charge of the Colonel's case, and Judith was hard put to it to decide which of the two men she disliked most. Mr Jones's air of depression might exasperate her, but nothing, to her mind, could have been more out of place than Hume's cheerfulness. His voice was loud, and hearty; as he followed her up the stairs he talked all the way of trivialities; and when he entered the Colonel's room it was in a noisy fashion and with a rallying speech on his lips.

The Duke's visit had considerably tired Audley, but he roused himself when Hume came to the bed, and managed to smile.

'Well, now, and what is all this?' Hume said, taking his pulse. 'I thought I had seen the end of you when I packed you off from Mont St Jean yesterday.'

'I am more difficult to kill than you suspected, you see,' murmured the Colonel.

'Kill! No such thing! I did a capital piece of work on you, and here you are demanding more of my valuable time! We'll take a look at that leg of yours.'

The bandages and the fomentations were removed. The surgeon said something in a low tone, and was answered by a sharp: 'Rubbish! Why do you give up a man with such a pulse, and such a good constitution? He is doing famously! You have been fomenting the leg; excellent! couldn't do better! Now then,

Audley, I'll see what I can do to make you easier.'

He took off his coat and rolled up his sleeves, while Judith ran to fetch the hot water he demanded. While he worked upon the Colonel's wincing body, he chatted, perhaps with the object of taking his victim's mind off his sufferings, and the Colonel answered him in painful gasps. His matter-of-fact description of the battlefield, literally covered with dead and wounded, shocked Judith inexpressibly, and made her exclaim at the plight of the French soldiers left there until the Allied wounded should have been got in. He replied cheerfully that it was all in their favour to be in the fresh air: provided they were soon moved into the hospitals they would be found to have escaped the fever which had attacked those who were got immediately under cover.

'Do you know how the Prince of Orange is?' asked the Colonel.

'Do I know! Why, I've just been with him! You need not worry your head over him: he's going on capitally. Baron Constant came rushing in this morning while I was with him, shouting out: "Boney's beat! Boney's beat!" and you never saw anyone more obliged to take Lord Uxbridge's leg off, I daresay? He is as gallant a man as ever I met! What do you think of his telling us he considered his leg a small price to pay for having been in such an action?' He stretched out his hand for some clean lint, and began to bind the Colonel's leg up again. In a graver tone he said: 'Our losses have been shocking. The Duke is quite cast down, and no wonder! He would have me bring him a list of such of our casualties as came within my knowledge last night. I did so, but found him laid down in all his dirt upon the couch, fast asleep, and so set my list down beside him and went away. He had had poor Gordon put into his bed, you know. Ah, that has been a sad business! There was nothing one could to except to wait for death to put a period to his sufferings. The end came at three o'clock. I went to call the Duke, but it was over before he could get there. I never saw him so much affected. People call him unfeeling, but I can tell you this: when I went to him after he had read the list of casualties there were two white furrows down his cheeks where his tears had washed away the dust. He said to me in a voice tremulous with emotion: "Well! thank God I don't know what it is to lose a battle, but certainly nothing can be more painful than to win one with the loss of so many of one's friends."

Judith saw that Colonel Audley was too much distressed by the thought of Gordon's death to respond, and said civilly: 'Nothing, I am sure, could become the Duke more than the way in which he spoke to us of his victory. I have not been used to think him a man of much sensibility, and was quite confounded.

'Sensibility! Ay, I daresay not, but General Alava was telling me it was downright pathetic to watch him, as he sat down to his supper last night, looking up every time the door opened, in the expectation of seeing one of his staff walk in.' He straightened his back, saying with a reversion to his hearty tone: 'There! I have done tormenting you at last! You will be on your feet again as soon as Lord Fitzroy, I promise you.'

He turned to give some directions to the other surgeon; recommended the application of leeches, if there should be a recurrence of fever; and took himself off, leaving the Colonel very much exhausted and the ladies quite indignant.

His visit was presently found, however, to have been of benefit to Audley. He seemed easier, and assisted by a dose of laudanum, passed as quiet a night as could have been expected.

When Barbara came into his room in the morning, she found him being propped up with pillows to partake of a breakfast of toasted bread and weak tea.

He held out his hand to her. The old gaiety was missing from his smile, but he spoke cheerfully. 'Good morning, Bab. You see that I have rebelled against your gruel! Now you shall watch how deedily I can contrive with my one hand.'

She bent over him, and to hide her almost overmastering desire to burst into tears, said with assumed raillery: 'Ah, you hope to impress me, but I warn you, you won't succeed! You have already had a great deal of practice in the use of one hand!'

He put the one hand to turn her face towards him and kissed

her. 'That's too bad! I had hoped to hold you spellbound by my adroitness. Will you oblige me by going to the dressing-table and opening the little drawer under the mirror?'

'Certainly,' she replied. 'What do you want from it, my darling?'

'You'll see,' he said, picking up one of his slices of toast and dipping it in the tea. She opened the drawer, and found a small box in it, containing her engagement ring. She said nothing, but brought the ring to the Colonel, smiling, but with quivering lips. He took it, and commanded her to hold out her hand. The ring slid over her knuckle, but the Colonel still retained her hand, saying quietly: 'That stays there until I give you another in its place, Bab.'

She dropped on her knees, burying her face in his shoulder. 'Charles, dear Charles, I shall make you such a damnable wife! Oh, only tell me that you forgive me!'

He gave a rather shaky laugh, and put his arm round her. 'Who is the "dear fool" now?' he said. 'Oh, Bab, Bab, just look what I have done!'

Judith came in a minute later to find Barbara, between tears and laughter, mopping up the split tea on the sheet, and exclaimed: 'Well! This does not look like a sick-room!'

Barbara held out her hand. 'Congratulate me, Judith! I have just become engaged to your brother-in-law!'

'Oh, my love, of course you have!' Judith cried, embracing her. 'Charles, this time I congratulate you with all my heart!'

'Thank you!' he said, with rather a surprised look. 'What's the news in the town today? How do Fitzroy and Billy go on?'

'I have not heard, but of course we shall call to make enquiries later on. The Duke has driven out in his curricle to rejoin the Army, at Nivelles. We understand he has taken Colonel Felton Hervey on as his military secretary, until Lord Fitzroy is well enough to go back.'

'A one-armed man!'

'Yes, and that is what touches one so much. There is a delicacy in such a gesture: Lord Fitzroy must be sensible of it, I

425

am sure! I never thought to like the Duke as well as I have done ever since he called here yesterday.'

The Colonel smiled, but merely replied: 'He must be worse off than ever for staff officers. I pity the poor devils remaining: they'll find him damned crusty!'

Judith was quite put out by this prosaic remark, but Colonel Audley knew his Chief better than she did.

The Duke, rejoining his disorganised Army at Nivelles found much to annoy him. He was displeased with the conduct of various sections of his staff, and quite incensed by the discovery that Sir George Wood, who commanded the Royal Artillery, had, instead of securing the captured French guns, allowed a number of them to be seized by the Prussians. That was a little too much; those guns must be recovered, and there would be no peace for Wood or Fraser till they had been recovered.

His lordship, no longer a demi-god but only a much harassed man, sat down to write his instructions for the movement of his Army. There was no difficulty about that: the instructions were compressed into four succinct paragraphs, and borne off by a trembling gentleman of the Quartermaster-General's staff.

His lordship dipped his pen in the ink and began to compose his first General Order since the battle. The pen moved slowly, in stiff, reluctant phrases.

'*The Field Marshall takes this opportunity of returning to the Army his thanks for their conduct in the glorious action fought on the 18th instant, and he will not fail to report his sense of their conduct in the terms which it deserves to their several Sovereigns.*'

His lordship read that through, and decided that it would do. He wrote the figure 3 in the margin, and started another paragraph. His pen began to move faster: '*The Field Marshal has observed that several soldiers, and even officers, have quitted their ranks without leave, and have gone to Bruxelles, and even some to Antwerp, where, and in the country through which they have passed, they have spread a false alarm, in a manner highly unmilitary, and derogatory to the character of soldiers.*'

The pen was flowing perfectly easily now. His lordship

continued without a check: '*The Field Marshal requests the General officers commanding divisions in the British Army . . . to report to him in writing what officers and men (the former by name) are now or have been absent without leave since the 16th instant . . .*'

Short Bibliography

COTTON, Sergt.-Major Edward. *A Voice from Waterloo.* 10 edn. 1913.

CRAAN, W.B. *An Historical Account of the Battle of Waterloo.* 1817.

CREEVEY, Thomas. *A Selection from the Correspondence and Diaries.* Ed., The Rt. Hon. Sir Herbert Maxwell. 1933.

CROKER, John Wilson. *Correspondence and Diaries.* Ed., Louis J. Jennings. 1884.

DALTON, Charles. *The Waterloo Roll Call.*

D'ARBLAY, Mme. *Diary and Letters.* Vol. IV. Ed., Charlotte Barrett.

DE BAS, Col. F., and T'SERCLAES DE WOMMERSON, Col. Ct. J. de. *Campagne de 1815 aux Pays-Bas.* 4 vols. 1908

DE LANCEY, Lady. *A Week at Waterloo in 1815.* Ed., Major B. R. Ward. 1906.

ELLESMERE, Earl of. *Personal Reminiscences of the Duke of Wellington.* Ed., Alice, Countess of Strafford. 1904.

FORTESCUE, The Hon. Sir John. *A History of the British Army.* Vol. X. 1920. – *Wellington.* 1925.

FRASER, Sir William. *Words on Wellington.* 1900.

GALESLOOT, L. *Le Duc de Wellington à Bruxelles.* 1884.

GLEIG, Rev. G. R. *Story of the Battle of Waterloo.* 1847. – *Personal Reminiscences of the Duke of Wellington.* Ed., Mary E. Gleig. 1904.

GOMM, Sir William Maynard. *Letters and Journals.*

GREVILLE, Charles. *Diary.* 2 vols. Ed., Philip Whitwell Wilson. 1927.

GRIFFITHS, Major Arthur. *The Wellington Memorial*. 1897.
– *Wellington and Waterloo*. 1898.

GRONOW, Capt. *Reminiscences and Recollections*. 2 vols. 1892.

GUEDALLA, Philip. *The Hundred Days*. 1934.

HOUSSAYE, Henri. *1815*. 1903.

JACKSON, Lieut.-Col. Basil. *Notes and Reminiscences of a Staff-Officer*. 1903.

JAMES, Lieut.-Col. W. H. *Campaign of 1815*. 1908.

JONES, George. *The Battle of Waterloo, with Those of Ligny and Quatre-Bras*. 1815.

KELLY, Christopher. *The Memorable Battle of Waterloo*. 1817.

KINCAID, John. *Adventures in the Rifle Brigade*. Ed., The Hon. Sir John Fortescue. 1929. – *Random Shots from a Rifleman*. 1835.

LARPENT, F. S. *Private Journal*. 3 vols. Ed., Sir George Larpent. 1853.

LENNOX, Lord William Pitt. *Celebrities I Have Known*. 1876. – (An Ex-Aide-de-Camp.) *Three Years with the Duke, or Wellington in Private Life*. 1853.

LOW, Edward Bruce. *With Napoleon at Waterloo*. Ed., MacKenzie MacBride. 1911.

MALMESBURY, Earl of. *Letters*. Vol. II. 1845.

MAXWELL, The Rt. Hon. Sir Herbert. *Life of Wellington*. 2 vols. 1899.

McGRIGOR, Sir James. *Autobiography*. 1861.

MERCER, General Cavalié. *Journal of the Waterloo Campaign*. 1927.

MÜFFLING, General. *A Sketch of the Battle of Waterloo*. 1930. – *Passages From My Life*. Ed., Col. Philip Yorke. 1853.

NEVILLE, Ralph. *British Military Prints*. 1909.

OMAN, Sir Charles. *Wellington's Army*. 1913.

SHAW KENNEDY, General Sir James. *Notes on the Battle of Waterloo*. 1865.

SIBORNE, Capt. William. *History of the War in France and Belgium in 1815*. 2 vols. 1844.

SIBORNE, Maj.-Gen. H. T. (Ed.) *Waterloo Letters*. 1891.

SIDNEY, Rev. Edwin. *Life of Lord Hill*. G.C.B. 1845.

SMITH, G. C. Moore. *Life of John Colborne, Field-Marshal Lord Seaton*. 1903.

SMITH, Lieut.-Gen. Sir Harry. *Autobiography*. Vol. I. Ed., G. C. Moore Smith. 1901.

STANHOPE, Earl of. *Notes of Conversations with the Duke of Wellington*. 1888.

SWINGTON, The Hon. Mrs J. R. *A Sketch of the Life of Georgiana, Lady de Ros*. 1893.

WELLESLEY, Muriel. *The Man Wellington Through the Eyes of Those Who Knew Him*. 1937.

WELLINGTON, 1st Duke of. *Dispatches*. Ed., Lieut.-Col. John Gurwood. 1939. – *Supplementary Despatches*. Vols. IX and X. Ed., Arthur, 2nd Duke of Wellington. 1863.

WOOD, Sir Evelyn. *Cavalry in the Waterloo Campaign*. 1895.

ALSO AVAILABLE IN ARROW BY GEORGETTE HEYER

Black Sheep

Charming and wise in the ways of the world, Bath society-belle Abigail Wendover has tried hard to detach her spirited niece Fanny from a plausible fortune-hunter. Her efforts become vastly more complicated with the arrival of Miles Caverleigh. The black sheep of his family, a cynical devil-may-care with a scandalous past – why, that would be a connection more shocking even than Fanny's unwise liaison with his nephew!

Friday's Child

Rejected by Miss Milborne for his unsteadiness of character, wild Lord Sheringham flies back to London in a rage, vowing to marry the first woman to cross his way. And who should he see but Hero Wantage, the young and charmingly unsophisticated girl, who has loved him since childhood . . . ?

Venetia

In all her twenty-five years, lovely Venetia Lanyon has never been further than Harrogate, nor enjoyed the attentions of any but her two wearisomely persistent suitors. Then, in one extraordinary encounter, she finds herself involved with her neighbour, a libertine whose way of life has scandalised the North Riding for years.

arrow books

The Black Moth

Jack Carstares, the disgraced Earl of Wycham, left England seven long years ago, sacrificing his honour for that of his brother when he was accused of cheating at cards. Now Jack is back, roaming his beloved South Country in the disguise of a highwayman. Not long after his return, he encounters his old adversary, the libertine Duke of Andover, just in time to dispute at the point of his sword, the attempted abduction of a society beauty. But foiled once, the 'Black Moth' has no intention of failing again . . .

Sylvester

Endowed with rank, wealth and elegance, Sylvester, Duke of Salford, has decided to travel to Wiltshire to discover if the Hon Phoebe Marlowe will meet his exacting requirements for a bride. If he doesn't expect to meet a tongue-tied stripling in need of both manners and conduct, he is even more intrigued when his visit causes Phoebe to flee her home. They meet again on the road to London, where her carriage has come to grief in the snow. Yet Phoebe, already caught in one *imbroglio*, now knows she soon could be well deep in another . . .

arrow books

The Corinthian

The only question, which hangs over the life of Sir Richard Wyndham, notable whip, dandy and Corinthian, is one of marriage. On the eve of making the most momentous decision of his life, he is on his way home, when he chances upon a beautiful young fugitive climbing out of a window by means of knotted sheets . . .

Bath Tangle

The Earl of Spenborough has always been noted for his eccentricity. Leaving a widow younger than his own daughter was one thing. Leaving his fortune to the trusteeship of the Marquis of Rotherham – the one man the same daughter had jilted – was quite another.

Arabella

Impetuosity is Arabella's only fault. An enchanting debutante and the eldest daughter of a country parson, she should know better than to allow herself to be provoked by Mr Beaumaris, the most eligible Nonpareil of the day.

Reluctant Widow

Stepping into the wrong carriage at a Sussex village, Elinor Rochdale is swept up in a thrilling and dangerous adventure. Overnight the would-be governess becomes mistress of a ruined estate and partner in a secret conspiracy to save a family's name. By midnight she is a bride, by dawn a widow . . .

The Foundling

The shy, young Duke of Sale has never known his parents. Instead, he has endured twenty-four years of rigorous mollycoddling from his uncle and valet. But when the Duke hears of Belinda, the beautiful foundling who appears to be blackmailing his cousin, he absconds with glee. No sooner has he entered this new and dangerous world than he is plunged into a frenzy of intrigue, kidnap and adventure.

Charity Girl

When Fate and a chivalrous impulse combine to saddle Viscount Desford with a friendless, homeless waif named Cherry Steane, who else should he turn to in such a scrape but his old childhood playmate, Henrietta Silverdale?

arrow books

Frederica

Rich, handsome, the hope of ambitious mothers and the despair of his sisters – the Marquis of Alverstoke sees no reason to put himself out for anyone. Until a distant connection applies to him for help. Plunged headlong into one drama after another by the large and irrepressible Merriville family, which includes the beautiful Frederica, Alverstoke is surprised to find himself far from bored . . .

Faro's Daughter

Renowned gamester and entirely void of a romantic disposition, Max Ravenscar regards all eligible females with indifference and unconcern. But when he meets the beautiful Deborah Grantham, mistress of her aunt's gaming house, he finds himself ill-prepared for such a worthy opponent.

Sprig Muslin

Finding so young and pretty a girl as Amanda wandering unattended, Sir Gareth Ludlow knows it is his duty as a man of honour to restore her to her family. But it is to prove no easy task for the Corinthian. His captive in sprig muslin has more than her rapturous good looks and bandboxes to aid her – she is also possessed of a runaway imagination . . .

arrow books

April Lady

When the new Lady Cardross begins to fill her days with fashion and frivolity, the Earl has to wonder whether she did really only marry him for his money, as his family so helpfully suggests. And now Nell doesn't dare tell him the truth . . . What with the concern over his wife's heart and pocket, sorting out her brother's scrapes and trying to prevent his own half sister from eloping, it is no wonder that the much-tried Earl almost misses the opportunity to smooth the path of true love in his marriage . . .

The Spanish Bride

Shot-proof, fever-proof and a veteran campaigner at the age of twenty-five, Brigade-major Harry Smith is reputed to be the luckiest man in Lord Wellington's army. Yet at the siege of Badajos, his friends foretell the ruin of his career. When Harry meets the defenceless Juana, a fiery passion consumes him. Under the banner of honour and with the selfsame ardour he so frequently displays in battle, he dives headlong into marriage. In his beautiful child-bride, he finds a kindred spirit, and a temper to match. But for Juana, a long year of war must follow.

arrow books

ALSO AVAILABLE IN ARROW BY GEORGETTE HEYER

Lady of Quality

Independent and spirited, Miss Annis Wychwood gives little thought to finding herself a suitable husband, thus dashing the dreams of many hopeful suitors. When she becomes embroiled in the affairs of the runaway heiress Lucilla, though, she encounters the beautiful fugitive's guardian – as rakish and uncivil a rogue she has ever met. Although, chafing a bit at the restrictions of Regency society in Bath, Annis does have to admit that Oliver Carelton, at least, is never boring.

False Colours

The Honourable Christopher Fancot, on leave from the diplomatic service in the summer of 1817, is startled to find his entrancing but incorrigibly extravagant mother on the brink of financial and social ruin – and more than alarmed to find that his twin brother has disappeared without trace. The unfortunate Kit is forced into an outrageous masquerade by the tangled affairs of his wayward family – his rigid uncle, Lord Brumby, the surprisingly wily Sir Bonamy Ripple, the formidable old Lady Stavely and Evelyn's betrothed, Cressy – but in the face of Evelyn's continued absence, Kit's ingenuity is stretched to the limit.

arrow books

Georgette Heyer's Regency World

Jennifer Kloester

**A unique and beautifully illustrated companion to
Georgette Heyer's Regency Novels**

A bestselling novelist since 1921, Georgette Heyer is known
across the world for her historical romances set in Regency
England. Millions of readers love the period for its fashion, famous
people and events, and its elegant and often outrageous mayfly
upper-class. It was Georgette Heyer who created the Regency
genre of historical fiction in the 1930s and 40s with books such
as *Regency Buck* and *Friday's Child*. Since then, in many minds,
Georgette Heyer and the Regency have become synonymous.

Not a dry history book, but the ultimate, definitive guide to
Georgette Heyer's world: her heroines, her villains and dashing
heroes, the shops, clubs and towns they frequented, the parties
and seasons they celebrated, how they ate, drank, dressed,
socialised, voted, shopped and drove. An utterly delightful and fun
read for any Heyer fan.

'An invaluable guide to the world of the *bon ton*. No lover of
Georgette Heyer's novels should be without it.'
Katie Fforde

arrow books

THE POWER OF READING

Visit the Random House website and get connected with information on all our books and authors

EXTRACTS from our recently published books and selected backlist titles

COMPETITIONS AND PRIZE DRAWS Win signed books, audiobooks and more

AUTHOR EVENTS Find out which of our authors are on tour and where you can meet them

LATEST NEWS on bestsellers, awards and new publications

MINISITES with exclusive special features dedicated to our authors and their

READING GROUPS Reading guides, special features and all the information you need for your reading group

LISTEN to extracts from the latest audiobook publications

WATCH video clips of interviews and readings with our authors

RANDOM HOUSE INFORMATION including advice for writers,